W9-BSH-270

Also by Caris Roane

ASCENSION

BURNING SKIES

WINGS OF FIRE

BORN OF ASHES

OBSIDIAN FLAME

CARIS ROANE

St. Martin's Paperbacks

This is a work of fiction. All of the characters, organizations, and events portrayed in this novel are either products of the author's imagination or are used fictitiously.

OBSIDIAN FLAME

Copyright © 2012 by Caris Roane.

All rights reserved.

For information address St. Martin's Press, 175 Fifth Avenue, New York, NY 10010.

ISBN: 978-1-250-00853-4

Printed in the United States of America

St. Martin's Paperbacks edition / May 2012

St. Martin's Paperbacks are published by St. Martin's Press, 175 Fifth Avenue, New York, NY 10010.

10 9 8 7 6 5 4 3 2 1

To Carol Webb,
a wonderful friend.
Bella Media rocks!

ACKNOWLEDGMENTS

Jennifer Schober, what would I do without you?

Rose Hilliard, a million thanks for your warm and continued support!

Danelle Fiorella—thank you for the best paranormal covers ever! I get more compliments on them, especially at a signing when the books are all laid out together! Yummy!

Laurie Henderson and Laura Jorstad, the manuscripts are always in the best shape once they pass through your careful hands.

Liz Edelstein, *Heroes and Heartbreakers* is *the best*!

My special thanks to Anne Marie Tallberg, Eileen Rothschild, and Brittney Kleinfelter for getting the word out about my Guardians of Ascension.

And once again, many thanks to Matthew Shear, Jen Enderlin, and the superb team at SMP.

There's no place like home . . .

Who can change,
But the one ready for magnificence.

—*Collected Proverbs,* Beatrice of Fourth

CHAPTER 1

Thorne, out of ancient Britain in AD 11, stood outside a vile-smelling dive, a real shithole, somewhere in El Paso One, Mortal Earth. He took deep breaths trying to calm the hell down so that he didn't draw his sword, go back inside, and impale a beefy-looking mortal who was more innocent than guilty in this little flirtation drama.

He whipped his Droid Ascender from the pocket of his jeans, a sweet interdimensional piece of technology that allowed him to call home. He all but punched the screen. Shit, his hand trembled. He had so much adrenaline and testosterone flooding his system that, yeah, he was shaking like a drunk off a bender.

The phone rang several times. "Pick up, pick up, pick up."

Finally, Alison's voice came on the line. "Sorry. Had to get out of Endelle's office before I answered."

"Okay, good." In the past three weeks since he'd left Second Earth, he'd grown dependent on Alison for a couple of reasons. She helped him keep his head screwed on straight, and she kept him informed on that little detail called the war against Commander Greaves.

He was about to launch into his current dilemma, as in

what to do about his woman who was making moves on another man, when Alison cut him off. "Thorne, there's something you've got to know right away, and it's bad."

His body stilled. Alison wasn't given to drama of any kind. From the day of her ascension over a year ago, she'd been an equalizing force among the Warriors of the Blood and especially with Endelle, serving as she did as the scorpion queen's executive assistant.

His hearing became focused, laser-like, on exactly what Alison would say next. He took another deep breath. "Let me have it."

"It's been all over the news for the past hour. In three days, Greaves is conducting a spectacle-grade military review that will last four, maybe six hours. Rumors are that he's marching an army of two hundred thousand troops, his 'Ascender Liberation Army,' down the Moscow Two avenue."

Thorne's lips parted because he needed to keep breathing, but he wasn't sure his lungs were working.

Greaves had just upped the stakes at the same moment that Thorne had gone AWOL to chase after a woman who wanted nothing to do with him.

Perfect.

"Are you there?" Alison asked.

"What?"

"Thorne, did you hear what I said?"

"Yes. Processing. Shit." He shook his head—like Alison could see that. "This is a completely illegal maneuver. COPASS can't let this slide, not this time. 'No entity shall engage in a public display of military prowess.' The rules are clear."

"Marcus has been on the phone nonstop to the international COPASS HQ in Prague. Every answer he's been given goes something like, *The committee has the Commander's request for permits under review.* But we all know what that means."

"Squat."

"Exactly. I hate to ask this, but can you come home? This news has all of the High Administrators still aligned with

Endelle jumpy. Three shifted their alliance to Greaves just because of the announcement. *Three*."

"Oh, shit."

"Exactly."

He turned back to face the run-down building, which blared some lively Mexican music: trumpets, guitars, and a quick beat.

Marguerite, his woman, his vampire bond-mate, was in there, getting one huge motherfucker of a Mexican all worked up with her long, blood-red nails and short platinum hair.

He'd followed her to Mortal Earth because he'd had no choice in the matter. Much to his surprise the goddamn *breh-hedden* had hit him flush in the jaw and torn all his good sense from its usual strong footings. All the warriors had thought the *breh-hedden* was a myth; then Alison had shown up and knocked Kerrick on his ass—Kerrick, the one who had vowed never to marry again. Three other warriors had followed, like dominoes: Marcus, Medichi, and just a few weeks ago Jean-Pierre.

Now it was his turn.

And Greaves had decided this was the hour to let the world know that he'd built an army worthy of victory, and was getting ready to launch his takeover bid of both Second Earth and Mortal Earth.

Fucking great.

He turned again, to once more face away from the bar. He felt the call of his world, of Second Earth, and of something more, something vast that had begun pulsing in the center of his brain. He lived with two aches now, the heavy pounding in his head and the stiff pulsing in his groin.

He was a man torn, now more than ever, because of the implied threat of a spectacle-based military review. Damn, there'd be fireworks and massive orchestral music as well as hundreds of DNA-altered swans and geese. Second Earth lived for spectacle and Greaves knew it. The damn thing was genius.

He squeezed his eyes shut and tried to think. Alison,

thank God, had fallen silent, giving him space, the usual. She'd been a counselor before she ascended. She knew how to let a moment breathe.

Finally, he said, "I'm going to do everything I can to move things along here. But I can't leave Marguerite right now and it isn't just because of the *breh-hedden*. Because she's obsidian flame, Greaves wants her dead. She's unprotected if I just take off. You know Endelle was counting on her emerging power to make a difference in the war. At the very least, I need to bring her home with me."

"You're right," Alison said, some of the tension leaving her voice. "I'd gotten so wrapped up in this review, I'd forgotten about Marguerite's power. Don't worry. I'll talk it over with Marcus. He'll understand. More than anyone, he'll understand." Marcus was four thousand years old and had only recently returned to Second Earth and to the Warriors of the Blood after a two-hundred-year absence, his own form of desertion.

Yeah, if anyone would understand all the dilemmas facing Thorne, Marcus would.

"I'd better go," he said.

"I almost forgot, what did you call for?"

"Nothing. I mean, I'll work it out." He laughed as he pushed a hand through his hair and all but dislodged his *cadroen*. "I may be calling you later. I've got a situation in El Paso Two."

Alison's voice dropped. "Oh, shit, Endelle just walked into my office. Gotta go."

The line went dead.

A military spectacle review. Jesus H. Christ.

He returned his phone to his jeans. He lowered his chin and went back into the bar. He sure could use a drink right about now, but for this ride he'd stopped with the Ketel One. Everything was coming to a head fast and he needed to see things just as they were, not through a vodka haze. Still, it sure didn't help that Marguerite was flashing a smile at that goddamn good-looking Mexican.

He drew his mist in tight. He was good at creating the

preternatural disguise that kept him invisible to anyone around him, especially here on Mortal Earth. Anyone, of course, except Marguerite. She could see him even though she'd been ignoring him all night. By now she was used to his hovering presence—he'd been dogging her heels from the first night he'd touched down on Mortal Earth.

They'd argued plenty, but this was the worst she'd been, sitting as close as she was to her current prey on a tall stool. It looked as though she'd made up her mind that tonight was the night.

He took up his former station, leaning against the wall, close to the door. He crossed his arms over his chest. His biceps flexed involuntarily. His nostrils flared. His breathing was still pretty uneven, especially since even at this distance he could smell her rose scent, rich red roses. It was the one sure sign that this woman was meant for him.

Yet he had no real claim on Marguerite, even though they'd been lovers for over a century. She'd broken with him, needing to go her own way, because she'd been locked up in a convent for the last hundred years. Her parents had consigned her to the Convent in Prescott Two in hopes of getting her to conform to their fanatical religious beliefs. She'd survived the ordeal by sustaining the hope that one day she'd be free to live however she wanted to live. So as soon as he'd liberated her, she'd hopped down to Mortal Earth and started a new life away from Second, away from the war, away from him.

The problem was that she'd ended their relationship at the exact moment the *breh-hedden* had kicked in.

What a nightmare the *breh-hedden* had proved to be. Marguerite was his *breh*, his bond-mate, the woman meant for him. She even carried a decadent rose scent that only he could detect. The urge to be near her, to protect her, to be joined to her in every way possible had overruled his common sense and even his duty as the leader of the Warriors of the Blood. That she also carried the red variety of obsidian flame power was just one more reason he'd felt compelled to follow her to Mortal Earth. Somehow he had to convince her to return with him to Second. So here he was, his back pinned to a goddamn wall in a stinking bar, and without a single clue as to how to convince her to come back with him.

He stared at the new Marguerite. She was as beautiful as ever, an almost perfectly oval face, strong arched brows, and large brown eyes, eyes he'd looked into ten thousand times while making love to her. She used to have really long straight brown hair that he would hold wrapped around his forearm when he took her from behind. Now she had short platinum-blond hair, white-blond, and blood-red fingernails about an inch long.

She sipped a very crimson cosmo, her current favorite drink, the same color as the lights flashing in his head. She had her elbow on the bar, her long nails flicking the feathered spikes of her hair.

The bastard next to her had his left knee about a millimeter away from hers. His eyelids lazed low.

Shit. Thorne knew exactly what that look meant: that the only thought running through the bastard's head would be just how soon he could get this woman on her back, or settled on his hips and riding him hard. He shuddered through a few more deep breaths.

He wasn't entirely to blame. The *breh-hedden* had him hooked in deep, forcing him to look at Marguerite not just as a woman but as his mate, his fucking mate. His mind swirled with a variety of impulses that kept shouting things like *Use your fists and beat the shit out of that asshole* or worse, *Use your sword and take the smile off his face permanently.*

This particular mortal wasn't half bad looking if you liked a scruff of a beard, a scar on the right cheek, thick black hair combed back straight, and tats on the neck, shoulders, and forearms. He was big, too. Warrior-big.

This was so not going to end well.

Under-fucking-statement.

Even through the stench of beer, smoke, and male bodies, all he could really process was that light floral scent that kept his dick in an uproar.

The bastard made his move. He reached out and grazed

Marguerite's elbow with the tips of two fingers, then moved away, a smooth, quick testing of the waters.

Marguerite smiled. She leaned in toward him and reached out with her hand to stroke his bicep.

Stroke his bicep.

Stroke his bicep.

The red strobes in his head spun faster. His fists balled. Creator help him. His palm itched for his sword. He spread his fingers wide, ready to catch some steel.

For a split second he almost completed the mental sequence that would have brought his sword into his hand. He saw the carnage as plain as day: one asshole with his head split wide, one woman caught up under his arm and hauled out of this hellhole kicking and screaming.

He was so close.

His fingers trembled.

He wanted his sword in his hand.

He wanted the bastard dead.

He didn't so much as *have* the thought as *act* because in the next split second he dematerialized out of the smoke and re-formed in the deep night shadows, well beyond the bar, well away from temptation. He bent over. He shook. He came within an inch of puking his guts out.

Shit. He'd almost killed an innocent man. Thorne, Warrior of the Blood, protector of the innocent, preserver of life, keeper of the peace, and he'd almost killed an innocent man. Creator help him.

So here he was, almost losing the Buffalo wings he'd gorged on, tortured because his woman, who was not his woman, was pursuing her favorite hunting-sport: *men.*

There was only one real question to answer: How the hell was he supposed to keep from killing this man if she succeeded in taking him into her bed?

Marguerite Dresner's fingertips tingled as she played over the tatted barbed wire on the stranger's bare, thick, muscled bicep. Her quarry's smell rose up around her. He wore a heavy cologne, heavy like his muscles, like the male scent she was getting from him. She flared her nostrils and sucked in more of what he was giving.

Unfortunately, another scent crowded the space.

Dammit, cherry tobacco. Again. For the thousandth time.

Despite the fact that she knew the real source, she asked, "Do you smoke a pipe?"

He shook his head, leaning into her a little. "Nope. I'm a cigar man. You like cigars?"

She liked the shape well enough. Who didn't? But she didn't care for the aroma. She did like pipe tobacco, though, which was one reason the cherry aroma bugged the shit out of her.

"Now, why are you frowning?" he asked. "What's made you unhappy?" He had a slight accent and a deep voice, fitting for all that body he carried around. Her gaze fell in a free fall to his snug jeans. This man knew how to display, and when his knee shifted just a little, the bulge moved.

She felt light-headed. She had waited so long for this, to explore the world again, to cruise the Mortal Earth bars and know a lot of men.

Men different from the only one she'd known for the past century.

Aw, shit, why did she have to think of Thorne right now. He hadn't wanted her to leave Second Earth, but she'd left anyway. She'd had to leave. She had a life to live and men to devour. One hundred years in that godforsaken Convent, the one with canings, and strappings, and beatings, had left her needing so much more of life than what Second Earth could offer right now.

Why couldn't Thorne get that? Why couldn't he just leave her alone?

She saw from her peripheral vision that he was done with holding up the wall. Huh, so maybe he'd finally taken the hint. He'd glowered and looked so hot in jeans and a wife-beater shirt that it was all she could do to keep from going over there and attacking him.

But she needed him to get the message. She couldn't go

back to him and she sure as hell couldn't go back to Second Earth. As much as she knew this would kill him, she'd been putting off the inevitable for three weeks now. She'd spent some time getting her bearings, learning to drive, then driving through state after state and back again. It was late March and most of the lower states were a piece of heaven.

But tonight she was crossing over, ending her connection to the past. She was beginning the real adventure, the fantasy that had kept her sane during her hundred years in that Convent.

She forced memories of Thorne down deep.

She lifted her gaze to the dark brown eyes in front of her, the man flirting with her, casting out signals. His gaze was slung low on her chest, as it should be. She'd hardly covered her girls up at all, and even though the bar was a little steamy her nipples were firm and probably nicely puckered, pushing against the dark blue silk.

He leaned in close, his hand sliding up her leg and squeezing her bare thigh. The man had a nice firm, possessive touch. He whispered against her ear, "Let's get out of here. I've got a place close by."

Shivers chased down her shoulders and sides from all that breath over her neck. Her heart set up a racket in her chest.

She didn't answer him. She just slid off the stool, took his big hand, and headed for the door. This is what she remembered it being like, the excitement, meeting some stranger, getting worked up after a couple of drinks, wondering how good he'd be in bed.

She had a knack for picking men who knew how to work it. This man had *good lay* written all over him. God, what a body, almost as big as Thorne.

Thorne again! Dammit!

She reached the cool clean desert air and drank in a big gulp, hoping to clear her head. But there it was again, cherry tobacco, stronger now that she was outside. She looked to her left and could see him in the shadows but lifted her chin and moved on. She needed him to get a clue: He could glower all he wanted, but this was the life she wanted, the life she'd chosen. Hell, this was the life she'd earned after so many decades locked up.

But when she got a few feet down the sidewalk, suddenly he was just there, all misted up so her new man couldn't see him. He didn't try to touch her but she couldn't help looking straight at him. Oh . . . God.

Don't do this, his mind sent straight into hers. *Please.*

His hands had dropped to his sides and were balled into fists. She could tell he was holding on by a thread.

She dropped her gaze to his chest. She couldn't bear looking into his eyes. How could she explain the why of all this? But then explaining wasn't necessary. This was what killed her about Thorne: He got her, he understood her, he knew she had to do this, had to leave, had to move on. In his way, he was letting her go. He sure as hell could have just thrown her over his shoulder, and maybe that's what she wished he would do so that she didn't have to choose.

But she had chosen.

Thanks for not making a scene, she sent.

Fuck, he responded, probably not meaning to.

Let me go, Thorne. Please.

Another quiet *Fuck* left his mouth, but he dematerialized.

Her new man leaned down. "We good?"

She looked back up at him. "We're good." She still had hold of his hand so she gave it a squeeze.

But something deep inside her trembled. She felt an overwhelming need to get back to Thorne.

Would this torture never end?

Would she ever truly be free of Second Earth?

She forced the trembling to stop.

Forget all that.

She had a life to live.

She ran a hand through her short blond locks.

He put his hands on her waist. "What's your name?" He dipped his head low and kissed her cheek.

"Marguerite."

"That's a beautiful name. *Marguerite.*" He said it slow, like he was practicing, like he intended to say it a lot and at exactly the right time.

"What's yours?" she asked. He shifted her beside him and set them both moving slowly in the direction of a big Chevy Silverado, the kind with four wheels on the back. A big man needed a big truck.

She needed a big man.

"José. My name's José."

"Mexican?"

"*Sí.*" The word popped out like a whip. "Mexican okay with you?"

"You mean, do I discriminate?"

"*Sí.*" Again, like a whip.

She put her hand on his hip and moved lower, sliding her fingers so that she rested over the entire beautiful length of his erect cock, the jeans rough against her fingers. "Oh, I discriminate. Right here, José. Is that okay with you?"

She pushed.

He hissed. "Yeah, it's okay."

She smiled. "Let's go, José, before I change my mind."

This time he smiled. He had a wonderful smile full of big teeth. She wanted those teeth on her.

Thorne had big teeth, too. He'd use them nipping, pulling, biting, plucking. He'd done it for a hundred years and knew exactly how to work her up.

Dammit, Thorne again.

Thorne stood in the shadows of the building. He didn't know what to do. Her scent was heavy in the air.

He watched them get into the truck.

He created more mist. He lost his shirt and mounted his wings. He shot into the air high overhead and followed the truck.

The red strobes still flashed through his brain but at least some part of his mind was functioning because his rational side had begun to calculate, to figure this damn thing out.

The man, José, would die tonight unless Thorne got his shit together and connected some dots.

He could engage in fist-to-fist, a battle he would win. So at the very least, yeah, he was doing that. He'd leave the bastard unconscious so that he'd live, but Marguerite would be pissed. She didn't have the gentlest temperament, an understatement that made him smile. She was his wildcat, game for anything, and he loved that about her.

But in this situation, her fighting spirit limited his options.

So what the hell was he supposed to do now?

He could call the cops, create a little diversion, cause some chaos. But again . . . woman . . . pissed. The one thing he'd learned from being Endelle's second-in-command was a little diplomacy, a sense of timing, a sense of when not to go all shock-and-awe, when something less splashy was called for. Not that he'd learned strategic thinking from her; rather, he'd learned because of her scorpion temperament and her recklessness. Thorne wasn't reckless, which was one reason his current predicament was a total shitfest.

He'd like to let loose. God knew he would. He'd like to let loose, use every power in his arsenal, and fix this thing right now. But that was warrior thinking: *Shoot now . . . don't even think about asking questions later.*

No, this fucking conundrum required finesse.

The truck pulled in front of a house that was much nicer than expected given the man's tats and the overall sleazy nature of the bar. The rock landscaping out front didn't even have weeds. Huh. The bastard might actually be a fairly decent bastard. Thorne even liked the truck. He knew the score. A big man needed something that fit the size of his shoulders.

As the bastard left the driver's side and went around to Marguerite's door, Thorne touched down at least fifty yards away, keeping his mist tight. He drew in his wings. He knew that if Marguerite looked around she'd see him, but when José opened the door she pushed off the running board and leaped into his arms.

He caught her and wasted no time jamming his tongue down her throat. His woman ate it up.

Thorne watched both sets of jaws working like mad.

Aw, fuck.

Before he realized he'd thought the thought, he pushed his mind against José's and slipped through the back door of the bastard's head. He was inside the man's mind.

He ignored the firebomb of desire that flipped words like *tits* and *ass* through the bastard's head with rapid slingshot-like movements. Instead he focused on what he'd been missing for three weeks, the feel of Marguerite's swift darting tongue pushing into his mouth . . . well, José's mouth.

The experience was unusual to say the least, because it was as though he not only was inside José's mind but could feel what José was feeling. And there seemed to be a strange vibration to the whole experience, like a low level of electricity all through Thorne's body.

At the very least, he felt like he could take partial possession of José's mind and body and just enjoy the ride, but because the red strobes were still flashing in his head, he knew at some point he'd probably lose it and take every one of the bastard's brain cells with a pointed thought or two.

He forced his brain to work hard at a solution, even in the face of José pawing Marguerite's breasts.

Oh, dear God.

He had to figure this out. He started flipping through José's memories. He had a bunch of friends. He liked women, a lot. He knew how to use a blade. He sure as hell knew how to use his cock. There was a lot he liked about the man. He even earned his living buying and selling shit on the Internet. The bastard was a goddam entrepreneur. Okay, he really couldn't kill him now. He was a contributing member of society.

So what the hell was he supposed to do?

What could he do?

He focused on the strange vibration he was feeling, the ease with which he could feel all that José was experiencing.

He pulled out of his mind.

José drew back from Marguerite, slid his arm around her waist, and propelled her to the front door.

A moment later that door closed and Thorne was left alone in the dark.

The trembling through his body started all over again. Jesus H. Christ. He felt those impulses fall on him, to race after the bastard and strip his skin from his body, one inch at a time.

Instead of reacting, he worked on his breathing and focused on this new strange sensation. Something was going on, a new power maybe, something unexpected. That deep throbbing in his brain got a little worse as well, but mostly it was this strange vibration and an urge to put a hand on José, but this time not to hurt him.

What would happen then, if he touched him?

He once more slid inside the bastard's head and sifted through the man's recent memories. He found a recent interaction with a friend named Miguel. He could see Miguel's face, even hear his voice.

Thorne sped to the front door and pounded. He then moved back about ten feet, still cloaked in mist. He called out, "*Hermano,* get your ass out here," in just the way Miguel would have, the way he often heard Santiago speak.

Jose opened the door and peeked his head out. He was sweating and his shirt was off.

Thorne penetrated José's mind and offered a little thrall action. *Tell her you'll be right back. Your friend needs your help.*

He looked behind him. "Stay here. I'll be right back. My friend Miguel is having problems."

Thorne could feel Marguerite reaching out for him telepathically, but he shut his mind down hard. He guided José to his truck and told him to hop in the back and have a nice nap. José practically sprang inside, stretched himself the length of the bed, and was out.

Thorne, now balancing on the top of the side, looked down at him. Marguerite wouldn't remain where she was for very long. Whatever he was going to do, he had to do it quick.

He leaped into the bed beside José and went with his instincts. He put his hand on José's face and felt that same vibration, a kind of electricity. He let it flow until it streamed through Thorne's body. His mist dissipated.

He rose up and turned toward the house.

Uh-oh.

Marguerite stood in the doorway, topless, her arms folded beneath her beautiful oh-so-familiar breasts. She still wore her short skirt and stilettos, which somehow made the whole picture sexier than if she were completely naked.

He was in for it now.

"Well, you coming or not?"

Thorne froze. Why wasn't Marguerite mad? Or was she? She didn't look mad? Her lips were swollen and she was ready for the action she'd been chasing all night.

He jumped down lightly from the bed of the truck. He was about to explain that he didn't want to kill her date so he'd put him in a slight doze when he realized that he wasn't quite himself. He felt odd just moving his legs. His upper thighs seemed heavier than usual like he carried a few more pounds. He glanced down and saw . . . not himself.

He was . . . José.

Holy hell, he'd just morphed.

Well, didn't this change things up?

For a split second he considered telling her the truth, but when she lowered her arms and thrust her chest out, he thought he'd be a fool to do anything other than accept her invitation.

Marguerite looked her prey up and down. He was built like Thorne except beefier. She'd also felt the most important part of him and yeah, like Thorne, his assets were just right, maybe not quite as well endowed as Thorne but he'd do. God, yes, he'd do.

She smiled. She'd been waiting for this for a hundred years and three long weeks. She didn't know why she'd even put this off. Anticipation streaked through her in fiery flashes, and watching José move toward her now like he meant to devour her in one big bite made her smile broaden.

José smiled back.

"What were you doing out there?" she asked when he reached the doorway.

"You should be inside," he said. "I have neighbors."

"Thought I'd give 'em a thrill."

"You're giving me a thrill."

"That's all that matters." When he got close, she grabbed his arm and pulled him into the house then slammed the door.

He moved fast as he picked her up and lifted her high, really high, as in his-mouth-to-her-breast high. She slung her legs around his back. He slammed her against the door.

"You getting rough with me?" But she was panting a little.

"You complaining?"

"No."

He settled in for a suck, taking her breast in his mouth and tugging in hard pulls, just the way she liked it. She knocked her head against the door because his mouth felt so good. This was what she wanted. This was what she needed.

Thorne used to suck her breasts like this, like he was drinking from the fountain of life and couldn't get enough. She had loved it then. She loved it now. Did all men enjoy breasts like this? She didn't know. The memories of the men she'd had before Thorne were a century distant, all but forgotten in terms of technique.

"Hey, where did you go?" José looked up at her. She liked his accent.

"I want my skirt off."

All those big teeth gleamed in the dim light. He leaned back and let her slide to the floor. He stepped away from her, his lids at half-mast. She reached behind her and unzipped the tight red leather. The zipper could have been a little longer, but it made wiggling out of the damn thing the right kind of show to put on. It was a real trick to keep her thong on at the same time, but she managed. It was just a bit of lace and sheer red fabric, but he would probably appreciate a little more anticipation.

When José's gaze felt to her bare mons, he whispered, "Nice wax." And his eyes rolled in his head, then he licked his lips.

"Where's your bedroom? I wanna be on my back."

"I want you on your back."

He didn't give her directions; he slung one arm behind her back and the other behind her knees and she was airborne. He was just strong enough and she was just small enough that he tossed her in the air a little as he walked.

She giggled. She was so damn happy.

When they reached the master bedroom, he tossed her on the bed and she landed laughing. She spread her legs wide and because it was something Thorne had always loved, she slid her hand down her abdomen, beneath her thong, and massaged herself.

"You'll make me come just standing here if you keep that up." Yep, she really liked his accent. There was just something so smooth about a Latin cadence.

"You'll have to stop me."

His jaw trembled and he moved kinda slow so she kept rubbing. It felt good.

"You like your hand there?"

"Sometimes my hand is my best friend."

"Not tonight." But he leaned down and kissed the back of her hand and nuzzled her, pushing at her so that together they were giving her a thrill.

She liked José. She liked his style. Thorne would have done something like this. Thorne would have *loved* how bare she was.

Thorne again . . . and yet she didn't feel quite so guilt-stricken. He'd probably taken off, at last, and now she was free.

She felt free.

José finally seemed to reach his limit with her self-ministrations. He pulled her hand away and slid her thong off, taking his time, but his gaze was fixed on the full lips of her lower body and again his tongue made an appearance. She leaned back on the bed, stretching out. She pulled her knees up but kept them spread wide.

He took a good long minute to look at her. She could hear him breathing. He sounded a little strangled.

She took the opportunity to let her gaze drift down his body. The sight of his broad chest and muscular pecs, his abs rolling down and down, caused her body to give one full undulating roll that ended with a strong tug deep inside. "I could come just looking at you," she said.

He smiled. He unbuttoned his jeans and pushed them down. But unlike her, he caught his briefs at the same time so that his package sprang free and now it was her turn to lick her lips. Yep, almost as big as Thorne.

Funny how she kept thinking about Thorne and yet it no longer bothered her. Guess she was making progress.

About time.

José grabbed her ankles and pulled her to the edge of the bed. He knelt, then he got busy.

"*Muy bueno*," she murmured.

Obsidian flame, above all else, requires surrender.
And surrender is never for the faint of heart.

—Collected Proverbs, Beatrice of Fourth

CHAPTER 2

Sweat popped all across Thorne's forehead, but he wasn't sure of the cause—whether it was the energy required to sustain the man he'd morphed into, or the sight of his woman bare, completely bare.

Oh . . . God.

His pulse throbbed in his neck. He wanted to sink his fangs and give her the potion she loved, but he couldn't. He wasn't even sure if in this form he could use his fangs.

Pity.

God, the things he wanted to do to Marguerite. Now that the *breh-hedden* had slammed him hard, all the usual desire he felt for her had about tripled so that he wept from his erection and his pulse pounded at every hinge of his body.

He lowered to her mons and swept his cheeks over the smooth soft skin. He kissed her repeatedly, savoring all that bareness as well as her familiar whimpers of pleasure. In the Convent, where he'd made love to her just about every morning at dawn, he'd cast a tent of mist over them both to keep the noisiness of their lovemaking from reaching other parts of the building.

He didn't have to do that now.

He trembled as he slid his arms under her knees. Her deep red-rose scent perfumed the air and worked him up. He was hard as a rock.

He didn't know what to do first—kiss her or lick her or just stare at what was to his eyes so beautiful, a perfect work of art.

He kissed her some more, his lips against her moist, swollen lips, plucking, adding a little nip then a suck. He kissed her in a line all the way to her opening . . . but that's when things went a little haywire because she was already thrashing on the bed and he was working to hold her tight but dammit, his tongue decided he had to have her.

He thrust his tongue in and out of her hard, like he was fucking her, like he couldn't get deep enough. She came rising up off the bed but he kept her hips pinned down. Was she aware that she was using her preternatural strength and that only with a matching power did he keep her from flying off the bed?

Probably not, because as he thrust into her and thrust and thrust, she screamed her orgasm. But he kept it up, looking up at her when he could, watching the ecstasy on her face, savoring the pleasure she felt. He brought her a second time and a third.

He was in trouble now, though. He could feel the vibrations in his body and had to work to keep from changing back.

At the same time, he had to have her.

He rose up and while she was still caught in the remnants of an orgasm, he shoved himself deep inside, which sent her once more flying up. He landed on top of her, pressing her into the mattress, grounding her.

He fucked her, hard. Shoving into her, pulling back, shoving in, watching her thrash some more beneath him. Her moans had turned into wild grunts and cries.

He was two men now, one in the throes of sex, the other struggling to hold his shape as José. His lower back tightened, his balls ready to fire off.

When the orgasm came, when he began to jerk, he lifted off her, supporting himself with his arms, his hips bucking into her. He looked down at her. "Look at me," he commanded.

She opened her eyes, which were wild with passion. She could hardly focus. He kept pumping as he held her gaze. This was his woman and he loved her. This was his woman, Marguerite, and he had a drive toward her now like nothing he had ever known. He had loved her for a long time in the Convent, but not like this. He spent every last drop his body had made for her, the body pretending to be José, but his seed belonged to him, couldn't belong to anyone else, and that's what he put inside her.

The vibrations were getting stronger now. Despite the fact that he had a powerful desire, even a need to remain connected to her, he had to get away. Now. Or he'd morph back.

And like hell was he going to reveal this little secret. It might just be the only way he'd keep from killing her lovers if she continued down this path.

He pulled out. He didn't like abandoning her like this, but he had to keep up his ruse.

He grabbed his jeans from the floor and went into the bathroom. He counted to ten. "My brother just left a text," he called out. "He needs a ride. I gotta go."

He dressed in rapid movements. When he reached the door he looked back at her. She looked so beautiful sprawled as she was. She looked confused as well, but he couldn't help himself as he said, "You know the way out. Call a cab. Just don't be here when I get back. My brother has a temper and besides, I don't like women in *mi casa* in the morning."

Okay, maybe that was mean, but she shouldn't have been bonking José.

He saw her eyes flash and knew her temper wouldn't be far behind, so he hightailed it. He ran out to the truck, and because he wasn't sure if Marguerite would cheat and use her folding skills to reach the front door, he got into the vehicle the old-fashioned way by opening the door and sliding in. He did, however, ignore the key as he touched the ignition to start the truck. He wasn't surprised that just as he started backing out she opened the front door.

He almost stalled out, his foot jerking away from the accelerator, because there she was, buck naked, and flipping him off.

There was so much he enjoyed about Marguerite, but it was her spirit that got him. She stood in the doorway, facing the front yard, without a stitch on and not caring who saw her. She was the kind of woman that would go down battling, nothing less.

"Asshole," she shouted.

He almost put on the brakes. He wanted to head straight back into the house, carry her into José's bedroom, and do her all over again. But the vibrations were getting stronger and he was sweating into his jeans.

He looked away and gathered his wits. He pointed the truck in the direction of the bar. When he was at last in a different part of town, and several miles away, he pulled the truck over, morphed back into himself, then released a long deep breath.

He was covered in sweat and gave one full-body shiver. Well, that was fucking weird.

He jumped into the back of the truck, woke José up, handed him the keys, and wiped his memory. He folded back to Marguerite's hotel room and heard the shower running.

He stretched out on the bed and waited.

He smelled roses and what do you know, he was smiling.

Okay, was it wrong to be enjoying himself?

The truth was, he couldn't remember the last time he'd smiled like this. Maybe a century ago, before his sister Grace had sequestered herself in the Convent, and before her twin, Patience, had been killed by death vampires. Yeah, maybe that far back.

Owen Stannett had everything set up, ready and waiting, candles lit, incense burning, shutters drawn to dampen the noise of Mexico City nightlife. He'd even had a new red leather chaise-longue made up for his favorite activity. This would be his first venture into the future streams since leaving Second Earth.

He'd spent the last three weeks hunting for Seers through all the known rogue colonies on Mortal Earth and hadn't found a single one. However, since these colonies weren't in any way hidden from Second Earth, they were accessible to Greaves. The Commander had probably already done his own reconnaissance and removed any Seers he found to his favorite Second Earth Fortresses in Mumbai, Johannesburg, and Bogatá.

Both Endelle's administration and COPASS knew where these rogue colonies were and kept track of all movements in and out of them. Designated liaison officers from Second Earth interfaced with the local governing entities to make sure that everyone was behaving and not alerting Mortal Earth to the presence of either the dimensional world of ascension or the inflammatory nature of vampire biology.

His search had been a huge disappointment given his plans to create his own Fortress in Mexico City One. However, he was convinced there had to be a conclave of Seers somewhere, maybe someplace secret, maybe heavily misted by an unknown entity.

So tonight he would begin searching in the future streams, something he'd been avoiding. One of the drawbacks of future stream work was that any Seer's activity could be detected by other powerful Seers. Granted, there were only a handful on Second Earth who had that level of power, but it sure as hell only took one, and the one he was avoiding was Marguerite Dresner.

Essentially, his activities in the future streams were only as successful as his ability to remain undetected. What he had going for him, however, was fairly substantial, since Marguerite hated being a Seer and avoided the future streams. So despite a certain vulnerability, he'd made the decision to launch his new life on Mortal Earth, which meant he needed to round up a batch of Seers, lock them up, and put them to work on his behalf.

He stretched out on the chaise-longue, the back of his heavily embroidered leather cowboy boots hitting a protective cloth covering. By nervous habit, he ran his hand over the carefully styled wave of hair along the right side of his head. The motion soothed him, eased his nerves.

The time had come. He could feel it in a smooth vibration of energy through his body.

Something big had been moving through the future streams for the last year, big but invisible, like a leviathan that surfaced in the ocean to taunt sailing ships, only to disappear beneath the waves, always pursued, never caught. He felt pretty certain this had something to do with obsidian flame, which had finally lifted its head just a few weeks ago with the blood slave Fiona, as well as with Marguerite. The women had worked together, coordinating efforts. The demonstration of their combined power had been impressive.

Yet he also understood that obsidian flame always came in threes, so another woman was destined to form the third leg of the triad. To date, she hadn't shown up.

He let his arms rest next to his sides. He closed his eyes. The strong scent of patchouli surrounded him now, and because the air-conditioning kept a gentle stream of air flowing around the room, he could see the candlelight flicker behind his eyes.

He took deep lingering breaths as though the bottom of his lungs were somewhere near his intestines.

Slowly he let his mind open. If he moved too fast, the future streams would crash down on him, rendering him immobile and vulnerable. This at least he'd learned to manage over the centuries.

With his Seer's eye barely open, he saw a broad spectrum of color, ribbons of light that went on, yes, forever, away from him, away from this point in time. His heart swelled and pleasure flowed through him. This was what he enjoyed most, this unexpected connection to what was his most essential gift.

He released a deep purifying breath and opened his mind just a little more. The ribbons began to move now, shimmering and rippling in waves. From his Seer's eye, he moved to stand before the ribbons and lifted his right hand as if preparing to offer a minister's blessing.

He lived in extraordinary times, as though the future had suddenly gotten in a big hurry and rushed toward Second Earth and Mortal Earth. He recognized the power behind this force—and it emanated from Commander Greaves. He was putting pressure on the world, on two worlds. Greaves had not lacked for ambition or for money. He had acquired the majority of Second Earth's mineral wealth long before the value of the minerals was known. He could afford to build an army, two armies, a thousand armies.

But in response, as though the earth couldn't easily tolerate the ambitions of sociopaths, new powers had emerged to contest Greaves's megalomania. The Warriors of the Blood, always an extraordinary if small force against Greaves, had begun growing in power with the appearance of powerful mates, or *brehs,* in their lives.

And now obsidian flame.

He still couldn't quite comprehend what such a powerful gift, based on a triad of connection, would mean for Madame Endelle and her administration. If he'd understood recent events, the first of the obsidian flame powers, belonging to Fiona, gave her a profound ability to channel the powers of others and even to allow a possession, which increased the preternatural power of both parties exponentially. Fiona had allowed a possession of Madame Endelle and together they had folded twenty thousand people from an arena disaster to safety. He could not fathom this level of combined power.

He knew that Marguerite was the second leg of this triad, that she had the red variety of obsidian flame, which meant that her already significant Seer abilities would be enhanced by her obsidian connection.

He positioned himself across from Marguerite's ribbon. She was incredibly powerful. In the Seer realm—and this perhaps frightened him more than anything else—he strongly suspected that because of obsidian flame, she would now have the capacity to reach pure vision, or 100 percent accuracy in her visions. It was something he could not do, nor could any other Seer he knew. A Seer who had the capacity for pure vision would be of inestimable value to the person who had charge of her: She would be able to see events as they unfolded in the future exactly as they would happen.

He was tempted to enter her future stream ribbon to see what she was up to, but he hesitated because of her power—and because he valued his own skin. Her level of Seer power wasn't the only significant preternatural ability she possessed. A couple of weeks ago, he'd tried to abduct her from Mortal Earth's I-10, a major highway that crossed the lower continental United States. She'd been driving a convertible, top down, in the New Mexico area when he'd stopped her car, ready to apprehend her. But she'd delivered a hand-blast that had shot him deep into the sky as though he'd been nothing more than a rag doll. He'd been able to fold to safety midflight, but it had required the rest of the day to heal from all the burns. If he'd been a lesser vampire, he would have ended up very dead.

Basically, he'd given up on acquiring her, so he now turned his attention toward locating, if possible, a group of Seers that might be living in some kind of protected facility on Mortal Earth. If they existed, he'd find them in the future streams. Very little was hidden from him once he entered the ribbons of light.

So instead of taking chances with anything having to do with Marguerite, he focused his thoughts very specifically on *hidden Seers of power.*

As he let his mind go very loose with this thought held foremost, the future streams began to move slowly, then gathered speed until he was watching a blur of color that became very light in hue, almost white.

Hidden Seers of power.

Finally, the line of ribbons began to slow and to differentiate into specific colors until the entire band stopped and a ribbon of burnished dark gray metal rose above the rest directly opposite him.

A female, a Seer, became visible to him.

He smiled. Yes, he enjoyed his power very much.

The woman was tall with some freckles, straight black hair to her shoulders. She had tattoos, and a hair-sized silver loop pierced her right eyebrow. She also had a small amber jewel just above her left nostril on the side of her nose. Her eyes were an unusual color: gray. A very pure gray.

Her name came to him.

Brynna.

He picked up the ribbon and it was like fire in his metaphysical hands, a wicked amount of energy flowing through his fingers.

He let her future come to him, images that began to move very swiftly; daylight, a cabin, a woman behind her, a knock on the door. He tested the women. His heart began to race. They were both Seers.

The location? He panned around and saw forest, a very thick dark forest, not pine, more like fir. He looked up toward the sky and saw mist, but not the usual white lace pattern, something with a strange green hue. He panned back and the door opened: Marguerite stood there, behind a screen door. He held his breath, waiting to see what would happen next, but Marguerite's Seer power, whether activated by her or not, could have an effect.

He saw her lips move. The stream began to fade until it disappeared.

He cursed. He needed to know where this was and what had happened, or rather what was going to happen. Because of the strange mist, he thought this place might be exactly what he was looking for: a hidden colony of some kind.

He had to continue. Had to learn more.

He still held Brynna's ribbon, so he ordered his mind and began to rewind the image, letting it flow backward until he could see the mist again. He had some skills when it came to the future streams and he used them now. He held the ribbon steady and froze the moment while still inside the vision.

This time, he focused on the location again and panned skyward, pulling back and back as though rising into the air, higher and higher until the mountains grew small and other towns appeared, until he could see the coastline of, yes, the Pacific Northwest. This colony existed in the Cascade range in the state of Washington, Mortal Earth. He then concentrated on the timing of this meeting. He could feel that the women would meet . . . tomorrow.

When he sat up, the incredible nature of his discovery flew around in his chest like a bird that had just been set free. He was astonished at his find. He ran a hand lightly over his wave. So there was a hidden colony, with Seers in residence, on Mortal Earth.

His mind began to order his next steps. He would confer with the leader of his small attack force, comprising eight powerful death vampires. He would make an advance visit to the location and establish the when and where of the attack.

He grew relaxed and content now that he had a plan. His new life on Mortal Earth commenced tonight. There would be no bureaucracy to manipulate, no Madame Endelle to sidestep, no Warriors of the Blood to avoid. He could do what he wanted because these Seers were living under the radar. With a little care and planning, he could simply appear, search through the colony, and take what he wanted.

He smiled as he left his meditation room and moved to a veranda that wrapped around the entire central courtyard. Very clever, these houses that looked like nothing from the outside but were elegant and lovely inside. A deception. He loved deceptions.

He crossed the courtyard to the large room opposite where his Mexican death vampires lived and plotted their nightly forays into the surrounding communities. The size of Mortal Earth's population, especially the number of people living in major cities, made for easy pickings for the pretty-boys.

Marguerite had been in the shower a long time and still she scrubbed herself silly.

She was so pissed.

She couldn't believe that José, a mere mortal, had actually told her to get out. She'd never been more shocked in her life. She'd had her own speech ready, right on the tip of her tongue, to the effect that she'd had a great time, but she just wasn't interested in seeing him again. Then José had said he had to split and she shouldn't be here when he got back.

The nerve.

At last, she turned the water off and stepped out of the shower. As she did, her fury eased up and in its stead was something very close to remorse. Essentially she'd just cheated on Thorne, even though she'd already dumped his ass. But then, the fact that she felt even a nanosecond of regret pissed her off all over again. She'd already told Thorne to get lost. She'd made it clear in a thousand different ways that she was done with him and her life on Second Earth.

Through all the decades locked up in the Convent, her dream of a new life on Mortal Earth had kept her going. She'd always seen herself this way, living free and hooking up with as many men as she wanted, hitting the road at dawn every morning, and travelling to the ends of the earth, then starting all over again. She didn't want to be accountable to anyone or anything.

On the other hand, Thorne didn't deserve to be put through this. Maybe her dreams of freedom had kept her going, but Thorne's presence in her life had kept her sane. But why had he followed her? He knew what she'd intended. She'd never made it a secret that once she got free, she was going on a prolonged man-hunt, maybe for a millennium.

She spread her towel on the toilet seat and sat down. She leaned over, put her elbows on her knees and her chin in her hands. The trouble was, she kinda felt like two people and torn right down the middle. She wanted Thorne. Aw, hell, she craved him.

But there was another part of her that also craved freedom and self-determination the way her lungs craved air, as though she would die without it.

Then there was Owen Stannett and Commander Greaves. Either of those major pricks would be oh-so-happy to strap a new ankle guard on her leg, hook her up to a Seer milking machine, and never let her see the light of day again. So what the hell would she do if Greaves or Stannett started a major campaign to acquire her?

There was nothing about her current predicament that was simple. Above all, she wished she could get rid of her obsidian flame ability. Unfortunately, once a preternatural power arrived, it was just there, forever.

At least her obsiddy power, as she liked to call it, seemed to be sleeping for now, thank you, God. She and Fiona were sisters in obsidian flame, and supposedly one day there would be another. Once they joined powers, they would be able to make some kind of cosmic orchestral music together—not literally, but something as yet undefined.

The night she'd left Second Earth, Madame Endelle had promised her all sorts of freedom if she would stay and help out her administration. But Marguerite hadn't been tempted, not even a little. Her experience thus far with administrators of any kind was that they would say one thing then do another, usually with the help of, yeah, an ankle guard.

A promise of freedom? Nothing in her experience told her she could count on that promise, from anyone.

So she'd left and here she was, feeling guilty as hell because she'd just cheated on Thorne even though she wasn't even with him anymore.

She let go of a really big sigh then heard whistling from the other room. At the same, she caught a whiff of cherry tobacco.

Thorne.

Her first reaction involved a slight jumping of her spirit so that she rose to her feet and almost smiled. Thorne would never have told her to just get out of his room. Never.

Thorne.

But the moment she let his name drift through her head, guilt powered down so hard she nearly fell to her knees. She'd just had some amazing sex with José, some of the best of her life, but now her vampire boyfriend of the past century was in her hotel room.

She cared about Thorne, she really did. But he needed to move on, get his own life, get back to the war.

She dried off her hair in rapid swipes of the towel over her head, shuffled her fingers through to even the strands out, then shrugged into her white terry robe.

When she left the bathroom, her heart lurched at the sight of him. He was sprawled on the bed, no shirt, looking as yummy as ever. He had on jeans and she knew he would be commando because that was his style. He reclined on his side facing her.

"Aw, you're wearing a robe." He clucked his tongue a couple of times.

She sighed again. She hated being this torn. And she really did need him to move on.

"What are you doing here?" She turned away from him and hunted through her suitcase. She had a bunch of new clothes. Shoplifting was just plain fun. She'd even let herself be cuffed and put in the back of a police car. When neither of the officers responded to her overtures, she'd just wiped their memories and folded to the Holiday Inn.

She smelled his cherry tobacco again. Dammit, she liked that scent way too much, and it liked her, right between her legs. For a long hard moment she thought about jumping his bones, just for old times' sake. But in the end, she needed Thorne to quit following her around. He needed to stop with all the protective bullshit and get on with gettin' on.

"You're beautiful," Thorne said.

At that, she stopped pushing all the mixed-up crap around in her suitcase and turned toward him. "I guess we need to have this out."

But he just smiled. He had an ease to his eyes that was very familiar.

Her mouth popped wide. "You just had sex."

"I did." He grinned. The bastard had the nerve to grin.

Marguerite closed the distance to the bed preternaturally fast so that before she knew what she was doing, or even intended to do, she straddled him, her robe falling open, which only made him grin some more.

"Who was she?" She thumped his chest with her fist.
"Tell me her name. Did you find her in one of the local dives
or maybe out there in the lobby?"

"I'm a gentleman," he said, lacing his hands behind his
head. "I don't fuck and tell. You know that."

She was so mad she couldn't think straight. She started
pounding on his thick muscled pecs with both hands. She let
out a strange keening sound she didn't think could ever have
come out of her throat. She hated the thought of Thorne with
another woman.

The next second he grabbed her arms and flipped her over,
pinning her. He put his mouth on hers and kissed her . . .
hard. She tried to fight him but he was six-five and really
built, lean, tough, and hardened by war. It was like struggling
against steel.

After a moment, when she'd quieted a little, he pulled
back.

"I'm so mad."

"You? Mad? Impossible. You have the gentlest temperament."

"Screw you." But he kissed her again, and because he
smelled delicious, like her favorite pipe tobacco, her muscles grew lax and she let him put his tongue in her mouth.

She shouldn't have done that. She really shouldn't. She
loved Thorne's tongue. Aw, hell, she loved Thorne, she just
didn't want this, all this closeness and connection, all this
future she could feel pressing down on her.

After a moment, he pulled back. She wanted him to understand, she really did. But the truth was, she didn't understand it herself.

"Isn't it killing you not to be with the brotherhood? Not
to be in charge, although I'd bet just about anything that
you've been issuing orders all this time."

His smiled was crooked. "Yeah. I put Kerrick in charge,
but he didn't like that job. I just turned the reins over to
Luken." He frowned slightly. "Santiago and Zach are feuding, something about me, I guess."

Guilt started piling up again. He was chasing her but he knew where he was needed. "You should go back."

He searched her eyes. "I will when it's time, but right now I have something I want to ask you, something I've always wanted to know." She could guess. "You never told me, not in any real detail, why you hated your childhood. I know you said you think we should have this out, but maybe I can't let go because I don't get it, not all of it. Tell me something, Marguerite. Let me in a little."

She looked up at him. He had such a gorgeous face, high pronounced cheekbones in sharp lines, low slightly arched brows in that sandy color that matched his hair. She loved his hair, all that thick, coarse mass, sun-burnished as if it had been painted with gold. His jawline met in a firm chin. But the pad of his chin was raised, round, and soft. She rubbed it now. His lips weren't full but compressed and strong. His eyes mesmerized her, a thousand different shards of gray and green, gold and light brown that somehow blended to create a smooth hazel look.

She reached behind his neck and removed the pick from his *cadroen*. She tossed it higher up on the bed and pulled his long warrior hair forward. "I love your hair. It almost has a wave and it's so thick."

"You're not answering my question."

"I'm thinking." She wondered what she should tell him that could explain her heart, or in some way help him to understand her drive to be free. "Do you know why I cut my hair?"

"I thought you wanted something new. I love it, by the way."

She was surprised. "I thought you'd hate it."

"Well"—he smiled—"when it was long, it did have one advantage."

Her neck tingled at the reference. He had taken her from behind a lot, wrapping her long, long hair around his forearm, holding her back toward him, constraining her.

Of course those images weren't helping and she really

did need to talk this out with him. "I cut my hair because the fanatical sect that my parents were part of forced all the girls to wear their hair long."

"You know I was born a Twoling in the good old Midwest, Second Earth, right?"

"Yes, that much I do know."

"Well, my folks were abusive, I just wasn't aware of it at the time. I thought what they did in the name of religion was normal. But getting lashed in a barn till the blood ran, all in the name of the Creator's purpose and discipline, did not endear either my parents or their beliefs to me."

She felt him stiffen and she was pretty sure she could hear him grinding his molars.

She sighed and twisted a strand of his hair around her finger. "As young girls and teenagers, we were required to keep our hair long and braided down the back, no exceptions.

"But that braid was a torment for years when I was young. In my sect, there was a group of bullies, girls, who would catch me and one of them would take me by the braid and drag me around until I was screaming and crying. Oh, they'd get punished, but the day I started fighting back, hitting and scratching, you wouldn't believe what the church regulators did to me.

"One of the regulators used a group of three switches bound together that she called, 'righteousness, purity, and love.' My father approved although he preferred his whip to anything else. Both my father and the regulators would make me strip to the waist. At least the regulators didn't bind my wrists and string me up. Beyond that, there wasn't much of a difference. It was all done in the name of religion."

She paused, unwrapped the strand of hair. She watched his chin tremble. She knew he was mad, but these were her burdens, not his. Thorne had enough on his plate as a warrior without being stuck with her problems. And she was only telling him now because she needed him to understand why she craved her freedom.

"Anyway, the Convent under Sister Quena's rule wasn't

much different from the sect I grew up in. I think sister-bitch really enjoyed delivering the canings and whippings. The devotiates were rarely touched, women like your sister, Grace. But then, they abided by all the rules because of their religious fervor, which does make sense.

"But there were at least a dozen of us who had been consigned there by relatives for 'religious instruction,' a polite euphemism for 'beating the sin out of us.'

"I admit I was the worst. I had no room left in my heart for what Sister Quena and her regulators were selling. In my opinion, there was no love in what any of them did. We were simply bad women and were treated in kind.

"But the truth was, most of the 'bad' women," and she succumbed to using air quotes, "weren't bad at all. They just weren't there by choice and they didn't agree with the teachings of the Convent."

He leaned down and kissed her forehead. His gravel voice flowed over her. "Grace told me you often took their whippings for them."

"She wasn't supposed to tell you."

"You forget, every once in a while I would see the results and even to my mind, you couldn't have deserved that much of Sister Quena's wrath, all by your lonesome."

"I hated her. I know I'm not supposed to hate, but I hated her. Sometimes, it gave me pleasure to pick a fight with her when I could see she was ready to take apart one of the 'bad women' for some absurd infraction like not folding your napkin exactly right after dinner was over. I mean what was the point? All the linens went to the laundry. But no, we had to fold them in a perfect rectangular shape, then they could be hauled to the laundry.

"I think sister-bitch used any excuse she could to hurt one of us. I think she used her rage and the whippings to take her mind off her own inner demons."

"I wanted to take you out of there so bad."

She thumbed his lower lip. "I know. But then you would have been hauled up on charges for interfering with Convent business and Greaves would have had the excuse he needed to haul your ass in front of COPASS and demand the death penalty."

His eyes hollowed out at that moment. "I was stuck."

"We were both stuck. But don't you see, we're not anymore. We're free, or at least I am. And I need this. I need to pick up where I left off during my wild college years. I lost my childhood and I need to be free, and in charge of my life, my days, what food I eat, where I go, what I do."

He frowned. "So I'm getting more of a picture here. But you've never talked about your college years much or how it was you got sent to the Convent in the first place."

She didn't want to tell him. He wouldn't like it, not as a warrior and her *breh*, but he should know the truth.

"Well, as much as I don't want to, I'll tell you straight out. Before I was sent to the Convent, and still in my teens, I totally rebelled. If I was going to get whipped by my father, it was going to be for real reasons. I found pleasure in sex, a lot of sex, with a lot of different men. I took up drinking, too, which fit the lifestyle and really bugged the shit out of my parents.

"Later, when I went to college, on my parents' dime, I got to partying a little too hard and my grades tanked. When my parents got wind of it, I laughed all through the supposed intervention until I realized that my folks weren't putting me in some early form of rehab, but rather they'd essentially jailed me in the Creator's Convent thinking to work religion into me.

"I remember thinking I was going to die but that's when I met you." She stroked his cheek with the back of her hand. She smiled. "Do you remember that first time we met?"

He nodded and a low growl left his throat. "I don't think I'd ever been more turned on in my life."

"I'd never seen a Warrior of the Blood before. Then there you were: Thorne. The leader of them all. When I think about it now, you were like this unexpected miracle in my life. You were exactly what I needed."

"I know what you mean, but it wasn't just the sex. You got

me. You accepted me for exactly who and what I was: a warrior."

She smiled. "I was so bad. I'd been facedown on my cot getting some old-fashioned relief with my hands when suddenly I felt the air move and there you were. I thought, *damn, all my prayers have just been answered.*"

He laughed, but he kissed her. "I thought you looked a little flushed. Then Grace showed up and you dipped behind the door so she couldn't see you. That's when you showed me your peaked nipple."

"I wanted you to see my orgasm. I think you got the point."

"Oh, I got the point."

"And you came back at dawn just like you promised."

"I couldn't not have come back. I thought about you all night while I was out there at the Borderlands. Night had never been so long. I thought the sun would never come up."

"You'd come straight from battling."

"You didn't seem to mind."

She smiled and stroked his cheek a little more. "Of course not. I knew what most of the hypocrites of Second Earth refused to acknowledge, that without all the blood you and your brothers spilled every night, Second Earth would have fallen to Greaves centuries ago."

He kissed her and ground his hips against hers. "I need you with me, Marguerite. Please don't do this to us. Please."

He looked so earnest and she almost wanted to just nod and tell him, "okay," but she couldn't. She shifted her gaze to his chin once more. She couldn't exactly tell him "no" if she kept looking into his eyes.

She shook her head. "I can't. I've . . . I've imagined my freedom for so long, and how I want to spend it that I can't stop now. I just can't. But I don't want to hurt you."

"So." Since he offered a long pause, she met his gaze. He continued, "You won't mind if I bury this"—and here he ground the hard length of him against her—"in another woman, or lots of other women? You don't feel any particular claim on my body? Seems to me I can remember dozens of times when you'd be holding my cock and whispering in my ear, 'This is mine.' Remember, Marguerite?"

"I remember." Jesus, how guilty was he going to make her feel? She scowled at him. "And, yeah, I'll hate it, but I'm not changing my mind about anything. I don't want a life with you on Second Earth, or anywhere. I want my own life."

But he didn't let her go. Instead he dipped low and began sucking on her neck.

She shoved at him in earnest now. "No," she cried. "None of that."

"I want your blood. Let me have it one last time." Oh, damn, he'd split his resonance, and she was almost helpless when he did that.

She shoved at him some more, but he didn't exactly budge and her vein started to rise, willing him on. She grew very still. She had to reach an understanding with him. As much as her body was on fire with sudden need and with the most pressing desire to let him sink his fangs and take what he wanted, she drew in deep breaths and willed all that insane need and want and passion away.

He must have figured it out, because he drew back and frowned at her.

She stared at him for a long time then said, "I have to do this."

His shoulders dipped slightly. Finally, he nodded and rolled off her. He ended up on his side and looked so serious.

She slid off the bed and turned to face him, pulling the belt of the robe tight. "You should probably . . ."

But she didn't get any farther. The goddam future streams suddenly opened up, an intense skyline of light-filled ribbons, stretching across the horizon as far as the eye could see.

One ribbon rose, expanded, and moved toward her then crashed hard, just as it had over three weeks ago when she had first made contact with Fiona, her fellow obsidian flame.

No, not again. She didn't want this. She didn't want any of this.

She fell to the floor.

Suddenly she was just inside the future streams, inside

one very specific vision. The sky was dark, a beautiful night sky, and the forest surrounded her, a forest of incredibly tall trees with straight trunks, close together. She heard noises in the forest, movement—not of animals but of people—a stealthy sound.

Death vampires.

She turned around and saw lights, many lights, but not from electricity, softer, like candlelight or oil lamps. She began running in that direction. She had to issue a warning. But the death vampires swarmed from behind, moving past her and through her. This wasn't her future, this was the future of whatever or whoever inhabited the glowing forest lights.

She thought the thought and propelled herself into the air and forward, flying without the usual wings, but soaring, speeding, getting ahead of the attack to try to understand where she was.

Higher and higher she flew, straight up through the tall fir trees. She soared over the tips now and began to fly above the glowing lights. Higher and higher until she saw dwellings, like cabins, some square, some round, some large, some small but all with the glowing lights, a river of lights. Higher she flew until she could see the coastline from a distance of several thousand feet. She recognized Puget Sound and she could feel that this was Mortal Earth.

She let the location seep into her mind.

She returned back to the forest and the glowing lights.

She understood then that she was looking at a hidden colony on Mortal Earth. From deep inside her mind, her obsidian flame power vibrated softly, as though amplifying her intuition. Then she knew, without a doubt, that this colony was a refuge for Seers.

Seers have been abused for millennia, their rights buried in the needs and wishes of the more powerful. In a domestic situation, this would be prosecuted as abuse. *In the name of government, this is called* for the common good.

—*Treatise on Ascension*, Philippe Reynard

CHAPTER 3

Thorne had no idea what the hell was going on but oh, damn, he felt sure it had something to do with her obsidian flame power.

He held Marguerite in his arms and spoke to her softly, her face cupped in his hand as he stroked her cheek with his thumb. He kissed her lips. "Come back to me."

But her lovely brown eyes seemed to rove over something else, something probably in the future.

She trembled, a very faint trembling all over her body. Her fingers twitched and flared as though she was reaching for something over and over.

He knew she was powerful, but he'd never seen anything like this before. "Marguerite, can you hear me?"

No response.

Shit.

If this was the future streams, then this new kind of vision left her vulnerable to attack. Which also meant that if she'd been alone just now, and the enemy had shown up, she'd be fucking dead. And she wondered why the hell he couldn't just leave her alone; why this wasn't a simple thing for him to let her live as she pleased.

He rocked her gently.

A familiar wave washed over him, of the war, and of the despair he'd lived with for so long. The last hundred years in particular had been a supreme shitfest.

He didn't want to think *of her*, of Grace's twin, but for whatever reason the memory descended on him of Patience and the last time he'd seen her. He'd been flying with his sisters through the canyons of Sedona, up and down their favorite inlets, catching the air currents, laughing, enjoying family time.

While the three of them had been airborne, the death vampires were just suddenly there. The attack came from the east, from the Mogollon Rim. There were only two. He'd thought, *Piece of cake*, because he'd folded his sword into his right hand, a dagger into his left, then flown like lightning in their direction before he'd so much as blinked.

At the same time, he'd communicated with the twins telepathically, ordering them to draw close to each other and to stay behind him as he fought the enemy.

That's when all hell had broken loose. A light like he'd never seen before flashed through the sky, blinding him for a few precious seconds. He'd turned in a circle, slashing his sword wildly in case either of the vamps got anywhere near him. His blade, however, never struck a thing, of that he was absolutely certain.

But when his vision returned, Grace was in a downward spiral, one of her wings broken, and Patience was nowhere to be seen.

He'd flown like a rocket in Grace's direction and caught her just before she struck one of the rock outcroppings. He'd steadied her and looked around.

No Patience. No death vampires.

He recalled closing his eyes and having the strangest sensation that he'd touched something bigger than Second Earth—but what, he couldn't say. Grace kept repeating, "The Creator, the Creator," as though she'd been caught in a spiritual event. He hadn't bought that, not even a little. Something had come, or someone, probably from one of the Upper Dimensions and completely without legal sanction.

He had left Grace sitting on the deep red rocks. He flew in an ever-enlarging circle, until he found blood, lots and lots of blood on the side of a gully, so much blood, enough from one person, maybe more. But there had been no feathers, no body parts, nothing like a battle, just blood, a torrent of blood.

He knew then that Patience was gone; taken and probably killed. By whom or by what, or for what reason, he doubted he would ever know.

He had returned to Grace, dropping to sit down beside her. He told her Patience was gone, her twin, the sibling with whom she had shared a womb. He had held Grace in the same way he was now holding Marguerite. Grace had stared up into the sky as though willing Patience to return to her, to draw her blood back into her body, and to come back to life.

But through all that time, Grace had remained adamant that Patience had not been killed; she'd been taken from Second Earth.

Thorne knew the world better. All that blood had spoken the truth to him. He had never argued with Grace. What would the point have been?

He had rocked her, and petted her cheek, and kissed her forehead as he now did with Marguerite.

He loathed the war and he felt something deep inside him begin not just a shift but an upheaval, a strong swell of sensation that started with disgust and ended with something close to determination. Something needed to change. Now. Tonight.

The war had been eating at him for decades, especially since Patience's death. But this angry sentiment had crystallized a little over a year ago during Alison's rite of ascension, the night that he'd sat near Endelle in the Tolleson Two arena and watched a frightened, overwhelmed Mortal Earth human woman, Alison, pass through the ropes that divided the black battling mats from the cement floor of the building. He'd watched her, an untried innocent, forced into a battle for which she was in no manner prepared. He had watched

Commander Greaves sit so calm, so still, so confident in his plans, the bastard who had orchestrated the event and turned it into a spectacle for all of Second Earth to view. His intention had been for his servant, General Leto, former Warrior of the Blood and supposed traitor, to slay Alison.

Instead Alison had won the contest with amazing feats of power, all for Greaves's pleasure.

Thorne had come to understand so much that night: that Greaves had been toying with Endelle and the Warriors of the Blood for decades, that he enjoyed the sport of war as much as he intended to one day be victorious, that he didn't care who suffered, that a woman's suffering meant nothing to him. Mostly, he'd understood that Endelle and her weak administration would lose this war, that defeat had become inevitable.

When Thorne thought of Endelle, something deep within bucked and raged. He loved her and he respected the sacrifices she had made for millennia. But right now she was part of the problem, a problem that had to be solved or two worlds would fall into slavery. He didn't have an answer right now, but one thing he knew for certain: Once he got back to Second Earth, once he was assured of Marguerite's safety, his working relationship with Endelle had to change. He couldn't go back to the way things were. He'd blocked their shared mind-link and as soon as he was able, he would insist she break it.

He'd had enough. Change needed to happen now.

As for Marguerite, she'd been his only comfort. Yet despite the fact that she was caught in something neither of them understood, she was more determined than ever to live life on her terms.

He didn't blame her. God knew he didn't blame her. But she was in danger.

He felt the future crowding him as he had never felt it before, holding his woman in his arms, smelling her rich red-rose scent, until he ached, body and soul.

Marguerite made a slow pass over the valley. There were dozens of farms and what looked like small homes and cabins, each with an attached vegetable garden, clustered along one portion of a long winding lane near the forest.

As she drew close to the upper portion of the valley, she thought she recognized one of the Warriors of the Blood—Fiona's *breh*, Jean-Pierre. He'd helped Thorne bust her out of the Superstition Seers Fortress, and later he'd been in Endelle's office. He was tall like Thorne, well muscled, but leaner.

Was Jean-Pierre in this village?

As she flew lower to the ground, however, she realized that it wasn't him, but rather someone who was built like him and had similar features. He was also younger than the warriors, not quite a man yet, but neither was he just a teen—somewhere in between.

She hovered in place watching him. He spoke quietly with another man, taller than him, with green eyes, dark skin, and long cornrows dotted with beads. This man's arms were muscled and bare. He wore a vest made up of some kind of sculpted animal skin. He looked solemn as the young man said, "Death vampires. They're here. In the forest."

The young man already had a sword in his hand.

The death vampires came: three, four, five . . .

The vision drew away from her, like a receding tide, and finally disappeared.

She felt something on her face, a callused thumb perhaps, then something softer and very moist. Lips, soothing lips.

"Come back to me."

Thorne.

Her eyelids fluttered. She was back in her hotel room. She was tired, so very tired, but then she'd traveled around the entire world how many times?

Thorne held her close and for the longest moment she felt safe, really safe.

And yet she couldn't stay like this.

As she drew out of the future streams completely, as she returned to consciousness, she sat up and slid off Thorne's lap. She felt like puking. She could hear Thorne talking to her. He stroked her arm and her thigh, gently, but she didn't want the distraction. The vision was still real in her mind.

She batted her arm in his direction and he stopped touching her.

The young man, so familiar.

"I . . . saw a warrior . . . who looked similar in build, in features, in stance to Jean-Pierre, but it wasn't him. More like a younger version of him."

"You had a vision then."

She drew in a deep breath. She realized she was on her hands and knees, the robe hanging open. She felt dizzy and sick, like she'd had the flu for about a week.

She pushed back to lean on her heels. She squeezed her eyes shut and took several deep breaths. "Thorne, we must do something. There will be an attack, very soon. I'm trying to determine the timing. I saw a young warrior standing with a black man, a leader, very tall, in a sort of village of round and square cabin-like houses somewhere in the Pacific Northwest. The Cascades?"

"Okay."

"We must go there, but I don't want to. Thorne, I don't want to."

"You're afraid."

She shook her head. Fear was not what she felt. The threat was not to her life, but to her freedom. She felt it like a rock in the pit of her stomach.

She turned toward Thorne. He had a dark look in his eye and something more, almost like panic. "What's wrong?" she asked.

"If I hadn't been here . . . Marguerite, do you know how vulnerable you were just now? This thing . . . this vision you just endured lasted at least ten minutes."

"Sweet Christ," she cried. "That long?" A fine stream of profanity flowed through her head. None of this was what she wanted: the visions, being completely out of control during them, and the awful responsibility of such deadly content.

Goddammit.

Yet the vision was here. If this colony was in danger, especially since it seemed to be some kind of refuge for Seers, then she couldn't just sit by and do nothing while death vampires went on a rampage.

But like hell she was going back into the future streams alone. She reached for Thorne's hand and opened her eyes, glaring at him. "You're coming with."

He nodded.

"And I don't care if it splits your head apart."

But the damn warrior just smiled. "Oh, I think I can take it."

She rolled her eyes, but closed them once more so that she could open her Seers window. She saw the ribbons spread out along the horizon, as was usually the case, but this time, perhaps because it was her choice to enter the future streams, there was no crashing of a vision, just the beauty that stretched on to both left and right forever.

She thought the thought, holding the young warrior's image in the front of her mind. She had expected the line of ribbons to move, which always happened when searching for something or someone specific in the future streams. Instead, as though waiting for her, the young man's ribbon rose, but this time she had control. She searched for the ribbon in a swift scan of power.

She found it, a deep green, like the forest in the early evening, the needles almost black but not quite. She reached for Thorne mentally at the same time and felt his presence. *Are you with me?* she sent.

Yes. And there he was, in her mind, and with her. Thorne had power, lots of it, if he could be in her mind like this so easily while she was engaging the future streams.

Can you see what I see?

Glowing lights and what looks like a mountain village.

Exactly. There isn't an obvious source for electricity although there could be one.

I see what you mean. Most of that light comes from oil, but it doesn't account for how well lit the house on the hill is.

Solar, maybe?

Maybe.

The future began to move in steady waves, and the images of the impending attack began to flow but not as fast this time. She heard Thorne's harsh breathing as the death vampires moved through the forest.

She thought the thought and the vision shifted to the tall black man. His name came to her, Diallo, and the young man so much like Jean-Pierre but more youthful—not quite a man, but close. Arthur.

She *felt* time move over the vision.

Looks like we have ten minutes, Thorne sent, *but I have no idea where this is. Do you?*

Yes.

And will you take me there? I can feel your reluctance.

Reluctance doesn't begin to describe what I feel. She sighed, a heavy rush of air that emptied her lungs.

But will you do it?

There was only one response involving one word, but she so didn't want to bring that word to life. She hated that word. She wished she could drown that word in a bucket of worms. That word, more than any other she'd spoken during the evening, threatened her plans. She knew it in her gut, which was maybe why she felt so sick, dammit.

But she knew what had to be done, so she sent the horrible word straight into his head. *Yes.*

She shook the vision off and felt him pull out of her mind. She rose to her feet. "But I'm getting dressed first." She went into the bathroom and folded on her black leather pants, a low-cut red tank, and her tight-fitting black leather jacket. Just for effect she added red-hot stilettos and long red-feather earrings with a silver heart and blackened skull and crossbones for good measure.

She headed back to the bathroom to fluff her drying hair and put on some makeup. If she had to go to the edge of a battlefield, she damn well wasn't going without mascara, a lot of it. She thought about toning it down, but this freak-ass colony could just suck it if they didn't like the way she dressed.

When she emerged from the bathroom, she saw Thorne, gasped, and did a full-body shiver. Holy shit. Gone were the jeans. He now wore flight battle gear: a black leather kilt and a belted weapons harness that spread over his chest and shoulders and supported two daggers. The harness ran in a leather strip down his spine to allow for wing-mount.

He was adjusting silver-studded, black leather wrist guards when he turned suddenly and looked at her. His nostrils flared. "What the fuck is with all the . . . rose. Oh . . . shit. You look hot as hell." A deep resonant growl left his throat as a wave of cherry tobacco hit her hard.

Her gaze fell to his stiff battle sandals and shin guards. Definitely an ancient Roman influence, but for some reason the whole effect, with his hair drawn back in the *cadroen* and his cheekbones in strong relief, spoke to something deep in her bones, something primal and very female.

Whatever the *breh-hedden* was or wasn't, it was damn mutual. She knew one thing: If they weren't headed out right now, she'd hop on the bed and crook her finger at him.

As she looked him up and down, one truth hit her square in the chest: *This is my man.*

Sweet, sweet Christ, she was so screwed.

Arthur Robillard stood on the porch of his cabin and extended his vision deep into the forest beyond the various houses opposite. He'd been uneasy all day, as though his body knew something his mind could only perceive in little flashes of awareness.

He lived in a secret Mortal Earth rogue colony after having jumped ship a few months ago, leaving Second Earth behind, much to the despair of his parents and the rest of his large extended family. He stood on the porch of his cabin, the one he had built with his own two hands, with a saw, a hammer, nails, with chisels and planers, and with the muscles the Creator had given him. It wasn't a big cabin, but it was his.

He didn't feel young, but at nineteen he was, by both Mortal Earth and ascended standards. Yet his shoulders were weighed down, pressed down by the war. Whatever his youth had been, it was gone, blown into a million pieces when his girlfriend, Nicole, died in a firebomb attack at the Ambassadors Reception a few months ago.

They were going to be married. His family railed against making such a decision when neither of them had even started college. But he'd been with Nicole for two years. He *needed* to be with her, in every way possible, and it seemed to him that marriage was the only answer, because, for whatever reason, he craved Nicole.

Her parents, well connected in ascended society, wanted her to follow the usual course of affluent ascended females: an eastern college with the junior year spent on Mortal Earth in one of the European universities. Nicole had received all the necessary training on how to function on Mortal Earth in order to keep their Second Earth vampire world a secret. The Sorbonne was very popular, and she'd been studying French since she was eight.

That was how he'd first met her in his junior year. She'd been a sophomore. She had asked if his name was French, which it was. He had been caught by the way her eyes almost disappeared when she laughed and her beautiful red hair, which fell in ringlets to her waist. He'd fallen in love, hard, the way he did just about everything. He'd been committed from day one, his arm around her shoulders, despite the fact that he'd been the brunt of jokes of his small circle of friends. Much he cared. He was with *his woman*.

He'd even taken blood at her wrist.

And she'd taken his.

If either family had known they were doing that, sharing blood, she would have been shipped off to an aunt who had a beachfront home in Panama Two. But he'd discovered the capacity to heal, if just a little, and the bruises left by doing the forbidden had been removed by holding his hands a couple of inches above the fang-marks.

But he'd loved it, savored the sweet burn, the burst of power. Of course it didn't help the other situation, which meant he'd become a bastard and had started begging for what he shouldn't have begged for. Nicole had almost caved, as hungry as he was.

That's when they decided they should just get married and make legal everything that they were about to do anyway.

Then the Ambassadors Reception had come and it was only by a fluke, a twist of fate, that he hadn't been with Nicole and her family that night. Now they were all gone, burned up, decimated, and his heart had become a rock-like thing that hung suspended and unmoving inside his chest.

Something else had hardened inside him as well, crusting over his innocence like drying cement. The war against the death vampires had raged all around him but had never, *never* gotten this close. If he hated the war before, he loathed it now, almost as much as all the political BS that Commander Greaves streamed around the world constantly. Maybe Greaves was the sole reason that the world was in trouble, but Arthur had other ideas—for instance, what about Madame Endelle? She was at fault, wasn't she? As Supreme High Administrator of Second Earth, she'd had the power for two millennia to contain the monster and she'd failed.

So now he was here, in a Mortal Earth rogue colony, a hidden, secret place. He'd sent a message to his father saying he was perfectly fine but that had been that. He had refused to reveal his location. He had things to figure out, his future for one, and he just couldn't bear the thought of being in a place that stood for everything he'd lost.

He loved this colony, this hidden place on Mortal Earth, where the war remained so distant, so far away, the people safe beneath an unusual layer of mist that combined the traditional lace-like element with some kind of moss-based component. He could see the dome of protection, even though almost everyone else here couldn't. The mist kept the locals undetectable, especially the hundreds of Seers who had sought asylum in the world Diallo had created for those ascenders who had gone rogue.

He had told Diallo just today that he meant to make his home here. He needed to speak with his father, of course, to break formally with him and with the rest of his family. He was very young in ascended terms. But in experience? He'd lived a century.

He couldn't keep pretending that he could follow the path laid out for him, to enter his father's import business, which had extensive dealings with Mortal Earth export firms run by Second Earth expats who still lived on the grid and were monitored by the bureaucracy of COPASS.

What had begun as a simple organization, the Committee to Oversee the Process of Ascension to Second Society, had turned into an administrative monstrosity with fingers in every lucrative pie to be found in the financial sector of Second Earth.

Arthur's disgust was profound.

He'd learned only a week ago that he was related to one of the infamous Warriors of the Blood, Warrior Jean-Pierre, a circumstance that explained so much from a genetics standpoint. He had always excelled at sword-work and at hand-to-hand combat. He'd received Militia Warrior training from the time he was eight, the youngest age a boy or girl could enter the various youth programs that focused on weapons training and military discipline.

He'd taken to it all with ease and with a superior skill that kept Militia recruiters knocking on his parents' door once a week for the past decade. Now that he was nineteen, they received personal visits even from Colonel Seriffe's staff, and the colonel at times headed the entire Militia Warrior operation worldwide.

As he stared out into the dark night, as he felt the future looming closer and evil not far distant, he stepped back into the shadows and changed into flight battle gear. He'd gotten really good at making the change and only had to do a minimal adjustment at the waist this time, although one of the two daggers he sported needed to be secured a little deeper into the sternum piece.

Yeah, he was uneasy. He even tied back his long hair with a strip of leather. He might have been teased about pretending to be a Whatbee, the nickname given to the Warriors of the Blood. But when you were six-five, weighed 220, and bore the weight of a man's muscle even if you still hadn't reached the legal age to drink, people left you alone.

He flexed his right hand. Even though his sword wasn't in his hand, it needed to be. He felt it with every breath of his body.

He heard an infant cry, a distant sound. Someone coughed. A couple argued. The village was settling in for the night.

He nodded to one of the villagers, a good man who patrolled at night, a three-hundred-year-old ascender who served as a Militia Warrior for the colony. Much good he could do if something really bad came into the village. He wasn't military-trained. Maybe he could sound an alarm or maybe he would be dead before a shout of alarm could leave his throat.

He thought about going to Diallo's house, waking him up, but Diallo's gifts ran in a different direction.

Diallo was a brilliant administrator, a leader. He had vision, kindness, and empathy. More than anything else, he rehabilitated Seers who had been abused on Second Earth.

The vibrations through Arthur's body got stronger. He stepped off the porch and once more wanted his sword in his hand, but he waited.

He paced in front of his cabin then began moving in the direction of Diallo's large house, the biggest house of the settlement, which overlooked the entire valley. He stretched his preternatural vision and slid deep into the surrounding forest.

Something was there.

Something was definitely out there.

Waiting.

For orders, maybe.

He just wished like hell he knew what to do.

Movement to his left dropped him into a crouch, a fighting stance. In the moonlight, he recognized Diallo's tall, lean shape. The vampire wore an animal-skin vest, his bare arms exposed to the cool March air. He was well muscled but no fighter. His dark skin caught the light as he moved toward Arthur. Diallo lifted a hand to sustain the silence.

Arthur nodded.

Diallo had never worn a more serious expression, his black brows low on his forehead. "Do you feel it, Arthur?" The accent was slightly British.

Arthur nodded. "Yes. What do the future streams say?"

"They are quiet, which I don't understand at all." His voice was deep and rich. "Something is wrong. It's a very powerful force, perhaps powerful enough to shut down the future streams. There is only one I know of with this kind of power: Owen Stannett, who recently fled from the Superstition Seers Fortress."

"You think he might be here?"

"I think he might have found something in the future streams to draw him here, yes."

"After our Seers?"

Diallo looked down at him and smiled. "Yes, after *our* Seers."

The word had flowed easily from Arthur's tongue. He was committed to the colony. The Seers were definitely his as much as anyone's, his to look out for and to guard. Diallo treated the Seer population extremely well, and brought Fortress refugees here anytime he could. He often had his most powerful Seers hunt for refugees whenever they were called to enter the future streams.

"What do you think he wants with them?"

"What they all want: foreknowledge and therefore power. If he succeeds, he will incarcerate them."

That which waited began to move.

Arthur thought the thought and at last brought his sword into his hand.

That which is hidden,
Will be made known.

—*Collected Proverbs*, Beatrice of Fourth

CHAPTER 4

Thorne had his arm around Marguerite's waist, a tight grip, too tight perhaps. The vibration took hold of him, the unique sensation of gliding through nether-space. He could feel Marguerite gliding as well. A brief blanking-out occurred, then awareness as his feet touched down.

As he materialized, he was immediately confronted by the young man from the vision, who crouched, sword in hand, then moved in front of the black man, a protective maneuver that Thorne approved of.

Both the young warrior and the black man spoke at once, but kept their voices low. "Warrior Thorne."

"My God," the black man said. "A Warrior of the Blood, here in our colony."

So they knew who he was. That was a damn good thing.

"And you are?" he asked, his voice perhaps too loud in the sleepy night of the village.

The black man spoke. "Diallo. I preside over this colony." He gestured to the young warrior. "This is Arthur Robillard."

Thorne stared at him. "Robillard. Then you're related to Warrior Jean-Pierre."

The youth nodded, a slow dip of his chin, his lips a grim line. He didn't seem happy about it.

Diallo's gaze shifted to Marguerite, and he sucked in a sudden breath. "You are *the one*."

"What the hell does that mean?" Marguerite responded.

Thorne's hand tightened around her waist. "*The one* what?" Again, his gravelly voice was a little too loud.

"She's a Seer of vast power."

"So?" Marguerite snapped.

"You are the one destined to change everything."

"Oh,w hatever."

"I don't like to break this up," Arthur said, "but there's something out there."

"You feel it then?" Thorne asked. He met the young man's gaze, just a glitter in the dark.

"Like something crawling over my neck."

Thorne nodded. "And how are you related to Jean-Pierre?"

"I'm his great-grandson but I just found out a week or so ago."

"You have the look of him. When I saw you crouch, I saw him. Have you had any battle experience?"

"Some."

Thorne narrowed his eyes. "How much?" He thought *War games maybe,* the kind done through youth military training exercises.

"Over the last year, I've killed death vampires. That kind of how much."

The boy clearly had an attitude but . . . shit. "How many, for Christ's sake?"

"Enough."

"Ballpark?"

"Maybe twenty."

Thorne's neck whipped up and back. How the hell was that even possible? "And why are you out killing pretty-boys?"

"Well," he drawled. "Someone has to get the job done."

Thorne wanted to grab this young man by the nape of

his neck and shake him hard. What right did he have to bust Thorne's chops about the need for more dead death vampires—and what the fuck was he doing risking his life by attacking them in the first place? Even Militia Warriors, trained for years, had to work in squads of four just to bring down one pretty-boy. And this kid was killing them single-handedly? Unless . . .

"You work alone?"

"Sometimes."

Sweet God almighty. "You mean there are others taking such stupid risks?"

Arthur's jaw turned to flint. He even took an aggressive step toward Thorne. "I only speak for myself." So the answer was yes. "When there ain't anybody else around to do a job, then yeah, I do it. Have you got a problem with that, Warrior?"

Essentially, no, but this kid was young. "How old are you?"

"Nineteen."

He wanted to knock some sense into the kid, but now the hairs on *his* nape rose. From long experience, he knew exactly what that meant.

He released Marguerite and stepped away from her so that he could fold his identified sword into his hand. Swords could be identified to the Warriors of the Blood and to Militia Warriors as well. Just touching a sword identified to someone else would cause death. "Diallo, I'd appreciate it if you'd take Marguerite somewhere safe while Arthur and I tend to business."

"Hey, don't I get a say in this?"

Thorne just looked at her, his fingers working the grip. "You do if you can fight death vampires, because by my tally, my sense of what's moving in the forest, we have at least eight pretty-boys coming straight at us."

She lifted both hands. "Point taken." She turned to Diallo. "So what kind of digs do you have in this place?"

Diallo smiled. "I have a cabin ready for guests at all times, but I also had a feeling."

"You've been expecting us?"

"One of my Seers, Brynna, had a vision of you in the cabin a month or so ago. That was all I needed to hear."

Thorne glared at them both. He needed his woman away from what he knew would quickly turn into a battle zone.

Marguerite glanced at him, her brows raised. "My boyfriend's getting impatient with us. You up to folding us out of here?"

Thorne mentally tripped over the fact that she'd just called him her *boyfriend*. Well, fuck him for liking it so much.

Diallo said, "Yes, of course."

Diallo put his hand on Marguerite's shoulder, a gesture that tightened Thorne's stomach despite the necessary and innocuous nature of the contact. Even in a critical situation like this, the *breh-hedden* would have its say. The pair vanished.

He turned toward Arthur. "How much battle training have you had at the various camps on Second Earth?"

"Since I was a kid. I took to it."

"Why aren't you with the Militia Warriors?"

At that, something seemed to settle inside the young warrior. "I didn't think the war would follow me here."

Thorne so got that. Well, it wasn't his place to judge why Arthur Robillard, great-grandson to Jean-Pierre, was here in a Mortal Earth rogue colony. But he also understood that even though Arthur's intention had been to escape the war, the war had found him anyway, and probably for a reason that would be a blessing to the villagers.

"They're coming," Arthur said.

"Yep." Thorne turned in a circle, stretching his preternatural hearing. He could hear the soft pads of footsteps through the forest.

"I'm hearing seven, maybe eight."

Thorne glanced at him. "You can hear that?"

Arthur nodded, his gaze fixed forward.

"Looks like Jean-Pierre's genes found a home."

Arthur smiled just off to the left side of his mouth. Sweet Jesus, he'd seen that smile on Jean-Pierre's lips. The Robillards had kinda strange lips but he knew for a fact that the women went for them, a full lower lip and the upper more pointed than most. It was so strange seeing Jean-Pierre in this kid's face.

Thorne looked up and down the village. The homes were scattered down a narrow valley on opposite sides of a stream. The air was cold, maybe forty degrees.

Arthur frowned at him then asked, "How do you want to play this? Do you intend to mount your wings?"

"Only if I have to. When I battle with my brothers, we keep things about nine feet apart and try to maintain a back-to-back posture. That will keep these bastards from getting behind either of us. So how many have you fought at once? And tell me the goddam truth. I need to know what I can expect out of you."

"Not many," he said. "Five, I think."

Thorne about dropped his sword. "You battled five, all at one time, by yourself, and lived to tell?"

Arthur raised a brow. "Like that's hard?"

Thorne chuckled. The kid knew how to front.

Arthur crouched slightly and inclined his head slightly to the northwest, up the valley and toward the wall of trees. "There."

Thorne glanced in the direction of Arthur's gaze and the first three pretty-boys emerged.

Arthur offered a raspberry sound, which brought them turning as a group in Thorne's direction.

"You always taunt death vampires?"

Arthur just smiled that smile again. Damn, he looked just like Jean-Pierre.

Thorne glanced down the valley then inclined his head. "We've got a few more on the other side of that building."

"Looks like we're going to have to split up."

"You think you can handle this?"

Arthur narrowed his eyes. "Blow me," he said, turning on his heel. He started to move then blurred away from Thorne. Only Kerrick could move as fast as that. Shit, what the fuck was he looking at? He knew. He already knew. A future Warrior of the Blood.

By this time, the party from the north was almost on him.

He'd been listening to their breathing and their whispers. When he turned, he raised his sword. It was game on.

These were big motherfuckers but fairly new in death vamp years. They still had leftover Hispanic attributes. Though the unification of features had already begun, as had the bulking-up of muscles, there was definitely a paling of all that fine brown skin.

He folded behind the group and took out the hamstrings of the bastard on the far left, cutting through the kidneys of the middle asshole and turning to meet the sword of the last pretty-boy high in the air. The sound was loud in the night air, a heavy clash of metal against metal. He half expected ascenders to come running from their homes. Instead lights went out one by one.

The villagers were well trained.

He spun and folded, then from behind took the last pretty-boy's head straight off. The heavy *thunk* on the hard earth was a familiar sound.

He crouched and turned in a circle hunting for more death vamp sign. Nothing.

He moved at a dead run, adding a burst of preternatural speed, in Arthur's direction. He could hear the fighting but the battle had shifted behind a cabin, near the stream.

He rounded the corner and stopped in his tracks. He would have joined the fray but there were two bodies on the ground and Arthur was fully engaged battling the remaining three death vamps.

The young man moved like lightning, just like Kerrick with a little of Jean-Pierre's loose style thrown in. His sword skills were mesmerizing. He could use some practice with the warriors, but goddam he was good.

One of the death vamps fell. The bastard to the left moved in as if for the kill and Thorne almost folded to intercept but instead, Arthur disappeared then reappeared behind him, grabbed the pretty-boy's long straight black hair, pulled his head back, and drove the short knife on the hilt into his neck then jerked.

The last death vamp didn't seem discouraged at all.

He matched Arthur in height but outweighed him no doubt by eighty pounds of sheer bulk and muscle.

Thorne backed away to gain a better visual of the street. To the north he could see bodies on the ground, none of them moving. To the south, the village was quiet and dark. Yep, the population was well trained. Diallo's doing? Shit, there was something to be learned here.

He extended his hearing beyond the grunts of the death vamp as Arthur put him through his paces. The ground sloped in the direction of the stream, but none of that seemed to matter to Arthur's quick feet.

Once more, Thorne scanned the dark forest beyond, but nothing returned to him. His hearing would definitely have picked up on another death vamp.

Whatever this attack was, Arthur had the last death vamp engaged in battle.

After half a minute passed, Thorne frowned. Why the hell was it taking Arthur so long to finish this guy off? The bastard was licked, moving sluggishly, and sweating like crazy.

"Need help there?" he offered. Maybe Arthur was tired.

But that familiar off-the-side-of-the-mouth smile appeared. The pretty-boy's sword scraped awkwardly all the way down Arthur's blade.

Arthur backed up, whirled, and at the same time flipped Thorne off. Then he got back to business and kept on fighting. He engaged over and over, thrust and parry, fending off the habitual straight-on attacks with ease, with agility.

When the death vampire finally fell to his knees, sucking in every breath like he was drowning, Arthur raised his blade high.

Shit, a rookie mistake.

The death vamp shifted position, brought his sword in a swift arc in the direction of Arthur's legs, and caught some skin as Arthur moved just a hair too late.

But at the same moment Arthur brought the sword down and took off the pretty-boy's head.

He hopped around on one foot for a moment. "Shit" came from between compressed lips.

When he finally stopped the hopping and put his foot down flat, Thorne smiled. The wound was hardly anything, maybe four inches across, an inch deep, not even what the Warriors of the Blood called a skin burn.

Thorne told him to sit on the ground. Arthur plopped. Thorne didn't have extensive healing abilities but he could take care of this one.

He squatted and put his hand over the wound. "You've got some goddamn beautiful moves."

"That was a dumb-ass mistake," Arthur said.

Thorne chuckled. "I've made the same one a couple of times a century, ever since I ascended. I'm lucky I still have both my legs. Once, I even got stuck through my gut. Now, that fucking hurt."

Arthur chuckled. "We good?" He jerked his head in a northerly direction.

"Yep. Have you folks had death vamps in this village before? I'm just wondering what we're supposed to be doing with the bodies. I've noticed you've got some kind of intricate mist going on."

"You can see it?"

He kept his hands steady but just looked at Arthur. "Yep."

Arthur's half smile emerged. "I guess Madame Endelle's second-in-command would have some power."

"That's what you'd think all right. How does that feel?"

"Good. A little achy."

"You want me to kiss it, make it all better?"

But Arthur just laughed.

After a minute, with the wound nicely closed, Thorne sat back on the ground. He met Arthur's gaze. "You're Warrior of the Blood caliber. You know that, right? Militia Warriors can't do what you can do."

Arthur's gaze grew fogged and he looked away. "Not interested, Warrior Thorne. I used to dream about it. I thought it might even be my calling, but . . ."

"But what?"

Arthur shifted and met his gaze. "If you had a son, would you want him doing what you do?"

Everything that the war had become pressed down on Thorne hard. "No one knows what to do," he whispered.

Aw, fuck. He was not going to unload on a kid. He jumped to his feet and slid his warrior phone from the pocket of his kilt. He swiped.

"Jeannie here. How may I help?"

"It's Thorne."

"Yes, I can see that by the identification." She fell silent.

"Is someone there?"

Still silent.

He felt certain it was message to him. Maybe Endelle had set up a system to track him, to get to him. Hell, yes, she'd done that. At the very least, she'd done that.

"I have eight bodies, Jeannie. I need them disposed of but we've got a protective shield overhead. I'm not sure you can find us."

"What part of the world are you in? That would help narrow the search."

Thorne glanced at Arthur. "Where is this place?"

Even though the night was dark, Thorne expanded his vision, and it was as though a light shone on Arthur's sudden mulish expression. He shook his head and clamped his lips shut.

Great. He had eight dead death vampires, one stubborn teen, and no way to dispose of them. Shit.

"We'll cremate them." Diallo's voice reached through the dark night. "On a pyre."

Thorne turned to his left. Diallo drew near, his braids heavy on his shoulders.

Thorne nodded. He brought his phone back up to his ear. "Belay that order, Jeannie. We're making other arrangements."

Her voice dropped. "When are you coming home?"

He stared at the ground. Well, that was the big question, wasn't it: When was he coming home? He wished he could fold back to Second Earth right now and get back to his real job, to leading the Warriors of the Blood, to serving Endelle. But he couldn't and something deep in his chest told him it wasn't just that Marguerite was vulnerable, or that he'd just discovered a secret colony, or even that the colony had been attacked by death vampires and needed his protection. No, the real reason went deeper and had something to do with Endelle herself, but like hell he was going to grapple with those issues right now. "I don't know. Gotta go. Take care."

He didn't wait to hear a good-bye or anything else she might want to say to him. He was torn and didn't want to feel any more guilt about his desertion than he already did.

He slid his thumb across the card's strip, ending the call, and returned it to his pocket.

Arthur gained his feet and walked around kicking his leg out, testing the recently healed cut.

"This is a terrible night," Diallo said. He had a very deep rich voice, a voice people would listen to.

He closed his eyes and within less than a minute several men began running in Diallo's direction. Apparently, he'd just sent out a telepathic summons to several people at once.

Interesting.

Who the hell was this man?

He looked past Diallo then looked around. "Where's Marguerite?"

Diallo met his gaze squarely. "I've given her a cabin, the one over there." He turned slightly and gestured with an elegant sweep of his arm. "The one with the planter by the front post, with the arched lattice frame over the walkway." It was about thirty yards from the battle site.

"Thank you." Jesus, he had so many questions, but the most critical one rose to the surface. "Through Marguerite, I saw the vision of this event and also the sense that this colony is a refuge for Seers. Is this true?"

Diallo nodded. "Yes, we have Seers here from all over Second Earth. And yes, we protect them."

"But you understand the larger implication?"

Diallo drew in a deep breath and let it out slowly. His expression grew thoughtful as though he was searching to find exactly what he either could say or needed to say. "Yes. That a very powerful entity has discovered our location with the intention of securing some of our Seers." He lifted his chin slightly. "With the exception of your woman, there is only one Seer powerful enough to disrupt the mist that protects this colony, or to overcome the blocks that we've had in place for centuries in the future streams."

"Owen Stannett," Thorne murmured.

He was the monster who had, up until three weeks ago, been the High Administrator of the Superstition Mountain Seers Fortress. He'd tried to rape Marguerite for the purpose of impregnating her. The bastard was intent on creating a super-race of Seers. He'd already raped a number of the Superstition Seers and fathered children by them. Looked like he was still intent on collecting Seers even though he'd gone rogue on Mortal Earth.

"Precisely."

Thorne held his gaze. "Then you're familiar with recent events on Second, in particular with regard to the Superstition Seers Fortress?"

Diallo offered a faint smile. "We know all that happens, Warrior Thorne. We're a hidden colony, not an ignorant one."

"I meant no offense."

A number of men drew near.

"Warrior Thorne," Diallo began in his most carrying voice, which resulted in a shocked murmur among the approaching villagers. "I wish to thank you for this service tonight and to welcome you to our colony. We'll talk tomorrow and I will answer all of your questions then. Arthur and I will tend to the dead. For now, you may have use of the cabin for as long as you wish. *Y pro nai-y-stae.*"

Thorne smiled. It was an old expression that essentially meant "You may stay for eternity." "That's very kind of you."

As he started to move in the direction of the cabin, the hairs on his nape moved ever so slightly. He turned back to the forest. Arthur did as well.

But his senses settled down almost as quickly. Whatever had been there was gone now.

Arthur met his gaze. "Stannett?"

"Maybe. Wish the bastard would show his face."

"Heard he got a bunch of his Seers pregnant."

"All part of his plan to create a super-race."

"Prick," Arthur muttered.

"Couldn't have said it better."

"Arthur," Diallo called out, waving him forward.

Arthur turned toward Thorne and held out his hand. "I'm glad to have met you. If you have some time tomorrow, maybe you could show me a couple of your moves."

"You got it. Just hunt me down."

Arthur turned abruptly and joined the work detail. When the villagers headed in a westerly direction, Thorne finally made his way across the lane.

Vegetable gardens grew at either the side or the back of every house, lush gardens that shouldn't have been growing like this in late March, so high in the mountains. But these were ascenders, and no doubt a few weather modifications had been put in place to keep the colonists well fed and self-reliant.

A light glowed from within the cabin. Thorne's heart began doing its jackhammer routine because he was going to see Marguerite again, the woman he'd begun to crave like wildfire.

She stood leaning against the doorjamb behind a screen door, her arms folded across her chest. "So how many were there?"

"Eight."

"You kill them all yourself?"

He glanced back. If she had tried to watch the battle, her view across the street was blocked by a thriving garden. The one up the street would have required she step out on the porch. Marguerite was many things, but she wasn't foolish.

He shook his head in response to her question. "I took three. Arthur handled five."

"That kid?" she cried.

He smiled. "Are you going to let me in?"

"Diallo gave this place *to me* for the night. I don't recall him saying anything about you."

His smile broadened. Was she starting *that* game? It was

one of his favorites, and she had a look on her face that said maybe she was.

"Let me in, Marguerite." He used his resonance, a low number, only three.

He heard her soft intake of breath but still wasn't surprised that she replied, "Not gonna happen."

He split his resonance five times. "I said let me in." He wanted in, all the way in, and not in the form of José or anyone else.

The rest of the night was his.

Marguerite held her ground because the longer she did, the more Thorne would get worked up—and she loved seeing him get worked up. She was in the right mood, as well, though she wasn't certain why. She'd already been with a man, but this was different. This was Thorne, and she knew him really well. And she'd always loved the way he'd taken care of her when she had need of him. Besides, he wouldn't kick her out of bed when he was through. He'd hold her, and tonight she might even like that.

Ever since they'd touched down in this strange secret ascender colony, she'd felt as though something called to her, something deep within, tugging at places in her heart she'd never quite known before. She felt unsettled, knocked out of stride, and she was never knocked out of stride. Pissed off, maybe, but she always knew what she wanted, where she wanted to go, and who she wanted between her legs.

"I can't let you in tonight, Thorne, you know that," she teased. "We're done, remember? You got me out of the Superstition Fortress then I left Endelle's office and now I'm here but only because of a stupid Seer's vision. But you can sleep on the porch if you want."

The scent of cherry tobacco sifted through the screen mesh. Her nostrils flared, intent apparently on catching every last bit. Sweet Lord in heaven, but that smell he gave off when he was thinking impure thoughts about her sure worked some magic down low. She started feeling tight and achy.

A faint growl sounded and Thorne caught the small handle and started to pull. Fortunately, there was a handle on the inside so she pulled back. The nice thing about being an ascended vampire was the simple fact that you got some overall strength without having to weight-lift. So she held tight.

Of course, it was only an illusion. The man could incinerate the screen with a lift of his palm. He had serious handblast capacity. He was also built as hell so that the whole time she'd been looking at the side mounds of his pecs that weren't covered by his weapons harness. She wanted her hands on him, then her lips.

Thorne tugged on the door again. *"Let me in, Marguerite."* More resonance. She felt light-headed and couldn't quite breathe. That had to be seven resonances. The man had a gift. When he worked up to fifteen and spoke straight into her ear, he could make her come so fast. He was some kind of magician, real Merlinesque, the bastard.

The thing was, of all the men she'd ever known in her life, she trusted Thorne, even when he slipped into caveman mode.

He tugged harder on the door. She had a slight advantage because of the doorjamb so she held on to the handle and leaned back, letting her weight work for her.

Then he began to pull in earnest. Even in the faint glow of the oil lamp she'd lit, she could see his biceps tightening up and swelling into the most gorgeous heap of man-muscle. She wanted to bite down on that hard, feel him jerk underneath her.

He kept pulling and he pulled her with him. She just held on to the handle as her feet slid onto the porch. The whole time, her gaze stayed fixed like an idiot straight on that muscle.

She was such a basic female. She loved a man's body, as in *loved* it, every facet and bulge and dip and firm jut. This was her weakness, all Thorne's physical strength, and the fact that he made war. What did it say about her that even though he was grimy with sweat and blood from the recent battle, she didn't care? She never had. Not once in the last hundred years. From the first she'd been able to accept who and what he was, a Warrior of the Blood, a protector of Second Society, a destroyer of death vampires.

And right now, God forgive her, he was hers and she was going to take him.

"Looks like I'm coming in."

She smiled. His voice was a damn gravel pit. Still, she said, "Forget it, Warrior. Not a chance." But his arm was around her waist and now he dragged her against him. He'd have to repair the screen tomorrow because it hung off its leather-straph inges.

His mouth was as familiar to her as her reflection in the mirror. She knew his lips, every millimeter. His tongue was thick and he worked it now, in and out of her mouth, making beautiful promises of everything he would do to her . . . as long as she didn't have another one of those stupid visions.

The memory of the vision, of how it had crashed down on her, rendering her blind and mute while it held her captive, caused her to stiffen, even to ignore that beautiful tongue.

Thorne drew back, slid his hand to the nape of her neck, and caressed her gently. "Hey," he whispered. "What gives? You just became an ironing board in my arms."

She pulled away from him and went into the house. Sweet Christ, she never pulled away like that.

"What's wrong?"

"Why did I have that vision? I don't get it." An oil lamp on the narrow wooden table by the wall lit the room in a soft glow. She crossed to the brown leather couch and curled up. She hadn't mean to end the moment, but she needed some answers.

He followed her into the cabin and closed the door. He pulled the surprisingly nice linen over the wide bank of windows that faced the street.

He remained by the window, popped his *cadroen,* and took a few deep breaths. His kilt was lumpish. She'd kind of stalled out at the wrong time.

"Hey, I'm sorry," she said.

He shrugged but smiled and bent over. "Damn, you work me up."

She heard him chuckling and watched all that thick hair fall forward.

After a moment, he lifted back up and met her gaze, but he was somber this time. "I think it's simple. You have emerging powers and it's no fucking picnic. But there's something else I need to tell you. Diallo and I believe that Stannett is behind this attack. He's powerful enough to disrupt the colony's mist."

At that, her body jerked. "Stannett and death vampires?"

"Why not? The man's desperate. We believe he was after the Seers who live here."

"You know, that makes complete sense. He probably went into the future streams hunting for exactly that, a secret stash of Seers or something."

"So you can hunt by subject?"

"Sure. I mean, mostly you hold the image of a person in your mind until you find their corresponding ribbon of light, but you can also do a subject. At least I could and no doubt Stannett can, although I think I might have been better at it, which is why he used me when I was locked up in the Convent." She pursed her lips. "But there's something more. Stannett would have had the power to get through this strange mist. Most Seers wouldn't be able to even see it."

Thorne held his arm out. "Shit. I'm sorry."

Marguerite's gaze slid over streaks of red over his arm and black wrist guards. There was at least one black feather stuck to him, but it didn't bother her. She'd been with him plenty of times after he'd battled all night.

But he turned to her and said, "The thing is, Marguerite, it doesn't matter what Stannett does, or Greaves. You've got to face the fact that you've got emerging powers. You've got to start dealing with them. Otherwise it's just going to get worse and I think you know that. You're the righteous red variety of obsidian flame, and you can't run from that."

"I'm not running." She twirled a lock of her hair around and around her finger. She could feel her brows pinch together.

"Looks like running to me." He shifted to stand in front

of her—and truth? She liked that he was straight with her. She'd never been a gentle flower. She never would be.

She leaned her head back into the cushion and looked up, way up. Jesus, he was tall. "I'm running *toward* something, Thorne, you know that. I want my freedom. I want to live how I choose, new powers or not. That's the least I deserve after a century in that shithole."

His shoulders did a little dip. "I know. Why do you think I'm not screaming at you?"

She narrowed her gaze at him. "This must be killing you."

"What?"

"Being away from the warriors, from your duty? I know that much about you."

He shrugged. "You're right. I'm hating every minute of this because I abandoned my post, except for one thing."

"What?"

The man almost smiled. "You're worth it. I mean, your temper isn't and sometimes I want to strangle you, but a warrior takes care of the woman he loves. Simple."

"You are such a bastard to be so nice to me."

Thorne reached down and took her hand. "Come here. Come shower with me. The hell if I'm going to keep talking to you with death vamp guts all over my chest."

Life is full
Of a thousand firsts.
Savor each one.

—*Collected Proverbs*, Beatrice of Fourth

CHAPTER 5

Marguerite laughed. She shouldn't have, not when he spoke of death vamp guts. She didn't know why she wasn't squeamish, but then she never had been. What he said should have made her puke. Instead this all just felt so normal. After he lifted her to her feet, she led the way into the back bedroom. The cabin was fairly small, three and a half rooms total.

The bathroom had a roomy shower but no tub.

Thorne moved to the shower and flipped on the water. He got rid of his clothes with a wave of his hand. He still faced the shower so she had a fine view of his ass. She tilted her head and sighed.

His skin was golden in color like it was permanently tanned, and there wasn't a line on him. His hair hung down his back. She loved his long warrior hair, always had.

He stretched out his hand beneath the water, testing.

His left butt cheek flexed and his hamstring tightened; his calf muscle, too. She wasn't sure but her jaw may have just trembled. The man was gorgeous.

He stepped inside and turned toward her, a beautiful profile view. His cock was partially erect and in terms of pure beauty, this was her preference. He wasn't standing upright but he wasn't limp, either. She wanted to be on her knees right now and worshiping.

She waved a hand and lost her leathers. Then took a little extra care with her feather earrings, settling them on the counter.

When she turned toward him, his gaze fell to the juncture of her thighs. She'd almost forgotten how different she was down there from the last time he'd seen her.

"Wow," he murmured. "A beautiful peach." His eyes fell toh alf-mast.

She knew that look. She savored that look. Then suddenly she realized he'd had sex with another woman just a couple of hours ago and her temper flared. She jumped in the shower and punched his left pec.

"What was that for, hellcat?"

"You slept with someone else."

She turned into the spray and he was suddenly up behind her and moving what was now completely solid up and down her butt cheeks. He had to bend his knees to get there. This was the only thing she didn't like about their disparity in height: Some adjustments were necessary.

His hands found her breasts as the water hit her face and drenched her hair.

"You smell like roses."

"I thought you wanted to talk about my visions."

"In a minute. I'm not clean enough yet."

She laughed. "No, you're not."

She grabbed a bar of soap and made a big bubbly lather between her hands. She turned into him and spread the bubbles over his shoulders and chest. He was so big. The top of her head barely reached his shoulder, which put her face at pec level, a really fantastic place to be.

She started scrubbing and getting him clean. The whole time he touched her, his hands rubbing over her shoulders, down her arms, lightly over her breasts, her waist, her hips. He teased her mound a little with the crook of his knuckle, but mostly he just let her wash him. She found she enjoyed it.

It dawned on her that because there had never been private showers in the Convent, this was the first time she'd bathed with Thorne.

She stepped aside and let the shower spray hit all that foamy soap. She helped rinse it off his chest. She lathered up again and cleaned his thighs. There was a lot of man to cover, and she went all the way to his feet.

She then ordered him to turn around. She performed the same ministrations on his back and shoulders. He sighed a couple of times. She wasn't sure what that meant.

She spent extra time on his ass, working the muscles slowly, cleaning down the crack and gliding over his balls from behind. A sigh became a familiar groan.

But she wasn't done. She soaped up the backs of his legs, savoring the feel of the hair all the way down.

Of course, she'd saved the best for last. As she rose up, she demanded that he turn around once more to face her.

"I'm going to use my hand now and make sure you're really clean."

A kind of growlish-grunt came out of his mouth but he said, "I like your short blond hair. I thought I'd miss all that brown length but I don't. This look suits you."

She smiled up at him, craning her neck. "I must look like a drowned rat."

He shook his head. "Nope. You're beautiful." He dipped down and kissed her. "Now, what were you saying about getting me really clean?" He smiled and suddenly her chest felt on fire. Oh, God, she couldn't really be in love with him, not *really* in love with him, could she?

She glanced down and his length bobbed in front of her, hard and ready for her hands. She slid her soapy fingers over him. His back arched and his thighs flexed. "Shit, that feels good."

That same fire-laden sensation continued to invade her chest as she worked his cock, gliding up and back, taking her time, thumbing the broad crown. She liked this man. She always had. She pretended to be completely engaged in her task, but her mind had spiraled elsewhere. She kept digging up images of Thorne coming to her at dawn at the Convent, making love to her on that horrible bed, enjoying and savoring her body, each time as intense as if it might be the last.

But here she was in the security of a strange unknown colony on Mortal Earth, hidden away, and she was actually spending time with him, and taking her time. She'd always been afraid that Grace would come back—and wouldn't that have been embarrassing for brother and sister.

So here she was taking pleasure in doing something she'd never done with him before, just stroking him and playing with him.

The soap had a slight floral scent, but the shower had filled with that fragrant cherry tobacco scent of his, which had begun working like a couple of quick perfect fingers between her legs. Desire spun through her.

Thorne released a rush of air like he was holding back a cyclone, then spun her gently away from the spray and eased her against the shower wall, still facing her. He was breathing hard.

"I need you," he whispered. He got in close and spoke into her ear. The whole time she worked his cock, all the way to the base and back.

"I need you, too." Her voice sounded like rocks covered with mashed potatoes. She cleared her throat. Okay, so they were both breathing hard.

He grabbed her around the waist and hoisted her up, letting her back stay snug against the wall. She knew where he was headed, so she wrapped her legs around his waist. The position put her closer to eye level so she didn't have to look so far up.

"Do it," she whispered, but she planted a hand on his chest and pushed just a little. "Not so close, though. I want to watch."

That beautiful smile of his appeared again.

She looked down and this time she smiled because her wax gave her the best view she'd ever had of Thorne's cock entering her. She tilted her hips a little. His knees were bent and his thighs flexed as he pushed, just a little at a time. His cock was dark pink and rigid, a solid pole entering her, and as his body pulsed and pushed, a hiss slid from between her teeth.

"So good. I love this, Thorne. I do, I do."

"Oh, yeah." Could his voice get any deeper? "I'm almost all the way in. Shit, Marguerite, you're so damn tight. Almost like ear—I mean, like all those other times."

"All those other times?"

"Yeah, in the Convent. Never mind. Shit you feel so good."

He'd almost said *earlier*. She was sure of it. Had he done some kind of mind-diving when she'd been bonking José? Could he do that kind of thing?

She might have pursued it, but he'd reached the end of her and now he was pulling back out, a slow, sensual withdrawal that brought a deep moan out of her throat. She arched her neck, and he didn't wait for further invitation. He licked her throat and her vein rose so fast that she wasn't surprised that he struck quickly and started drinking.

Oh, God, she sent. She hadn't meant to do that, to enter his mind, but there she was.

You taste so good.

You're so hard, rock-hard.

He thrust in a steady driving pace and it was heaven. Between all that thickness moving in and out and the feel of his mouth sucking hard at her neck and taking her blood, she was on the cusp, heavily on the cusp.

But it felt different somehow, different in a really good way. That she'd thought of mind-diving made her wonder what it would be like. She knew she had power, lots of it, and she also knew that being deep in the mind of another vampire could trigger some added pleasure.

Thorne?

Yeah, baby. Oh, God, your blood. I can feel it working my muscles. I feel stronger. Just . . . just tell me what you want but damn I'm close.

I want in, as in deep-mind engagement. Now.

He'd never allowed it before because Endelle had a mind-link with him. He'd always feared she'd discover the truth and ship Marguerite's ass to the Superstition Fortress.

A long pause. Maybe he was figuring out the question. Or maybe the hesitation meant something else.

The sucking slowed, as did the surge of his hips.

You sure?

Yeah.

He resumed the heavy sucking and began pushing into her with deep thrusts. *Do it,* he sent.

She hissed and mentally gave a big push and suddenly she was just inside his mind as deep as she could get.

He groaned long and loud but kept pulling at her neck.

But the image that hit her brought pleasure streaking through her, bringing her close. She could see Thorne over her, making love to her, but he wasn't himself, he was José, or in José's mind, or something.

Maybe she should have been mad. Instead, she gave a cry because it was hot as hell and Thorne began to pound into her, the sound of his flesh against hers a loud slap even with the water still hitting his back.

The orgasm crashed down on her almost as hard as the recent vision so that she was suddenly clinging to him and experiencing pleasure like she had never known before. Being in his mind was a ride or maybe *the* ride, the part of the experience she'd needed all this time, all these decades to really go through the roof.

And it just kept rolling, over and over, sharpening along her bare clit, streaking up the inside of her until she was pulling hard on Thorne's cock, begging him to give her what she wanted.

Give it to me, she practically shouted within his mind.

Fuck, came back to her.

He shoved into her hard, released her neck, and shouted at the ceiling.

She could feel his release and because she was in his mind, she could even experience his pleasure, which triggered hers all over again, so that as he thrust hard, she came and came and came, crying out and pressing her mound against him.

It's never been like this.

"No, it hasn't." His movements slowed, but his breathing was a harsh rasp in the shower.

"I'm shutting the water off," he said. "Damn, that got cold." He must have used his mind because he didn't let go of her and suddenly the water stopped spraying. "I don't want to let go of you yet."

"You'd better not," she said. She slid her arms up around his neck then kissed him. "I like being inside your head. That was the best we've ever done together."

He nodded and chuckled. "You're a pain in the ass, Marguerite, but I love the way you talk to me."

"I'm gonna leave your head now," she said.

Again, he nodded. His lips were parted as he sucked in air.

She pulled out of his mind and it was the strangest rubbery sensation, like pulling taffy or something, until at last she left him. Still, he remained in the shower, holding her ass firmly in both hands and keeping them joined.

She wiggled her hips so that she could feel him deep inside. "This feels good," she said. She looked into his eyes, gorgeous hazel eyes. Usually they were bloodshot, but not now. Of course, he'd been off duty for three weeks chasing her across the country and back, which meant he'd been off the Ketel One.

Now here they were, joined like two people would be joined who'd been making love for a century. Only this had been better. Of course, they'd only had sex while she'd been held captive and he'd been worked to death as a warrior.

There was, however, one issue she needed clearing up.

"So what the hell was that with José?"

"Oh, was that his name?"

"You know damn well that's his name. You were in his head, weren't you? And when you'd had sex, you didn't mean with another woman, did you? What was this, like some kind of ménage à trois?"

"I guess," he said, with a slight shrug. "Worked for me. And it kept me from killing him."

Her shoulders dropped, and she leaned her head against his neck and sighed. "I'm glad. I couldn't stand the thought of you with another woman. I know that makes me the worst kind of hypocrite when I shagged José, but I think I'd kill her. I'm beginning to understand why that woman with the long dark hair was so upset with me. What was her name? The one bonded to that tall gorgeous Italian?"

"Parisa."

"Yeah, she about ripped my face off when I flirted with her man."

"I remember." His arms tightened around her.

"I'd be like that if we took this much farther. I'd want to kill any woman who looked at you."

"Then tell me you understand my dilemma a little."

She lifted up, her arms still hooked around his neck. "So you wanted to kill José?"

"Yeah. I almost did, too. Then I worked it out in my head."

"Or his head."

"I guess you could say that."

She yawned. "You want to sleep with me tonight?"

"Thought I already did."

She thumped his shoulder. "In bed, idiot."

He squeezed her ass. "Did you actually think I was going anywhere else?"

She laughed. "No, I guess not."

He shuddered.

"What?" she asked.

"We get to sleep together . . . all night."

"Thorne, please . . . please don't get too used to this."

He gave her a soft smile. "No worries, not right now. Let's just get some rest. We'll figure things out tomorrow. And since there are Seers in this colony, maybe they'll have some insight about your visions."

"Okay."

He thumbed her cheek and stared into her eyes.

His gaze was full of something she didn't quite recognize

except that it warmed up her chest all over again and made her put her lips against his. He kissed her fiercely, pushing his tongue inside her mouth, a kind of claiming.

She wrapped her arms more tightly around his neck.

He kissed her for a long time. Because he'd firmed up inside her again, she wondered if he was headed toward a second round. She wouldn't have said no, but suddenly she was really tired.

"Okay, bedtime." But he sighed heavily as he withdrew from her, as if he didn't like being apart either.

He flipped the lever and the cold water came on. "Sorry, there's no hot water left."

She didn't mind the cold so much. She'd been used to it for decades in the Convent.

He stepped out of the shower as she finished up. When she finally emerged, he had a towel waiting for her, holding it wide. She stepped into it and he wrapped her up from behind.

Why the hell did he have to be such a nice guy? Didn't he know this was killing her?

After a night of working the darkening, in which she lost sleep keeping death vampires from being shipped to the Metro Phoenix Two area, Endelle wasn't in the mood to be polite. She had never been so fucking agitated in her entire life. She felt like a thousand little ants were gnawing on her nerve endings. Where the hell was Thorne and why hadn't he come back, preferably with Marguerite strapped across his back?

Fucking morons.

She paced the weird tree room in Jean-Pierre's house, having decided she needed a break from her office in her administrative HQ. Fiona sat on the huge branch that bent sideways from the main trunk, swinging her legs and smiling up at her warrior from time to time. He stood behind her and had his arms draped over her shoulders.

These latest lovebirds gave her the scratch.

"I had to get out of the office."

"You are always welcome in our home," Jean-Pierre said, his French accent as easy as a wet dream.

She waved an arm. "What the hell kind of room is this anyway and what's with the walls? They have to be ten feet and then there's this huge-ass tree growing straight through the floor."

"I built the floor around the tree when it was young and trained this branch. I often sit here to think. It is an Arizona sycamore. The fragrance is very sharp from the leaves, especially after a rain."

"Whatever." She slapped her leather skirt and watched both pairs of eyes drift to the floor and back. She looked down. "Shit. These garden-variety snail shells just aren't holding up like I thought they would." She had glued them in a nice curve right over her crotch, but most of them were busted up and there were bits and pieces on the thick glass that made up the floor of the strange round room.

Fiona started biting her lip and examining her nails.

"What? Are you laughing at my skirt?" She was so not in the mood to be laughed at.

Fiona pinched her lips together and shook her head. Then she started coughing.

"You are such a ninny."

But that apparently set Fiona off, and she started laughing really hard. "I . . . I haven't heard that expression in decades. Ninny? Really?" She laughed some more.

For some reason, the moment broke Endelle, but not in a good way, and she collapsed to sit on the floor. Her heart ached and she didn't know what to do.

Thorne had been gone for three weeks now and she had this horrible feeling he was never coming back. She couldn't even contact him because he'd somehow managed to block their shared mind-link.

As she spread her knees to sit cross-legged, the bending of the skirt sent a bunch more shells breaking apart. Much she cared. She ran her fingers lightly over the starfish that covered her right boob. She'd started experimenting with sea crap to enhance her fashion design. The nubby texture kind of soothed her.

Since Jean-Pierre had turned around and was now staring up into the budding branches of the tree, she realized she was probably fully exposed—her skirt was short, and her modesty had disappeared sometime during the Roman conquests on Mortal Earth. Today's thongs, while awesome, really didn't cover a whole helluva lot.

So the fuck what.

Fiona hopped off the branch and folded a somewhat lumpy, multicolored throw in her arms. She crossed the space and spread it out over Endelle's lap. Endelle didn't even complain. She just sighed heavily.

"Endelle, is there anything I can do?"

Fiona dropped to sit in front of her, also cross-legged, but she wore jeans. This couple preferred jeans to anything.

Jean-Pierre turned back around. "*Oui*, Endelle, we would like to help, if we could." He now leaned over the branch, his forearms balanced on the smooth bark, his hands clasped in front of him.

Endelle looked at his current position as well as the height and flatness of the smooth tree limb. Her brows rose. "That branch is at a really good height, if you know what I mean."

The fact that Jean-Pierre's gaze whipped to the back of Fiona's head and Fiona's face turned a sudden crimson color spoke volumes. Endelle snorted. "You two are about as hard to read as a turkey on a Thanksgiving table."

Of course her gaze went right back to the branch. It was wide and would make a perfect platform. It really would.

Her thoughts then turned as they did way too often toward Braulio, that prick of pricks who'd suddenly shown up in her life and started making her want a man bad. They'd been lovers a few millennia ago and then he'd died, or she thought he'd died. Apparently, Luchianne, the first vampire ever, had hauled his ass out of the River Styx, so to speak, and hidden him away on Sixth Earth all this time.

Now Braulio was back, performing some sort of service

for the ruling council there with hopes of keeping Greaves from taking over two worlds. She might have gotten excited about the idea of Sixth getting involved in her difficulties—but one thing she knew for sure, when it came to government, forward movement was about as fast as trying to get ketchup out of a glass bottle. She'd need to stick a big fat butter knife up somebody's ass to get a little progress.

When Fiona had recovered her complexion, she rephrased her question. "What can I do to help? That's why you wanted to see me, right? Because Marguerite and I share the obsidian flame power?"

"No. I don't know. Maybe. The hell if I know."

Endelle got that sick sinking feeling again, the one that had hit her when she found out Thorne had dropped to Mortal Earth and disappeared off the grid. "I've never felt this lost before. I mean, the war has been a shitfest for a long time, but I always had Thorne with me"—she tapped her forehead—"here, in my mind. Now he's shut me out."

"Did he break the link with you?" Jean-Pierre asked.

She'd had the mind-link with Thorne for centuries so that she could reach him telepathically day or night. She'd set it up, and with mind-links only the person who'd established the link could break it.

She shook her head. Holding the multicolored throw in place, she brushed broken snail-shell bits from the upper creases of her skirt. "He can't break the link, but he found a way to block me. I think he might have emerging powers. I can't reach him. I can't even read his thoughts—and I've always been able to read his thoughts. The only good thing about this whole fiasco is that he has to be with Marguerite. He has to know where she is, has to be protecting her, and God knows we need her. My only hope in this whole fucking situation is that he'll bring her back."

She met Fiona's gaze. "So, what about Marguerite? Have you heard anything from her in these last couple of weeks? If I remember, you two could reach each other when no one else could."

"Nothing. I'm sorry. I honestly thought I would have because we kind of connected when she was in the Convent. But to be honest, the sense I have of her is that she wanted to shake the dust from her sandals. She was done with Second Earth."

Endelle still couldn't believe that obsidian flame had finally shown up on Second Earth. She had been so excited when she'd first learned that Fiona had this power: Each individual identified as obsidian flame would have emerging preternatural abilities, and—because the flame phenomenon always worked in the form of a triad—there would be two others.

Marguerite had already been identified as the red variety, and with her advanced Seer capacity, Endelle was really hoping that her contribution would involve her Seer skills. The third woman hadn't yet emerged—but what good would it do if Marguerite was still traipsing around on Mortal Earth, apparently intent on living however the hell she pleased? Though she had never seen an obsidian flame triad in action, she understood that the potential was enormous.

God knew they needed a weapon of this magnitude in order to fight Greaves. She could feel in her bones that what had always felt centuries distant was about to fall on Second Earth in the form of Armageddon. The fact that Greaves was holding his military review spectacle had simply solidified this truth.

And now Thorne was gone.

The ultimate warrior.

The man she'd always counted on.

She once more rubbed the little lumps on the starfish's back, but she stared now at nothing in particular, her heart aching. Her emotions were all over the place as well, but they seemed to revolve around two specific poles; one that was pure grief, like now, and the other so filled with fury that she'd nearly lost her mind with rage.

Jean-Pierre left his humping position on the branch and sat down on the glass floor behind Fiona. He surrounded her with his long legs so that she could lean easily against his chest.

This couple's relationship had traveled light-years since they'd completed the *breh-hedden* about three weeks ago.

The goddamn *breh-hedden*, that really infuriating vampire mate-bonding ritual that had half her warriors in heat—and now Thorne had been struck down as well. He'd been so out-of-his-mind that for the first time in two thousand years he'd actually abandoned his post.

Jean-Pierre wrapped Fiona up in his arms, which caused her to turn her head slightly and kiss him just over his vein. Endelle saw the faint puncture marks of a recent tap.

She looked away. For some reason this display of tenderness and intimacy was a shard straight through her heart. Maybe she was just missing Thorne, but damn she felt lonely. She hadn't realized how her ability to reach him day or night with just a thought had kept her feeling not just secure but connected as well. Since he'd left, she'd been like a ship without a rudder. She was getting damn sick of the feeling, like she'd begun moving in endless circles.

"Thorne needs to get his ass back here."

Jean-Pierre nodded. "We all feel it as a terrible loss. I did not realize how much we depended on him. Zach and Santiago are having a war of their own, and even Kerrick got into a very big fight with Luken. Thorne is a leader of men, it is as simple as that."

"He kept me grounded."

"*Oui.* All of us, I think. We are missing him very much."

"And now Greaves is making a show of his army to the world."

"Were you with Marcus when you got word of the spectacle?"

"Oh, yeah. He put a hole in the wall. I've never seen him quite that enraged. He was moving around so erratically that Havily suddenly folded into the space demanding to know what was going on and why his hand hurt."

The completion of the *breh-hedden* had one telling feature: Each partner could experience the other partner's external physical sensations. When Marcus had punched the wall, Havily had felt it as well.

"That must have been awful for her," Fiona said. She held tightly to Jean-Pierre's arms. "When he fights, I have to close down the sensations or I'm not able to sleep at all."

"Yeah, Havily was pretty upset. Hell, we all were. To show his military strength to the world? Shit."

"*Mon dieu.* We are so fucked."

"You got that right."

"Greaves is a madman," Jean-Pierre muttered.

"Yeah, well, at the very least he's insane. His current line of propaganda goes something like, 'The war has been nothing but a misunderstanding,' and he 'hopes for a permanent resolution by the winter solstice.' Imagine, the 'winter solstice.' Isn't that the most beautiful new-age crap you've ever heard?

"He's invited COPASS to attend as well. Apparently, most of the committee members have accepted his invitation. And did you hear the latest, that COPASS members are being granted British-style forms of address and corresponding ranks? Even Harding, that prick of pricks, must now be addressed as my Lord Asshole?"

"Are you shitting me?" Jean-Pierre said. But because *shitting* sounded like *sheeting,* all she could do was smile. She wanted him to say it again. His accent could melt ice in ten-below weather.

That Fiona kissed his neck again didn't surprise Endelle, but she got the feeling by the way he looked at his *breh* that Endelle would have to fold out of this weird tree room or she'd have another kind of spectacle to watch.

As she rose to her feet, the knitted throw and a bunch more bits of snail shell fell to the floor. Before she could reach for the throw, Fiona folded it into her arms. She'd only recently completed her ascension, and she practiced her folding skills any chance she got.

"We're going to lose more High Administrators because of the review. Well, I've taken up enough of your time." She glanced at Fiona. "You'll tell me if Marguerite contacts you?"

She nodded. "Of course." Fiona then reached out and touched her arm. "Thorne will come home soon. Don't worry."

But her heart plummeted again. Jesus, if she didn't get the hell out of this place, she'd start weeping onto her starfish boobs, and like hell she was going to do that.

Fuck Thorne, anyway, for taking his little goddamn *brehhedden* holiday on Mortal Earth.

With that, she lifted her arm and folded back to her palace.

She needed to be alone for a while before she returned to HQ.

How can a traitor ever redeem his actions?
He can't.

—*Collected Proverbs*, Beatrice of Fourth

CHAPTER 6

Darian Greaves, the Commander of the Ascenders Liberation
Army, protector of the disenfranchised, soon-to-be leader of
two worlds, approached the first of two enormous transport
cages. He wore a fur hat, necessary over his bald head. The
Russian spring was very cold, especially since it was nearly
ten at night. His nostrils sparked when he breathed. The re-
hearsal had been going on since one in the afternoon and
would probably continue until the early hours of the morning, although the DNA-altered swans and geese that had been
trained to fly in squadrons had already been sent to their
designated resting grounds for the night.

The white tigers within the cages were restless, pacing
back and forth. He kept them hungry because hunger put
them in motion, a very consistent law of nature.

He understood the concept extremely well. He had been
hungry his entire adult life.

He patted the side of the cage and the tiger sprang at him,
screaming and slashing.

Good. These cats would make an excellent part of the
spectacle parade. He had one goal: intimidation, implied
threat. He wanted all the Territories of Second Earth to

understand that he would punish severely any who did not align with him before the final battle took place.

His Seers were working hard on his behalf, as well they should. The military review spectacle looked very favorable in the future streams. The several he'd viewed telepathically through one of his more advanced Mumbai Seers had shown the exact level of magnificence he'd been hoping for.

Even so, he felt vaguely uneasy, an unusual state for him. He had such confidence in his plans that he wasn't used to even the smallest wiggle of anxiety.

If he could locate Owen Stannett, he'd put him on the future streams just to be sure. But Stannett was off the grid and had enough power to hide from Greaves, unless of course Greaves really wanted to find him. Not yet, though.

As for the tigers, he was well satisfied. He lifted a hand and signaled to the trainers and drivers to take them away. "Send them to General Leto at the viewing platform. I want him to have a look. Get his approval." He was in full inspection mode, but not just where the parade was concerned. Unfortunately, tonight he had to deal with . . . Leto.

He was disappointed in the truths that had emerged over the past several weeks about his dearest Warrior-of-the-Blood-turned-general. And yes, even a little surprised, despite the fact that he was rarely surprised by anything. The human-vampire nature was a restless thing, seeking for some kind of communal oneness and connectedness that could never really be achieved.

Leto had taken dying blood on the first day of his defection. What truer statement could there ever have been of purpose and intention? He had all but sold his soul to be part of Greaves's glorious mission to transform both Second Earth and Mortal Earth into the paradise he envisioned.

He felt really sad that Leto would not be part of the new world he would create. The pyramids of Egypt, the Great Wall of China, all the great European cathedrals combined would be nothing to the monuments he intended to build, or rather have built, by the great supports of Mortal Earth.

Some would call it slavery. He would herald such acts of sacrifice as the finest form of service for the good of all.

He was nearing the fulfillment of all things. The vibration of his growing power sang in his veins, a strong powerful composition full of cymbals and drums and trumpets. His army was almost complete and beautifully well trained.

Greaves was the *coming one*. He could feel it now, chosen by destiny to transform all six dimensions. This first part of his plan was essentially just the beginning.

Still, he sighed. All well and good but there was just something so *lowering* about discovering an unhappy and unsuspected truth.

Leto was a spy.

If Greaves hadn't been bereft of a heart he would say his heart was just a little bit broken. Absurd, of course, but he'd always liked Leto in an essential way. There was nothing of either the simpleton or the braggadocio about the man. There were times he even had *feelings* toward him, and Greaves had never been particularly homosexual. He'd always preferred women, but Leto was wonderful to look at. He had incredible blue eyes, very sharp and piercing, the color clear like crystals.

He sighed. Perhaps he'd had a little crush on the man after all. How else could he have explained being so blind to his activities for nearly a century.

Leto also had kept his hair warrior long and constrained by the ritual *cadroen*. From the first, Greaves had approved this affectation because it was a constant reminder to his followers that he had successfully turned a powerful Warrior of the Blood, one of Endelle's own elite force.

Leto had been a feather in Greaves's cap, at least until the truth had finally surfaced, or rather when Greaves, just to make certain of his general, had sent a very gifted IT hacker into Leto's files. He really should have done it sooner, but Greaves preferred to trust those closest to him until proof surfaced to the contrary.

But Leto's conduct had become erratic over the past few

months, ever since Alison's rite of ascension, actually. Leto had several times stopped taking dying blood until Greaves forced it on him. Leto was in that state even now, pretending that he wasn't gripped with the resulting cramps because he'd refused to imbibe his allotted portion of the addictive substance. Maybe that's what had forced Greaves's hand, what had prompted him to finally set one of his dogs on Leto's trail.

But that trail had unearthed the unhappy news that Leto had been deleting files for years, which had been causing a corresponding amount of chaos at his Estrella Mountain War Complex for the past two decades. In terms of a scheme, not half bad, really. But what else had Leto been up to? Naturally, Greaves had set more than one of his trusted counter-intelligence workers on the entire host of Leto's activities, especially anything from the past year, which encompassed Greaves's push to a final, decisive battle that would cover all seven continents of Second Earth.

And now he knew the truth.

How utterly unfortunate.

Greaves looked down the long avenue lined by enormous wintry trees, not yet leafing out. He loved everything about the location. He'd spent a fortune lighting the route since the event would begin in the late afternoon and continue into the night to best display the fireworks. The forecast was perfect: snow on the day before the event. He wanted everything cold and gray, preferably overcast. Steely skies would be absolute perfection.

He drew his phone from his pocket and mentally touched the screen. He was rarely forced to make personal calls, but this one was necessary since Casimir couldn't be reached with a simple bolt of purposeful telepathy. Casimir, as a Fourth Ascender, had sufficient power to create an almost impenetrable mist around his Paris apartment.

Greaves hadn't wanted to bring Casimir into his plans, but the advent of *royle* wings with Warrior Medichi and his woman, Parisa, had forced his hand. He needed a powerful ascender on staff, but loathed having to ask for help. Casimir was an undisciplined vampire who tended to act in his own best interest, despite his professed alliances.

He really despised the man on so many levels, but right now he needed him. Leto was one powerful vampire; only a Fourth Ascender would have a shot at rendering Leto unconscious so that Greaves could turn him over to his specialty death vampires. Neither Greaves nor Casimir, under the current law of the land, given their respective power levels, could directly murder anyone. There was, however, nothing on the books against assisting the occasionally necessaryp rocess.

Casimir picked up on the third ring.

"Five minutes, at the platform. Just fold directly to it."

"No greeting, Darian? I'm disappointed beyond words."

Greaves didn't make use of profanity, or at least not very often, but right now he knew a strong impulse to let loose. Casimir's manners, how should he put this, *bugged the shit out of him.* Always, the man attempted to get up a flirtation.

But rather than let Caz goad him into a display of temper, he drew a very deep breath and smiled. "Five minutes," he said quietly. He mentally thumbed his phone and put it back in his pocket.

Five minutes and he'd take care of one more nuisance.

Warrior Leto was through. He'd reached the end of his rope and he knew it. There was nothing more to be done.

Despite the cold, perspiration beaded on his upper lip.

He wore a heavy wool coat over thick wool trousers, regulation. It had snowed in Moscow Two, just a couple of inches, nothing significant, but it was fucking cold. He had on gloves and a fur Cossack hat.

He stared down the long, extremely well-lit avenue, five miles straight and very wide. This avenue was the prime reason Greaves had worked so hard to turn the High Administrator of Russia Territory. Moscow Two was a perfect stage.

Some of the most beautiful buildings of Moscow One had been re-created in the Second city: parts of the Kremlin, St. Basil's Cathedral with its onion domes in a bunch of different colors, and the Kutuzov Triumphal Arch. In some ways the Second city was a caricature of the ancient city that had developed over centuries. But sending Greaves's army, the one he'd been building for decades in secret, the one drawn from Militia Warriors and death vampires from all over the world, would produce spectacle at its finest.

Camera crews were set up all along the route. Right now the flying bots zoomed back and forth, the remote operators testing all the equipment. Grandstands also lined specific parts of the route, each one built tall and hung with Greaves's newly created insignia, a stylized mythological phoenix in black, maroon, and gold. Each grandstand would house hundreds of hired actors to shout and applaud nonstop.

As for himself, he was ill, in the only way that a death vampire could become ill. He hadn't taken dying blood for over two weeks. The cramps were nearly unbearable at this point. He'd even taken to using ibuprofen to ease some of the pain. Unfortunately, his vampire healing capacity tended to throw it off, just not the withdrawal-based cramps. He'd made a decision to let the addiction run its course. The abdominal seizures would become unbearable but he wasn't taking dying blood again. Never again.

Eventually, he would be unable to eat. Therefore, though ascended, he would die of starvation, a process that would take months.

Too fucking bad.

When he'd learned the source of the dying blood—that Greaves kept women as slaves, killing them once a month then bringing them back to life with bags of regular blood and defibrillators—he'd reached his limit. Of course, the blood had to come from somewhere, but he'd blinded himself to that reality until now. That Warrior Jean-Pierre was now bonded with a woman who'd been put through that hell for over a century had finally pushed him over the edge.

He just couldn't do it anymore.

He no longer cared that his handler, James, wouldn't receive his regular reports on Greaves's activities, or that Sixth Earth would be unable to properly monitor all that was going on, in preparation for what? What could Sixth Earth do? Nothing. Upper dimensions had rules about involvement in lowerd imensionsp olitically.

Yeah, he was fucking done.

So be it.

This was one of the prices he'd paid all these years as a spy. From the first, Greaves had insisted on turning him as proof of his defection from the Warriors of the Blood. As with all of the High Administrators and members of COPASS whom Greaves had turned, he supplied both the dying blood and the drug that hid the telltale signs, so that those addicted didn't have to look like they partook of something so heinous. Hypocrisy at its best.

A faint chime sounded deep within his mind. He ignored the nausea and dove inward toward the sound. James's telepathic voice resonated. *Leto. You are in mortal danger. When the woman comes, go with her . . . no questions, no debate, though you will want to refuse . . .*

The message ended.

He was done with this as well, the brief commands, without rhyme or reason, without debate, from his Sixth dimension handler.

Would he go?

No.

He was finished. If Greaves had finally stumbled on all his relatively ineffective sabotage, and was coming to finish him off, he thought the timing damn fine.

A shudder passed through him. He felt feverish now. The vomiting would start soon.

Grace sat on a wood stool in front of her small desk, holding a pen in her hand, the old-fashioned kind that required an ink pot. She had written pages and pages of her erotic poetry already today. She had begun writing this forbidden verse during the first year of her internment at the convent. And always, for reasons she couldn't explain, one man, one warrior had been the object of her imaginings, partly because she'd known him forever: Leto.

Warrior Leto and Grace's brother, Thorne, had been friends for the past two thousand years. She had known Leto that long as well, although perhaps not as well as Thorne knew him. Leto had always lived a warrior's life while Grace's preference for religious study in the course of her two thousand ascended years had taken her all over the world, on both Second and Mortal Earth. She had even lived in a Chinese Buddhist monastery, outside of Beijing Two, but that was six hundred years ago. She was as different in her life's pursuit from Leto's as two vampires could be. He made war. She worked to understand how all the religions of the world strove to make sense of life. But every once in a while, their paths would cross and she had always enjoyed speaking with him. He was a cultured man and she had always admired him.

She had been extremely surprised when she'd learned that he had defected to Commander Greaves's faction. No one was more loyal to Endelle or to his warrior brothers than Leto, which led her to believe that there had to be an explanation. So when Thorne had told her that Leto had been a spy for the past century, his conduct had finally made sense to her.

According to Thorne, Leto had served the Council of Sixth Earth as a spy on the council's behalf and his purpose in Greaves's camp had been to document the Commander's activities and to report to the council's liaison, James, with all pertinent information. The council's purpose in having Leto do this was still unknown. Thorne had then warned her to hide the information from Sister Quena, the High Administrator of the Convent, or any other powerful ascenders, since Leto's precarious position could be endangered by a careless thought.

Of course she had deep-shielded the information, which involved the creation of a powerful but very small shield over the specific data deep within her mind. She actually visited the shield daily as part of her meditations and said a prayer for Warrior Leto's safety and for his safe return to the Warriors of the Blood.

Because she'd sat for an hour or so, the wood stool had

created a numbness on her backside. It was hand-hewn and uneven but very smooth from centuries of use. She turned the pen in her hand as she stared down at a poem she had written at least a decade ago. She smiled because she thought it beautiful and obscure, the perfect verse: *He took me to the grotto, And explored the damp, weeping walls.*

She sighed. This sensual part of her had always required an outlet, but it was something of a mystery. Nor did she understand exactly why she held Warrior Leto as some sort of romantic, sexual figure in her imagination. Of course he had embarked on his journey at about the same time she had gone into the Convent, a coincidence that had increased her sense of mysterious connectedness to the warrior.

She thought the dichotomy in her personality a great paradox, but contrary to much spiritual teaching, across religions, she didn't try to suppress these longings and imaginings. She gave them form, in verse, and when she did that normally she felt satisfied and could move forward with her devotions.

However, of late, especially since Marguerite had been taken from the Convent, Grace's longings had increased in both fervency and frequency.

She had been writing a lot of verse over the past three weeks.

Today in particular had been full of new strange sensations. The earth seemed to be moving beneath her feet and her mind had a strange, loose quality, as though all the doors were open and a breeze blew through constantly.

And also, for inexplicable reasons, she was missing Marguerite this morning more than ever. She had truly loved her cellmate even though they were water and oil.

They were even different physically, since Grace was tall and Marguerite relatively short at five-five. In complexion, Marguerite was dark and Grace was fair, her skin almost white. Marguerite's eyes were a dark brown and her hair long and of a color to match her eyes, while Grace's hair hung in thin blond ringlets to her waist.

As for temperament, their dissimilarity continued.

Marguerite was wild, without sexual restraints. She had a worldly outlook and often spoke of men as something to be worshiped with her body. She had been Thorne's lover, the one who eased Thorne from his duties as a warrior, from almost the beginning of her residence in the Convent.

Grace was chaste. During her life prior to the Convent, she'd only had one lover, her husband, since divorced. She blamed herself for the divorce since she knew she was a rather strange ascender. She had been chaste before him and chaste since. She worshiped in chapel, her head bowed, her eyes closed, her heart completely open to all the mysteries of the universe.

Yet with all this disparity of inclination and temperament, she had loved and valued Marguerite as a sister. She had prayed for Marguerite every day, not with a hope that Marguerite would accept Sister Quena's harsh and oftentimes brutal discipline; rather, she prayed for Marguerite's freedom because that was what her Convent sister had wished for more than anything else in the world.

So the day had come when Marguerite had been granted her freedom, and Grace had rejoiced for her even though Thorne in turn was devastated. And therein lay one of the great mysteries of life: how one person's deepest desire could hurt another person to the core.

But Grace had compassion for Marguerite. Her life had been exceptionally difficult from the time she was a child. She was also quite young in ascended terms, just over a hundred and twenty. And most of those years had been lived in a state of duress behind the stone walls of the Convent.

Then quite suddenly, everything had changed for Marguerite. Endelle, acting in her capacity as the Supreme High Administrator of Second Earth, had finally approved a transfer for Marguerite to the Superstition Seers Fortress. However, the transfer had been granted by Madame Endelle on the sole condition that Her Supremeness be allowed access to the Fortress.

When the High Administrator of the Fortress, Owen Stannett, denied access to Madame Endelle, she in turn authorized Thorne and Warrior Jean-Pierre to break down the front doors of the fortress and to remove Marguerite by force if necessary. In doing so, the warriors found a nightmare awaiting them since it was revealed that High Administrator Stannett had been siring children by the Seers under his care in an effort to create a super-race of Seers.

So Marguerite had been given her freedom, and though Madame Endelle had believed that Marguerite would join forces with her and serve her administration in support of the war against Commander Greaves, Marguerite instead had made her escape to Mortal Earth.

Grace had always been amazed by Marguerite, by her spirit. Again, water and oil. Grace had never been powerful like Thorne or like her twin sister, Patience. Grace had been the one to sit back and smile at their antics, to *glory* in who they were in all their strength and brilliance.

Her thoughts had always been inward and upward.

She had been on the sidelines, cheering them on, in everything they did. Patience had been wildly powerful, almost a warrior like Thorne. Her disappearance—for Grace still could not believe or even *feel* that her sister was truly gone—had been a shock.

As for Thorne, Grace had always thought that his symbiotic relationship with Endelle had held him back, had prevented greater powers from emerging. She had tried to tell him many times of her beliefs, but he had replied that he was doing his duty—and for a Warrior of the Blood, there was no greater honor.

Shortly after she had joined the Convent, Marguerite had arrived. To some extent, though she could never explain it, Grace had always felt that her fate was linked to Marguerite's, a very strange intuition, to be sure, given that they were, yes, water and oil.

But she loved Marguerite, and though she had been gone just a little over three weeks, she missed her.

She turned the pen in her fingers. Her joints ached. In late

March the stone cell was icy cold and the inmates weren't allowed to wear more than their handwoven gowns, day or night, rain or shine, winter or summer.

As she dipped her pen in the inkwell, sudden, inexplicable longings surged yet again within her, a swell of her heart and lungs that caused her for a moment to lose her ability to breathe.

This was new.

What on earth?

Then the experience took a turn, a sudden hard turn. She dropped the pen on the floor and rose from her stool. She moved to the center of the small chamber. She held her hands palms-up and tilted her head back just a little, her eyes closed.

Spiritual fervor, surely.

She was almost in pain.

She could feel a vibration now, but it came from below, beneath the stones on which she stood.

The vibration intensified and fear suddenly shot through her. She didn't understand what was happening.

But even as the fear came, a wave of love followed that eradicated the fear so that she spread her arms wide and smiled. She let the love flow. She had a sense of weight, of strength, of vitality, of life force, and of the earth.

Yes, of the earth, a power that seemed to be flowing through her. She had the sense that something enormous had come to her.

The object of her forbidden poetry came into her mind: *Leto.*

She saw him as clearly as if he were standing next to her. He shivered in the cold. He wore a dark fur hat that just covered his ears and looked very Russian. The sky overhead was both the dark of night and yet the muted gray of clouds overhead. Snowflakes fell. He stared ahead, the sharpness of his blue eyes as vivid as she remembered, beautiful.

The power and the love she felt flowing through her, from the source she didn't understand, coupled with the affection she had always felt for this brother-warrior of Thorne's, poured through her in an increased rush. Just like that she stood next to him . . . sort of. In some mystical way, she knew herself to be in two places at once.

He stared at her, wide-eyed, stunned. "Grace?" he murmured. His lips were tinged blue from the cold but she could see that his skin was clammy, as if he was ill, something highly unusual for vampires.

"I'm here," she said. Her focus was all for him. She could feel that she was not with him in a corporeal sense, and yet she was able to stand next to him. She didn't question the situation.

"What . . . what are you doing here?"

She shook her head and looked around. Extraordinary white tigers, one in each cage, paced, restless and . . . starving. This she could tell because of the power within her.

She looked to the left of the cages. She stood with Leto at the head of dozens of stairs that flowed down to a broad empty street, a long avenue lined with bare trees. She looked back at him. "I was thinking about you and now here I am. Where is this place?"

"Moscow Two. I . . . I have not seen you since you went into the Convent."

Grace smiled. "Over a hundred years ago." As she stood next to him, she could suddenly smell him. The scent was erotic, very much a man but laced with forest, like the ponderosa pines of northern Arizona.

The power once more flowed over her in a great wave of understanding. She didn't so much have a vision as she simply *knew* what was happening and what was needed. "You are in mortal danger and you are to come with me. I am to tend your wounds."

Leto knew he shouldn't go. He was all that was abhorrent to such a sweet spirit as Grace. Besides, his presence in her life would put her in danger. He was sure of that.

A double shimmering appeared in front of the tiger

cages. Casimir and Greaves arrived together, forming a purposeful front. He didn't harbor even the smallest doubt as to the meaning of their sudden appearance.

He felt something inside him relax and give way, as though he hadn't really breathed for the last hundred years.

It was over, finally over, the ten thousand games he played, all the ways he hid his subversion, all the ways he'd tried to sabotage the tasks Greaves assigned him, all the dying blood he had consumed.

So now he had a choice to make: to go with Grace or to die here, on this platform. He felt in his gut it would be much better for him to leave the earth now, permanently, than to involve Grace in one more moment of the chaos that would ensue should he go with her.

He was ready to die. That would be his decision today. He would simply refuse to take her hand.

He turned to Grace but she had a funny look on her face as she shifted to stare not at Greaves but at Casimir.

Leto, too, glanced back at Casimir and saw that the Fourth ascender's attention had suddenly become fixed on Grace, his dark eyes wide, almost surprised. His lips moved. Leto thought he might have said, "Beautiful." Then he whispered, "I'm smelling a meadow, soft grasses, fragrant wildflowers all combined."

Greaves turned slightly and scowled at him. "What did you say?"

But Casimir ignored him. He took a step forward. Then another.

So Casimir could see Grace but Greaves couldn't. What the hell did this mean?

Leto turned back to Grace. Then he smelled it as well, the gentlest fragrance of a meadow, all that verdant growth, the earth, a combined scent of indistinguishable flowers.

Breh-hedden shot through his mind. A flash of fear followed swiftly at the singular truth that the Fourth ascender also smelled Grace. If all that he knew of the *breh-hedden* was true, he was both experiencing and watching the inception of what had always been a myth on Second Earth. Only what the fuck did it mean that both he and Casimir could scent the same woman?

Oh, God, no.

"Grace," he said, calling to her. She turned to look at him and in that same moment, from his peripheral vision, he watched Casimir lift his hand in what would no doubt be a monstrous hand-blast, aimed not at Grace but at him.

"You must come now," she said.

When she stretched out her hand to him, a semi-transparent limb with an iridescent sheen, he looked at the cupped fingers, the small white hand, and he placed his palm over hers and held on tight.

He saw Casimir's energy release toward him but at the same time, a strange kind of vibration flowed through him. Suddenly he whipped through nether-space, dematerializing and blanking out for a split second, only to touch down in a dark stone cell right next to . . . Grace.

He let go of her hand and spun in a circle, folding his sword into his hand and preparing for the Fourth intruder, but nothing more happened.

A wave of abdominal cramps caught him and he lurched forward and gasped. He released the sword back to his weapons locker deep in the bowels of Estrella Mountain where Greaves had one of his primary military compounds. The sword was identified to him and therefore dangerous to Grace. He dropped to his knees.

"You're in pain."

He nodded, gritting his teeth, unable to breathe. After half a minute, the spasm eased though much of the pain remained. Struggling, he regained his feet. "Intruders," he whispered, wanting to call his sword back but afraid he would completely lose control.

"Don't worry, the trace is blocked."

"You have that kind of power?"

She shook her head. "No, but the power that possessed me does."

"What power?" He looked around, expecting another ascender to step forward, James perhaps, but there was no one else in the room.

She shrugged. "I can't explain it, since I'm not sure exactly what just happened to me. But I felt a power from there." She swept a hand in the direction of the floor. "Then the power flowed through me. Suddenly I was thinking of you, and then there I was next to you."

He pinched his lips together. Nausea swirled in his gut.

He focused on her. She looked like a goddess with her long blond hair streaming in ringlets all the way to her waist. She wore a long gown, somewhat nubby and rough in appearance, perhaps handwoven, very beige. Her eyes were large and a light goldish green. Her eyelashes were light-colored as well, which added to her almost angelic look. Her chin had a faint dimple, just as he remembered.

And her scent was much stronger now that he stood beside her. His body reacted, wholly inappropriately, and as he turned to face her, as her meadow and wildflower scent continued to pummel his senses, he began to grow aroused. The muscles of his thighs, abdomen, and chest flexed and relaxed, then trembled in need. But all that sudden physical sensation, like he needed to take her to bed now, caused a new wave of nausea to flow.

What was he going to do? He'd never seen such a spare room with so little he could use.

"You're going to be ill."

He felt the clamping of his cheeks. He nodded.

She held out her hand and a wooden bowl appeared. "I'll get into trouble for this."

He took the bowl, turned away from her, and puked his guts out. Great, just great.

I have heard it said that freedom is the ability to do what you want, when you want to do it. But I have come to believe that true freedom is the ability to help other people do what they want, when they want to do it. But then, I am a hopeless idealist.

—*Memoirs,* Beatrice of Fourth

CHAPTER 7

Marguerite was alone in the cabin and had been for a while. Thorne was out hunting down Diallo, that tall gorgeous black man.

Now, there was a fine piece of . . .

Okay, she needed to keep her thoughts pure, at least while she was sharing a bed with Thorne.

She sat on the brown leather couch, cradling a cup of hot, hot coffee, wondering whether she should just take off. Everything about being here felt like another cell into which she was being shoved one push at a time and without a say.

She'd awakened to Thorne spooning her, which of course had led to an early-morning romp. All those wonderful chemicals were still jumping around in her veins, shouting in alternate fits of air-boxing, *Yippee!* and *Stay with Thorne, you fucking idiot!*

And yes, she'd enjoyed it, but she had this really bad feeling that the longer she stayed shacked up with Thorne, the harder it would be to leave and get on with her real life.

She sipped her coffee and stared through the bank of

windows out at some beautiful tall fir trees. But that didn't help. The sight reminded her that she wasn't where she wanted to be.

She lowered her chin and scowled as she took another sip. The cabin had a small kitchen with a decent coffeemaker and cupboard stocked with Seattle's Best. Apparently, the colony had generators or something, which supplied the homes with some electricity. So yeah, she'd turned on the coffeemaker and sighed when it lit up.

She didn't need more than coffee, not first thing, although her stomach seemed a little more rumbly than usual. Probably nerves. She'd always had coffee in the Convent. Sister Quena had at least given her devotiates a big cup to start off the morning. Come to think of it, coffee at breakfast was about the only nice thing the woman had ever done.

Whatever.

The trouble was, she had the willies again, irritating little shivers that kept climbing all over her back and down her sides, bugging the shit out of her wing-locks.

Ever since Thorne had related his belief that Owen Stannett was behind last night's attack, he'd been on her mind big-time. If he'd hired some death vampire mercenaries to get his job done, would he recruit another couple of teams and try again?

As she rolled the warm mug between her palms, she tried to figure out exactly what she was feeling, why she was so uneasy. Yes, she had reasons—Stannett being on the hoof, was one—but something more was going on, something inexplicable, something *big*, something within her. She rubbed her itchy back against the couch.

Maybe Thorne was right. Maybe she needed to just settle down for a minute and confront the fact that she was obsidian flame, whatever the hell that might mean for her in the coming days, weeks, and months.

Her power was emerging, vibrating deep into her bones, making her wing-locks swell and retract and, yes, itch.

She took a deep breath. It was either take deep breaths or throw the coffee cup against the window. She didn't want this. She didn't want any of it. She didn't want obsidian flame or her Seers power or any of her advanced powers.

She could even go into the darkening like Havily and Endelle, something Thorne didn't know she could do. She was a smelter of preternatural power. Maybe it was a good thing for the world she lacked ambition as well, because sometimes she had the sense she had as much power as Endelle. Aw, shit.

She had to get out of this cabin, leave this colony. She had to get rid of her association with Thorne. She wanted a new life, a simpler life, a life with one goal: *shagging a bunch of hunky men*.

There was just one problem—that stupid Seers gift of hers had started crashing down on her and leaving her wide open to who the hell knew what. And Thorne had been right: If the enemy had been around last night . . . Stannett, for instance . . . she'd be locked up right now, a new ankle guard around her leg, trapped in a cell probably forever.

She took a few more deep breaths until she calmed down.

She set her mug on the massive coffee table in front of her and fluffed her damp hair. Well, that was something positive she could focus on. She loved this cut. If she wore it loose, it clung to her neck and face in nice wisps. If she wanted to go clubbing, she could use a curling iron and create a nice sexy cloud of white. A heap of dark red lipstick and she was good to go.

But when the hell could she go clubbing? Especially since she'd looked up and down the lane of this colony and all she'd found were rustic cabins, a few nice houses, and a whole bunch of farms. Maybe this was some kind of ascended Amish colony. There were vegetable and flower gardens everywhere, and she could hear kids out there playing, yelling, crying, all of which supported her theory. A few dogs barked. This was mountain-based suburbia. It didn't exactly lead her to the conclusion she could continue her forays into freedom here.

Unless there was a bar somewhere down the road.

A girl could only hope.

A knock on the door put her on her feet. Thorne wouldn't have knocked—or death vampires, either, for that matter. Yeah, she was jumpy, even with all that mossy mist keeping the colony hidden. But the attack last night meant the lid was already blown off this little piece of Eden.

She moved to the window and looked out. To her left, she could see a group of men, big men not far from the cabin, all wielding swords and intent on something. But she couldn't see what because—and wasn't this just the best news ever— there were two women on her porch.

Shit. Two females. She wasn't exactly "girlfriend" material in the platonic sense. And if they'd brought a plate of brownies, she might just scream.

She sighed and opened the front door. The lead woman wore jeans and had enough cleavage showing from a snug tube top to support a bunch of nicely folded "ones." She had straight black hair just past her shoulders, some serious black eyeliner, and a spiderweb tattoo on her neck. Her right eyebrow was pierced with a thin silver loop and she had a second piercing, a small amber jewel, beside her left nostril. Her eyes were steely gray and damn, the woman was tall, maybe six-two. She leaned against the doorjamb and narrowed her eyes looking down at Marguerite. "Heard we had a new Seer in town."

Well, wasn't this a surprise. No brownies, just attitude.

But Marguerite was so not in the mood. "Screw you." She slammed the door but was really surprised when she heard the women laugh and the other one say, "Told ya she wouldn't like it, Brynna."

Told ya?

Curiosity got the better of her and she reopened the door. "What the hell do you want?"

The woman next to Brynna, a shorter chick with red hair, said, "Neither of us could get a reading on you in the future streams—which can mean only one thing, a Seer of power. Brynna"—she jerked her thumb at the Amazon next to her— "just wanted you to know that we're not your typical Seer outfit."

Huh. Maybe she needed to rethink her "Amish" theory.

"Well, I guess you'd better come in and tell me what the hell is going on then."

She headed back to the leather couch, picked up her cup of coffee, then curled up in the corner. She would offer them a cup as well, but she wasn't in the mood to play hostess. She felt that same overwhelming need to get out of this colony . . . now.

Brynna crossed the room to straddle the rounded edge of a big leather club chair, but Red moved to the windows to watch the men just down the street.

Brynna said, "We hear Arthur and one of the Warriors of the Blood slaughtered some death vamps last night."

"Yep. Eight of them."

"We've never had them here before."

"Never?" That was another surprise. She glanced at the window. In the distance, above the trees she could see the mossy mist. "You've got some interesting protection. I guess that's kept them out."

"You can see it then?"

"Can't you?"

Brynna shrugged. "Yeah."

Red called out, "But the rest of us can't. Brynna's the only one with power like Diallo, and Arthur, too, I guess."

Marguerite shifted her gaze back to Brynna. "So you're powerful?"

Brynna shrugged again, but her lips got a pinched look and she didn't meet Marguerite's gaze.

"Well what do you know," Marguerite said. "You don't like having all this power, either. I thought I was the only one."

Brynna shook her head and now stared at the rag rug beneath the coffee table. "I . . . I hate it. I've felt like a goddamn spectacle most of my life and of course my parents, *my loving parents,* always pushed me forward making me perform. It really sucked."

"So let me understand. Your Seer power is not your most potent gift?"

Red turned to face the room. "She can go invisible all the time. It's really annoying."

Marguerite looked at Brynna. "You mean like folding?"

But Brynna faded to nothing really slowly and said, "Not like folding at all." She fell silent.

Marguerite could feel her move, though, almost like a ghostly presence. She sensed that Brynna's hand was near her head so she reached up and caught it, trapping her wrist in a tight fist. She looked up into surprised gray eyes as Brynna made herself visible.

She nodded, but this time she actually smiled as she said, "Well fuck me, this time. No one has been able to do that, ever."

Red faced her. "Not even Diallo."

"Nope." Brynna added, "I don't know about Arthur. But he's a little too young to mess with."

Marguerite frowned. She knew she was powerful, but it sometimes surprised her just how different she was from most ascenders. She glanced at the mist again then back to Brynna. "How long have you two been here and where did you come from?"

Brynna had been in the colony a couple of hundred years. *That long?* Red, less, just forty years. And her name was Jane, come to find out.

"Do you miss Second Earth?" Marguerite asked.

"Sometimes," Brynna said. She plucked at the buttons on the flannel shirt she wore loose around her tube top. "I miss the air. The air is different on Second. And of course I miss the gardens. We don't have public gardens like Second does."

"Why did you come here then? Why did you leave?"

At that, Brynna and Jane exchanged a glance.

Oh, shit. "Tell me."

"We're Seers Fortress refugees. Jane escaped from the Atlanta Two Fortress and I'd spent one day in the St. Louis Two Fortress but like I said that was two hundred years ago. Diallo found us on the run and brought us each here, far from our families—or at least it was far away at the time."

Marguerite nodded. The whole Seer system was for shit. Any time an ascended child or the occasional young adult was discovered to have Seer ability, the families of the gifted would be persuaded through land grants and wealth to relinquish rights to the individual, always of course with the promise that the child would be given an excellent education, rich lodgings, and all that an ascended vampire could wish for on Second Earth. The families were also encouraged to consider the profound honor the child would have as a Seer in Second culture since most Seers assisted their territorial High Administrators. That the Creator's Church sanctioned and encouraged children to be removed from their homes and placed in Seers Fortresses only added to the pressure families experienced to give up their gifted children.

Though the occasional High Administrator of a Seers Fortress was liberal-minded, kind, and followed through on the promises made to the families, for the most part abuse seemed to be the order of the day. Over the centuries, the Fortresses became locked-down facilities and the Seers subject to the kindness or villainy of whatever disposition the administrator possessed.

All in all, Seers' rights had devolved to squat.

Marguerite had always thought it some strange kind of miracle that her parents had refused to ship her off to a Fortress when she was small since her Seer ability had been well-documented by the time she was eight. But then, her abusive parents had always preferred having control of her. They only sent her to the Creator's Convent in hopes of having the devil beaten out of her after she'd gone wild at college.

And right now, if either Jane or Brynna was caught on Second Earth, they'd be sent to any of hundreds of Fortresses throughout the world. Only, with the new technology, they'd be strapped with ankle guards just as Marguerite had worn in both the Convent and the Superstition Seers Fortress. They'd never escape a second time.

"Okay, so just how old is this colony? And how is it no one knows about it on Second Earth?"

"Diallo said he worked for centuries to create this mist. He tested it and retested it until he was certain it was impenetrable by even the most powerful ascenders. So you can see why we're shocked that you're here today. Right now, the colony's council is in an uproar. We left the meeting. Too many men, and a few women, yelling but doing nothing. Same old, same old. Anyway, he created the colony in 909 BC."

"Holy shit." Marguerite frowned then apologized. "Okay, sorry for the profanity. I'm not exactly house-trained."

Brynna smiled. "What the fuck are you apologizing for? We're Seers, not saints."

Jane laughed but then sighed with some gusto as she continued to stare out the window. "That's some pair of shoulders. Wow. I mean I knew that some of the Militia Warriors from Florida had folded in for some training, but *damn*." Her tongue made an appearance and she swiped her lower lip. "I'd like to lick the sweat off that."

Marguerite had seen the men outside with swords. They were grouped in an arc maybe watching some kind of demonstration. The lattice arch and angle of the building hadn't allowed her to see what kind of man-candy was showing his stuff or apparently his shoulders.

Jane was now fanning her face, her nostrils flaring with genuine female interest. So at least one of the Seers wasn't shy about expressing her overall interest in the male species. It might be fun to check out the local talent with a couple of girlfriends.

Of course, guilt about Thorne roared once more and she winced. Which of course pissed her off all over again. With her back up, she had a couple of questions she'd like answered. "So what do you do for entertainment around here? Or do you slip over to Seattle One? Down to Portland One maybe? Hit some clubs?" Maybe if she could get things settled with Thorne, she'd follow these Seers to their favorite hunting grounds.

But neither spoke up to answer her question. Instead, she felt a sudden tension in the room. "What? Don't tell me you don't get out much? I mean Mortal Earth has some damn hunky specimens."

Brynna shrugged. "It's complicated."

Marguerite had a feeling exactly where this was headed. As for complicated, no it wasn't. "Let me guess. Because you're Seers, and maybe because you're women, too, you aren't allowed beyond the boundaries of the mist."

Brynna narrowed her eyes. "Not sure about the 'women' part, but the Seer part is right. We get the reasoning. We're wanted, as in *wanted*, as in if we're discovered by other rogue ascenders unattached to our colony, then we could get reported, and the whole setup could get blown."

Marguerite sipped her coffee, but it had cooled off and she preferred hers scalding. She set the mug on the table at her elbow. Her temper, on the other hand, was starting to fire up just fine. "This is such bullshit. For half a second there I'd almost started to like this place. Now you're telling me you don't have the same rights as regular vampires?" She crossed her arms over her chest.

"There's not a one of us here who isn't grateful for this refuge. We all live as we choose and to a certain degree we respect this law. We know what waits for us beyond the protective mist: potential informants, death vampires, or, worse, Greaves. Our choices are a bit limited." Brynna then lifted her brows in a really in-your-face kind of way. "But if you think it's unjust, what do you intend to do about it? You've got power, unlike most of us who are only moderately blessed with Seer vision."

"I'm not going to do anything. When did that become my job?"

"Then what exactly are you complaining about? See, it's really easy for you to sit there and judge, but are you going to stick around, get involved, challenge the status quo? No, of course not."

Marguerite clamped her arms over her chest. "Oh, whatever." She knew she sounded childish but she did not like the direction of the discussion.

"Brynna," Jane called out. "Stop busting our visitor's chops and come look at this hunk. He kind of reminds me of that guy you bonked at the club in the colony outside Portland

One, the one who stripped at Jake's Fangtap. But this one's taller and bigger, uh, *everywhere*. The last time he spun and levitated, his kilt flew up. I got a good look and can I say, again, wow." She followed up this statement with, "I need me a man."

"Maybe it's Warrior Thorne."

"Just git your ass over here. You, too, Marguerite. We heard you'd come in with Warrior Thorne. You can tell us if this is him, because if it's not, and it's one of the Florida Militia, I'm all over it. By the way, are you together *together*?"

Good question. "Yes . . . no . . . not exactly. We were at one time."

"So you're not now?"

Marguerite needed things to change. Maybe this was the moment to start. "No. We're not together." But she felt dizzy speaking the words aloud. Did she really mean it? Want it? "So I know you can't leave the colony, but where can a girl grab a drink?"

The women exchanged a glance.

"Uh, just so ya know, I'm sort of crawling out of my skin here and I could really use a girls' night out." But as the words left her mouth, she realized that this was new territory for her. Other than Grace, she'd never had girlfriends before. At the same time, her freedom quest reared its head, so she added, "And I'm serious. I'm crawling out of my skin. I'm not exactly used to all this. I've sort of been locked up for a while." To say the least.

Brynna narrowed her eyes. Jane looked at Brynna. "Well," she drawled. "There is a club, at the edge of town. We go there sometimes."

Jane snorted. "You're there every other night."

"Girl's gotta have a hobby."

At that, Marguerite smiled. She really liked where this was headed. "Are you maybe talking about a club that features men who *move*."

"Oh, yeah." Brynna's voice had dropped about an octave. "To music."

Jane swayed on her feet. "And sometimes their clothes fall off."

Marguerite closed her eyes and her body responded with a head-to-toe shiver. "Now you're talkin'." If Thorne had an objection, and he would, she would just have to make him understand that this was her choice, what she needed in her life, right now, tonight.

These women definitely understood.

"How about eight o'clock?" Jane glanced at Marguerite over her shoulder. "Devon's performing. He's fantastic."

Brynna chuckled. "Yeah, he's good. Eight works for me."

Marguerite met her gaze, and some of her tension fell away. "That would be great."

Brynna gave some really simple directions, which settled the matter.

Jane, whose gaze was still fixed hard out the window, suddenly gasped. "That warrior's kilt just flew up again. Oh, my God. Brynna, you've got to see him."

Brynna slid off her chair-arm perch and joined the petite redhead staring out the window.

Jane waved Marguerite over. "Come here and tell us if this is Thorne, although I'm still really hoping it's one of the Florida boys."

Marguerite rose to her feet. She doubted it was Thorne, since he'd intended to meet up with Diallo for the morning. Still, if it was some hot ascender, she might just have a look; she was essentially on the hunt. Sort of. Oh, shit, her conscience hit her all over again. She ought to have at least a small sense of loyalty to Thorne. But how could she explain to anyone how she really felt? She wasn't rejecting Thorne. She didn't want to be committed to anyone. She wanted to be free.

Marguerite moved to look out the window, standing behind Brynna. She had to lean a little because Brynna was built on big lines, but, yep, there he was, *her man,* going through some strange kind of maneuver with the sword, almost in slow motion. There were at least two dozen Militia Warriors grouped around him, watching intently. There were a number of good-looking ones, too.

But it was Thorne her new friends were staring at. "Yep, that's Thorne."

"I'd heard of him," Brynna said. "But I've never seen him before. Damn, he's gorgeous."

Jane issued a soft groan. "I've never seen a Warrior of the Blood before." She palmed the window then dragged her fingertips down the glass. "Arthur's not too hard on the eyes, either. Too bad he's so damn young." The two warriors seemed to be putting on some kind of training exhibition for the Militia Warriors.

"No shit," Brynna murmured. "But Thorne. He's all grown up. Oh, God, I think I might be ovulating."

The women chuckled.

Marguerite blinked and looked at Thorne through the eyes of two women who were seeing him for the first time. He had his long hair pulled back in the *cadroen* so that the sharp lines of his cheekbones stood out. He had a strong face, a warrior's face, a way of holding his head and putting his gaze on another person that commanded attention.

Whenever he put his attention on her like that her knees buckled.

He held a sword in his hand to show young Arthur some moves. Arthur wore a weapons harness and kilt. Thorne was stripped down to just his kilt and battle sandals. Sweat glistened on his golden skin, his ridiculously broad shoulders, the breadth of his back. As he turned to face the cabin, his nipples were hard pebbles. Her breath quickened.

His pecs were thick pads that she'd sucked on about a million times. Was there a part of his body she hadn't taken in her mouth? His abs were a roll of muscles she'd tongued. The kilt dipped just below his navel. He had the right amount of hair on his chest and stomach. She knew the line that led all the way down, one of her favorite places for the tip of her tongue.

His every move flexed a new set of muscles.

Time slowed.

She had to admit she'd never seen him like this, doing what he did best. She heard his laughter and watched as he caught Arthur playfully with his palm on the back of Arthur's neck.

Arthur rolled his eyes, spun, and resumed the warrior position, knees bent, feet apart, sword in both hands, upright, ready.

Thorne called out a command.

Sweet Lord in heaven, even through the window that voice of his could work her like nothing else. It was all rough-hewn, like he gargled with sawdust. How many times had he used just his voice, a little resonance thrown in, his body suspended over hers, to bring her.

But had she ever really *seen* him before?

It struck her that he was *magnificent,* like something biblical that would ride in with enormous wings, his flaming sword held aloft, his hair flowing back in long waves, gilded by the sun. She had the strangest sensation that she had just seen exactly who he was and this vision of him thrilled her, striking a chord deep within. She blinked a couple of times, removing the strange image from her mind.

"I'll bet he really knows how to work his other sword."

The women laughed.

Aw, hell. Thorne was putting on one fine show for the women even though he probably had no idea they were watching him.

"Man, I'd like to get some of that, right between my legs. I'd heard about Thorne, but I didn't know any man could be so . . . perfect."

"Yes" was Jane's response, and the word carried a whole lot of estrogen. For the first time since she'd taken Thorne into her bed, Marguerite realized she might have been a little shortsighted in understanding his appeal to women generally.

She backed away from the window and looked down at her hands. Both were curled, and her inch-long red nails held the shape of a fine set of daggers. She felt another weird vibration go through her and before she could prevent it, a growl emerged from the base of her throat and rumbled through the room.

Jane and Brynna turned to look at her, eyes wide as they planted their backs square to the window.

"What gives?" Brynna asked. "You said you weren't together."

"He's mine." She'd added resonance, which caused Jane to wince.

Brynna stepped forward, both hands out and up in the universal sign of surrender. "Hey. I'm sorry. Jesus, what the hell is going on? Marguerite, I would never step on the territory of another woman. That's one of my rules. But you said—"

"I know. I know." She couldn't exactly breathe. Her winglocks had started to thrum. She bent over and worked at her breathing. "I'm in trouble here. Oh, man. And now I'm pissed as hell! I didn't ask for this. He's been my lay for a hundred years but we're not exactly, uh, monogamous." Well, *she* wasn't. She'd screwed José. That Thorne had been in his mind and enjoyed the ride as well was completely incidental. She had no right to Thorne, to insist he was hers, and she didn't even want him like that! What the hell was this?

As if she didn't know.

Goddamn the *breh-hedden*!

Jane and Brynna drew close, moving to stand directly in front of her.

"We can help with this," Brynna said.

Marguerite stayed bent over, her hands on her knees. She was shaking and damn close to mounting her wings.

"You're gonna mount, aren't you?" Brynna asked.

Marguerite nodded, swallowing hard.

She folded off her shirt because her back was a mess with weeping. She had enormous wings. The small living room wouldn't be tall enough to manage them. Letting them loose now would cause some damage and a whole lot of pain. She had to control this mount.

"Let us help," Jane said. "We can help you."

She strained to look up at the women. "What the hell are you talking about? How can you help?"

Brynna nodded. "We're Seers. We have group power." She frowned. "Or . . . don't you know about that?"

"I have no idea what you're talking about." She was pissed, her favorite, go-to emotion. She felt in control when she was mad so she was probably mad more often than she was willing to admit. But realizing that these women were lusting after *her man*, well, it had hit her in the gut, made her ready to fight, and her wing-locks, in response to all that aggression, were about a breath away from a full-on mount.

Goddammit.

But before she could say anything, the women were on her, both pairs of hands touching her shoulders and her head.

Her first response was to jerk away from them, but they just followed. She felt their warm comforting stream of energy and knew they were doing her some good, but she hated being touched like that. Her wing-locks responded instantly and began to settle down. The streaming fluids just stopped.

But she hated all this nearness, this closeness. She couldn't bear it.

She tried to pull away but found she couldn't, not even a little. A war began to rage within her mind, a battle between *This feels so good I could stay here forever* and *I'll kill them both for touching me.*

But the women didn't let up. The feels-so-good sensation kept flowing and her body grew quiet. Unfortunately, the more calm she felt the angrier she got, two sensations that couldn't live within the same body at the same time. She ground her teeth together and small grunts came out of her mouth. They needed to back off.

Her wing-locks had completely settled down and even the muscles of her back that had swelled, readying for the release, were thinned out and normal. But something in her mind began to spin in ever-widening circles. Wider and wider. Suddenly the wood floor of the cabin rushed up fast.

Warrior's Lament, fragment
I bloodied the dirt, blood on my heel
My sword cared not the cost
And though I won, thus was I lost

—*Collected Poems*, Beatrice of Fourth

CHAPTER 8

Thorne was breathing hard. "Good workout." He clapped Arthur again on the back of his neck and shook him for good measure. Arthur smiled. He wiped his forehead with the back of his wrist then shook off the sweat.

They were both dripping.

Glancing at the Militia Warriors, Thorne addressed the leader. "You've got good men, here, Ettgers. Why don't you take your troops and work what you've seen here. In my experience, this is the best time to get in some good drilling."

"Yes, Warrior Thorne." He turned to his troops, which included at least three women, and gave a short brisk order to head down into one of the local pastures. Almost as one, the unit turned and moved at a quick jog down the shallow grade toward the lower farms.

Thorne put his hand on Arthur's shoulder. "Your instincts are good, your speed better. Speed is your biggest advantage. Only Warrior Kerrick might be faster. He could teach you what I'm not sure I can.

"What I can tell you, though, is that you need training, persistent, day-to-day training, by one of us. I don't care which one. Jean-Pierre might be the best choice because you're lean in the way he's lean and you move like him."

Arthur glared at him and set his jaw. "I'm not leaving the colony. With all due respect, Warrior Thorne, you need to get used to that right now. And the hell if I'm joining the Warriors of the Blood."

Thorne smiled. He couldn't help himself. He knew that look well. He'd seen it on eight warrior faces for the past several hundred years. Basic belligerence seemed to be a defining trait for this level of skill and power.

Thoughts of the warriors, however, and the post he'd abandoned, dropped a stone in his heart. Shit, he had to get back. What the hell was he doing here anyway?

He'd been able to talk for an hour to Diallo, who'd invited both Thorne and Marguerite up to his house for lunch.

Thorne had been making his way back to the cabin when Arthur had waylaid him and asked for a training session. He had strong instincts about the boy, and something more, a hint that the future lay with this young man, even though he couldn't imagine how yet. So he'd accepted.

Ettgers had joined in with his group.

It had been a good session.

Besides, he knew Marguerite had needed some time to think, to work things out in her head. He had no doubt that his woman was anxious to leave, despite the great lovemaking. She had itchy feet, and that wasn't going to change anytime soon.

He looked up and down the lane, always on the alert, always hunting for death vamp sign, or maybe just for some clue as to how to get himself out of this mess.

"Now you're pissed at me," Arthur said.

Thorne looked back at him. "I don't know what you're seeing, but this isn't pissed. If I was pissed, you'd be facedown on the ground with my foot on your neck."

But Arthur smiled that half smile. "Good to know. Let's hope I stay on your sweet side."

"Just so ya know, not sure I have one."

But Arthur laughed. It was a good sound.

Jesus H. Christ. The kid had killed five death vampires last night. No question he was Warrior of the Blood material, but Thorne had just enough to compassion to know that he didn't want that for Arthur. He wanted Arthur to stay all bundled up in this secret society, to stay safe and as innocent as he could for as long as he could. But how innocent was a young man who had just gone into battle and come out with a whole lot of blood on his hands?

"So why are you here?" Thorne asked. "Why aren't you back on Second figuring out an occupation, going to university, dating, all the usual? You must have friends you left behind?"

The minute the last question left his mouth, Thorne regretted opening the lid to this goddamn box. Arthur shifted his gaze away from him and narrowed his eyes. Damn if he didn't look just like Jean-Pierre right now, and with a familiar haunted expression that told Thorne the war had already become personal to Arthur.

Which of course meant that someone he loved had died. Wasn't that always the way?

Arthur remained silent but Thorne sure as hell wasn't going to press him for more information. He wasn't exactly built for exchanging confidences and shit.

Then Arthur seemed to come to a decision and shifted his gaze back to Thorne. "You've been straight with me and you haven't tried to order me around. So here it is. I was engaged to be married and before you tell me I was too young to know what I wanted, you'd be wasting your time. I was in love with her, we were engaged, then she died in the fire-bomb attack at White Lake during the Ambassador's Reception."

Oh, shit.

Thorne got that sinking feeling in his gut again, the one that weakened his leg muscles, that felt like the earth was pulling him down, that gravity had suddenly tripled in strength.

Maybe there'd been more than one reason he'd dropped

down to Mortal Earth in pursuit of Marguerite. The attack at the Ambassador's Reception a few months ago had been aimed at one of the warriors' women, Havily Morgan. Her warrior, Marcus, had almost been killed. Marcus had done what he could to put distance between himself and the bomb, taking the attack away from a lot of innocent people, but he'd gotten shredded and almost died.

It had been a horrible night, not least because the fire-bomb had taken eleven civilian lives. He had never known who the victims were. Hell, he hadn't wanted to know. Battling at the dimensional Borderlands every night had been its own form of torture. Having close contact with grieving families—well, he couldn't keep doing his job if he did that.

Now he stood looking into the haunted gray-blue-green eyes of a young man who had once been committed to love, to a woman, to life. There was no more innocence for Arthur.

Thorne turned away from him. He couldn't keep feeling the depth of his goddamn despair, that the war just kept rolling on, stripping people of hope and of a future.

That big thing began to move within him once more, maybe a need for change, maybe a great unwillingness for things to continue as they'd been. Anger boiled as well, but then that was nothing new. All the warriors felt it, a persistent fury that never stopped, rage against death vampires and against Greaves and his fucking minions, against a war without end.

But this whole encounter reminded him that he needed to get back to Second Earth, especially with Greaves turning up the heat with his military spectacle review.

On the other hand, once he got back, what the hell was he supposed to do?

He was used to command.

He liked command. He'd never questioned his job.

But he sure as hell had questioned the war.

He would do things so differently.

He could only imagine Endelle's fury that he'd jumped ship. Talk about a tempest. He'd hate to be Alison right now. Alison served as her executive assistant and now Thorne had one more thing to feel guilty about: that he'd brought trouble down on Alison's head.

Whatever.

But even as a sharp twinge deep within his mind told him that Endelle was trying yet again to bust through the shield he'd put around their shared mind-link, he knew that change wasn't possible with her, not if things continued as they'd always been. Endelle had a lot of excellent qualities, and yes, he admired and respected her, but for a long time now he'd had a very different take on the war and what ought to be done about Greaves.

Thorne glanced down at the sword in his hand. He'd been using a practice sword, not one identified to him. The identified swords were capricious and would always result in death if grabbed by the grip by someone other than the owner. But sometimes an accidental touch could result in death as well.

His practice sword, which belonged to Arthur, had a nice weight, evenly balanced.

"Well, fuck," he stated. In a quick flick of his wrist, he sent the sword skyrocketing and spinning. He hadn't done this in decades, maybe not in centuries. It was a kid's trick and something you never did with a sword, any sword. He blurred in the direction it would come down; as it reached the apex then began to fall back to earth, he waited, worked out the trajectory to within a hair's breadth, then caught it by the grip.

"Some move," Arthur said.

Thorne glanced at him. "Don't ever do that." But he laughed. Arthur had reached the age of magnificence, the certain belief he always knew best. He would do whatever the hell he wanted and there wasn't a damn thing to be done. Arthur was a teenager.

"Warrior Thorne." A woman's voice called to him from the direction of the cabin he'd shared with Marguerite the night before. He turned and saw a short redhead wave him forward. "Can you come here for a minute? Something's happened to Marguerite and we're not sure what to do."

"Of course."

He tossed the sword to Arthur without thinking. It was a natural reaction. He would have done the same to any of the warriors, but Arthur wasn't one of the warriors.

But Arthur simply shifted sideways and caught the sword by the grip as though he'd been doing it all his life. Yep, an inch away from being all grown up.

Thorne moved in a blur toward the house and onto the porch. Once inside, he found Marguerite unconscious, on the floor. A very tall woman with shoulder-length black hair and a web tattoo on her neck had her hand on Marguerite's arm, but his woman's body twitched and spasmed. She was naked from the waist up.

He thought he understood the problem, or at least one of them.

"Don't touch her," he barked, his gravel voice acting like fire to two pairs of hands. The women jerked back, rose to their feet, and moved to stand together by the window.

"What happened here?"

The tall woman said, "She was really upset about something that happened earlier and couldn't seem to breathe. We're both Seers, Jane and I, and all the Seers in the colony take care of one another as a community. We sent her what we thought was hands-on healing assistance and it did seem to calm her. Sort of. I think her wings were ready to mount, which might have been a problem in this small space. But in the end she passed out. We thought we could bring her around but nothing we've done has helped."

He pulled her onto his lap. Her back was wet, which meant the apertures of her wing-locks had been weeping, readying for a mount. Why the hell had she been about to release her wings?

She was out, completely unconscious, a limp doll in his arms. "Did she see something in the future streams?"

"No, we don't think so. The situation didn't have the flavor of a vision." She drew a deep breath. "We honestly don't know what happened except that she seemed to be very intent . . . on you."

Okay, he didn't quite know what to make of that, but he asked, "Did you have your hands on her the entire time?"

She nodded.

He looked back at Marguerite, sliding his fingers through her hair. Her forehead was damp. He knew what her life had been. "She doesn't like to be touched."

"What?"

He looked up at the woman, his lips tight. "Marguerite doesn't like to be touched."

"Oh . . . I see." The tattoo lady frowned. The women looked at each other as though trying to make sense of this or maybe communicating telepathically.

"We'll leave you, Warrior Thorne, unless there's something more we can do."

"No. And . . . and thank you for preventing the wingmount but I'll take it from here."

They left, silent, concerned.

When he was alone with her, he rocked her gently, his gaze still on her face. Her complexion was very pale, almost as white as her hair.

How could they understand? He wasn't even certain he could make sense of all that she had suffered. That she'd been physically beaten in the name of religion was a big part of the problem. How does the mind reconcile love and that kind of violence?

After about a minute, as he stroked her cheek with his finger and just held and rocked her, she began to stir.

She sat up still in his arms, a hand planted on his damp chest. Sword instruction was sweaty work.

"Did you have another vision?"

She shook her head. "No." She tugged at the few fine hairs between his pecs. "You aren't wearing a shirt."

"I was showing Arthur a few things. So you didn't have a vision?"

She shook her head. "No, I . . . shit, I must have fainted."

He chuckled, relieved. "Okay, why did you faint? What the hell happened in here and who were they?"

"A pair of Seers who live here in the colony. They touched

me, put their hands on me." She pushed away from him and struggled to her feet. He joined her and because she was barefoot, he towered over her.

She stared up at him and scowled. "I have to get out of here, Thorne. Now. This is the wrong place for me." She rubbed her arms like she was cold.

The movement jiggled her chest, which caused his gaze to fall straight to her breasts. And like any normal male, he lost sight of the subject at hand. His woman had beautiful breasts, full, weighted at the bottom, with large areolas. The nipples were peaked in the cool air. Before he could prevent it, a soft growl rumbled in his throat.

She rolled her eyes and folded her robe on, covering up all that beauty that suddenly had his cock doing gymnastics.

"I'm leaving," she said. "I'm going back to the Holiday Inn." She lifted her right arm, a sure signal she intended to dematerialize.

But before a nanosecond had passed, he blurred to her and grabbed both arms. "Not without me, babe."

"Don't you dare 'babe' me." But her shoulders eased down and she lowered her arm.

"Please don't leave, Marguerite. I'm begging you for at least that much. I know this situation sucks, but you feel it, too, don't you, that we need to be here? Tell me that you feel it. That somehow fate has brought us here, together, to a place that has been hidden for almost three thousand years."

She glanced up at him. She opened her mouth then closed it as though there was something she needed to say to him. Something was going on. "Spill it," he said.

She met his gaze straight-on but her hands were planted on her hips. "All right, I'll stay. I have to stay because of the visions, but I will have my own life." Her cheeks worked. "I'm going out with the girls tonight. We're meeting at a club for drinks."

He frowned. Seemed harmless enough but she still looked so damn belligerent, not a good sign. "Okay," he said, knowing full well there was a second shoe in her other hand.

"Apparently, there's entertainment." The slight lift of her chin also did not bode well.

"What kind of entertainment?"

The shoe fell. "Dancers."

He lifted his brows. "*Male* dancers?"

She nodded. She also stared at him, hard, one big challenge in those large brown eyes of hers. His wing-locks swelled and he felt sudden moisture on his back. His breathing hitched up, high in his chest. He stepped toward her, his feet moving before he'd made the mental command.

"Cherry tobacco," she whispered. "What are you doing?"

He took her arms and held her. He looked down into her face. His woman was going to a place where she would be staring at other men's naked bodies, lusting after them.

He wanted to tell her not to go, but his mind had started flashing again with red strobes.

She blinked. Her eyes dilated. Fear, maybe? Desire? He wasn't sure he cared which it was, but as his nostrils flared, he caught her rose scent and it thickened in the air.

Thorne? she sent.

He didn't respond. He wasn't certain he could. He had seen a small yard out back, a stretch of rough lawn, a picnic table. At this point, he didn't have much of a choice. This time, his wings were on the edge of mounting and just like Marguerite, if he mounted them inside the cabin he'd do some serious damage.

With his hands on hers, he folded her to the backyard.

She protested, but he still didn't care.

He glanced around. It was a private yard except for Diallo's large house on the massive outcropping of rock. Some of his windows faced this direction. Maybe they'd be seen. Maybe not.

Again, he didn't care.

The rational part of his mind seemed to be slipping away in quick stages.

He dragged her to the picnic table and flipped her onto her stomach so that she hung off the ground, her bare feet just touching the ground.

"You can't do this," she cried.

But he smelled a rush of rose so strong that he threw a quick dome of mist over the yard and released a sudden cry because his wings flew through his wing-locks. Releasing wings was always pleasurable, an intense rush, a release of endorphins, and very sexual. He roared, his chest aimed at the sky. He beat his wings in strong thrusts as he held on to the table. He kept her pinned with the strength of his thighs.

He folded off his kilt.

"Your wings," she whispered, her voice low and rough. "So beautiful."

He didn't say anything. He just rubbed his erection down the slick line of her leather-covered ass.

"Get my pants off."

He rubbed her back. His wings wafted and because they were so big, a breeze flowed.

"Oh, your scent. It's grabbing me low. Thorne." She sounded in agony. Good. About damn time.

She was pressed against the picnic table. He put his hand on her ass and folded off her pants. He stroked her ass, running a finger deep, then he pushed her legs apart. Her hips were already rocking into the table.

"Fuck me," she whispered. "Oh, God, just fuck me."

He put his hand on her shoulder and folded off her robe. Her back was a mess. Her wing-locks were swollen and weeping. She wasn't far away from a mount herself, but he knew of one sure way to keep the wings from releasing.

He leaned over and began to suck. He started at the upper left wing-lock and gorged on the moisture that wept from the aperture. The taste of roses flowed down his throat and kept him stiff.

She cried out over and over beneath his mouth. She moved her hips wildly, trying to get a connection that would give her some relief. But he was pissed that she would even think about going to a male strip club and he knew exactly how to punish her. He kept her orgasm just off shore. In the meantime, his hips rocked and he teased her with his cock sliding along the insides of her legs.

"Please, Thorne. Please."

Forget it, sweetheart. Sounds like you'll be getting your kicks tonight. I don't think you deserve my cock. What do you think?

She tasted so good. He sucked harder on the next wing-lock. Her back arched. She tried to slide her hand under her hip, to give herself some relief, but like hell he would allow that. He grabbed her wrist and held her tight.

Please, Thorne, I'm begging you.

He released her suddenly and backed away, his wings shimmying with the tension in his body. He held his cock in his hand and stroked himself, moving to the side to let her see.

She rose up, her eyes widening, her gaze fixed low.

"If you want this, you're going to have to work for it."

He forgot how fast she was, though. She had speed like a warrior and before he knew what she was doing, she had slid on the grass on her knees right at his feet. He meant to prevent her from doing anything, but she took him in her mouth and began to suck.

Okay, he was too far gone with need, desire, and a kind of primordial possessive rage. He caught the nape of her neck and helped her suck him.

She knew what she was doing and took him deep, as deep as she could.

Thorne, give it to me. Give me all you've got.

He was so close to letting go, but he held back. He moved away from her, holding his cock, thumbing the tip.

She sat on her knees, staring at his groin, panting. Her nipples were hard buds.

Shit. For a moment, he'd intended to come in her mouth and leave her.

He put out his hand, palm-down. She nodded.

He leaned down and picked her up, a movement that caused his wings to sweep all the way to the ground and for a moment cover her in a tent of feathers.

But this had to be finished between them and because he was who he was, he couldn't leave in her agony. He carried her back to the picnic table but settled her on her back this time.

I want your blood, he sent.

She said nothing, just arched her neck, and the vein rose without a single swipe of his tongue against her skin. He pushed her legs apart, positioned himself, and drove in. At the same moment, he turned his head, closed in on her throat, and bit deep.

Her body jerked, but a heavy waft of rose flooded his face as he began to suck. He gripped her arms, pinning her, his hips working her low, his mouth sucking hard.

She held still for him, but he could feel the tightness in her well and she'd begun to whimper softly. The lowest part of her began matching his thrusts, tilting into him and creating the familiar rhythm. She was a fist now pulling on him.

He didn't ask permission this time. He just pressed against her mind, then pushed hard.

She cried out, but he saw her pleasure begin to streak, and as she pulled on him, he could feel the pulses and the ecstasy that had her screaming.

Her blood had created a furnace in his body.

He was ready. *Oh, God.*

Yes, Thorne, give me all you've got.

His balls tightened and even if he'd wanted to hold back, he couldn't have. He let out a roar as he came, pleasure riding up, straight up as his cock released into her. She kept up just the right rhythm, as though savoring him, just as she always had.

His wings wafted slowly through the air, back and forth, as his body settled down.

You're all man, came from her mind, a subdued tone.

Finally he withdrew from her and at the same time retracted his wings.

He didn't say a word as he headed to the back door.

He couldn't exactly put a name to what he felt as he reached the doorway to the bathroom and he wasn't sure he'd actually enjoyed the orgasm.

He put a hand to his chest and closed his eyes—then it hit

him. Dammit, he was hurt . . . to the quick. Did she care so little for him that despite her understanding of the *breh-hedden* she would even think about going to that goddamn club?

Marguerite was cold as hell as she lifted off the table. She remained standing for about two seconds then fell to the grass, completely naked. She stretched out. She was wet between her legs and her eyes burned. Some of her frustration had eased, but her guilt had about tripled.

What was she doing? This was a good man and she was treating him as though he was a boyfriend she'd grown tired of. But she wasn't tired of Thorne, not even a little. She just needed . . . her freedom and some sense that she had the smallest control over her life.

Please God let him understand that much. Please. Please.

She rubbed her fingers over her lips. Her throat felt inexplicably tight. She folded the afghan from the foot of the bed onto her body. The air was cold in the mountains in March.

She felt Thorne's presence before she heard him. She didn't even have time to move before he lifted her into his arms, afghan and all.

He looked upset, but much less hostile, just really . . . sad. She stroked his face. "I'm sorry I can't be what you need right now."

"Don't worry about it." She could hear the shower running, and since the cabin was so small, the next minute he was pushing the afghan off her and carrying her beneath the spray. This time, he lathered up and washed her body.

He was so somber.

"I'm sorry," she said again, her hand on his wet hair.

He put his finger beneath her chin. He leaned down and kissed her, a deep probing kiss. "I love you. And I'm sorry that I got all caveman on you. But the thought of you looking at other men—"

She leaned up and kissed him hard. He locked his arms around her and deepened the kiss, his thick tongue searching every crevice.

Oh, God, what was she doing?

She pulled back. "Thorne, please try to understand. I'm holding on to this dream, the one I've had for the last century, of doing whatever I wanted to do, of having real freedom. And I'm so afraid that the longer I'm with you, the more I'm getting trapped in a different kind of prison. You're a Warrior of the Blood. I know what you do every night. You battle death vampires. I don't want to be hanging around your house, waiting for you to come home, wondering if you will make it through the night."

"I know." His rough voice filled the tight space, water flowing down her back. He kissed her again. "Just forget it, all of it. You need to go out tonight. I'm not going to stop you." Then a smile touched his lips. "But I may tag along."

She stroked his cheek. "Thank you for understanding or at least trying to."

"I don't like it. Any of it. I want you to have your freedom but this fucking *breh-hedden* . . ."

"I know."

The water stopped. Thorne must have mentally shut it off again.

"Okay, sweetheart, let's dry off, get dressed. Diallo invited us to lunch. He's also given us one of the guest rooms in his house while we're here. He thought it would be safer than the cabin."

Lunch. Her stomach turned over a couple of times. She wasn't exactly hungry, but then it was hard to have much of an appetite when she was so damn stuck. "Okay," she said.

But as Marguerite dried off and brought the rest of her shoplifted clothes from her hotel room to the cabin, she couldn't ignore the tightening of her chest. The future was rushing at her in hurricane-like blasts now. And the harder she fought for her freedom, the farther away it seemed to move.

How do you build a new world
Out of one that is broken?
Slowly and with great care.

—*Collected Proverbs,* Beatrice of Fourth

CHAPTER 9

Thorne saw the clever nature of Diallo's home, the easy flow of room to room. He could see the colony's council in a social setting, the tempers dialed down with food and drink, critical jurisdictional and administrative concepts discussed with a smile instead of over a blaring microphone or with a sword in hand.

The house was built in a U shape with a large central courtyard. The front of the house faced west, while the east backed up to the forest. The principal front rooms had a meandering effect, lots of sofas and big low chairs, the palette in soft greens and beige, some in leather, some in soft-looking fabrics.

He got it. He understood the entire purpose.

"People would settle down in here," Marguerite said.

He wasn't surprised that she saw it, too. Maybe it was her nature or that she'd been in such a cold, harsh environment for so long, but she felt the intention of the layout as sharply as he did. "Yeah, they would."

Thorne had a house in Sedona that he used just for himself, but as he looked through the living room and the enormous glass windows with a view that covered the entire length of the valley, he felt the need for a new home.

No, not a home, something more. Something with purpose, something Endelle's palace should have been but wasn't: a gathering place.

Endelle had built a series of vast domed rotundas, all connected, one to the next, the entire edifice built out from the side of the McDowell Mountains on the west-facing slopes. But the place was only used for the occasional ascension ceremony or formal dinner. It wasn't even furnished except for a few dining tables and chairs.

Endelle had never quite grasped the need for state functions, the reception of dignitaries, the bringing together of ambassadors from around her allied Territories, the need for public address, diplomacy, and presence. She was a woman from some of the first tribes that had roamed Mortal Earth and in a very basic sense she should have been a warrior, not an administrator.

He withheld a heavy sigh. She should have ascended millennia ago because the level of her power was tremendous, but the Upper Dimensions had kept her on Second since there had been no one of an equivalent power to balance Greaves. Second Earth would have long since fallen without her darkening work and the sure threat that if Greaves ever once personally used his preternatural power to strike, she'd be able to take him on.

So COPASS had been formed by a majority vote of all the Territories during their bi-century worldwide congress, a committee designed to oversee the process of ascension to Second Earth and to define the rules of engagement for both factions. The original intention had been to keep powerful ascenders safe during the ascension process—Greaves had been systematically killing them off before they could ascend.

Unfortunately, from the moment COPASS had been formed, the Commander's subtler skills of manipulation had been able to take full flight and he'd been steadily turning members of the committee. In turn COPASS had step by step begun moving all the rules and regulations in his favor.

Endelle had ended up hamstrung by a specific COPASS law, which stated that no person was allowed to cross the threshold of a Seers Fortress without the express permission of the High Administrator of that fortress. So guess who had operated the Superstition Fortress? Owen Stannett.

And between Endelle and Greaves, Stannett feared Greaves a thousand times more. Endelle might have been ineffective, but she was essentially law abiding. She wouldn't act against Stannett, which meant he'd shut her out from the information his Seers could provide her about the future streams for the past hundred years.

Her administration therefore had been flying blind.

And failing.

While Greaves, who did whatever the hell he liked, was succeeding.

So as Thorne glanced around, he saw tremendous potential in a house like this.

Diallo called from the hallway, "If you'll come with me, we'll be dining in the garden." He smiled as his gaze landed on Marguerite. "The temperature is controlled."

Thorne's mind began running in all sorts of new directions. He didn't know if it was because of Diallo's home, or the nature of the colony, or what, but his heart had begun to beat in a hopeful way for the future of his world, maybe for the first time in a very long time.

Marguerite felt Thorne's hand at her back, and it was a perfect pressure, but her skin crawled. She felt something emanating from him, some new power or something, and it was bugging the shit out of her because it spoke of the future and of purpose.

She had to get out of here. This colony kept spinning sticky spidery filaments all over her, tying her up, trapping her.

She sat down to a lovely bowl of melon pieces, cantaloupe

and honeydew, a few strawberries thrown in. Each piece she swallowed stuck in her throat. Chicken as a second course would be arriving soon. The thought of it didn't help. She just wasn't very hungry.

Diallo responded to Thorne's questions, which he'd been firing off in rapid succession from the moment they'd entered the garden.

She glanced around. The garden was beautiful. Horticulture defined Second Earth and Diallo had brought some mad skills to the art form, spreading them around in a super-sized courtyard that had to be at least thirty yards long. The arrangement of beds was lush, something possible since, yep, the air temp was controlled as well as the humidity. As she glanced up, she could see that the entire area was covered with a special shimmering shield.

The table had been set up in a very large open space in the center of the garden, an area covered in pavers. Beyond the dining area, she could hear the quiet sound of a gentle waterfall. A gazillion plants of every size, shape, and origin created a setting as verdant as any tropical environment, just without the bugs and excessive heat.

Using her linen napkin, she dabbed at her lips and eased back in her chair. Both men stopped talking and looked at her.

She glanced at them.

"We've been ignoring you," Diallo said.

She knew both he and Thorne were being polite, and she could tell Thorne wanted to talk to this extraordinary man. "Would you mind if I retired to our room? I'd like to rest for a while."

She rose as she spoke, as did both the men. Her gaze fell on Thorne.

You okay? he sent.

She nodded. "I'm fine, really. I need some alone time and I promise I'm not taking off."

At that he narrowed his gaze at her. *I've heard that before.*

But you knew the truth then. You knew I was leaving. What do you think right now?

At that his shoulders relaxed. He could read her like nobody's business. He nodded. Aloud, he said, "Yes, get some rest."

She thanked Diallo for the lunch, even though all she'd had was a few bites of melon that still sat uneasily in her craw. She just wasn't herself.

As she crossed the courtyard to the south-facing rooms, she realized that for the past few days, she'd been feeling a little off. But then she'd been doing so many outrageous things. She wasn't used to so much freedom and of course then there were the crashing visions and more Thorne than she'd ever had. Sort of like going to the fairgrounds, gorging on junk food, then throwing up after a trip on the roller coaster. Yeah, that about described the last few days for her, except Thorne wasn't exactly junk food. More like filet mignon. Lots and lots of filet mignon.

It occurred to her that if she continued on with him like this, they ought to start thinking seriously about birth control. Although the fact that she'd been with him for decades in the Convent and had never gotten pregnant had pretty much convinced her that she was barren or Thorne was shooting blanks.

She had an uneasy feeling that she needed to be more responsible just in case her ascended vampire body decided to heal up the parts that didn't work and she ended up with child. Which would really suck. She was so not the maternal type.

A chill went through her. And dammit, she'd shagged that asshole, José, completely without protection.

Okay, must be more responsible.

The room assigned to them on the southern-facing side of the house was strangely white and romantic looking, almost bridal except that the fabrics were cotton and not all lace and satin.

The bed was king-sized with tall mahogany posts and a layering of mosquito netting. She moved to the oversized plate-glass window. She could see the valley below. She could see the Militia Warriors practicing their sword fighting.

There were vegetable gardens and fruit orchards everywhere, each with that shimmering shield overhead, just like Diallo's courtyard garden. Food would never be a problem in the colony.

Suddenly she was just tired.

Tired of everything: of longing to leave but feeling compelled to stay, of craving Thorne yet hating the thought of him with other women, of knowing that this colony was officially up shit creek because of Stannett, but above all tired of the feeling that she couldn't bear it if she never saw Thorne again.

She turned away from the window and crossed to the bed. She pushed back the top, fresh-smelling comforter. She sniffed it and realized that it had the smell of the outdoors. The Convent gowns and bedding had the same wonderful smell because everything was hung outside to be sweetened by the air and the wind.

She released a deep sigh, crawled beneath the covers, and when her head hit the pillow she drifted into sleep faster than she had thought possible.

Greaves sat behind his desk in his Geneva penthouse. He had his elbows on the arms of his chairs and his hands joined just at the fingertips, tapping slightly. He hadn't brought his claw forward, not for these two men. His left hand could transform into a claw at his command, a little DNA experiment that had proven both successful and quite useful through the decades. He often used it for intimidation, but he had a strong feeling a show of power wasn't what was needed at all in this situation.

Owen Stannett stood with his proverbial hat in hand, but he'd come with phenomenal information in the form of a hidden colony, perhaps even several hidden colonies, on Mortal Earth that contained refugee Seers. He'd also come with a list of demands.

Fascinating.

Greaves had asked Casimir to attend the meeting for several reasons. The Fourth ascender lounged in his usual position on the black leather couch to Greaves's left, his legs spread wide. He wore his habitual tight leather pants with everything on display. Caz knew Stannett quite well and Stannett knew everything Caz displayed quite well because Stannett had been a slave to Casimir for a couple of hundred years a few centuries back.

Greaves almost winced. All that mass would have *hurt*.

The whole situation was so very interesting to Greaves. What twist of fate had brought the men together again in this very room, in Greaves's Geneva penthouse, his current place of administration? He owned the entire building and in the basement was his Round Table, very Camelot-esque— in a more modern way, of course.

But as he met Stannett's gaze, he saw nothing of the submissive in this man. Nor was he dominant, an intriguing circumstance all on its own. It made him a conundrum in terms of handling. If he went too hard at Stannett, the man would simply vanish. Not hard enough and he wouldn't cave.

He glanced at Caz, a mere sliding of his gaze then back, a very subtle signal.

Caz folded instantly to a position right behind Stannett and slid his arm over Stannett's chest, a very ownership-based move.

A wave of hatred flowed over Stannett's face. So Stannett hadn't exactly enjoyed servicing Casimir. But then from everything he'd understood, Caz had a strong sadistic tendency, much stronger than even Greaves's proclivities.

"Why don't you just tell the Commander what you want, Stanny? Save us from wasting the night away." Caz strengthened his hold on Stannett, tightening the arm around his chest.

Stannett's gaze hardened. He met Greaves's once more. "I'm not playing these games." For good measure, he sent a little shock wave flowing through his body that popped Caz right off him.

Casimir looked both surprised and excited. He rounded Stannett to stare at him. He smiled. "That actually hurt. You've learned a few tricks."

But Stannett was playing this smart. He ignored the sexy

monkey and, keeping his gaze aimed at Greaves, laid his cards on the table. "I have a number of Third Earth powers, the most significant being my Seer abilities. I can hinder activity in the future streams. Right now, even Marguerite, the second of the obsidian flame triad, cannot follow my path, cannot know what I do."

"This is power, indeed. Now tell me why you didn't take your offer to Endelle?"

"She will be angry about the children I spawned in the fortress. She will be . . . *unforgiving.*"

At that, Greaves smiled. In this one thing, he could admire Stannett: that he'd attempted in recent years to create a super-race of Seers out at the Superstition Fortress. "I suppose she wouldn't appreciate the long-range vision of your plan."

Stannett smoothed the wave alongside his head and his lips actually smirked. "No, she would not."

For half a second Greaves approved. He understood the full scope of Stannett's quandary. "So, what you're asking in exchange for your services, and once the war has been decided, is a palace, a fortune, and a permanent waiver from all government agencies. In addition, you want the Seer, Marguerite, sequestered in your fortress."

"Yes."

"And what of me?" Greaves asked. "Will I be allowed to visit?"

Stannett bowed. "Of course . . . *master.*" Just the right emphasis on that last word.

And there it was, the subservience he sought. "And will you be willing to partake of dying blood and the accompanying antidote? I require this of all my servants."

"No." Stannett's chin dipped. "I cannot agree to this since there is some evidence that dying blood by its nature affects a Seer's ability in the future streams."

The response was reasonable. Still, Greaves didn't like that he wouldn't have some external command of the man once the agreement was struck.

He tapped his fingers together once more. "I will agree to your requests on one condition."

"Anything, master."

His take on Stannett was that the man would do whatever he needed to survive, including betray Greaves. However, if Stannett could actually fulfill his requirement within the future streams, then he would have earned Greaves's support.

He waved Casimir back to his couch. Caz folded in the blink of an eye.

To Stannett, he said, "I'd like to test your abilities. We have a little situation that needs tending to. Thorne's sister, Grace, appears to have some sort of emerging power of an inexplicable nature. Although I was unable to witness her manifestation in Moscow Two, Caz tells me that she somehow appeared beside General Leto before Casimir could initiate the prearranged hand-blast that would render him unconscious.

"I have recently learned the Leto has engaged in subversive activities against me, and he must be eliminated. Because Grace was instrumental in saving him, I want her taken care of as well. You will work with Casimir to get the job done. Use your control of the future streams to organize your strategy. And I want this accomplished before the military review."

Though Stannett's expression hardened, and he still refused to glance at Caz, he bowed once more. "Yes, master."

Greaves repressed a smile. He had several pleasures in his position and in his life, but one of the most satisfying was the pairing of one unhappy force with one dominating force to get a job done. The resulting friction always satisfied some dark place in Greaves's soul.

But as he glanced from one to the other, he finally did allow himself to smile—though not in amusement. Stannett had Third Earth abilities and Casimir was a Fourth ascender. Together they had as much power as Greaves. If they were smart and got this job done, well, his future was made.

Especially since what Grace had accomplished made it a strong possibility that she was the third member of the obsidian flame triad. Of all the tasks before him, making certain that these members did not combine their power was one of his most pressing concerns.

"You have to get him out of here," Sister Quena cried, her sharp cheekbones flaming. "He is a traitor and a man. Everything about his presence here is offensive in the extreme."

Grace sat on her stool beside her bed and pressed a cool, damp cloth against Leto's forehead. Hours had passed since she'd brought the warrior from Moscow Two but instead of improving, his pallor now matched the cloth, a sort of grayish white. Sweat poured from him and he shook from head to toe. She didn't know what to do. His addiction to dying blood was tearing his body apart and it shouldn't be.

She'd gone to the Convent's library and researched this part of a death vampire's suffering—how long he could survive without dying blood and what sort of symptoms would accompany the deprivation. Essentially, Leto's withdrawal wasn't running the usual course.

Unfortunately, she suspected that the aberrations he presented had something to do with the terrible call of the *breh-hedden* on his body.

Grace could no longer pretend she wasn't Warrior Leto's *breh,* or that he wasn't hers, as strange as that seemed. But with his scent thick in her nostrils, her sinuses, her brain, all the poetry she'd written throughout the years, the erotic, forbidden verses, kept rushing back at her until she ached so fiercely she wanted to scream.

At the same time, she was so worried for this warrior that her heart kept pounding in her ears. She just didn't know what to do. But her instinct, above all, was to protect him while he was in such a vulnerable state.

"Are you listening to me?" Sister Quena shouted. "I want him removed. I shall contact Madame Endelle myself to let her know that her faithless one has somehow tried to seek asylum in my convent."

"I'll leave," Leto said, but the words came out little more than a whisper. He tried to rise but he'd grown as weak as a kitten and simply fell back against the hard mattress.

After another breath, he tried again.

Grace put a hand on his shoulder holding him down. "Rest, Leto. I will see to this."

"James," he whispered.

"What?" She leaned closer.

"Find James."

"Who is James?"

But his eyes closed and his breathing grew to a light pant. She understood then that he was near death.

"Devotiate, I will call the regulators if you do not step out of this cell. I will call Madame Endelle and she will take him."

But the thought that Sister Quena, High Administrator of the Convent, would jeopardize her warrior, forced Grace to leave his side, to rise from her stool, and to turn to face the one Marguerite had always called "sister-bitch."

Grace felt the earth below her rumble, that same power she had felt before. It drove upward, flowing into her feet, up and up, until she tingled with power.

She opened her arms wide and let some of that energy flow toward Sister Quena. She would not think of hurting her, or even disrupting the authority she had over Grace, but she could not allow Leto to leave her cell.

When she spoke, her voice, much to her surprise, split-resonance. *"You will leave us and you will forget that you've seen Warrior Leto here this day. You will forbid anyone to approach this cell."*

Sister Quena blinked three times and finally bowed. "As you wish, devotiate." The tall woman, aged in appearance despite her immortal vampire nature, turned and left to walk very slowly down the hall.

Grace took a breath and willed the energy to leave her, which it did, draining down her body and through her feet, perhaps back to the earth. She glanced down at the floor. What was this new power that had come to her, which seemed so separate from her yet was hers apparently to call at will?

The same power had allowed her to save Leto.

Small gasps behind her caused her to whirl and once more assume her post. When she sat down, she once more dabbed the cloth over Leto's forehead. He reached for her arm and his eyes opened. "Thank . . . you," he murmured.

But it was the connection of his hand on her wrist that sent her mind whirling with understanding. She had what he needed. She rose up and leaned over him, shifting sideways to sling her arm around his head and over his left shoulder.

She positioned her wrist over his mouth. "Drink," she said. "Take what you need."

He tried to open his mouth but couldn't.

Grace didn't understand where all her boldness was coming from, but using her other hand, she slipped her finger and thumb into his mouth and stroked his gums until his fangs emerged. Of course such intimate contact caused her to press her legs together. Even touching him brought all that desire rushing to the fore.

Leto groaned and his scent suddenly flooded the room, that beautiful forest smell. With a sudden jolt of unexpected energy, he jerked forward and struck.

Grace cried out, her neck and back arching in surprise and then in the utter sexual pleasure that swept over her. Desire flooded her in deep, exhilarating waves. Leto held her wrist to his mouth with both hands as he suckled. He looked up into her eyes.

She put her free hand on his hair and let her fingers glide through the thick black mass.

His color began to return, deepening to a beautiful rich olive tone, so beautiful against the crystal-clear blue of his eyes. She wanted him to live, he had to live. She felt this deep in her soul, that he was necessary to the future of Second Earth, and to her, and to the children she would one day bear for him.

She felt and saw all this as she looked into his eyes. But was any of it real or just her imaginative sensibilities? What she did know was that she craved him, in the way she knew that other women, associated with the Warriors of the Blood, grew to crave their men.

Leto stared into pale green-gold eyes and so much innocence that he felt blinded by Grace, her beauty and her purity. How could someone as lost as he was, as damned by his actions, be here in the presence of such goodness?

He knew only one thing. He had been near death, though he couldn't understand the why of it. The addiction to dying blood, when left unsatisfied, could only result in death after months of agonizing starvation.

But as the hours had passed in Grace's company, with his body on fire with his need for her, not only had the cramps reached an intolerable level, but his heart and lungs had begun to fail him. He'd been on the verge of heart failure for the last hour.

How had she known that her blood would relieve at least part of these symptoms, even abate the abdominal seizures to the extent that he could take deep breaths and remain stretched out instead of curled up in agony.

Oh, God, Grace.

If he stayed here, he put her in jeopardy.

He sat up. He had to get out of here. He had to make contact with James, maybe even Endelle. Yes, Endelle. He had to let her know the truth about Greaves's army.

But the sudden movement sent black spots flying before his eyes. He fell back on the bed.

He felt Grace's hands on him again, and her rich, earthy meadow scent flooded his body with new drives, new cravings.

"Rest," he heard her whisper.

He wanted to talk to her, but the room spun and all he could do was focus on his breathing. He really needed to get his shit together. But how?

That evening Marguerite ordered a cosmo and munched from a big bowl of popcorn in the center of the table. She seemed okay with the popcorn, but the cosmo was bugging her stomach. Yep, she had to admit, her nerves had gotten the better of her.

She sat at a small elevated table, her feet hooked on the lower rung of the tall bar stool. The club was noisy with feminine chatter but she could hear her new friends just fine.

She was just too tense and more than once thought about taking off. Earlier, Brynna had introduced her to Devon the stripper. What a hunk. He was tall—but not nearly as tall as Thorne—he had reddish bronze hair that hung in waves just to his shoulders, his eyes were a vivid blue, and his proportions, from broad muscular shoulders, to narrow hips, to lean thighs, took her breath away.

He had even taken her hand and squeezed her fingers. He'd sent, *I'm yours. Just say the word. Right after my performance, if you're willing*

She was so freaking tempted. Ever since she'd left Second Earth, her hormones had been in overdrive.

But what about Thorne?

He was nearby, cloaked in mist, and holding up a wall like he'd done in El Paso One. Jane couldn't see him but Brynna could. She scowled because of it. "He looks mad," she whispered, leaning close. "Are you sure he's not going to tear the building down?"

"Don't worry. We have an understanding." Sort of.

Brynna shrugged. "Your funeral," she said, but she smiled, if a little sloppily. Brynna had been drinking vodka tonics and now had two empty glasses in front of her and a third she'd almost finished.

Yeah, maybe it was her funeral. It was certainly her agony. Thorne had listened in on Devon's offer, but he hadn't said anything. She had expected a quip or two like, *He's so short, just six feet* or *His hair smells like some kind of pansy-ass perfumed gel*. Instead, he was as somber as when he'd picked her up off the grass earlier.

Brynna interrupted her thoughts. "So is there anything you want to ask us about our Seer methods?" She covered her mouth and barely disguised a burp.

Marguerite stared at her cosmo. She didn't mind the

diversion from Thorne's dour presence. "Well, why have I never heard about this group Seer stuff before?"

Brynna laughed. "Actually, it's not done on Second Earth, at least not that we know of. This was something that developed over time. Diallo encouraged us to give it a try, and it took quite a few decades to perfect."

"So how does it work? Is it kind of like meditation or something?"

Brynna slid her fingers into the side of her hair and leaned her elbow on the table. "Kind of like a meditation, but more like a reaching out telepathically until we all meet in the middle."

"Sounds interesting." Truth? She was a little bored. She had no plans to continue her Seer work. She didn't really need to on Mortal Earth. She could certainly handle bar-hopping without having to dip into the future streams to figure out who her next lay would be.

"You don't really seem into your Seer self," Jane said, but she was smiling.

"Not too much. I just never really saw the point of it all except as another form of slavery. I mean, what good has it done the colony? Have you ever thwarted attacks or civil unrest?"

Both women laughed, but Jane glanced in the direction of the stage then at her watch. "Five more minutes." She sat up a little straighter.

"I've been working the future streams for about two centuries now," Brynna said, "and I've learned that I can focus on certain kinds of events and on neighboring colonies to see if issues might surface that Diallo's council of elders can begin addressing before bad things happen. For instance, we had a series of floods in the early nineteen hundreds that wiped out a whole bunch of farms. We worked together and formed a strong enough vision to warn the inhabitants of that area so that no lives were lost. Diallo and the council set up a relief program for flood victims way in advance. A lot of machinery, furniture, and livestock were saved." She lifted her tumbler to her lips and finished her drink. She waved to the waitress then pointed at her empty glass.

Marguerite was surprised. "That's the first time I've heard of the future streams being used for good. Stannett was all about gaining more power, securing his fortune and his safety, but this actually makes some sense. Although I know for sure that if I worked for Endelle, she'd mostly want information about Greaves and his plans." A big *whatever*.

Marguerite glanced from Jane to Brynna. "So mostly, you're about helping the colony."

"And each other," Jane said.

The women looked at each other and laughed. Shared secrets maybe.

The general good humor and camaraderie that flowed between the two women reminded her of her relationship with Grace. And for the first time, she realized she missed her cellmate, really missed her. She even missed Fiona, which was a surprise. She would never have believed that one day she'd actually care about her female friendships—or any friendship really.

Brynna glanced in Thorne's direction and shook her head. "Any more like him at home?"

"A bunch more," Marguerite said, smiling.

She opened her mouth to give a fine recounting of the warriors she'd met, but suddenly the music hit the loudspeakers, the lights dimmed, and the stage spots began to flash in every color imaginable, moving wildly across midnight-blue velvet drapes that created a strong backdrop for the performers.

Jane, who sat on Marguerite's right, leaned close and all but shouted, "You're gonna love this."

Devon appeared in flash of smoke, no doubt having folded to the center of the stage as soon as the smoke popped.

He wore some kind of shiny gold jumpsuit and he held in his hand a matching space helmet with two really stupid-looking antennae sticking out of the top. Was that duct tape holding them in place?

The first thing he did was lose the helmet, sending it in a

whirling sideways spin across the smooth black tile of the
stage floor, a trick that for some reason made the women go
wild.

Jane was the first one to leave her tall stool. She whipped
past Marguerite so fast that she brought a kind of wind flowing along behind her.

It wasn't long before Brynna abandoned her perch as well,
heading for the edge of the stage, especially since Devon
wasn't wasting any time. He was already bared to the waist
and swinging his spacesuit jacket around as he gyrated his
hips in a mind-bending circle.

She glanced at Thorne, wondering if he intended to start
badgering her, but his gaze was on the floor at his feet, even
more somber than before.

Thorne? she sent. Now she was just worried.

He turned in her direction and finally just gave her a lopsided smile. *Have fun.*

He lifted his arm and was gone.

Marguerite set her cosmo down; otherwise she was sure
she would have just dropped it. Thorne leaving was the last
thing she'd expected to happen this evening.

She glanced in Devon's direction.

By now her Seer-mates were at the side of the stage
screaming their guts out.

She knew only one thing, this wasn't for her, not tonight,
not with her man giving her so much space and being so
damn *mature* about the whole thing.

She sent Brynna a telepathic message: *Hey, I'm heading
home.*

She didn't know if Brynna could possibly "hear" her given
the show that now involved a hunky man in a G-string pumping his hips right in front of her.

But Brynna turned around and winked at her.

Marguerite smiled as she lifted her arm, thought the
thought, and folded out of the club.

From the archives, only one reference to the extraordinary myth of obsidian flame exists and it is as follows, "Intuitive vision is the defining attribute of obsidian flame."

—*Treatise on Ascension*, Philippe Reynard

CHAPTER 10

When she arrived back at Diallo's home, it took her a minute to find Thorne. He was reclining on the couch in the expansive front room. He wore a white tank and jeans. He was barefoot. If she hadn't been feeling so worn out from all her guilt and indecision, she might have savored how he looked.

His arms were crossed over his chest.

A single oil lamp glowed dimly across the room.

He turned to look at her. "You left?"

He seemed neither surprised nor particularly interested. "Yes."

He nodded and stared in the direction of the window. "Get some rest and just so you know, I'm headed back to Second Earth tomorrow. You can come with, you'll always be welcome, but I'm done following you around."

"Good. You should go back."

At that, he sat up, swinging his legs to plant his feet on the floor. "So that's it?"

She sighed, feeling dull inside. She found herself chewing on the inside of her lip; it seemed funny to her because it was more something Grace would do than something she ever did. "Yeah, I guess that's it."

"Why did you come back tonight then, if you don't give a flying fuck?"

She laughed and threw her hands out in front of her. "I don't know. It seemed like a point of honor. I'm not a bad person, Thorne. I just . . ."

"You just want your freedom."

He settled back against the cushions. "I get it. I'll be gone tomorrow, although I hope you'll stick around in this colony, under Diallo's protection, until you get this damn vision thing sorted out. As for myself, I'm feeling the pull back to Second. I'm needed there. I have a big job to do. I'm just starting to get that, so yeah. I'm leaving."

Marguerite's throat felt really tight. Were they actually saying good-bye? She nodded several times. "I . . . I think I want a hot shower."

She didn't wait to hear him say one more thing. Besides that, her eyes were burning again, which they seemed to be doing a lot lately. She lifted her arm and folded straight to their shared bedroom.

She took her shower and the warm water soothed her. She was a bit of a mess. Her muscles kind of ached, and there was this constant dull throbbing in the center of her brain, and now her heart hung like a sack of sand in the middle of her chest.

After the water turned cold, she hopped out of the shower, toweled off, and decided there was one thing she did want right now. She wanted to sit next to Thorne, really close, kind of draped over him so that she could press her ear to his chest and just listen to his heartbeat. She'd done that a few times after their more brisk lovemaking sessions when she was in the Convent. She'd always loved it.

Yep, that's what she wanted.

The fact that she was pretty sure Thorne would simply open his arm and draw her close had the effect of once more closing up her throat and burning her eyes.

But as she stood beside the bed and folded on a pair of jeans and a soft red sweatshirt, she felt a familiar roiling sensation deep within her mind.

Oh, no, no, no.

"Thorne," she cried out.

In the next split second, as the vision began to crash, he appeared in front of her. She held her head in her hands and strove to keep the vision at bay. "Help me."

"Vision?"

She nodded.

"Tell me what to do," he said, sinking down in front of her. He put his arms around her but she pushed him away, her own arms stiff. Tears began to stream down her face because the pain of holding back what felt like an entire ocean was overwhelming.

She listed sideways. She had to figure this out.

"Please, Marguerite, tell me what to do. What can I do?"

But she just shook her head. She couldn't tell him because she had no idea what needed to be done.

He put his hands on her face and looked into her eyes. He held her gaze. She let herself fall into those wonderful hazel eyes—and suddenly he was inside her mind.

I'm here, he sent.

Yes. But her telepathy was barely a whisper.

I can feel the pain and I can see the vision. You're holding it off but only by the strength of your will. There has to be a way to manage this, maybe if we worked together.

She couldn't say anything. She just trembled.

He took her in his arms and held her. *Enter my mind*, he commanded.

It will hurt you.

Doesn't matter. Do it.

Marguerite gave a push and suddenly she was inside his head, but this time she could tell that the vision remained outside.

She took a deep breath and slumped against him.

Better?

Oh, God, yes.

Good. Now let's see if we can figure this out.

She took more deep breaths and suddenly a different kind of vision came to her, not of images but of *knowing*. All of this was about her obsidian flame power, including the crashing visions. The *knowing* whispered through her mind. This was her power, the one she didn't want, but it was here, demanding her attention.

She stopped battling the truth, that whether she liked it or not, this damn power was here to stay. She sighed heavily against Thorne's chest as he caressed her arms and her back then embraced her. Well, there were worse things that could happen to her than to have a warrior like Thorne holding her, keeping a vision from dominating her mind, and just anchoring her until she could figure things out.

She closed her eyes and while still inside Thorne's mind, she let the truth of obsidian flame come to her.

Truth.

Her truth, no one else's.

That she had carried the stripes that belonged to someone else, even when she was a child and her father had whipped her. She had borne the pain of someone else's fear and loss and suffering.

She had felt Sister Quena's whip so that others wouldn't have to. She had done it willingly because her resistance to instruction had been the woman's greatest frustration and Marguerite's only weapon against her brutality.

But the result had been her own disconnection from others, a deep fear, even resentment of connection. She hated being touched or embraced by others. Only Thorne had been allowed in.

Yes, these were her truths.

Out of those truths came a singular understanding: She had to allow Thorne to breach the barrier of her obsidian flame power, to allow the connection, so that she could access that power.

Had she been avoiding this moment? Yes.

Would breaching this barrier alter her life forever? Probably.

Thorne? she sent.

Yes? How close he felt when she was in his mind while communicating telepathically.

I need you to do something for me but it's not going to be pretty.

Anything, sweetheart. And this was the truth about Thorne: No matter what request she put in front of him, his answer would always be the same.

Maybe that's what made this moment tolerable, maybe even possible.

I need you to pierce my obsidian flame power, to open it. And don't ask me how I know this is what you need to do, I just know.

Okay. But . . . uh . . . how do I do that?

You need to follow me back into my mind then you need to dive very deep. Just dive and dive, go with your gut on this one, until you find my obsidian flame power. Then break it open. I can feel it pulsing and waiting. But you need to breach it in order to release it.

The evolution of powers among Second ascenders was always a mysterious experience. Thorne knew nothing about obsidian flame except that it had enormous potential, like splitting the atom, and now Marguerite had asked him to pierce hers, to open up her power.

This was no small thing—either that she had asked him to do it, or that he would be doing this for her. He valued that she trusted him, but what would the result be? More power?

Would she then draw even farther away from him, be more inclined to leave him, to live on her own, to pursue her own interests because now she would have more power?

The selfish part of him resisted, held back. To do this thing, should he even be able to do it, would change their relationship. He could feel it deep in his heart, in his soul, in his spirit.

Power always changed things.

But in his two thousand years of ascended life he had come to understand at least one thing: When a new power emerged, the best course to take was always to go with it, take it to its limits, explore every damn facet, and work it, work it hard. To do less would always leave the ascender open to the enemy. Always.

So he set aside his own self-interest and followed Marguerite's instincts.

He pulled back and met her gaze, staring into those beautiful brown eyes. He took a deep breath. "Ready?" he asked. He was in tune with her instincts and he could tell this was going to be difficult, very difficult. When she had said "pierce," she meant that some part of her obsidian flame power had to be cut open in order to be engaged.

"I'm ready. But as soon as I pull back into my own mind, do what you need to do as fast as you can because I won't be able to hold the vision for long."

"Got it."

He felt her leave his mind but he followed in tight formation, right on her mental heels, and moved with her back into her mind. The vision loomed and he felt her pain as she once more expended the energy to keep the vision from crashing.

He closed his eyes in order to focus on his internal quest. As he took in the breadth of her mind, he saw the dark aperture. Just as she had told him, he dove into the tunnel, mentally moving as fast as he could

He flew down deep until the tunnel became very dark, obsidian black, no light escaping, But he pressed on. Her memories wanted to fly at him, from every angle, to drag him away from his purpose, memories that mostly looked like the Convent. Sometimes even his own image, his body moving over hers, would show up, but he ignored it all until from the blackness emerged a pinpoint of light that grew larger as he flew toward it.

He could hear Marguerite shrieking now but he somehow knew that it wasn't the vision causing her pain; rather it was his journey, as though this flight down this long tunnel had hurt her. He could now see the sheath that needed to be pierced—and whatever her current pain, this would be infinitely worse, as though her obsidian flame power had needed to be cloaked until exactly this moment.

* * *

Marguerite had never known such pain. She felt as though Thorne had taken a flame torch with him and just burned her mind up as he went. The only advantage seemed to be that while he made this journey, the vision lumbered above her unable to crash down as it usually did, maybe because she was in such pain.

Hold on, came from deep within her mind. Uh-oh, this was about to get worse.

She grabbed Thorne's arms and dug her nails in.

The penetration was ferocious, a blinding stab of pain that made her earlier shrieks sound like kitten meows. But his first effort wasn't successful.

Oh, shit.

This shield is tough. I'm sorry, Marguerite, I've got to try again.

Just do it! She sank her nails harder, probably too hard, but Thorne held rock-steady.

This time when he punched, her arms spasmed, but at the same time she felt the barrier break apart. She also heard Thorne from deep within her mind holler, *Holy shit. I'm on my way out. Look out.*

This time, however, the pain was gone and in its place was a kind of euphoria she'd never known before, a rising stream of pleasure that rushed up through her mind and kept rushing until she saw stars and more stars, until she was looking at the universe above her, the entire galaxy spinning around and around.

She didn't know how long it was before she came back to earth, or back into her body, or whatever this was exactly, but when she did she knew something had changed. The power she had always experienced as a Seer felt more rounded and complete, certainly bigger and stronger and just there, omnipresent.

She couldn't yet see Thorne. She was too lost in the middle of the experience.

But she was aware enough to know that she still had hold of his arms and that he was rubbing her back very gently.

Her hands were wet, but she didn't know why. Her fingers even slid around.

So this was obsidian flame, the breadth of it. She tried to measure it but what she felt the most was how easily she now held the vision at bay—as though it had moved several feet from her and sat limp in the air, powerless to affect her anymore. From this time forward, no vision would ever again crash down on her.

She didn't know if she should feel relieved. Certainly she had more control, but a corresponding thought sliced through her: What would be the price of such control? What would be left of her life now? Where would her precious freedom be?

Thorne, thank God, didn't intrude on her thoughts; nor did he speak to her. He just continued his gentle touch on her arms, her shoulders, her back, soothing her, comforting her.

He was a good friend, tremendous support, an anchor. Who else could have done for her what she needed? Who but a warrior could understand that sometimes pain just had to be tolerated?

She smiled when it occurred to her that he'd essentially just popped her obsidian flame cherry.

She finally drew back and looked him in the eye. She could tell he was no longer in her mind. She was pretty sure that obsidian flame had shot him the hell out of there. "So did you get fried or anything?" she asked.

He smiled and shook his head. "I got a taste of what you endured, but it was more like a punch in the ass when I left the center of your power."

"You know, you seem really pleased with yourself."

"Not with myself. I'm pleased because I can feel the difference in you, in your obsidian flame power. It tastes complete, and very big, as though before it was just a shadow of what it could be. But how did you know you needed it pierced?"

She shook her head. "I remember Fiona went through something similar but it wasn't Jean-Pierre who had done the deed. It was Endelle."

"Well, I'm sure it was no picnic."

"I felt like you were carrying a blowtorch and had it lit

the entire journey. And once you got there, you used a chain saw to cut through some really sensitive tissue."

"Good to know. Okay, so tell me about the vision."

"It's just there, waiting. When I'm ready."

He smiled. "That's fantastic. So obsidian flame has done this for you, given you command of these visions?"

She nodded. "I think so, at least to the degree that they can't just incapacitate me." Her hand slipped down his arms. She drew back and gasped. "Look what I did to you?" Her horrible inch-long nails had dug into him and created a bunch of small wounds. Blood oozed down his arms. "Oh, God, I'm so sorry."

But he scoffed. "Please. You really think I'm not used to much worse? Besides, I could tell how much this recent penetration hurt you."

At the sound of the word, she smiled. "I haven't had a penetration hurt that bad since I was fifteen."

"Oh, now, please don't bring that up. That is so not the kind of thing I can handle."

She rolled her eyes. "Thorne, how old are you?"

"Two mil."

"And, uh, just how many women have you *penetrated* in the past twenty-four centuries?"

He could only grin, so she leaned up and kissed him full on the lips. "Wish you'd been the one, if that makes you feel better."

"It does."

"But man, with the size you are, that would have hurt a helluva lot worse than what I went through."

"Again, I need to remind you that I don't want to hear about you with other men, even if you were just a teenager. I'm also guessing we need to take a look at this most recent vision."

"Right." She frowned as more of her intuition kicked in. "I have a feeling this vision concerns you, just like the last one, so maybe you should just jump in."

"I agree." He took a deep breath then pushed his mind against hers.

This vision was like a black cloud, which really didn't bode well for the contents. She held her obsidian flame power at the fore and very slowly opened the door to the future streams. The images wanted to rush, but she simply thought the thought and they slowed.

She was back at the Convent, inside the cell she shared with Grace. That sight alone was enough to almost make her want to shut the whole thing down. Instead she held steady and let the next images come. It was as though she stood in the center of the cell facing Grace's bed, her former cot behind her. As she began to pan toward the wall with the desk that sat between the beds, the images simply became murky and unrecognizable, something that never happened in her visions.

She felt uneasy. She had a sense that there were two people in the room, Grace and someone else.

I don't understand. Why did the images stop? Thorne sent. *I mean, what the hell happened to them?*

She thought for a minute. She extended her senses toward the vision once more, then she knew.

Oh, shit, Stannett.

You mean he's interfered?

Exactly.

Sonofabitch.

She prompted the vision once more, hoping that perhaps there was a way to enhance her obsidian flame power in order to overcome the interference. But she could feel that her new power was flowing in a perfect stream—yet there was nothing she could do to affect what Stannett was doing. He was one powerful vampire.

She closed the vision down and pulled back to look at Thorne. He disengaged from her mind so that the familiar rubbery sensation followed. She was alone within her mind once more.

"That was your Convent cell," he stated, frowning.

"Yes, it was." She felt restrained in her spirit.

He put his hand on her arm and met her gaze. "What are you not saying? I can feel your hesitation. What's going on?"

She looked up at him, at his somber expression, the pinch of his lips. It was simple: She didn't want to go down this path.

Unfortunately, this path involved saving Grace, her friend, her cellmate. She even suspected that it would involve all the devotiates in the Convent as well.

"Is this an attack?" he asked.

"I don't know." That at least was the truth. "All I know is that Stannett is blocking the vision. Maybe he suspected I'd be reading it, or maybe he's just taking precautions. I don't know."

"And you think this is serious?"

"I know it is." She let her gaze fall to his chest. His tank was cut low so that she had a view of the swell of his pecs and the fine hairs on his chest.

She didn't want to say the rest—that she also suspected she would be able to see the hidden part of the vision if she had help. She would have to involve another Seer in the situation, to engage with another Seer in the future streams, to create a connection that she did not want to create.

She squeezed her eyes shut. She didn't want this to be happening, for aggressive visions to be the reality of her life; she hated that she had been thrust onto the stage of world events because she was a Seer of great power and because she was obsidian flame.

But there was another truth here, a very dark one. She didn't have to respond to this vision and she didn't have to take her place in ascended society. She had a choice. She really did. She could go her own path, especially now that she would be free of the crashing visions. She had control.

She still had a chance at the life she'd dreamed of for so long, she really did. She could taste it. All she had to do was back away from this, not take it to the next level, a level she saw so clearly it made her dizzy.

But what would happen to Grace if she failed to act?

Truth? She didn't know for sure, but it wouldn't be good.

Her gaze fell to the carpet. She was only faintly aware that she was breathing hard.

She put a hand to her forehead.

"Marguerite, what's wrong?"

The next level.

Connection. That thing she despised.

She wanted her freedom.

One obscenity after another rolled through her head. Though she remained physically close to Thorne, in her mind she was mounting her wings and flying up and up and up, into the stratosphere. Never mind that she couldn't breathe or that her wings were icing over.

Oh, God, this could not be happening. She wasn't ready for this. She didn't want this, not even a little. She was at a crossroads and the choice was simple: either go forward with what she knew to do and save Grace and how many other devotiates, or leave this colony right now, live her life the way she wanted to live it, embrace her freedom.

She didn't want this. It wasn't fair.

"Marguerite, talk to me."

She pulled back. Her gaze fell to his arms and to the blood now dried in swaths where her long nails had pierced him and her fingers had slid around. It looked like a child had finger-painted on him.

But Grace was her friend and she would die if Marguerite didn't act. She could feel it now in her bones. This much she knew, this much Stannett couldn't hide from her, that Grace would die this very night without her help.

The next breath she drew had a singing quality, part hiss, part gasp.

In the end, however, there was no choice, no choice at all. Grace was her friend, had helped keep her sane, had shown her respect when everyone else was afraid to. Only Grace had stood up to Sister Quena on Marguerite's behalf.

Though her heart was breaking because the freedom she had fought for was now disappearing, she lifted her gaze to Thorne. "I need to reach pure vision and I need to do it now. If we want to save your sister, and the other devotiates in the Convent, I have to reach pure vision."

"Oh, God. What do we do? Do you need Fiona?"

She shook her head. "I've thought of her, of course, but I know that for what I need to accomplish, only another Seer will do. I need Brynna. I need you to go to the club and bring her back here. Will you do that for me?"

Thorne met her gaze squarely and dipped his chin a little. He nodded. "I'll be right-fucking-back."

As he lifted his arm and vanished, she drew in a deep breath. What did it say about him that he simply stared into her eyes, made an assessment, and took charge? That familiar swelling in her chest happened again, the sure knowledge that she loved him and trusted him.

But did he understand even a little what she was giving up tonight, forever?

Would anyone?

You are beloved.

—*Collected Proverbs,* Beatrice of Fourth

CHAPTER 11

Thorne had needed every ounce of patience he'd learned over the past two millennia in order not to push Marguerite. He had felt her restraint and he knew something was terribly wrong, but he hadn't been a leader of men and women, of powerful warriors and powerful vampires, without having come to recognize a pivotal moment, a moment of dynamic change.

He had feared the worst when she had hesitated: that she wouldn't be able to make the leap, wouldn't be able to accept and embrace the challenge in front of her. No, he didn't comprehend the scope of what she was going through, but he felt the weight of it, the size of it. After all, he had pierced the sheath protecting her obsidian flame power and he had hurt her. The entire experience had spoken the truth to him about who she was when it came to her most essential courage and what she was going through.

But the nature of the broken vision had stalled her out, had meant something terrible to her—a personal loss so great that she couldn't even speak her thoughts out loud. He'd been tempted to steal inside her mind and read exactly what was going on, but that was a violation he would never commit.

So he had waited. And she had chosen.

She had chosen for Grace and for the Convent devotiates.

She had chosen against her life of freedom.

He folded directly to the club and found Brynna half sloshed with four empty tumblers in front of her. He leaned down to her and looked her in the eyes. "Marguerite needs you. She asked for you specifically. Will you come with me?"

Brynna squinted. "Goddamn, you are so handsome. Oh, I shouldn't have said that. Okay, yeah, sure." She turned to the other Seer with the red hair. "I have to go. Don't know when I'll be back. Marguerite and this hunk need me. Maybe a threesome!" She laughed at her joke then turned serious eyes on Thorne. "I don't do threesomes."

He had another quelling moment of fear. Would Brynna be of the least use in this state?

Well, he hoped like hell a few fingers of vodka wouldn't matter.

"I'm going to fold you out of here. You ready?"

"Sure. Fold away, gorgeous."

He thought the thought, and the next moment they were back in the bedroom. Marguerite was outside on the patio, standing in the cold in her bare feet, her jeans, and her red sweatshirt. He felt her sadness, a deep pain that he would probably never understand. But she was so young by ascended standards, just a little over a century, and her life thus far had been brutal on many levels.

Brynna went to her. Thorne was right on her heels.

"Whadya need, Sister-Seer?"

Marguerite turned to her and blinked. "You're drunk."

"Yeah . . . little bit. Whazzup?" She giggled.

"Brynna, I need you to help me get to pure vision, right now. We have an emergency. Can you do that for me?"

Brynna threw her arm forward. "Pure vision? Shit, yes. Piece a cake. Of course I've never done it before." And then she laughed. "Okay . . . emergency . . . must focus. Here's the thing. I can barely achieve 70 percent accuracy, but I'll do what I can."

"Good. How do we do the communal work, you know, more than one Seer at a time?"

Brynna put her hand on Marguerite's shoulder and said, "Like this."

Thorne couldn't imagine what went on between the two women, but what he could observe was that each head jerked backward, as if lightning had just shot back and forth between them.

He felt Marguerite call to him telepathically. He didn't wait, but pushed into her mind, and oh, yeah, his woman had power because there it was, the vision, complete, perfect and moving at exactly the right speed to be seen and understood, to be witnessed.

But for a long time, what he saw there didn't make any sense at all. Yes, it was the Convent. Yes, he saw Grace at times, then not at others. There seemed to be some kind of strange cloaking substance, very much like mist, but it moved in strange patterns.

What is that? Marguerite sent.

I think it's mist.

And those are death vampires, in the long hall where the cells are located. Is that . . . Leto?

Yeah. Why the hell is he at the Convent? Shit, he really doesn't look so good.

It's weird that he's there, Marguerite sent. *But why is he separated from Grace when they're in the same cell?*

That's the mist.

Oh, shit . . . that's Casimir, isn't it?

Thorne finally understood. *This is Casimir's doing. I think this is a kind of mist called shifting mist.*

Thorne was stunned. Shifting mist required enormous power and he sure as hell had never seen it before. So this was definitely an attack. Death vampires, a Fourth ascender, and shifting mist: Holy hell, how was he supposed to orchestrate a battle against shit like this?

The vision ended with death vampires slaying the devotiates, Leto dead, and Casimir folding Grace straight out of her cell, taking her back to his home in Paris One. He could sense the level of Seer accuracy that the women together had not only overcome Stannett's future stream block but had achieved pure vision. There was no question in his mind that what he was seeing was exactly what would happen if he didn't intervene.

And what the fuck was Leto doing in his sister's convent cell? How did he even get there? Had he folded to her? If he had, why would he have done that? Why would he have put her in jeopardy like this?

Okay, one dilemma at a time.

He withdrew from Marguerite's mind in order to make certain of one thing: whether or not he could replay the vision in his mind. He focused on what he had seen, and yes, there it was, the entire vision from beginning to end. If he wondered for a moment how that was possible, he let it go. Time later to dissect the how of things because he had only minutes to take care of business.

He let go of the images for a moment to make sure Marguerite was all right. She stood wide-eyed with shock, even trembling.

Brynna blinked several times. "Sweet mother of God, they're all going to die."

He put a hand on each shoulder and looked from one woman to the other. He squeezed. "Listen to me, no one is going to die tonight except all those fucking death vampires, have you got that? This is what I do. Will you both trust me to get this job done?"

Two nods.

"Good. Now come back in the house and get warmed up. It's goddamn cold out here." The temperature-regulating shields weren't universal to the colony site. Even his feet were cold.

Marguerite hooked Brynna's arm, and though the Seer stumbled a little, she guided her back into the bedroom.

As Thorne closed the door, he knew one thing. He was going to need some major Warrior of the Blood help on this one.

* * *

Change.

From the window of his hotel suite, Casimir stared at the Eiffel Tower all lit up, a lively backdrop to a night sky and his favorite city in the world, any dimension, Paris. He had lived at the Plaza Athénée for a decade, one of his favorite residences ever. His children had lived here since the day they were born. He'd made a good life for himself on Mortal Earth. His current support of Greaves was earning him another small fortune.

But after seeing Grace in Moscow Two, holy fuck, he was in trouble.

He'd lived in all four dimensions during the course of his life, his very long and in many ways satisfying life, but he'd never faced this; an unexpected erotic scent of a woman, an ascended vampire, a devotiate, which had only one but quite impossible interpretation: the *breh-hedden*. He honestly didn't know what to do. And he always knew what to do.

He still couldn't believe the vision or whatever it was that had taken Leto right out from under his stasis power. If he hadn't hesitated, Leto would already be trussed up and in Greaves's tender care. But he'd stood there for a few seconds too long, in frozen hell beside Greaves, on the main stage of the forthcoming military review spectacle site, ready to incapacitate Leto. Then an angel had appeared beside Leto, with really long blond hair, light eyes, and a glow around her entire being.

He'd just never seen anything like it before, the opaque quality of her presence, the power that beat in waves all around her, and the stunning sight when at the moment Leto put his hand in hers, they both vanished. But it was perhaps an even bigger surprise that Greaves had been completely unaware of her presence.

After Leto disappeared, all Greaves had done was complain about Casimir's hesitation, blaming the failure of Leto's capture on that. Of course he was right, yet just as he'd opened his mouth to explain his hesitation to Greaves, he had held back. If Greaves hadn't had even the smallest perception of Grace, then this was very significant in ascended terms. Caz had a deep gnawing sensation that this could become critical to him in the future, perhaps even a point of negotiation or survival.

But how the hell was it possible, in any dimension, for this woman to be his *breh*? Even if he wanted to pursue Grace, what could they possibly have in common? He was a Fourth ascender and she was a saint. He was a sadist, a hedonist. He might be a devoted father, but in terms of good qualities, that was pretty much it and he knew it. Which made him completely unworthy of Thorne's sister, and frankly not interested *at all*.

But here he was with a perpetual hard-on because of his sensory recall of the woman's scent, like fresh earth and sweet wildflowers. He wouldn't have minded displaying his oh-so-worthy arousal except that in addition to being aroused beyond comprehension, he'd stopped craving the woman currently sharing his bed.

The exquisite Julianna matched his sadistic tendencies and enjoyed sex with equal abandon. But a woman who had spent the last century in a convent would really not enjoy an S&M threesome with a Goth abducted from a seedy local club, fucking her and drinking from her until she was almost drained of blood.

Right now he was screwed. He couldn't see how to move forward but he knew he couldn't stay where he was. How strange that one moment in time had altered his life forever.

He could hope that Grace would die as Greaves intended in their forthcoming little Convent adventure, but even as he watched the Paris lights twinkle, he knew he had to bring Grace home with him.

He hissed softly. He needed some relief. Now.

He walked to the master suite, gently gliding his fingers up and down his erection as he moved. At this hour, his boys were asleep along with their au pair, so he didn't have to worry about being seen in the act.

He found Julianna asleep, which was good.

In a very swift move, he folded off his clothes then tied her spread-eagle to the four posts of the bed. As he positioned

himself to straddle her neck, she blinked up at him ready to
squawk. But he was too needy, and when she opened her
mouth to yell at him, he inserted himself. He grabbed the
headboard and mouth-fucked her as the image of Grace
swirled through his mind, as the recollection of her scent
brought him close to the edge.

He didn't care that Julianna was struggling beneath his
rough efforts. All he cared about was giving himself up to
what he needed now more than life itself.

He came shouting. He came and came as he imagined
burying himself between Grace's legs and drinking at the
same time from her neck.

When he was done, he rolled off Julianna, who was gag-
ging with all that he'd given her and struggling against the
bindings.

When she could finally talk, she glared at him. "I might
have enjoyed that if you'd let me participate. What is wrong
with you? You've been in a weird mood since you returned
from Moscow Two. What happened out there?"

"Do you want to go back to Greaves?" He released her
from the restraints then stretched out on the bed next to her.

She sat up, wiping a hand over her mouth.

He couldn't look at her. He just stared up at the mirrored
ceiling. He had his arm thrown over his forehead. He closed
his eyes.

She drew close and stroked his fingers very lightly. "I've
grown fond of you," she said, her voice small. "I . . . I thought
you enjoyed my company."

"Something's happened, something completely beyond
my control and I know I can't give you any longer what you'll
need of me."

"So . . . you're dumping me after having stolen me away
from my heart's desire? You're letting me go because of
something mysterious that I'm guessing you won't even tell
me about?"

"It's not personal, Ju-Ju. I've even had a few times with
you in recent weeks that I thought maybe we were soul mates.
We certainly are evenly matched in bed. It's a fucked-up

ascension thing. The problem is, I won't treat you right during the next few days or weeks or however long it takes to resolve this situation and you need to go."

But he felt the woman vibrating with rage next to him. He understood who she was, that she would find some way to punish him for being so summarily dumped, so he simply thought the thought and she was gone.

He rose, showered, and prepared for battle.

The hour had come.

Time to destroy Leto. As for Grace, he could hardly wait to see her again and to draw her meadow, wildflower scent into his nostrils.

Greaves was in the bathroom, flexing the DNA-altered claw of his left hand, when he heard a woman shouting, and not far from him. He frowned slightly, since he recognized the woman's voice.

He was naked and aroused because working his claw was connected to his cock. Both were symbols of power. Flexing his claw therefore brought lovely ripples of excitement deep into his groin.

He held his erection in his hand as he left the bathroom. He found Julianna standing near the foot of his bed, naked, her back arched, her arms spread wide, her head tilted toward the ceiling and screaming profanities the likes of which he had never heard leave her throat before.

"Trouble in paradise?" he asked, walking calmly toward her.

He was both glad to see her and yet extremely suspicious of her sudden return to his bedroom. She'd been his lover for a few heavenly months until Casimir had required her as one of the prices he'd demanded for serving Greaves. He had hated parting with her, and deep within his mind he'd promised himself that Casimir would pay for having insisted on her.

Yet here she was, inexplicably back in his Geneva bedroom.

She turned toward him. Her body was perfection. She

had perfect large breasts, which were peaked because of either the chill in the room or her rage. He somehow doubted she was aroused.

"What did you do to him?" she cried.

He spread his hands wide. "I don't know what you mean." He snapped his claw, which brought her attention momentarily to one of her favorite tools. Her eyes flared, but she wasn't to be so easily distracted.

"Casimir sent me back but he wouldn't tell me why. He said it was some kind of ascended bullshit so of course I figured you must be involved."

He pressed the claw to his naked chest. "You wound me, my dear. I've had nothing to do with this and I have no idea what you're talking about."

She turned her head to the side but eyed him up and down. When her gaze hesitated on his cock, he reached down with the claw and stroked himself. She'd always enjoyed his claw.

She sighed and her shoulders relaxed. She even took a few steps toward him. "I don't mean to be a bitch and I missed you, but he dismissed me like I was some sort of ordinary prostitute for whom he had no further use."

"You are anything but ordinary, not in any respect." He snapped his claw again.

He watched her shudder. "Now tell me exactly what Casimir said so that I can interpret the situation for you. I am convinced you have somehow mistaken his intentions."

She turned and sat down on the edge of the bed. She told him everything, including the recent invasion of her mouth. He moved toward her, gently rubbing the crown of his cock. Now that she was here, well, she was simply delicious.

"So what was he thinking about when he took you in that brutal manner?"

"I have no idea."

"You didn't enter his mind?"

Julianna tilted her head. "You know very well I don't have that kind of power. Certainly not with a Fourth ascender."

But Greaves had a suspicion that something had happened in Moscow Two when Casimir failed to acquire Leto with his stasis skills. There had been just the smallest hesitation on Casimir's part, as well as an astonished expression. But what had caused it?

Even Leto's whereabouts had been a mystery until Stannett had reported that the future streams showed him in the Convent, in Thorne's sister's pitiful cell.

And now Casimir had sent Julianna back.

He dropped to his knees before her and spread her legs. He rubbed the claw along the inside of her thigh. "Let me take the sting from your pride. Let me love you the way I used to."

Julianna sighed. She even smiled. She put her hand on his bald head and stroked. When she began to sink in her nails and continued the exquisite pressure, she said, "You always knew exactly what I needed to ease my heart."

With her nails embedded in his flesh, both hands now, he made liberal use of his claw.

When she began to scream, he knew she was content.

But as he sank into the completely delightful business of making Julianna bleed, he pondered a few interpretations of his own, about exactly what had happened to Casimir in Moscow. And Leto. And exactly what Grace had to do with all these strange occurrences.

Thorne wanted to fold on battle gear, but he was still caught in a disagreement with Marguerite. Brynna had folded home to get sober. He had hoped she would stay with Marguerite but as soon as he and his woman had started arguing, the Seer had taken off, asking only for an update later to ease her mind.

Marguerite had her hands planted on her hips. "I'm coming with," she stated . . . again.

"No, you're not. Death vampires, remember? And let me just add that one of those motherfuckers looked big, really big, so the answer is no, you're not coming."

She met his gaze, but her brown eyes flashed and he understood that look of determination. Over the centuries, he'd known a lot of warriors, both male and female, and this was one of the many things that made no difference when it came to gender: pure stubbornness. Marguerite would have her way and she would go to the grave before she gave in.

He released a heavy sigh.

"This will be dangerous, Marguerite. I've never encountered shifting mist before—and exactly how well do you think I'll be able to do my job if I'm worried about your safety?"

She blinked a couple of times, and some of her belligerence dissipated. "I understand your dilemma," she said, "I really do, but I'm not just being capricious here. I'd prefer not to go. But I can sense that I need to be there."

Oh, great. She'd just given him the one reason that would force him to acquiesce. He hated this. And the thought that she could either be wounded or die made him jumpy as hell.

Okay, he did not have time to argue, and given her level of power he was obligated to respect her instincts. However, the thought that at any given time she'd be within a few yards of extremely powerful death vampires put a chunk of ice in his chest.

But he went with his gut. "You've seen the vision, you've seen where the action will be. If you can get to your old cell and stay there, with Grace, that would be best—that's where the Fourth ascender will be and he's not a fighter. If you can't, then place yourself in any of the outlying regions: the chapel, the sanctuary, the cellars, the dining hall. The shifting mist wasn't in any of those locations."

She lifted her chin and straightened her spine. "Understood."

It was so the right word for her to speak that he almost smiled. Instead, he murmured, "Thank you."

He waved his hand in a quick flash and folded on flight battle gear. Another wave and he folded his weapons harness on, a snug fit molded to his chest. He secured his *cadroen* then checked his daggers.

He brought his warrior phone from his Sedona house and thumbed.

"Jeannie, here, how may I help?"

He started in. "This is an emergency, Jeannie. I have a handful of minutes to orchestrate a protective operation within the Creator's Convent in Prescott Two. As quickly as possible, please fold Warriors Luken, Santiago, and Zacharius to Sister Quena's administrative office. Contact Colonel Seriffe and have him send squadrons to each of the Borderlands to replace these warriors until further notice."

"Very good."

Pause. He knew the question without needing her to voice it. "And please let Endelle know that I will be in contact with her during the next twenty-four hours and that Warrior Leto will be with me."

"Leto? I mean, yes, of course, I'll let her know. Anything else?"

"Yes, I'll be calling for cleanup, but we're dealing with a special kind of mist in this situation. Just stay tight."

"Got it. I'll get the boys now."

He thumbed his phone. He trusted Jeannie. She'd served as a liaison among all the warriors for centuries. She had exceptional telepathic abilities, which had been her primary tool for transmitting critical messages among the warriors prior to the twentieth century. However, she was a modern woman now and infinitely preferred the phone, the grid, and everything else electronic. If this job didn't get done, it wouldn't be her fault.

He slid his phone into the narrow slit at the waistband of his kilt and turned in a circle, surprised that Marguerite had left the room. "We need to go," he called out.

She folded in front of him. She now wore a flight suit in a deep red, almost burgundy color. "Where did you get that?"

"I contacted Brynna"—she tapped her head—"and she just sent it over. It bags a little around the ankles because the woman's an Amazon, but otherwise, I'm good."

He could see that she was.

"Let's go." He put a hand on Marguerite's shoulder and thought the thought. The trip through nether-space, an entire dimension, took a little longer, an extended blinking-out then sudden awareness as his feet touched down and he released her.

"What is the meaning of this?" Sister Quena glared at Thorne then Marguerite. But when she caught sight of the latter in a flight suit, her expression turned to a sneer.

How had Marguerite tolerated this woman's domination for all those decades?

Before Sister Quena could begin her tirade, however, he said, "Your Convent will be under death vampire attack in approximately four minutes. If you have a lockdown drill, implement it now, or many of your devotiates will die tonight. Your choice, Madame High Administrator."

Whatever else the woman might be, she was a ruler first.

She reached beneath her desk and clearly pressed a button because a split second later, bells rang shrilly and at sharp intervals, echoing from one end of the long building to the other. Beyond the door to her office, he could hear soft-padded running—but not a single spoken word or cry of alarm.

He glanced at Marguerite. She sent, *We had regular drills. No one will be the wiser as to what's really happening. Everyone will obey.*

He nodded. He despised the methods used to exact this kind of discipline, but in a moment like this one, he valued the result because lives would be spared.

The air shimmered and by long habit, even though he knew who was coming, he stepped away from Marguerite and folded his sword into his hand. He crouched.

Luken arrived first, sweating, blood-spattered. Bits of black feathers stuck to his arms. "Thorne," he murmured. His light blue eyes had a haunted look. *We need you,* came rushing into Thorne's head, followed by, *Sorry, boss. We're good.* He nodded several times, but he flashed his sword into his hand as well. "We under attack?"

"Yes. I've summoned Santiago and Zach."

"They're feuding."

"I know."

Nothing more was said.

Sister Quena stood tall and straight-backed behind her desk, very serious. She had a clicker in her hand and pointed it in the direction of a bank of monitors on the west wall. She clicked one after the other. Security cameras popped online. There were at least a dozen of them.

Thorne shifted his attention and his gaze moved briskly from one to the next. All the areas of the Convent were clear.

The air shimmered once more, on opposite sides of the room. Thorne dropped into yet another protective crouch, stepping between the closest shimmer and Marguerite. Luken matched his movements.

Zach and Santiago.

Thorne felt a sudden rush of emotion. He'd missed his men. He'd hated being away from the action, away from his responsibilities. Christ, he'd only been gone a week or two. Why did it feel like a century?

He shook off the sensation.

The newcomers didn't look at each other, but they were so fixed on Thorne that even if he hadn't known there was a problem, he'd have smelled it a mile away. Santiago and Zach were good friends, close friends. So what the hell?

But he didn't have time to ask the usual questions or even to knock their heads together.

He folded his sword away, drew the men in close, and explained that he'd have to do a quick, very painful mental download for any of this to work, that their friendly Fourth ascender had set up a shitfest on Leto's behalf, that yes, Leto was in the Convent, and that no doubt Greaves had orchestrated this little party.

"Madre de Dios," Santiago murmured. "Leto is here?"

"Yes, but in the vision he didn't look so good. I don't think he can fight."

"So he's finally giving up his spy gig?"

"Looks like it." Thorne glanced from one familiar face to the other. "You boys ready for this?"

Luken smiled. "Hell, yeah. Do it."

Thorne started with Luken, putting his hands on his face

and letting the images fly. Luken jerked and emitted a faint groan indicating the damn thing hurt, but he hung on. The download lasted fifteen seconds.

He did the same thing to Zach then to Santiago. When all three men were up to speed, he gave his commands in shorthand.

Sister Quena called out, "The monitors. What is happening?"

Thorne turned to glance from screen to screen. It was as though watery waves cloaked half of them. Through the waves, dark figures floated through. "It's started. Let's go."

He turned to Marguerite. "Do what you feel is best from minute to minute. I trust you."

She was white-faced but she nodded.

Grace turned in a circle. She didn't understand what had just happened. She was now alone. "Leto?"

But nothing returned to her except the low beautiful sounds of church bells.

"Hello, Grace. Don't be afraid. This won't last very long."

She turned around as a feeling like dread and excitement all jumbled together passed straight through her chest. She could sense the darkness in the stranger, but his voice did something to her, sent a vibration swirling in her lungs. She was so drawn to him she couldn't breathe.

He was recklessly handsome, with long curly black hair, well past his shoulders, and he had dark glittering eyes. He wasn't nearly as tall as Leto, closer to her height. He had a narrow attractive nose and full lips. His skin was very pale in contrast with his hair and eyes.

Death vampire? She didn't think so.

The vibration she had come to know, that was peculiar to her, rumbled beneath her. The stranger looked down at the stone floor and his brows rose.

She drew the power into her and stretched out a hand to him. He looked at her fingers and frowned. When the power reached him, he arched and his lips parted, but then he seemed to settle down even though he appeared to be in pain.

She could see inside him. He was dark and he was light, so very human, so very good and so very bad. He was a being torn apart by the choices of his life, and he had lived a long time, five millennia. She could sense these things but she couldn't read his memories, only the aftertaste of his decisions, the happiness, the decadence, the bounty of passion, and more often than not the guilt. In this, the stranger seemed very much like Leto.

She had a sense, however, of the man he could be, one full of great acts of kindness and of self-sacrifice. But right now he was a terrible cynic, the worst she had ever known.

"What is your name," she asked. "And where is Warrior Leto? What have you done with him?"

He approached her and she lowered her hand. She didn't fear him and yet part of her knew she should because the darkness in him was very dark. He wore very tight black leather pants and a silk shirt that caught the light in muted purples and green. The cuffs and collar were broad and the sleeves almost billowing. "My name is Casimir."

"I saw you in Moscow Two." He smelled of something spicy and something more, like mulled wine—like he would taste extraordinary on her tongue and for reasons she couldn't explain she wanted a taste.

He put his hands on her face and slid them deep into her hair. He didn't blink. "This isn't what I wanted," he said. The heavy bouquet of his wine scent buckled her knees.

She groaned and then his tongue was in her mouth, deep, so deep. He drove into her and then his body was pressed up against hers, moving in a fluid, snake-like motion, utterly sexual, reminiscent of her poetry.

Grace, he whispered through her mind. *I need you so badly, desperately. I need you to come with me, to come home with me and live with me, to be my wife and a mother to my two small boys. Say you will come.*

She wanted to. She felt that everything he had just asked of her was her destiny, her calling.

She drew back ready to tell him yes, but from deep within her mind she heard another voice, a woman's voice, one that had been as familiar as her own for the past hundred years.

Can you feel my presence, Grace? I'm here in the Convent. Thorne is here, too. You're in danger. I'm going to fold into your cell right now, so don't be frightened.

She pulled out of Casimir's arms.

Danger?

She glanced around her at a strange moving partition in the small cell. The mist that had created a division in the room, separating her from Leto, began to move. Casimir grabbed her and pulled her in the direction of the door.

Still no Leto. And no Marguerite.

Goddammit. Marguerite's voice was within her mind, as well as one of her favorite words. *Where are you? Are you still in the room?*

Once more, Grace felt the vibration at her feet and the power surged up through her body. *I'm near the door.*

But Casimir drew her against him and inhaled at her temple. "You smell of the earth and this power of yours is so erotic. Come with me."

She felt a movement of air next to her and Marguerite was suddenly there in a blood-red flight suit. She at first didn't know what to say, but it was Marguerite who turned to Casimir and said, "Why is it I hear church bells when you're around?"

"You can hear them?" Grace asked.

Marguerite nodded.

Grace glanced at Casimir. "So do I. And you're the source?"

Casimir shrugged, a slight lifting of his shoulders. "One of ascension's little jokes." She felt very confused by what was happening and even though Marguerite spoke of danger, that wasn't what she felt or intuited. Instead she continued to experience a pressing need to be with the dark vampire in front of her.

Grace shifted her attention to Marguerite. "What did you mean, I'm in danger?"

Marguerite's large brown eyes opened wide. "This asshole is here to destroy Leto, or didn't he tell you that? He's also here to take you away, to take you to Paris One, to live with him, to never see your friends or your brother again, or the Convent."

Grace turned to him. "Yes, he said as much. I feel drawn to you, a sense that I must be with you, but I can only go on one condition."

"I'm not fond of conditions. You should know that about me. I prefer to rule in my own small petty way. But tell me your condition."

"That Leto be allowed to live."

He laughed. "No. Non-negotiable, as is your coming with me or not. You will come with me and then *you will come with me, repeatedly.*" She'd been married. She didn't mistake his meaning. He continued, "You will learn to love your life and I already know some of your tenderness. I believe you will come to love my sons. They are very young and miss their mother, who died recently. As for all this repression"—he swept an arm to encompass the cell, most of which was still hidden behind the shifting swirling mist—"today, you will leave that behind as well."

"I will not go with you." She backed up. "Not if Leto dies." She felt torn, ripped apart inside. She felt drawn to this difficult man as much as she was drawn to Leto, as though both men were intended for her, as though somehow their fates were inextricably linked together. To lose one was to lose the other. Here was a great mystery.

He moved into her fast and put his arms around her. But Marguerite did the same thing from behind, her arms wrapped tightly around Grace's waist.

She felt Casimir's fourth dimension power. She felt herself begin to leave, to fold, right out of Marguerite's tight grasp.

But suddenly the vibration beneath her feet, that power that came from the earth, increased, flowing in a new, heavier wave up and up. At the same time, this earth-based power recognized Marguerite. That was the only way Grace could explain the meeting of Marguerite's power with her power. When the two touched, Casimir's attempt to fold her out

of the Convent ceased as well. Her feet landed back on the
stone and Casimir flew away from her, slamming against the
wood door of the cell. He looked down at his arms as though
they were burned. He was breathing hard, his dark eyes wide.

Then he stared at Grace and murmured "no" in a long
slow sweep of air.

She felt Marguerite shift to stand beside her. She met the
woman's surprised stare. "Did you feel that?"

Grace nodded.

"But what was it?"

Grace shook her head. "I'm not sure yet. It emerged yesterday for the first time and helped me bring Leto out of
Moscow. Greaves had discovered that Leto was a spy and
meant to have him killed. But . . . just now, while you were
touching me, the power grew stronger, as though it recognized you. Did you feel it?"

"Hell, yes, I did." She glanced at Casimir. "Surprise, asshole."

"Grace, you must listen to me," Casimir cried. She turned
to meet his eyes, which were almost wild. "You're obsidian
flame, the third leg of the triad. Now you must come with
me. I'm the only one who can protect you."

Grace shook her head. "Obsidian flame? I don't think so."
But even as the words left her mouth, from deep within she
felt the call, heard the whisper, *obsidian flame*.

Now she understood. Over the last few weeks, her wings
had changed from a predominantly light blue with a smat-
tering of black dots toward the base of each, to blue with a
black flame marking. Obsidian. Flame.

She said as much to Casimir, adding, "But Sister Quena
said it was the mark of the devil."

Casimir drew close once more, although this time he held
his hands up as if in surrender. "Grace, please listen to me.
Greaves intended for you to die today. He will not let obsidian flame stand. If you want to live, you must come with me."

In a very swift movement, he lifted his arm and before
she could protest, the mist shifted a third time, separating

her from Marguerite and forging a new barrier in a diagonal through the room. What choice did Grace have now?

She lifted her chin. "I will not go with you," she stated.

Casimir smiled. "I'm not exactly giving you a choice." He put his hand on her shoulder, and she half expected to feel herself whisked away from the Convent. Instead he leaned close and sniffed her skin right at her temple.

Shivers chased down her neck and over her shoulders. His spiced wine scent cascaded over her so that she breathed him in deeply. His lips, which were moist, ran in a line of slow kisses over her cheekbone heading toward her lips.

She couldn't help the desire she felt. Her mind was clogged with a heady aroma of mulled wine and her thoughts dissipated, spreading out and becoming very loose so that all she could think about was how heavenly his lips were. She began to turn her face into him and up so that with two more kisses, his lips were on hers.

Heaven.

Absolute heaven.

There are numerous detailed stories about the occasional, but rare, visitation of Third Earth entities to Second Society. The decoration of hair with long, narrow braids, studded with ceramic and glass beads, is a persistent theme within these anecdotes.

—*Treatise on Ascension*, Philippe Reynard

CHAPTER 12

Thorne rarely fought in such tight spaces, and he'd never fought when the mist could twist and turn so abruptly. He'd had his sword lifted high ready to strike down a pretty-boy; then the mist shifted and suddenly his sword met Luken's. His arm vibrated from the strike so badly that his bicep cramped.

Luken was one big motherfucker. He grinned as he said, "Sorry, boss, but looks like we're right on schedule."

At least it gave them a break, the ability to breathe for a minute, to wait. Thorne bent over at the waist and planted his hands on his knees. Damn, there were a lot of death vampires in this fucking hallway. Sweat poured from him.

But honest to God, the waiting was worse. Or maybe it was the lack of sound from anywhere else in this compacted battleground. Nor could he reach anyone telepathically. The mist had that effect as well.

He'd tried to reach the other warriors but nothing returned to him.

His arms and legs shook. He had so much battle adrenaline in his system that he could have puked. The only thing he knew was that the mist shifted when it shifted, and nothing could happen until it did.

He rose. "I was afraid I'd find death vamps inside the Convent cells, but I haven't, have you?"

Luken's mouth was a grim line. "No. I found one pounding on a locked door and laughing. He didn't giggle for long."

Thorne smiled. "No fucking doubt."

"You got that right." Luken had large light blue eyes, but his somewhat angelic appearance with his mass of long wavy blond hair was completely misguiding. The man was a massive killing machine with heavier, meatier muscle than any of the warriors. Luken had been the one, just a few weeks ago, to knock Thorne unconscious in Endelle's office when the *breh-hedden* had taken possession of Thorne's mental faculties. That was the exact moment he'd caught Marguerite's rose scent for the first time, an event that had coincided with her disappearance from Second Earth and the beginning of her bid for freedom.

Luken glanced up the hall then down. "If I remember the vision correctly, I should be on this side of the mist when it shifts. There will be three death vampires in this location"—he grinned at Thorne—"and two for you. After your little vacay, think you're up to it?"

Thorne laughed and as the mist shifted, he flipped him off. Luken grinned a little more.

Thorne turned and two death vampires were on him, long black hair gleaming, dark eyes glittering, and that pale almost bluish skin a beacon in the dimly lit Convent halls. They both came from his left.

He turned and, with his left hand, grabbed a dagger from his weapons harness. In a single smooth stroke he jammed it into the throat of the pretty-boy whose sword was high, inches away, and ready to cleave Thorne's head in two.

Thorne dropped and with preternatural speed rolled beneath the second death vamp, then thrust his sword up. He caught the second bastard in the gut. The momentum of both death vamps, one with a knife in his throat, one with his stomach slit open, forced them into a collision. They bounced off one wall and fell into a writhing heap.

Thorne did what he had to do.

He took the head of the pretty-boy he'd gutted. The other one, trapped beneath his buddy, stared up at him, the hilt bobbing as he tried to swallow or breathe or maybe both.

Thorne reached down and grabbed the dagger, pulling it out. Blood spurted with each thump of the bastard's heart. It wasn't long before his eyes glazed over.

Two more down. His tally was already at five. The vision had shown about thirty death vampires in all. Casimir wasn't taking any chances. Too bad he hadn't known that Marguerite would be able to reach pure vision.

He had half a minute or so before the mist shifted again. Sweat dripped down his face. He folded a cloth into his hand from his Sedona house, wiping his face then his knife. He slid the dagger back into its sheath on his weapons harness. He really hated this fourth dimension shit and all this silence.

He withdrew his phone from the pocket at his waist and thumbed. Ten seconds later Jeannie began her cleanup job. He couldn't imagine trying to battle on these stone floors, all slippery with pretty-boy blood—not to mention the sheer gymnastics it would take to circumvent these big bodies while trying to wield a sword.

"Close your peepers," Jeannie said.

He did. The light flashed. Thank God for Jeannie and the women at Central.

The mist would shift soon. He could feel it now, a very faint vibration in precise timing with Marguerite's vision. He dropped into a half crouch, his sword in both hands and upright.

But when the mist shifted again, he faced one huge-ass death vampire, bigger than any he'd ever seen on Second Earth. In the vision, the bastard had looked smaller. What the hell? He had to be at least as tall as Medichi, maybe even taller.

As he engaged the first sword-strike, however, he caught

the scent of rose. Shit, that meant Marguerite was somewhere nearby. Was she safe?

If he hadn't been battling for centuries, his worry for
his woman might have caused him to falter, but he wasn't a
Warrior of the Blood for nothing.

Leto sat on the edge of the bed, breathing hard, spots still
dancing in front of his eyes. What the fuck was going on?
Where was Grace? He had to get to her. But he couldn't hear
anything.

He stared at a wall of mist that kept shifting and changing its location in the cell. He'd never seen anything like this
before.

His stomach had started cramping again. He rose to his
feet, fighting the urge to vomit the whole time. Sweat poured
from him. He was shaking, but he wanted to be ready since
the mist would probably shift again.

He shuffled his feet apart to get his balance. "Grace," he
shouted.

All that returned to him was his voice in a series of
echoes. Casimir had to be behind this. No Second ascender
that he knew of, including Greaves or Endelle, had the power
to make mist that moved around.

"Grace," he called out again. His arms shook, but not
from weakness. This time, his need to get to her took control of him, even strengthened him. Some of the nausea
eased, and he found he could move.

He paced the cell, if slowly, and wiped his sleeve over his
forehead. Jesus, he still wore the wool from Moscow. He
shed it now, even though the cell was frigid. Grace lived in
the vilest of places.

Oh, God, he had to figure this out.

He stopped moving and drew in a deep breath. That's
when he caught her scent. The mist could do many things
but it couldn't keep her earthy wildflower scent from him.

He took another step forward, in the direction of the hallway, where the door would be on the other side of the mist.
The scent grew stronger.

She was there, near the door and not far from him.

He tried to reach through the mist but couldn't. It was as much a physical barrier as a shroud over the space between.

But one thing he knew to be true—the mist would move again. And when it did, he wanted to be as close to her as he could get.

Thorne?

He heard Marguerite's voice in his head like a sharp bell. He was surprised because though he couldn't communicate telepathically with any of his warriors, he could hear her. *Breh-hedden,* maybe?

He wanted to answer her but damn, he'd never seen such a big-ass death vampire in his entire fighting life. And the bastard had mad sword skills.

Little busy here, he finally managed between heavy grunts. *You okay?*

Yeah, I'm fine. I'm safe. Never mind, I'll figure this out.

The confines of the hallway and the physical barrier of the mist left little room to maneuver, to get in a killing strike. He'd seen the bastard in the vision, but yeah, he'd looked smaller, probably because he'd been alone and there hadn't been any other pretty-boys to compare him to.

The death vamp whirled, caught him with a fist against his chest, and slammed him against the way-too-solid mist. Thorne jumped back, crouched, sword upright. This asshole had to be six-eight and built like Luken. He'd been around a good long time. Besides the usual faint bluing of the skin, he also had darker blue markings in curves just in front of his ears. He wore braids to keep the hair out of his eyes.

"I've been waiting for this a long time," the vamp bellowed. He spun, raising his sword, and before Thorne could get in a thrust the bastard brought his sword down fast, preternaturally fast, almost as fast as Kerrick. Thorne blocked with his sword, but shit, what the hell was this?

His arm vibrated from the blow and his shoulder muscle seized, but like hell he was going down for this prick or any other death vamp. He grunted hard, spun and tried for an upper thrust, but the pretty-boy's sword was just there. And he wasn't even sweating. What the hell was he looking at?

He folded behind the pretty-boy, using one of his best spinning moves, but that asshole was again right there with him as he materialized and once more that sword-strike sang up his arm.

What the fuck?

The bastard's eyes glittered. "Something wrong, Warrior Thorne? You out of your depth here?"

"You're what's wrong, you stinking pile of blue shit."

Something deep within, however, whispered to him, some kind of preternatural intuition. Then he understood. He was looking at a Third Earth death vampire, something new in Greaves's arsenal—or maybe this was Casimir's idea.

It didn't fucking matter. Thorne was officially up shit creek. Right now, he needed more power, plain and simple, or he was going down. He might have stood a chance if the space hadn't been so tight, but the size of this mother-fucker, and the power he wielded, made movement all but impossible.

From deep within his mind, that same intuition moved and shifted about. What came to him in a blinding flash of awareness was that he needed Fiona and her obsidian flame power right now, the one she'd shared with Jean-Pierre more than once, the same one that Endelle had used to save all those people just a few weeks ago.

But how to get to her through all this fourth level mist?

Telepathy?

He moved backward, away from the blue prick, trying to give himself just a few extra seconds to figure this out. He wasn't able to reach his warriors telepathically. On the other hand, he could converse with Marguerite, but he had assumed that was a result of the *breh-hedden*.

What if it wasn't? What if somehow he was connected to her obsidian flame power? What if that was why telepathy worked between them?

Was it possible a simple telepathic message would reach Fiona?

He stopped debating the matter and sent a hard-driving piece of telepathy in a beeline straight at Fiona, holding her image as the bastard moved in on him.

The pretty-boy came at him hard and fast. Thorne sprinted, preternatural-style, doing a roll and coming up on his back only to barely block a heavy sword-swipe. He rolled and gained his feet, then sprinted back to where he'd begun.

Thorne, is that you?

Fiona, thank the Creator. Listen, I need your obsidian flame help now. Can you hook me up? I need to expand my sword speed fast.

There was a slight pause, then she said, *I'll have hell to pay with Jean-Pierre. He's a little possessive, as you know, but you got it.*

As he stood at the ready, crouched, his sword upright, his gaze glued to the death vamp's laughing eyes, he suddenly felt Fiona right beside him, her shoulder to his shoulder, her hip to his hip, then a kind of melding took place.

I'm right here, she sent. *Can you feel me?*

Yep.

Which power do you want me to enhance?

My sword-arm. I need a goddamn blur of speed.

Here ya go.

He felt the tingle, then the vibration all down his right arm. His muscles bunched in just the right way. He could feel the enhancement.

He blurred as fast as he could. He folded just two feet behind the Third asshole and caught him through the spine in a quick powerful thrust, faster than anything he'd ever done before.

And identified swords were fucking sharp.

The pretty-boy screamed and Thorne gave a hard jerk to the right, severing the spine, then withdrew. As the death vamp started to fall and as though time just about stopped, Thorne turned so that his shoulder squared up to the bastard. Without missing a beat, he continued making use of Fiona's channeling power and with incredible speed took the pretty-boy's head. It hit the stone with a thump, but the body landed on solid knees and wavered. Thorne shoved his foot against the asshole's back and the whole thick meaty body flopped forward.

Good.

He was breathing hard, sweat streaming. There was blood everywhere.

Thorne?

Yeah, Fiona. I'm here.

We good?

He smiled. *We're perfect. Thank you. But I want you to know, I owe you one. Just let Jean-Pierre know that I was battling a Third Earth death vampire.*

What?

Yes, you heard me right, which is why I called on you.

I guess Greaves has turned up the heat again.

Afraid so. You'll let your breh *know.*

Of course. There was a beat, just a short one, of silence, then a very quiet, *And Thorne?*

Yeah?

Come home soon. We need you.

He withheld a sigh. *I will.*

He felt her separate her channeling powers from him then depart. That was one fucking gift Fiona had, to combine forces like that. She'd saved Jean-Pierre more than once because of her ability. Now she'd just saved his ass. Obsidian flame had some goddamn righteous potential.

Could the other warriors call on Fiona? On Marguerite?

Fiona had been right to be worried about Jean-Pierre's reaction to her connecting with Thorne. Warriors didn't share their women . . . ever. So just how would he feel if all his brothers had access to Marguerite?

The dangerous vibration that lanced through his body was answer enough. Okay, there was a lot of shit to work out. But not right now.

He called Jeannie and once more closed his eyes for the powerful flash of light that would take dead bodies away and leave no trace behind. He thanked her and thumbed his phone.

But why was he able to communicate with the obsidian flame women, and not with his own men?

He didn't have time to contemplate the subject, since the mist shifted—and what do you know, three more blue assholes appeared in the newly created space. This time they were Second-ascender-sized, though, so he smiled.

Marguerite tried yet again to fold into another newly created space of mist that still kept her separated from Grace. She didn't understand why she was so limited when she'd been able to fold into the cell in the first place.

She was damn frustrated.

But even as she paced her small quadrant, jumping up on Grace's bed then hopping down, Fiona's familiar telepathic voice showed up deep within her mind. *Hey, sister, how's tricks?*

Something inside Marguerite relaxed. *It's great to hear your voice but what's going on?*

I just helped your man out and wondered if you were okay?

Sort of. I . . . we're at the Convent in the middle of a shit-storm. She explained everything in a few short sentences including the fact that Grace was their third leg of the triad.

Wow, but then she's Thorne's sister. In a way it kind of makes sense. That's one powerful gene pool.

The blah-blah was great but Marguerite's nerves were on fire. *I need to get to Grace but even though she's just a few feet away, I can't seem to fold to her. I think it might have something to do with this crazy-ass mist. Can you help me out?*

What if I tried to enhance your folding skills? Do you think that would do the trick?

Only one way to find out. Do it, obsiddy-sister.

She felt Fiona's presence first, matching up next to her shoulder then her hip. The channeling power just flowed. She felt it as the vibration that occurred right before doing a fold from one location to the next.

Fiona sent, *Just picture where you want to be.*

Grace came to mind. She focused. The vibration began and after a tiny blanking-out, she touched down behind Grace by barely a foot. But holy shit, Grace was in Casimir's arms and pressed so tightly against the Fourth ascender that the molecules between them had to be getting crushed.

Her mouth fell to the floor.

Fiona's voice intruded. *Everything okay? You went really still. What's going on?*

If I told you, you wouldn't believe it. Hell, I don't believe it. But listen, I'd better go. I'll fill you in later, okay?

Just tell me if Grace is okay?

She's fine. Really. I mean, she's definitely not in mortal danger.

Marguerite, I'd better go. Jean-Pierre just walked in and he looks as mad as fire. Oh, damn, I forgot. He's just experienced everything I just experienced.

Why would he be mad that you helped me out?

Not you. Thorne.

Oh, shit. No, your man's not gonna like that . . . at all. Bye.

The separation from Fiona was brisk and caused Marguerite to list sideways before she caught herself.

But as she stared at the subtle erotic sways and moves of Grace's body, she wondered what the hell she was supposed to do now.

Then the mist shifted. And though it didn't separate her from Grace again, it did bring a new problem.

It had taken another shift of mist before Leto finally had access to the space Grace inhabited.

But holy shit, the bastard had his arms around her, his tongue deep in her mouth, and dammit *his woman* was in a full state of arousal, her meadow scent flooding the room. He could hear each breath the Fourth ascender took, deep breaths through his nose as he kissed Grace, inhaling what belonged to Leto.

Without even being aware that he was thinking the thought, he found his sword suddenly in his hand.

The cramping was forgotten. The sweating. The nausea.

He saw crimson, a sheen of color over his eyes that pulsed with each rapid beat of his heart.

He lost his sense of hearing, but he could see. Everything began to move in slow motion as Grace turned toward him and mouthed something—something she must have said aloud but that still didn't reach his ears.

His gaze was fixed now on Casimir. The bastard turned slowly to meet his gaze, a smile slithering over his face.

Time resumed.

Casimir released Grace but he lifted his arm and threw a hand-blast that knocked Leto into the wall of mist.

Leto fell to the floor, his sword flying from his hand, bouncing off the mist and landing next to his foot. But he lifted his hand at the same moment and returned the hand-blast in full force.

Casimir looked surprised as he flew backward into the far stone wall of the cell. However, just as Leto gained his feet, Casimir righted himself.

"So the traitor has become a traitor," Casimir called out.

"Fuck you."

"Is that an offer? You're quite beautiful, Leto. I'd accept it wholeheartedly."

Leto began to sweat as the initial surge of adrenaline subsided. With a quick piece of levitation, he drew his sword into his hand and began moving slowly across the stone floor. Though some of his initial strength had waned, he still had enough juice to match Casimir. He lifted his left hand upright, palm-out, ready to fire off another blast.

"I don't want to fight you, Leto. You're weak. It wouldn't be fair."

"I'm not so weak that I couldn't take you right now."

"Oh, the words you speak to me." He put a melodramatic hand to his chest. "Yes, take me, please."

"Again, fuck you."

"Again, I'd be delighted."

"You're so full of shit." Leto moved fast.

Casimir moved forward, closing the distance in three

strides. He shoved his power straight at Leto's chest and blasted away. But Leto brought his sword down, which deflected the hand-blast energy. At the same time, he caught the tip of the blade against Casimir's arm, just a bite, but he sliced through the billowy sleeve and the blood flowed.

Casimir dropped to the stone floor, holding his arm. "This wasn't supposed to happen."

Leto moved in for the kill and lifted his sword high. Casimir lifted his hand once more, lowered his chin, and sneered. He wouldn't hold back this time and Leto was pretty sure this one would hurt, but like hell he was backing down.

However, a hand-blast from the side, from Marguerite, knocked the downward aim of Leto's sword, forcing the blade to fall harmlessly aside. Her second hand-blast, issued within a fraction of a second of the first, deflected Casimir's flow of power and shoved it in the direction of the bed Leto had been using. The blast hit the wall overhead and showered the bed and floor with a number of harmless silver sparks.

But the soldier in Leto went back to Casimir and lifted his sword once more.

Grace stepped in between and shook her head. "No, Leto. You must listen to Marguerite. She says he is not to die, that he has great purpose in the coming weeks."

Leto lowered his sword. He was breathing hard and his chest hurt. He blinked. Sweat stung his eyes. He shifted his gaze to Marguerite, who drew close to Grace. "What do you mean?"

She shrugged. "I don't know. It's something I've intuited for several weeks now. Strongly intuited. He must live."

But Leto shifted his gaze to Casimir, who still sat on the floor, holding his loose sliced-up sleeve over the wound. Blood pooled on the floor. Good, he'd cut him fairly deep.

Leto shook his head and addressed Marguerite once more. "He can't be trusted. He belongs to Greaves. He's allied with him."

Marguerite shrugged. "What can I say? I saw him in a

vision—not the particulars, just the sense that he plays a role on behalf of Endelle's faction in the coming months."

The nausea returned. Shit, he was dizzy all over again. But he glanced at Casimir and was appalled that the bastard was actually lifting the hem of Grace's gown. He heard him sniff.

Rage brought his strength returning and he lifted his sword once more, moving away from Grace. "What the fuck, Casimir? Both of these women are begging me to spare your life and you're deliberately taunting me? Come out from behind Grace's skirts and face me."

But Casimir leaned back so that now he sprawled on the dark stone floor, supporting himself on his elbows. His tight pants as well as his position left nothing to the imagination. "It doesn't matter to me whether I face you or face away from you. Both positions are equally pleasurable."

"You sonofabitch." He made a move toward Casimir, but Grace caught his free arm and her touch stilled him. He looked down at her, trembling all over again at her scent, her nearness.

"Enough, Leto. He must live."

"Yes, I must," Casimir said. "I scent her, Leto. You know what that means? I'm her *breh*."

"You fucking liar."

"But I scent her and if I've read Grace accurately, she scents me as well."

He glanced at Grace, ready to have her refute Casimir, but she didn't meet his gaze. Instead she stared at his chin, two spots of color on her cheeks. This couldn't be possible.

He turned to Casimir and narrowed his eyes. "You can't scent her. *I* scent her."

"Wildflowers and earth. A sweet spring meadow after a light rain."

Leto took a step backward. "This is not possible. She can't have two *brehs*."

Casimir grinned then looked Leto up and down. He even offered a sigh. "Looks like a ménage à trois made in heaven to me. I'm game and you've already offered to fuck me."

If Leto hadn't been feeling so damn weak, he would have jumped on the Fourth ascender and beaten him until that arrogant smirk could never return to his face, ascended healing or not.

But Grace suddenly left Leto's side. She dropped down beside Casimir and without a moment's hesitation folded a strip of clean fabric into her hand and began bandaging his arm.

Leto shook, not just with rage but with despair. What the hell did it mean that the woman meant for him was also scenting the bastard-from-hell?

Casimir didn't deserve Grace.

But that thought brought him up short since neither did he.

Neither did he.

Christ, what a fucking mess.

Casimir looked at the small white hands that bound his arm. He was charmed. Mesmerized and charmed. Her scent flowed into his nostrils and up into his brain until he was dizzy. He was aroused all over again as though he'd never understood arousal before. His desire for her trebled and he once more leaned close and sniffed. He couldn't get enough of her meadow, earth, and wildflower scent.

She tied the knot of the bandage and backed away from him. But he followed, caught her arm, and drew her wrist beneath his nose. He shuddered as he took in the fragrance of her skin.

"Stop it," she said, trying to pull away from him, but he held her fast. He pushed his own wrist beneath her nose. "Tell me what you smell so that I know I'm not imagining this."

He expected her to turn away, but instead she sniffed. He heard her sigh. "Like spicy mulled wine." She met his gaze, her beautiful gold-green eyes and pale lashes.

He nodded and smiled. "Intoxicating, isn't it?" He was pleased. Beyond words.

She shook her head. "I don't understand."

Leto dropped down behind Grace and put his arms around

her. She seemed to freeze at the intimacy. "You may not have her, Casimir. She is mine. *Mine*." The last word held such reverence that Grace gasped and leaned into him, reaching up to touch his cheek.

The woman was torn. This was not going to be simple.

Casimir's head spun, a dizzying sensation, like he was on a carnival ride that was moving too fast. He wanted to draw a sword into his own hand and take Leto's head here and now, but he had never learned the art and now regretted it. He wanted to do battle, but he'd never been a soldier. He made love, not war.

He heard a soft growling sound and realized it was coming from Leto and that Grace was leaning harder against him, her shoulder turned into his chest, her nose searching along his skin, her arm up around his neck. "You are the forest," she whispered.

Leto began to drag her backward across the cell.

Casimir started to follow and a new growling sound emerged, one that came from him this time. He couldn't allow this.

But a pair of legs covered in blood-red flight pants barred his way. He looked up, ready to sneer, but Marguerite held a wooden stool in her hand and it caught him on the forehead, spinning him to the side. He felt the cold stone floor as his face smacked against it.

Then nothing.

Marguerite turned toward Leto and Grace, who were now sitting against the far wall near Marguerite's old cot. She glanced left then right. The mist had disappeared. For the first time, she heard the sounds of battle outside in the hall, the grunts of men doing the work of war, the sliding rasp of steel against steel and the occasional cry or shriek when a blade found purchase.

But as her gaze returned to Grace and Leto, never would she have thought that her pious cellmate would have engaged with two men in the space of minutes. Perhaps there was more to Grace than she had ever imagined.

Leto's pallor had changed. For a few moments, while caught in a killing fervor, he'd almost regained a healthy look. Now he looked like a ghost.

Grace petted his cheek. She lifted her sleeve to wipe his forehead. "You're sick again."

He nodded, but caught her hand and kissed her fingers one after the other, over and over, perhaps trying to get rid of Casimir's scent.

Marguerite glanced back at Casimir. He'd already begun to stir. She tested her folding capacity with a quick thought. She felt the vibration but pulled back. *Thorne.*

You safe?

Yep. I've got Leto and Grace. I'm taking them back to Diallo's home.

Good. Looks like we're about done here. The mist has broken up.

Should have. I clobbered Casimir with a stool.

She heard him laugh. *That's my girl. And Santiago just got the last of these bastards. We'll do cleanup then see you in a few.*

Marguerite smiled. She loved that he'd just spoken to her as though she was one of his warriors. Damn righteous.

When Casimir moaned, she moved swiftly to Grace and Leto, put a hand on each, and thought the thought.

Once her feet touched down on the patio of Diallo's courtyard, and Grace and Leto were sitting at her feet in the same intimate embrace, she blocked her trace. There was only one problem: Leto now writhed in agony from the fold. If you were hurt or ill, a fold could be a real sonofabitch.

Thorne turned and looked up the hall. Santiago and Luken were headed his way. The mist was gone.

The other direction, Zacharius strode toward him, shoulders hunched, sword still in hand. He had thin streamers of blood in two stripes across his face. He'd lost his *cadroen* in the fighting, and his mass of thick curly black hair hung down around his shoulders and sides. Shit, his hair was long—at least to his waist now. Rumors were that he could make his hair move just with a pointed thought or two, but he denied it. Thorne sure as hell hadn't seen anything like that.

"All clear," he called out. Zach had a deep booming voice and large dark blue eyes.

He turned back to the two others. Luken had his phone to his ear. "Aw, Jeannie, you kill me." He even smiled. "Another time. Let's get this war wrapped up and then maybe I'll do it." He thumbed his phone, still smiling. The women at Central were the bomb, always had been, always would be.

Luken tipped his chin at Thorne and said, "She wants to set me up with her cousin."

Thorne laughed. Jeannie had been trying to set each of the warriors up with her cousin since the beginning of time.

He glanced from one warrior to the next. God, he missed this. No question, he needed to get back.

He was about to say something to that effect when Luken whipped his warrior phone from the slit pocket of his battle kilt. "Yeah, Jeannie." His expression grew somber. After a few seconds, he said, "We're on our way."

He turned to Zach. "We've got twelve death vamps at the Superstitions."

"Holy shit."

"Get out there, get me some blue skin."

Zach nodded, lifted his hand and vanished.

To Santiago, Luken said, "We've got another eight at the downtown Borderland. Gideon and his crew are barely holding on."

"On it, *jefe*." Another blink of the eye and he was gone.

The word stung. Santiago had always called Thorne *jefe*. But for now, that job belonged to Luken.

Luken turned and met his gaze straight-on. "Sorry, boss. I should have let you—"

"No, you shouldn't have."

"It's just that you've been gone and then you sent Alison that message to have me take over."

Thorne clapped him on the shoulder. "You did good. The job suits you."

Luken thumbed his phone then put it away. He smiled. "I'll happily give it up the second you come back. Which will be—?"

Thorne shifted his gaze to the cold stone walls of the Convent hallway. When would that be?

Now that Leto was coming in from the cold . . .

He shifted his gaze back to Luken. "I'm thinking tomorrow, but I'll let Jeannie know for sure."

"Tomorrow." The usual smile turned to a grin. Luken lifted his arm. "If you don't, I'm coming for you." He flipped Thorne off then vanished.

Thorne drew in a deep breath. He headed to Sister Quena's office to give a report and to make sure that none of her devotiates were harmed.

After that, time to deal with Leto.

Forgiving oneself for committing the most heinous of crimes,
Requires endless prayer and atoning deeds.
Even then, may the Creator have mercy on your soul.

—*Collected Proverbs,* Beatrice of Fourth

CHAPTER 13

Thorne paced beside the hospital bed inside the colony's infirmary. He still wore battle gear, and his heavy sandals sounded like thunder on the hardwood floor.

Much he cared since Leto looked like shit. His eyes were squeezed shut and his breathing shallow. He was so damn pale. Just how close to death was he? But then he was essentially a death vampire, so maybe this would be normal during the withdrawal process.

The vampire warrior was old in ascended terms. Thorne had known Leto from the first day of his ascension. He had fought beside him all those centuries ago. Leto had been one of them, a brother-in-arms for millennia, having ascended in 1201 BC and having served as a Warrior of the Blood most of that time, a good thousand-years-plus before Thorne's ascension.

Thorne had looked on him as a mentor given his age, his power, his general sense of fair-mindedness. His defection, so close to the time that Patience had died and Grace had gone into the Convent, had deepened Thorne's grief. He'd gotten drunk with Leto, laughed at his jokes, ignored his bad moods, scoffed at his professions of bedroom prowess, all the usual.

But as he paused at the bottom of the bed, stunned by Grace's tenderness toward Leto, he knew only one thing: He didn't want Leto to die. He wanted him to live, to have a real life in a world without war, to settle down with a woman, maybe even Grace, to father a dozen children, to see them grow up into decent vampire ascenders, for Christ's sake.

Which begged the question—even if Leto survived, what would Second Earth give him? More battling as a Warrior of the Blood? More death and destruction?

Thorne's chest swelled first with anger, then with purpose. He wanted more for all his men, a chance at life, a good life, but how the hell would that ever be possible given the current state of things, given the current administrator's inadequacies?

A faint hiss and arching of Leto's neck, a tightening of his features, forced Thorne to settle the hell down. Getting pissed about things right now wasn't going to help this situation. Leto was in deep shit on several levels.

From Thorne's conversations with Endelle, he knew that James, from the Council of Sixth Earth, had convinced Leto over a century ago about the necessity of serving as a spy on their behalf. They had needed him to provide the Council with an ongoing record of Greaves's war efforts. To what purpose, though, who the hell knew, because to his knowledge the Council hadn't acted once to relieve Second Earth of the burden that had become Darian Greaves.

Did this Council understand what they'd put Leto through?

Leto had been the finest of warriors. A fine, elevated grain ran through his temperament. He was smart and he'd studied throughout the centuries: philosophy, science, all the religions. And like any good warrior, he despised death vampires.

Did the Council understand what it had cost Leto to partake of dying blood?

Thorne understood. They'd ruined him. Even he could see that Leto's will to live had shrunk to the size of a tick's ass, and guilt was sinking him into the grave.

Now he was here, having been rescued by Grace straight off a massive spectacle platform in Moscow Two.

Thorne glanced at Grace. She sat beside the bed in an aura of calm, dabbing at Leto's forehead with a damp cloth. Her unoccupied hand rested on top of Leto's and he already knew the truth. The goddamn *breh-hedden* had found its next pair of victims, this time with a kicker. According to Marguerite, Grace was also scenting that bastard, Casimir.

Sweet Jesus, how had this become Grace's lot? Or Leto's? What kind of misery did this portend for his devoted sister, the spiritual one in his family?

Marguerite's voice rippled through his mind. *You have to help him.* Marguerite stood away from the foot of the bed. He turned toward her but shook his head. He didn't know what he should do.

Marguerite, however, widened her eyes pointedly then jerked her head in Grace's direction. Thorne thought he understood but he didn't want this for Grace, not the *breh-hedden* with Leto, or any other Warrior of the Blood.

He ignored his woman and turned to stare at Leto some more.

"Thorne," Leto called to him, but his voice had a pinched quality.

Thorne moved to the right side of the bed, opposite Grace. "I'm here."

"There are things I must tell you. About the . . . army . . ." But his body seized up on him. He grimaced, and it looked as though every muscle, in every limb, had decided to contract at exactly the same moment.

Shit.

The man couldn't even open his eyes. He glanced at Grace but she shook her head. She then pressed her eyes closed for a long moment, maybe tossing up a quick prayer, then opened them. He always forgot how pale her lashes were above her green-gold eyes. She met his gaze. "He's dying, Thorne. My blood will revive him, at least for a time, but he refuses to drink from me. Will you order him? Please?"

Thorne's chest tightened. His gaze shifted to Leto. That familiar brotherly affection rushed over him, for the man who had battled beside him century after century. Leto couldn't die, no matter what terrible things he'd done during his time with the enemy.

That big thing stirred inside him again, and a powerful intuition rose up strong and sure. Leto was critical to the terrible events soon to unfold—and his destiny was linked with Grace's. Together they had work to accomplish.

He gave himself a shake. All fine and dandy, but how on earth was Leto to survive a permanent withdrawal from dying blood?

And to have him drink from Grace? It seemed like an abomination. Grace deserved better. Grace deserved someone pure, someone not associated with the war, someone who wasn't a goddamn death vampire.

"I am not his commanding officer," Thorne said.

Marguerite moved up beside him and nudged him. He turned and looked down at her, meeting her scoffing gaze. "What?"

"Don't be an ass. Leto's guilt is holding him hostage right now and we need him here. Even I can tell that he will obey you if you say the word and that's not because I just had a special vision." She did air quotes and rolled her eyes. "Issue the goddamn order."

Shit. Fuck. Well, this was one thing Marguerite had always been able to do: clarify the situation.

"Fine." He leaned over Leto's face and said, "Take my sister's fucking blood, you sonofabitch. We need you alive, not dead. Try to look at it this way: The creator has a good goddamn reason for pairing you with my Grace. As in maybe, just maybe, you need to stick around to save her life. I won't be able to do it, not with the load on my shoulders."

Leto's eyes opened, just a slit. He lifted his left hand and Thorne grabbed it, holding tight. Leto's lips almost curved as he said, "You were always . . . such a prick."

Thorne chuckled. "Well, at least that's something we agree on. Now drink. Just wait till we can clear you some privacy." He took a deep breath. "Will you do that, Leto? Please?"

Leto searched his eyes and his fingers tightened on Thorne's. After a long moment, he nodded.

"Good. Good." Thorne's eyes burned, dammit.

Movement near the door caught his attention. He shifted his gaze and saw that Diallo was waiting for him. Thorne had asked to see him for a few minutes so Diallo had folded in from the sister-colony in Florida One. He looked back at Leto. "We need you, brother. Marguerite's right. I can feel it as well. We need you here. And we'll talk tomorrow, okay?"

Leto nodded.

Thorne released his hand.

He turned to Grace. "Will you be staying with him?" The moment he spoke the words, however, he knew the question was unnecessary. He understood her spirit and he could see her resolve. In fact, her chin almost looked mulish, tilted up as it was.

She nodded. He rounded the bed and put his arm around her shoulders. Shit, that earlier burning had put a wet sheen over his eyes. He squeezed, and she leaned her forehead against his shoulder. She stayed in that position for a few seconds.

After a moment, he met her gaze and sent, *Are you all right?*

Again, she nodded. "Don't worry. I'm very much at peace. This is my path." She put her fist against her chest.

Thorne cursed under his breath. Goddamn the Convent. That bitch, Sister Quena, would have taught *submission* above all things, but it was just so that she could wield her spiritual hammer over the devotiates.

You have choices here, Grace.

But at that, she lifted her chin a little more. "I know the difference between when to fight and when to relinquish control. I do know the difference."

He released her and took a step back. Her voice held resonance, even vehemence. Did he really know his sister? But then for the past hundred years he'd only seen her, only related to her, in the Convent setting. Now here she was, staring him down. "Fine," he said at last. "Understood."

Grace straightened her shoulders. "There's one more thing you should know."

He inclined his head but all he could think was, *Oh, God, what now?*

Grace took a deep breath, which lifted his blood pressure another notch. "It would seem I'm . . . obsidian flame, the blue variety, though I don't know yet what that means."

Thorne blinked. He couldn't have heard her right. Grace was the third member of the obsidian flame triad? How was this possible? He glanced at Marguerite, but she inclined her head.

Leto turned in Grace's direction and tried to rise up on his elbows, but failed. When he landed against the pillow, he said, "You're . . . obsidian flame?"

"I am. And the power I possess, which is what brought you out of Moscow Two, seems to come from the earth. I'm not sure of the implications." Here she glanced at Marguerite, then back to Leto. "In fact, I have no idea what this is or what it will mean for the future." She shifted her gaze back to Thorne. "Casimir made it clear that Greaves will want to destroy obsidian flame above all things. Both of you need to be prepared for that."

"Grace," Thorne whispered. He could sense it was true but he felt suddenly very sad. "I would not have wished this on you."

Grace tilted her head. "But it is on me and I'm welcoming this new power. I don't fear it. I have been praying for a very long time to be of use to my world, and now perhaps I can be. Do not pity me. There is nothing here to feel bad about."

All Thorne could do was nod several times in a row. He didn't trust himself to speak. He was way too angry about everything right now. That his beloved sister had essentially just been dragged into the front lines of the war started splitting something inside him very wide. The only thing that held him together was the fact that she seemed to *desire* what had come upon her.

Fine.

What-the-fuck-ever.

One last glance at Leto. "I'll bring Endelle by tomorrow. You'd better still be alive."

Another faint smile touched Leto's lips. *You know,* he sent, *you look like you could chew nails right now. Or spit fire.*

A familiar, leading comment.

In former centuries, Leto would have offered a remark like that, Thorne would have responded, then Leto would have perhaps asked a pointed question and drawn him out, part of all that *mentor* bullshit.

But those were former times and though Thorne might have at one time sought counsel from Leto it was not something he could do now. And it wasn't just that a hundred years had passed with Leto serving the monster of Second Earth. No, something was changing within Thorne's heart. Right now the only counsel he trusted was his own.

He turned to Marguerite and held out his hand. She was still at the foot of the bed. She stared at his hand and lifted a brow.

"Are you gonna give me trouble, too?" he asked.

"Hell, yes," she responded, but she rounded the bed and put her palm in his.

Thorne turned away from Leto's bed and shifted to put his arm around Marguerite's waist as together they crossed the room.

He had to let the situation go. Grace was right: There were times you just had to relinquish control. That Grace was now linked with Leto made this one of those times. This was her path, not his. His path, on the other hand, was running *her* thumb up and down his palm and working him up. Her rose scent was increasing, too, which meant she had something very specific on her mind. Given all that had happened, and all that he had just learned, the idea of taking Marguerite to bed really appealed to him.

When he reached the doorway where Diallo waited, the leader of the rogue colony turned into the foyer, let them walk past, then closed the door to the infirmary behind them.

Thorne was grateful. The last thing he needed to see or hear was his sister offering up her blood to Leto. He shuddered at the thought of it.

"Thank you for returning to speak with me," Thorne said.

"Of course. You would not have summoned me for a trifling reason and I promise you, Warrior Thorne, I will always do my best to come when called. That is my promise to you."

His words held a kind of weight that Thorne didn't quite get. But it was clear that Diallo trusted him, which was a good thing.

In short order, Thorne explained the events of the last few hours. He spoke of the battle, the shifting mist, the involvement of a Fourth ascender, and Brynna's role in helping Marguerite to achieve pure vision.

Despite the fact that he left out the very significant point about Marguerite coming fully into her obsidian power, Diallo turned toward her then met and held her gaze. "Your power has expanded significantly since I last saw you. I can sense it in you."

"Yes, my obsidian flame power."

"You are necessary, Seer Marguerite, in ways you do not understand yet, but I don't believe it is your ability to reach pure vision that Second Earth needs from you."

"How strange that you would say that when all my life I've been dogged for my Seer skills."

"Which means no one has seen your true gift."

"Which is?"

But Diallo smiled. "Your temper, of course."

"What the hell does that mean?"

Diallo shook his head. "One day, you'll understand." He turned toward Thorne. "In the meantime, I can't stay here for very long." He tapped his forehead. "I have a terrible gnat in here, in the form of one of the council's elders. We were having a wonderful argument when I got your summons and the dear man wants me back." He laughed as he spoke, a good-humored way to tell Thorne to get on with things.

"Unless you are opposed to the idea, I want to bring Endelle here in the morning, and I'd like for you to be here. She will need to speak with Leto, to figure out how to protect him, and he's ready to talk. But she also needs to be made aware of these hidden colonies." So far, Thorne knew of two others beyond the Seattle Colony, one outside of Portland and of course one in Florida, near Lake City.

Diallo nodded. "We've been debating the situation all night. Ultimately, however, we know that our choices became exceedingly limited the moment those death vampires breached our mist."

Thorne couldn't agree more. "Would it be better if I brought Endelle to you now?"

But Diallo placed a hand on his shoulder, and he felt a sudden familiar soothing flow of warmth. Alison had the same ability, to give ease and comfort with a touch. "I would advise both you and Marguerite to take your rest now. I've strengthened my mist against intruders—although if your Jeannie at Central needs to fold anyone to this location, it won't be a problem, your discretion of course. And if even one death vampire succeeds in getting through our mist again, alarms will sound this time and give you warning.

"Please, make use of my home. I will meet you there tomorrow. How does ten sound?"

"Good. That's good."

Diallo glanced in the direction of the door to Leto's current room. "If you like, we can create a second protective mist around the infirmary, if that would ease your mind about your brother warrior and about your sister."

"Absolutely." Thorne released a very deep sigh. He was more worried about the situation than even he realized.

Diallo extended his hand toward the front door. "If you'll come outside with me, I'll show you the mist technique in

case you ever need to use it. I believe both your powers are
strong enough to make use of it at will."

"Is it that simple?"

Diallo smiled. "Yes, I believe it is."

Thorne brought Marguerite forward to precede him from
the building. Once outside, he turned toward the smallish
cabin-like structure. Diallo stood next to Marguerite and
lifted his foot for both of them to see.

His rope sandal disappeared, folded somewhere.

Diallo then placed his foot in the dirt. "The trick to this
kind of mist is a connection to the earth. And the Pacific
Northwest is such a damp part of the world that the trees
often have moss growing on their northern faces. Picture
any tree in the vicinity then fold some of that moss into your
hand. You won't need much."

Thorne focused on a tree, and with a little mental scrap-
ing took moss from near the base and folded it into his hand.
He held the moss palm-up. Marguerite did the same.

"Marguerite, touch my arm. Thorne, touch her arm. We'll
form a chain and you'll be able to feel and resonate with a
like vibration."

Diallo was a man of action and he simply began the process. Thorne had created mist before, thousands of times,
but he had no idea whether Marguerite had or not.

But as the vibration passed through her to Thorne, he
watched her smile as she held up her arm, the moss pinched
between her fingers. All three of them began sending the
lace-like filaments, only now shrouded with a green tinge of
moss, toward the dwelling until it was completely covered.
Each of their mists, however, had a different quality, and the
end result, though powerful, wasn't exactly elegant.

Diallo laughed. "I'm not sure if I love it or hate it."

Marguerite laughed as well.

Thorne just shook his head. He could feel the power of
the mist and knew in his heart of hearts that if Grace and
Leto weren't safe beneath this protective shroud, they
wouldn't be safe anywhere.

He turned and offered his hand to Diallo. "Thank you for the mist. I'll sleep easier tonight. And thank you for the lesson. I have no doubt I'll be making use of this technique in the future."

"You can retrieve this moss from any point in the world with just a thought. And I have found that for some reason the moss from these fir trees works best, but you might want to conduct your own experiments."

Thorne smiled. "Hard to find this quality of moss in the desert."

Diallo laughed. "I suppose not. Well, I must away. Good night." He bowed slightly, lifted his right arm, and vanished.

Thorne suggested that he fold Marguerite to Diallo's courtyard. She agreed, sliding her arm around his waist.

He felt the vibration and the slight blanking-out, but as he touched down in Diallo's living room, he had a thought, a rather perfect one that he knew would please Marguerite. He glanced down at his battle-weary kilt and the blood spatters on his arms and legs.

Yeah, he needed to get cleaned up but there was something else as well, another powerful need that had to be tended before he could relax.

He squeezed her waist and said, "I forgot something, but I'll be back in about ten minutes."

Since she looked ready to argue with him, he chucked her chin, lifted his arm, and took off.

Grace stared into the most beautiful blue eyes that had ever existed in the entire course of mankind, clear and piercing, even though in this moment Leto was doused with pain. His lips were parted. "I don't want this for you."

She nodded. "Leto, it's all right." She glanced down the length of the bed. He filled it top-to-bottom. Even though from the time she could remember, Thorne had been warrior-sized and she was used to all the height and breadth, she often marveled at just how big these men were. "Maybe I could lie down next to you while we do this?"

"That would be . . . nice."

With great effort, he pushed himself to the opposite side of the bed. He was beneath a sheet and a soft wool blanket. He lifted the blanket and she crept beneath so that his very naked body was separated from hers only by the sheet. And her gown.

He pulled the blanket over her.

"Oh," she whispered, "it's so warm. I'm never this warm, at least not in winter or early spring. Or the fall for that matter. Summer was always nice, though."

"That building . . . was damn cold. Like Moscow Two."

She felt herself relax as she hadn't relaxed in a long time, despite all that had just happened. He slipped his arm around her so that she settled her head on his shoulder, but she drew back so that she could look at him. She also needed the angle to present her wrist again, but he pushed it away and turned into her, shifting to look at her neck.

When she realized what he wanted, that he wanted her primary vein, her whole body rolled and arched, which in turn brought a soft hiss from between his lips as his forest scent suddenly drenched the space. Oh, God, this couldn't be happening to her, that all her poetry was descending on her like a warm wave of the most erotic water, flowing over her, enticing her to do the forbidden.

She wanted to pull away from him and to offer her arm, to *insist* on her wrist or even the deep vein at her elbow, but she couldn't, especially since she was having trouble breathing into the depths of her lungs.

Grace, he sent. *Rest on top of me. Let me take you from your throat, just this once.*

She stared into his eyes and her breath caught in a series of desperate hitches—and then her body completely betrayed her. She rolled onto him. Through the sheet she could feel the strength and bulk of his warrior's body.

And that he was fully aroused.

She pulled her long hair over her shoulder to hang down her back. She lifted up and presented her throat. His lips settled on her skin as he enveloped her in his arms. She shifted

several different ways to make sure she was comfortable so
that once he started, he'd be able to keep drinking.

But the closeness and all the movement was very arousing.

"You smell of the sweet earth."

"And you, of the forest."

Oh . . . God.

He had enough strength to slide his hand over her nape
and hold her steady. He licked her neck in long slow sweeps
until her vein rose, which didn't take but a few seconds. The
next moment his fangs struck to just the right depth.

She cried out, not in pain. The sensation was exquisite.
She couldn't help what happened next as she spread her
legs and settled herself on the hard curve of his muscular
upper thigh. Her right hip was pressed up against his erection.

As he drank, desire for him spiked. She couldn't but roll
into him, taking pleasure on his leg. That she could feel how
hard he was at the same time as his erection slid up and
down her hip also kept her moving. She'd kept herself pure
for so long.

But the feel of his mouth on her skin, of his fangs buried
in her neck, of her blood leaving her body and flowing into
his mouth, of all her strength strengthening him—all this
worked like an aphrodisiac.

Her mind became a loose wandering thing and his body
the hardness she needed. Her hips moved faster and his thigh
rose in response, pushing back against her, increasing her
pleasure. He held his hand tight against her nape in order to
keep his fangs fixed into her throat.

He was groaning now. His free arm rubbed up and down
her back then his fingers were suddenly stroking her wing-
locks. Oh, God, she'd forgotten how good that could feel.

Leto. Leto. She had been married. She knew a man's body,
but should she touch him? Really touch him?

Leto.

*I'm here. Let it go. Let it all go. Let it happen. I'm right
here.*

He was giving her such pleasure. She smoothed her hand along the sheet and found his hip.

He groaned and sucked harder. She found the stiff length of him and rubbed up and down, pressing him into her hip on the other side as she moved.

Oh, God, Grace. I'm going to come. If you keep doing that, I'll come.

She didn't stop and his voice in her head and the suction on her neck took her to the brink as he sent, *I want my mouth on you.*

The thought of Leto taking her down low sent her flying over the edge. *I'm coming.* She moved hard against his rubbing thigh. She came and came and came as she rubbed his arousal faster. She felt his cock jerk as he began to release. His body arched suddenly and his fangs slid from her neck and he groaned long and loud at the ceiling.

She continued stroking him until his body finally quieted and he fell back against the bed. She followed, her legs still spread over his thigh, her body achy now and very tender. Her breathing began to ease. She rested on his chest, savoring the feel of his breaths, in and out.

Grace, thank you. That was . . . beautiful.

Yes, it was. But she felt greedy. She wanted more, so much more. Would he be able to go the distance with her? She wasn't sure any man could.

She drew back, planting her hands on the pillow behind his head, careful not to catch his long hair in the press of her palms. She looked into his eyes. Who was this man, really? She knew that her path was bound to his in some mysterious, extraordinary way, just as she knew she was also bound to Casimir. But what could the end possibly be?

His color had returned and he had her blood on his mouth.

His arms were still around her and he was caressing her very slowly up and down her back to her waist. She didn't know what possessed her but she wanted to taste her blood on him, she wanted to know what she tasted like.

She touched her lips to his but his scent interfered so that though she could taste a slight metallic flavor, her perceptions got completely lost in the smell of the forest that emanated from him, from his skin, even from his breath. When he parted his lips, she slid her tongue down the center of his and he groaned again.

She kissed him for a long time, then drew back. She shook her head. "Leto, why did you refuse my blood earlier?" Though she was pretty sure she already knew why, she needed to hear him say it.

His lips parted as though he meant to tell her, but he closed his mouth and sighed. His gaze shifted off to the right and he petted her hair in a long slow sweep that traveled over her shoulder and down her arm. "I've done terrible things in the name of my mission. I don't think, after all that I've done against Endelle's administration, that I'll be able to survive what's coming next. I don't even think I should. You need to know that, even though the *breh-hedden* seems to have snagged us."

"I was committed to the Convent, but I'm not sure I want to go back. I don't know. Tonight seems to have changed everything."

"Maybe it has, but never mind." He pulled her against his chest, and the air swooshed from her lungs. "Let's just get some rest. I suspect the next few days are going to be a bit rough."

Grace wasn't an idiot. Leto had been one of Greaves's right-hand men for a century. He was famous for his betrayal of Endelle.

There would be retribution.

Leto knew too much.

"What did you do for Greaves?"

He sighed in one heavy release of air. "I built and trained his army."

Oh, God.

Marguerite was fresh from the shower and wearing a simple long red cotton gown with thin straps. She leaned over the

side of the waterfall and let the cool stream of water run
through her fingers.

She was changed, she could feel it, she just wasn't sure in
what way.

She'd made a big decision tonight, to allow the communal
effort toward pure vision. Because of it, Leto and Grace were
safe beneath an awkward shroud of combined mossy mist.

It was a particularly strange experience to not only be
caught by the *breh-hedden* but see others struck down as
well. Grace had barely been aware of anyone in the room
but Leto, and when he could finally summon the strength to
open his eyes, they always seemed to turn toward her first.

She knew that feeling well: the need to ascertain the exact
location of *the other*, as though somehow her life depended
on it.

And yet, as she searched her heart, it didn't take long to
find that part of her that longed for wide-open spaces, for
infinite choices, for self-direction.

She sighed. She had never felt more sobered in her life,
more weighty within her soul, at all that had happened, from
communing with Brynna, to being in the middle of the battle
at the Creator's Convent, to getting Leto and Grace away
from Casimir and safely to the colony.

She shook her head and slapped at the water. She was supposed to be driving her stolen convertible up the eastern sea-
board right now, looking for bars with lots and lots of Harleys
stacked up outside, music blaring, and eating Buffalo wings.

She'd give anything to hear some Gaga right now and
bury her face in some hot wings and ranch sauce. Maybe it
was the battling, but she was hungry. Her stomach rumbled.
She really hadn't eaten very much lately, either.

She also had an itch and her heart was pounding. Would
Thorne never get back from wherever the hell he'd gone?
She needed a man and she needed him now, the same way
she'd been feeling for three weeks, like her hormones had
jumped into overdrive permanently.

She sniffed and rose. She was smelling cherry tobacco,

which made her very happy, but there was something else and then she groaned.

She turned around and Thorne stood there grinning at her. He held a foil-covered platter in one hand and two beers in the other. "Hungry?" He also wore jeans and a loose nubby blue cotton sweater that made his shoulders look about ten feet wide. He'd cleaned up for her.

But it was the second scent hitting the air that made her stomach rumble. First things first. "Starving. Is that what I think it is?"

He laughed. "I've been trailing you around so I know what you like. Here ya go."

"Wings," she cooed. "I am so in love with you." She meant it playfully, but his expression softened and her heart went all mushy.

Shit.

But he laughed. "Don't look so distressed. Come eat. Whatever you're feeling right now, this will make it better. Besides, at least half of these are for me. No. At least two-thirds."

He set the wings down on the table, along with two Dos Equis, plates, and a stack of napkins about two inches thick.

She forgot about all her musings as well as her need of Thorne. "I've never been so hungry," she cried. She settled herself in her chair, leaned forward, and dug in.

Thorne was right with her. Neither of them spoke for a good long while, until the bottles were empty and red oily sauce dripped down his chin. She laughed and wiped it off. He returned the favor.

"Is it always this way? Are you starving like this when you've spent the night battling?"

He met her gaze and smiled, but his eyes were lit with something other than laughter. The garden lights flickered over his face. He looked almost young in that moment. "Actually," he said, his rough voice sending a few shivers straight down her spine, between her wing-locks, "there was only one thing I wanted when I was done battling."

She knew exactly what he meant because she'd wake up

long before dawn, every single morning, waiting for him to show up beside her bed.

She reached over to him and ran a thumb over his lips. With a jerk of his chin, he caught her thumb with his lips and drew it into his mouth. Then he sucked. She hadn't been expecting that and a new shiver began at the point of contact, shot up her arm, and flowed over the rest of her body.

She suddenly lost all interest in the wings. Besides, all she could smell was Thorne's tobacco scent now, and since he seemed to be enjoying nursing on her thumb that scent only sharpened, flooding the cool night air.

Her gaze never left his and even though she wasn't in his mind, she could read it. She left her seat and climbed onto his lap and replaced her thumb with her tongue until she was plunging into his mouth and his hands were caressing her ass.

I need you, she sent.

I need you, too.

Are we alone in the house?

Oh, yeah.

Good.

I didn't know
The heights of love
Until my beloved
Took me in the air.

—*Collected Proverbs,* Beatrice of Fourth

CHAPTER 14

Marguerite slid off his lap, stood up, and took both his hands in hers. "Come with me." She had something very specific in mind and she hoped he'd be game. Of course, she couldn't remember when he'd ever said no to her, but then they'd never had so much room before. And this would be *big*. Her Convent cell, on the other hand, had been *small*.

He didn't say anything. He just smiled and rose to his feet. She dropped one of his hands and pulled him deeper into the garden near the waterfall. There was a white chaise-longue there, almost love-seat-sized, which meant it was big enough for a warrior.

He started to take her in his arms, but she planted a hand on his chest and said, "Would you mind if we did this my way for starters?"

His brows rose. "You want to take charge?"

"Yes."

A low growl formed in his throat until the airspace around her vibrated.

"I take that as a yes?"

He nodded.

She glanced at the chaise. "This probably won't make

much sense at all, but I'd like you to get good and naked then lie down for me, on your back."

He grinned. "Sweetheart, that makes perfect sense."

She liked him. God help her, she liked him so much.

He thought the thought, his sweater and jeans disappeared, and in that athletic warrior way of his, he stretched out, all his golden skin on the white of the cloth. He was almost fully aroused, which meant that her breath caught in her throat and for a moment she forgot what she meant to do.

"You like what you see?"

Her gaze drifted back up his abs and chest to settle once more on his face. *Oh, yeah.*

Good. Aloud, he said, "Okay, so . . . what do you want me to do."

She nodded slowly. "I want you to pop the *cadroen*. I need your hair free. I need my hands in it."

He reached behind his head, moving slowly, which had the wonderful effect of flexing a whole lot of muscles up and down his arms and across his pecs. Even his abs tensed.

But his hair was still wet. "You showered? When did you have time?"

He chuckled. "I'm fast. And I have connections."

"You mean you had Jeannie order the wings."

"Well, yeah. Had to get back to you. Now, what did you have in mind?"

A knee came up. His cock moved.

Oh, God.

Yet even as she looked down at his beautiful nakedness, even as anxious as she was to start tasting all this maleness, her vision of him began to alter, swirling through her mind. He seemed to be shrouded in an iridescent light, like something out of Mount Olympus. Even his wings had shifted to a beautiful silvery white shade.

And there was power. A lot of power. As well as a sense that destiny was moving through him in a new way, a commanding way, altering his life and his path.

That she was part of his path seemed to be a given, seemed preordained.

She had gone with him to the Convent, returning to a place she hated, because she'd believed she was necessary, and so she had been. She had kept Leto from killing Casimir. She had kept Casimir from taking Grace to his lair.

She was necessary.

She closed her eyes and lifted her face skyward. She held her hands out, palms-up, and the future was simply there: Thorne was on a promontory, and she was beside him. This was new, having the future arrive like this, without even picking up a ribbon of light. Her heart swelled as she looked at him, his long hair swept away from his face and flowing behind him. He looked different, made new, stronger as he stared toward the horizon. The western sun cast a fiery glow over his face.

How much she loved him.

She felt pressure on her fingers, and the vision dissipated. She opened her eyes and looked down. Thorne had hold of her hand.

He shook his head. "Not now," he said. "You may look into the future later. Now belongs to me."

With these words, the silvery white light around her god-like man also faded away. She blinked. What remained was the ache in her chest because she did love Thorne, so very much, despite her drive to be free. He was a silvery white light that lived in her heart.

The breath she drew was ragged and it took her a few more seconds to shake off the effects of the vision and to come back to this moment with him. It helped, of course, that his body was laid out before her.

As her gaze roved him once more, she slid the straps off the long, red gown, letting the whole thing fall all the way to the pavers. She was barefoot and she'd gone commando.

He didn't say anything but his gaze drifted over her breasts, down her abdomen, and low to the juncture of her thighs. He sighed, and the air once more grew spicy with his male tobacco scent as he leaned back on the chaise once more. Her legs quivered and she couldn't exactly breathe. Cherry tobacco had a sweet scent, something she had always enjoyed smelling, and now here it was combined with Thorne.

He started to rise up again, but she lifted a hand and shook her head. He eased back down.

Had she ever really seen this man before?

She approached the side of the chaise and smoothed her hand over the thick pads of his pecs, to the well-defined abs and the strong lines of his lower abdomen. His cock reached his navel. She drifted her fingers down his thick stalk, then over his legs, which had a fine dusting of hair.

She climbed onto the chaise next to him so that she was on her knees. She put her hand on his upper left thigh and stroked down to his ankle. His shinbone was sharp, his muscles lean and toughened from battle.

She moved back up the other leg.

So this was Thorne, the man who had made love to her for a century in the confines of that small, dark, pathetic cell. She glided her hand up the heavy muscles of his thigh, using her fingers to define each one. She leaned down and kissed his left thigh and licked him, up and up.

But when she reached his groin, she pulled back and looked at him, at his strong erection and at the heavy sack that made him all man. He was breathing heavily. She wanted to take him in her mouth, but she needed more from right now, even though she didn't quite understand why.

She felt so different with him tonight. She felt in some mysterious way that she was seeing him for the first time. He wasn't just her early-morning, after-battle lay. He was Thorne. *Thorne.* Leader of the Warriors of the Blood and her *breh,* her bonded mate.

And she needed him tonight as she hadn't needed him before. He was the anchor that had first helped her keep the vision at bay then who had pierced and released her obsidian flame power.

She put her hands on his abs, leaned up, and pressed.

He flexed for her so that she was pushing against a hard plane of muscle.

She met his gaze. *You're so strong.*

He nodded. His eyes had a strange expression, a kind of glow. He looked right now the way he often did in front of his troops, fully in command even though he lay beneath her hands.

She pushed upward until she had her hands over his pecs and his nipples. He flexed these for her as well and she squeezed, her fingertips digging in just a little. She glided her hand up around his neck and stroked the veins on each side.

Her mouth watered. She wanted so much tonight. God help her, she wanted everything.

When she reached his mouth, she didn't use her fingers, she slid to stretch out over him and kissed him as she dipped her left hand beneath his nape, deep into his damp hair.

His tongue pushed back until he entered her and rhythmically drove into her mouth. She eased her body down onto him until the tip of him touched all her wetness and readiness.

He groaned, his arms surrounding her and caressing her, his fingers gliding down her back.

Your wing-locks are soaked.

The minute he said the words, she knew what she wanted. She lifted up and met his gaze. "I want you to enter me and then I want to mount my wings. We could never do that in the Convent and I always wanted to. I wanted to be in flight when you came."

His body tightened head-to-foot as his cock found her opening and he pushed inside her. He held her in a powerful embrace as his fingers played over her wing-locks until she was crying out.

"You're thickening," he said, rocking into her slowly, drawing back, pushing in again.

"Yes." She could hardly breathe. Pleasure gripped her down low and her back was almost spasming.

He dipped to reach her ear and split his resonance, whispering, *"Just let them go. There's enough room on this chaise and with the surrounding plants. You can mount your wings. Just let them go."*

His presence deep in the well of her body, and the hard

erection along with his slow thrusts, kept her right on the cusp. Oh, what would this feel like to mount her wings while he was inside her. Oh. God.

She breathed hard focusing on her wing-locks. At the convent, all the devotiates were encouraged to mount their wings once a week, just for overall health. But wing-mounting was always done in private. Each time, she'd been wild with desire, and she often fantasized what it would be like if she was joined to Thorne while it happened.

Now the time had come and he was with her, so with her. She was almost hyperventilating as she held on to the moment. And then, as he pumped into her, a little faster now, they came, a swift glide, an intense pleasure that had her arching away from him. She screamed as her wings released into full-mount. She would have flown away had he not secured her with his hands around her waist, pinning her against him and holding his cock firmly in place.

Still, he pumped into her. He knew her body so well.

Still, the pleasure came.

Once more, she cried out.

He pumped hard and fast now, bringing her close to the brink again. She arched and screamed into the night air, her hips rocking and meeting his thrusts. She came and came. She gripped his arms, holding on tightly because her wings were enormous and all the movement had set them to wafting, trying to take her into the air.

Thorne groaned. "Oh, God, Marguerite. You're so tight."

She met his gaze. "Can you hold on? Can you get into position, still inside me, and mount your wings? I want you to feel this. We could never do this in the Convent and I wanted to. Oh, God, Thorne, I wanted to so much and I want you to have this experience right now." She was gasping for air.

"I need something more, first. Something to give me strength." When his gaze fell to her throat, she gave a cry and put her vein against his mouth. He sucked and licked so hard she nearly came again. She slung her arms around his neck.

Do it.

He struck and her blood began to flow.

That did it. Her body tugged on him, the size of him working her internal muscles so that this next set of orgasms was better than the first, more intense, sharper. He held her hard against his mouth so that her hips were free to pump.

Oh, God, Marguerite, you feel so good. Your blood is a rose fire down my throat. When her body had sort of calmed down, he shifted so that he sat on the edge of the lounge and she wrapped her legs around his waist.

Thorne didn't know how he was lasting. Of course two millennia of practice helped, but damn, sex had never been like this between them. The more of her blood he drank, the more the muscles all along his shoulders and down his arms tightened and strengthened. This, however, was the same, that her blood gave him strength. No other woman's blood had ever powered him. But hers did, and maybe she was helping him last.

The events of the past few hours had changed Marguerite. He could feel it in his bones and he approved. Some threshold had been crossed, some terrible barrier busted open. She was more present with him than she'd ever been.

Would she stay? Well, that was the question, but not one that would be answered right away.

He released her throat and drew back. He smoothed her short white-blond hair with his hands and kissed her.

Her wings were exquisite, a beautiful black with a red flame marking, one of the telltale signs of obsidian flame. And with each thrust of his hips as she straddled him, the wings moved a beautiful rhythm that pulled her away, which only added to the tight inner sensation between them.

He kissed her again, but this time her tongue was in his mouth, swirling around his. She had a small feminine tongue. *Mount your wings, Thorne.*

He groaned. The thought of releasing as she had released, of maybe even taking her up into the air, caused him to shudder. He kissed her more deeply, thrusting his tongue into her this time.

She groaned as he kissed her.

Hold on to me, he sent. He moved to the edge of the chaise. *Wrap your legs around tight because we're going to take off.*

She locked her ankles around his waist and her arms tight around his neck, keeping her seated against his groin.

You ready? I'm going to stand up.

She pulled back and looked at him. "I want this."

"Me, too."

Her wings were so beautiful, so big. The wafting moved all the plants around her in gentle waves.

He stood up with her.

She held on.

His back was wet. He could feel the wing-locks dripping. He could also feel how swollen all the tissue of his back was. He closed his eyes and as he pumped into her, rocking his hips slowly, he just let it happen.

He arched forward as the wings flew. The sensation, connected as he was down low to Marguerite, with her body stroking him as she rocked her hips against him, was unbelievable.

Hold on. Oh, God.

He arched a little more and she stayed with him, tightening her legs around him. His lower back tightened and he started to come. He heard his own shouting, as in some distant realm, because his mind was clogged with the intensity of the orgasm.

At the same time, his feet pushed off from the pavers, his wings flapped, and he rose into the air, his arms low around Marguerite's waist. The pleasure continued to streak the length of his cock. He knew they had begun to move in a slow spiral upward and he cast a net of mist around them.

"Thorne, I'm going to come again."

He held her ass tight and thrust in and out of her, a real trick in flight. She was so wet; the glide was like heaven. He had never done this before, never taken flight while making love. The sensation was unnerving and thrilling. Her blood had strengthened his body so much that he felt himself readying again.

His body trembled with so much adrenaline. They'd reached the upper limbs of some of the courtyard trees. "Pop into parachute-mount. I'll do the same."

She nodded and reshaped her wings, as did he, so that just at roofline level and in the canopy of several of the broad-leafed courtyard trees, he held her gaze and once more began to pump.

Marguerite didn't know it could be like this. She kept one arm hooked around his neck so that she could use her free hand and slide her fingers through his hair. She kissed him lightly and when pleasure began to build, she kept that tender pressure on his lips.

You're close again, she sent.

Yes. And you're so tight.

Take me, Thorne.

He groaned once more and while suspended in the air and using his wings to create a reactive pressure in order to hold them both steady, he used all his warrior strength and drove into her with tremendous force so that she orgasmed hard, her lips pressed to his.

She was breathing in fits and starts and her legs trembled. She really wasn't used to so much exertion and some of her muscles were screaming, especially her butt muscles and arms.

"I need to retract my wings," she said. By now, even her arms shook.

He smiled and said, "Bring your wings into close-mount and I'll get us down from here."

She looked down at the courtyard. The view was beautiful, especially through the leaves of the upper canopies of the various trees.

She pulled her wings in and within three seconds, like a fast, smooth elevator ride, he stood flat-footed on the pavers. Her legs were still locked around him as he kissed her, only now he supported her fully with both hands so that her muscles calmed down.

She felt so warm and fuzzy, unusual sensations for her. She could almost get used to this.

"I don't want to let you go."

She kissed him again, then buried her head into his shoulder and just held him. She let the tips of her fingers graze the feathers that were now in close-mount, the wings pressed up against his body. They were a light gray color, and honestly looked really great against her black-and-red wings. But she recalled her vision of him with silvery white wings and she wondered where all this was headed. What was happening to them both that she would have such a vision, that she would now be in this community of Seers, and that she'd actually achieved pure vision?

"I'm going to bring my wings in," he said right against her ear. She nodded into his shoulder and watched as he spread his wings straight out to the sides in the full-mount position. She felt his body vibrate and shudder as the structure narrowed to incredibly fine points and flew back into his body.

This was one of the great mysteries of Second Earth and of flight: that an ascended body could create and release such magnificence at will.

But her body was now trembling with fatigue. Without saying anything, Thorne drew back, pulling out of her. She eased down his body until her bare feet were on the rough pavers.

When she slid her arms from around his neck, he said, "Now let's get you to bed."

"It's been a long day."

"Yeah, it has."

She sighed and before she knew what he meant to do, he scooped her up and carried her in the direction of their white bedroom. There were times when having a warrior for a boyfriend was just plain awesome.

The following dawn, Thorne had his warrior phone to his ear, his arm around Marguerite and he was still in bed. God, a man could get used to this.

She was naked, a small warm body pressed up next to his. She faced him, her fingers sifting through the hair between his pecs. She kept sighing and each time she did, he smiled because he could feel her contentment.

He'd never had this kind of time with her at the Convent— half an hour at the most.

Luken came on the line. "Hey, boss. If I make slurping noises, Havily just showed up with her usual Starbucks run." Havily tried to do this every dawn for the warriors, when they finished their nightly battling at the Borderlands. She'd meet them at the Cave and bring sustenance. Suddenly, Havily's voice was just there, "We miss you, Thorne. When you coming home?"

Again he smiled. They were a solid group and when the pieces were missing, any of them, well, days felt like years. "Tell Hav we're headed back sometime today."

Luken shared the information and Havily squealed. "Is this true, boss?"

"Yep. Time to come home."

"Good. And Gideon's here. Duncan as well."

"The Militia Warrior Section Leaders?"

"Yep, Jean-Pierre thinks it would be good to include them since they have their squads battling now more and more."

Thorne drew a deep breath. He didn't want to ask the question, but he had to. "We lose any Militia Warriors last night?"

"Nope."

"Good." The sudden tightness in his chest eased.

"Yeah, Jean-Pierre's doing some hot-shit stuff with the Thunder God Warriors. You should see it. He's been able to bring more of their powers online and he does some kind of sensory download so that the warriors are doing better. A lot better."

He knew Jean-Pierre had ramped up his game. Ever since he'd completed the *breh-hedden* with Fiona, his ability to guide some of the more powerful Militia Warriors into greater powers had really expanded. This seemed to be true of the *breh-hedden* process: Once it was completed, both partners were stronger in power and capacity.

He hugged Marguerite and she responded by rolling her body against his, a kind of full-body hug.

Where the hell was all this going?

But he was missing the front-line action, so yeah, time to head back. "Sorry I was gone so long," he said.

"I got a good look at you last night. Your eyes look better. I think you needed this time away. But come home. I'm about ready to kill two of your warriors, if you get my drift."

"I do. Either Carla or Endelle will be in touch to let you know what's doin'."

"Got it."

"Get some rest."

He debated the next phone call. He released a sigh. He should just call Endelle, tell her what was doing, but dammit, he couldn't. He had a feeling the moment she got him on the line she'd give vent to her rage—that he'd taken off, that he'd blocked her mind-link, that he'd been incommunicado for three weeks—and the truth was, he didn't trust himself. If she so much as sniped at him about a hangnail, he had a feeling he would let loose with a thunderbolt of lightning.

He understood then that he was angry in a way he still didn't get.

With that knowledge, instead of opening up the mind-link to Endelle, or even using his interdimensional phone and giving her a shout, he did the only thing that made sense.

He called Carla. She was one of two women that he and the Warriors of the Blood generally dealt with at Central. There were others, but for the most part Carla and Jeannie were it. Carla had the day shift.

He thumbed his warrior phone and Carla came on the line. Because he wasn't exactly in the mood for small talk, and because Carla had the ability to sense his temper, she received without a single comment his instructions to call Endelle, to inform her of the hidden colony, and to have her fold to Diallo's home for a meeting at ten o'clock.

"Got it," Carla said. "Later."

He released a breath. He loved the women at Central for being able to read him.

He thumbed his phone then folded it back to his night-stand in his Sedona Two house. Unless he was battling for the night, Sedona was the only place he kept it. In the past he'd sent way too many of these specialized phones to Murphy's Laundry on Central. Soap, water, and electronics just didn't mix.

He leaned his head back down on the pillow wondering what the hell to do about the scorpion queen. For one of the few times in his life, he really was at a loss.

Marguerite sighed again. She couldn't help it. She didn't know what to think about all that was going on and it was really bugging her. Did she love this, lying in bed with Thorne, stretched out next to him? Uh, yeah.

She'd awakened to his mouth on her breast about half an hour ago, he'd brought her to a quick, roaring climax, and now she lying in his arms, her right nipple wonderfully sore, and wondering what the hell she was doing.

She wasn't discontent, exactly. She was just antsy, like she'd been for the last few decades in the Convent. She wondered if Thorne would ever understand.

Was she prepared to leave? To let him start bonking women at the Blood and Bite? By all his descriptions of that joint it was exactly the kind of place she would have frequented, often.

But what did it say about her, what deep flaw did it reflect, that she could have this bounty in bed next to her, this absolute perfection of masculine beauty and power, and she was still wishing for the Blood and Bite and a tumble in the red velvet booths?

She finally released another sigh, pulled out of his arms, then rolled to sit up on the edge of the bed. Only her toes touched the dark wood floor, the bed being on the tall side. The room was cool, but not cold like the Convent.

She fluffed her hair and made her way to the bathroom. Diallo had provided toothbrushes so she brushed vigorously, rinsed, spit, and tried to ignore a very sudden desire to be back in her convertible. Freedom called to her, a seemingly infinite voice, and she responded with every fiber of her being.

But why did she still long to leave? And would she always feel this way?

Last night had been amazing with Thorne, in the garden, sex in flight, connected through it all and experiencing such amazing orgasms. When her wings had mounted, she'd almost spun off into the stratosphere from the intense pleasure of the experience.

She wanted to do it again.

She wanted to do it again with Thorne.

And maybe that was what bugged her so much. She'd barely started to live. She'd only been out of her own personal hellhole for three weeks and a couple of days. How could she even think about settling down?

When she rinsed for the last time and rose up, her resident god-like warrior stood in the doorway, leaning sideways into the doorjamb and looking like he was holding up the entire house. "Do you have to be so goddamn handsome? It would help a lot if you looked like a troll."

He laughed. "What's got your ovaries in a twist?"

She lifted a brow. "My ovaries in a twist?"

"Well, I could hardly say your nuts. Come on, spill it."

Her shoulders dipped. "I don't know. I should be content, but I'm not. What the hell is wrong with me?" She waved a hand to encompass him from head to foot. "I mean, look at you. Even Brynna and Jane were practically ready to bear your children when they saw you practicing sword-thrusts with Arthur."

"They were, huh?"

"Oh, don't get cute on me."

"Okay. Fine." He brushed past her and walked into the shower, a nice big shower. He completely ignored her and turned the jets on, all seven of them, plus the rain-head.

She moved so she could watch him and he put on one helluva show as he turned in a slow circle, his face into the spray, eyes closed. Fit. Ripped. Handsome. Perfect. Thorne. Her lover. Her *breh*.

And oh, God, she loved him so much. This she would admit to herself. She ached for him.

Shit.

She opened the glass door and stepped inside. She pushed his soapy hands away from his chest and stepped up against him, wrapping her arms around him.

"Hey, I'm showering here."

"Just hold me, asshole."

"You're such a romantic." But he chuckled, then moved his wonderful massive arms and wrapped her up. "I take it you're struggling with being close to me."

"Yep."

"No worries."

"Nope. You are not allowed to say that. You are not allowed to be a nice guy."

She felt him sigh but he kissed the top of her head. Wisely, he kept his trap shut.

Endelle sat at her desk in her executive offices at her administrative building in Metro Phoenix Two, not far from South Mountain. She stared at her laptop icons but didn't touch the keyboard. She was just a little too upset. Okay, a lot upset. Her nostrils had been belching proverbial fire for the past three weeks and right now the air smelled of smoke.

Carla had just called and informed her that *His Majesty* was inviting her to a meeting, at ten o'clock, to a previously unknown rogue Mortal Earth colony that had apparently existed for three thousand years without detection.

And no, Thorne hadn't told her these things. Carla had. *Carla.*

Thorne apparently couldn't be bothered. No request, no by-your-leave, no *I'm fucking sorry for having abandoned you for the past several weeks and for blocking our mind-link communication and for walking out on my duties as the leader of the Warriors of the Blood.* No fucking nothing.

She leaned back in her chair trying to calm the hell down but failing.

Luken had just left. He'd reported to her about the night's

incidents, about the battle at the Convent in Prescott Two the night before. The fight was still on between Zach and Santiago. If Thorne had been here, he would have knocked their heads together by now. But no, Thorne just couldn't be bothered. He was chasing Marguerite around, that gifted Seer with obsidian flame power, who also couldn't be fucking bothered.

She reached for a coffee that Luken had brought her and she knocked it over. Goddammit.

The mess went everywhere and she hadn't even been able to call on her vampire speed and keep the thing from spilling.

Well, she had other ways to take care of this.

She mentally shoved the door to her office open and called out, "Alison, get your ass in here and bring one of those tea towels with you. Now."

Alison appeared in the hallway from her office and folded a tea towel into her hand. Her brow was slightly puckered as she moved up the hall.

Endelle sat tapping her marble desk and watched the blonde beauty walk toward her.

When Alison reached the doorway, she asked, "What do you need the tea towel for?"

Endelle tipped her head in the direction of her desk. Some of the coffee had reached the edge and was dripping over the side.

Alison lifted a brow. She didn't miss a beat, though. She walked up to the desk and started patting the lake until the tea towel was stained and sopping. Her mannerisms were dramatic, almost theatrical, because of course Endelle could have just *thought* the entire mess away.

The towel disappeared and Alison brought another dry one into her hands. She worked with increasingly exaggerated movements until Endelle was about ready to explode.

"Would you stop that?"

Alison sent the final towel away, probably to her laundry room in that mansion she and Kerrick now lived in together. She moved to stand directly opposite Endelle. "Would you please tell me what's wrong instead of ordering me to do ridiculous things? What the hell happened? Did you finally talk to Thorne?"

At that, instead of rage firing a missile through the top of Endelle's head as usual, her throat closed up so tight she could barely breathe. She shook her head. "No. Carla called, though." Her voice sounded like she'd squished it to the size of a pea.

Alison dropped to her knees in front of the desk, which meant she met Endelle's gaze straight on. That was the thing about Alison. She met you where you were and right now Endelle couldn't even stand up. She just sat in her goddamn chair trying like hell even to swallow.

"So you haven't spoken to Thorne, not once, since he left."

She shook her head. "He blocked the mind-link."

"I know. So what did Carla want?"

"To tell me that *His Majesty* wants me to fold to some strange hidden Mortal Earth rogue colony and that afterward he's coming back here but for who the fuck knows for how long. Leto's there. His sister Grace, as well." But Alison would know all this—Luken would have told all the warriors this morning.

"Leto is in serious danger then."

"Luken said he's near death unless Grace feeds him."

"You're kidding."

"He's a goddamn fucking death vampire, or didn't you know that? When Greaves turned him, he really turned him. No half measures with that bastard." She put her hands over her face. She didn't know what was happening to her. She was so not herself.

"Endelle, look at me. Talk to me. Why does Thorne want you to come to the colony?"

She let her hands fly apart. "How the hell should I know?"

"Why do you think?"

She shrugged. "To talk to Leto, I guess."

"Okay, that's good. No doubt Leto has a lot of things he needs to say to you and to Thorne, and Thorne wants you there. He hasn't cut you out of his life. He's just headed down a different path because of the *breh-hedden*. He'll come back to you eventually. Give him time. And space."

"Space? You want me to give him *space*? How about I walk away from the war? How about *I need some space,* so I go on a jaunt, find some NBA superstar to match my height and my proclivities, and I follow him around for a few weeks. I'll call it the *breh-hedden* so it won't matter because it's my fucking destiny. It won't matter that I have duties every night to go into the darkening and follow that bastard Greaves around to keep him from sending more death vampires to the Borderlands. Hell no. Yeah, Alison, that's what I'm going to do. I need space so I'm going to take some space."

Alison rose to her feet. There was too damn much compassion on her face as she said, "You're feeling lost because he's gone."

"Oh . . . fuck you!"

But Alison wasn't impressed. "So what are you going to do about it?"

"Well, for starters, I'm headed to Mortal Earth."

"Okay. And in the meantime, I'm going to plan a welcome-home party tonight for Thorne."

"Oh, well, let's at least do that. Let's reward Thorne for his fucking bad behavior."

"You know, I have to say, Endelle, you almost sound like you're whining. And as my boss once told me, there's no whining in ascension."

"Oh, shut the fuck up."

When facing the dragon,
Try not to lose your temper.

—*Collected Proverbs*, Beatrice of Fourth

CHAPTER 15

At a quarter to ten, Thorne opened the door to Leto and Grace. His sister was calm, but he could feel the tension in the air. Leto, still very pale, had a determined jut to his chin, which probably meant he'd come to some decision Grace didn't like.

Leto's planning to take off as soon as he talks to Endelle and to the Warriors of the Blood.

Thorne met her gaze and nodded. He tried to imagine what he would do in Leto's shoes. Yeah, he'd probably take off. The guilt alone must be killing him.

From the direction of the kitchen, he heard Marguerite. "Where the hell are the coffee filters?"

Leto laughed, a good sound. Thorne glanced at him and smiled. "That's my woman." In a louder voice, he called out, "Honey, we've got company."

Marguerite ran in from the right, the direction of the kitchen. She had on cherry-red socks and slid on the smooth wood floor on purpose. What an entrance. She also wore black leather head-to-toe and his whole body suddenly lit up.

"Hey, Grace, Leto," she said, smiling. "Sorry about the

greeting." She glanced at Grace. "I'm trying to get a pot of coffee together. Come help." She waved her forward.

Without waiting for a response from any of them, she took off on a run to slide her way back into the kitchen.

Diallo's house was expansive to say the least. Grace followed after, the loosely woven Convent gown dragging slightly behind her.

Thorne ushered Leto into the living room. Leto moved on slow feet. He crossed to the windows to once more take in the view. Even though the forest held Diallo's house in shadow, the valley below was flooded with morning light, revealing a whole string of small farms.

Leto drew up next to him and crossed his arms over his chest. "This is a nice place. Very peaceful. And you say Endelle has no idea these colonies exist?"

"Not to my knowledge, and she would have said something. She's not much into withholding information of any kind."

At that, Leto actually chuckled. "No. She's not."

Thorne glanced at him. "You must know that Grace communicated to me what's up, that you plan to leave. Permanently."

"Of course."

Thorne looked back over the idyllic landscape. In the distance, he watched a couple of preteen boys practicing their flight skills, flying up to the roofline of the house then gliding to a grassy slope along the side of the house. He'd done that when he'd first mounted his wings. It helped to use stationary objects as a point of grounding while learning to manipulate all those back muscles and to get a feel for how the wind currents affect the wings one second to the next.

"You do know that I've been AWOL for the past few weeks. I basically deserted my post."

"I have to admit I found it impossible to believe, but now I understand. This is about Marguerite, isn't it?"

"Yep." He frowned and turned toward Leto a little. "What do you make of it—the *breh-hedden*, I mean."

Leto shook his head. "Completely fucked up. If I ever find out someone is behind this kind of fated matchmaking, I'll kill him . . . or her."

"But you're not going to be around." Maybe he shouldn't have said it like that.

The haunted look came back. "You're right. I'm not."

At that moment he felt a movement of air and turned to see the shimmering. He whipped to face whoever it was and with the conditioned response of centuries folded his sword into his hand. Leto did the same.

In tandem, both men sent their swords back to weapon lockers.

Diallo put up his hands and smiled. "Sorry. I should have called first, given a warning." He glanced behind him. "Oh, good, I smell coffee. The elder in charge of the Lake City colony only serves tea. We've been up most of the night, arguing, and I want some java."

Diallo's arrival made Thorne suddenly and acutely aware that Endelle would be coming soon. He wasn't sure he was ready to face her, especially since he wasn't exactly feeling remorseful about leaving. If anything, he was just pissed off.

Another shimmering, and she was just there, facing away from him. He was grateful for the moment, because she wore a halter covered in small seashells. Her skirt was a strange collection of strips of something, seaweed maybe, the rubbery kind. Jesus, he couldn't quite tell.

But it was the smell of the ocean that struck him, and not in a good way. The seaweed was a little ripe. She turned around and his gaze flew up. She wore a starfish like the front-piece of a crown, which was sort of pretty against her mass of black curly hair.

"Poseidon," Diallo said. But he took a step or two back.

Thorne took another sniff and couldn't stop from moving away from her a foot or so. Leto as well.

She rolled her eyes, touched the seaweed, and the next moment it was gone, replaced by a short electric blue mini skirt, in leather of course. "It needs to dry." Her gaze settled on Thorne. "So where the fuck have you been?"

"Making sure my *breh* was safe."

Her mouth worked. She was mad and somehow her anger served to increase his own irritation.

"You could have said something to me, given me a warning."

"And what would you have told me?" The words came out really fast, with a little steam attached.

"You're going to get pissy with me? You do know that I could have you arrested, jailed, and thrown at COPASS's fucked-up maw for this little stunt? You know that, right?"

But Thorne didn't answer because the top of his head was about to come off.

Fortunately, movement from the kitchen distracted him. Grace emerged bearing a tray with some kind of pastries, napkins, a sugar bowl and creamer. Marguerite followed carrying a heavier load of six large coffee cups, probably filled to the brim. He glanced down and smiled. She still wore her red socks.

Endelle turned around. The shells on her halter, each one apparently hanging free, clattered. Not a bad sound, it was just weird but what else was new? She was the Supreme High Administrator of Second Earth and she dressed like every day was Halloween. His irritation ratcheted up another hard notch.

"Well, well, well, Marguerite, happy with yourself?" Endelle planted her hands on her hips.

Thorne felt his temper begin to spike. He was ready to go on the attack, but Marguerite's left brow rose. She paused for a moment and looked the scorpion queen up and down. As she put her feet once more in motion, she moved past her and said, "Love your skirt, that halter is to die for, and I am so diggin' the starfish. Who's your designer?"

Endelle's mouth opened; then she looked down at the seashells. She flicked a couple of them, which set up a rippling effect. "I make up most of this stuff myself."

Marguerite caught Thorne's eye and winked.

Thorne shook his head, and his temper eased up. His woman had some unexpected chops.

In the center of the room was a massive coffee table, and both trays found a home there. Diallo moved in first and lifted a cup, but handed it to Marguerite. "Thank you for this kindness. I'm very grateful."

He then offered a mug to Endelle. She took it, but rolled her eyes and sat down in a tan leather chair opposite the table. She leaned back and stared at nothing in particular as she sipped.

Thorne took a cup but moved to a matching tan chair at the long end of the coffee table. He sat down on the edge of the seat, holding the mug in both hands. The nerves that had been irritated were now jumping. In addition, he had that sensation again, of something big moving around in his chest. It wasn't anger this time but a feeling that something new was on the horizon.

Grace sat beside Diallo on the couch and Leto perched himself on the wide arm nearest her. He'd grabbed a mug as well and now sipped, but he immediately set it down on the table in front of him and put an arm over his stomach. He leaned forward and grimaced.

Great.

Was the coffee bad? It smelled like heaven. Thorne sipped and realized the coffee wasn't to blame, just Leto's current condition.

Which led him right back to the point of this difficult conclave. Though he was ready to get the ball rolling, it was Diallo who met Endelle's gaze and said, "I thought about coming to you, a thousand times over the centuries. But one of our rules if you live here is absolute secrecy. When someone decides to leave, I wipe their memories."

"What if they just disappear?" Endelle asked. "Jump ship. What do you do then?"

"I hunt for them and I do as much damage control as necessary." Some of his braids were caught up at the back of his head. He had strong, powerful features, high cheekbones, an almost aquiline nose, large deep green eyes.

"You're tall," Endelle said. "You seeing anyone?"

At that Diallo smiled. "My wife is in Hawaii, doing some healing work among the colonists there."

Thorne narrowed his eyes. "You have a colony in Hawaii?" He sipped his coffee.

"Florida, Hawaii, Oregon, Washington."

"Well, fuck," Endelle said. "Just how many colonies are there."

"Enough."

At that, Endelle rose to her feet and slammed her mug down on the table. "What the hell kind of answer is that? Enough? It isn't an answer, it's a fuck-you. So fuck you."

"Endelle, what are you doing?" Thorne rose to his feet as well.

She turned to face him. "And don't even get me started on you."

That weird thing inside him moved again, gliding around like something that had been hungry for a long time and was ready to start devouring.

But it was Marguerite who changed things around. She actually rose in a smooth leap to stand on the coffee table, straddling the trays. She was now at just above eye level with Endelle.

Endelle was so surprised by this sudden move that she took a step back, hit her calf on the back of her chair, and fell back into her seat.

Marguerite glanced from one to the other. "Aren't you both forgetting something here? Like *why* we're all here?" In a theatrical manner, she swept her arm in Leto's direction and flipped her wrist. *"Hello."*

Thorne couldn't help it. He laughed, and his temper once more stalled out. As he sat down again, keeping his mug level, his gaze shifted to Endelle and he was a little startled by what he saw. She was looking at him as though she'd been kicked in the gut about a hundred times.

She schooled the emotion soon enough and started glaring. But she'd opened a window, and he wouldn't soon forget that look.

Jesus, it hadn't occurred to him that she would actually be hurt by what he'd done.

Shit. Now his guilt roared.

She dipped her chin and shifted her gaze to Leto then back to Diallo, finally to Marguerite. "Point taken, blondie. You can sit back down."

"You sure about that?" Marguerite narrowed her eyes at her, cocked her head. She even tapped her foot. "If you don't behave I might just have to pop you one." She held up her fists, boxer-style. She was so not Endelle's equal that everyone grinned.

Endelle offered her a quirk of her lips, then a laugh. "Fine. I'll be good."

Marguerite stepped off the table. "I wasn't asking you to be good. What the hell kind of fun is that?"

This time Endelle did let loose with a stomach-roll of laughter. It sounded good.

Diallo addressed her. "I wasn't trying to be annoying. I'm not at liberty to share the details of our colonial structure and for the present, I hope you'll respect that. I don't run the show. We have a very fine council of elders who make those kinds of decisions."

"Fine, much good it will do when Greaves takes over this sorry dimension."

"The very point I've been arguing with the council for the past eighteen hours."

Endelle shifted her gaze to Leto. "Well, I guess this is all about you, then. What do you need to tell us? Greaves hasn't exactly hidden his forthcoming military review. His propaganda plays on just about every channel night and day."

Leto met her gaze. "Shall I be frank?"

"No," Endelle said sarcastically. "Be coy because that's what we need here. Or better yet, let me spend the next hour just guessing."

Thorne hated her tone of voice and he almost rose to his feet again, but Marguerite sent, *Ease up, Thorne.*

He drew a deep breath and turned to Leto.

The warrior released a sigh. His gaze fell to the floor in

front of him. "Greaves has a vast army, ten times larger than the one he'll be parading through Moscow Two."

Thorne frowned. "Ten times what?"

"He'll march two hundred thousand down the avenue. Yeah, it's going to be one long fucking spectacle."

Thorne jerked forward. "He has a working army of two million?"

Leto nodded. "And I trained it. That's been my primary job for the past fifteen years. I've basically laid the groundwork for his takeover of two dimensions."

Grace murmured a soft, "Two million. Oh, no."

The number astonished Thorne. And Leto had trained the army. He shifted his gaze to Endelle and stared at her. She didn't meet his eyes. She stared at the untouched plate of pastries. Who the hell could eat now?

Thorne leaned forward and put his mug on the coffee table. He put his hand on his forehead, elbow on his knee. Shit. Of all the things he'd expected Leto to say, that wasn't one of them: two million expertly trained men and women.

Sweet Jesus.

He leaned back once more. "Leto, what the fuck does this mean? You're saying that the Council of Sixth Earth approached you in order to have you spy for them, and the result is that you built an army for Greaves?"

Leto sighed heavily. "The purpose of my mission, the part that I was able to fulfill, was that I fed them Greaves's files continuously."

"How? How did you do that?"

"Through James. He has a lot of power. He could create specific shields when he uploaded the material, shields that Greaves wasn't even aware of. Sixth Earth knows what's going on, probably even more than I do because I didn't look at all those files, not even a fifth of them."

Thorne knew the rest of what Leto wasn't saying, that even with all of James's formidable Sixth Earth power, James wouldn't intervene directly in Second Earth affairs. He wouldn't lift a finger to stop Greaves.

"But an army of this magnitude. Jesus H. Christ. How

could the contents of those files possibly counteract an army of two million? This is a fucking nightmare."

Leto drew in a deep shuddering breath. The circles under his eyes looked deeper than ever and he was almost ghost-white. "I don't know what it all means, I just reached this point that I couldn't take it anymore, not the dying blood, not the antidote, not the training of Greaves's army. And now the Military Review. It's spectacle-grade, Thorne, and it will change things. The sight of even a tenth of Greaves's army will force a lot of High Administrators around the globe to shift their allegiance to the Commander unless something unexpected happens, some miracle.

"As for the army, oh, God. I did what I could to diminish my efforts, but you know what Greaves is. He was very thorough about the training. I wanted to sabotage parts of it, but I couldn't, not without jeopardizing my mission. Every time I pushed James on this, he pushed back even harder. He was adamant about the necessity of the files. He kept trying to tell me everything would work out, but how? Sixth Earth won't intervene once the battling starts. They never have in all of Second Earth history and to do so would be to violate their most basic non-interference rule."

Thorne shook his head. "So, somehow, we're expected to believe that everything else you've done will justify the creation of an army. Not in a millennium is this going to make sense to me."

Leto met his gaze. "James has been insistent from the first to trust in him, to have faith in the council's wisdom. But I'm with you: How could building this army be right?" He shaded his face with his hand. "But there's something else I have to tell you. It doesn't have anything to do with military power, but I have a sick feeling that it could be worse."

At that, Thorne could no longer remained seated. What could be worse than a standing army of this magnitude?

Leto, still sitting against the arm of the chair met his gaze then glanced at Marguerite. Thorne got a bad feeling.

Leto looked up at him again. "Greaves built five palaces

on Second Earth, one each in Africa, the Andes, Chicago, Siberia, and Hong Kong. He's already started moving Seers from his favorite Fortresses into these palaces. Of course *palace* in this case is a euphemism for 'prison.' They're designed to harness, and I do mean harness, Seers together in order to achieve pure vision. No more guesswork with accuracy rates and incomplete visions. Which means, of course, that he'll know the future."

Marguerite rose from her seat only vaguely aware that her feet had left the ground. Something in her mind had gone dark and twisted. She stared down at Leto. "What did you say?" she asked. "He's harnessing Seers together?"

Thorne stared up at her then for some reason blurred in her direction though she had no idea why except that suddenly she was looking down at him, way down.

She blinked and looked at the floor.

Whatever thought had stunned the levitation power into existence in the first place now fled her, and she plummeted. She would have hit hard but Thorne caught her.

"What the hell was that?" she asked. "What did I just do?"

"You levitated. I take it you've never done that before?"

She shook her head then pushed away from him. She headed toward Leto, who still sat on the arm of the couch as calm as you please, hollow-eyed but having stated so many horrible things that her body had started trembling. How could he have spewed so much horror and still be just sitting there? She wanted to hurt Leto, which wasn't in any way fair to him. But the thought of Seers treated so badly split something within her wide open.

She turned away from him and began to pace. Her heart ached something fierce. She rubbed between her breasts and made herself take deep breaths. God, it was almost as though she could feel those Seers crying out, wailing, or worse, living in such bleak despair that there were no more tears, no anguish, just a terrible wish for death. And death could not come to the near-immortal.

She walked in a big circle trying to calm down. Somehow

this feeling was associated with her obsidian flame power. She stopped pacing and bent over. The ache began to grow until it became almost unbearable. She panted and rocked back and forth. She couldn't breathe.

Thorne. She needed Thorne.

Help me, she called to him.

He came.

He rubbed her back. "What can I do?"

"I don't know. I don't know what's wrong with me."

"Endelle, can you help here?"

Marguerite lifted her head but Endelle shrugged. "This isn't my gift. You need someone like Alison or Mr. Feel-Good over here." She gestured to Diallo.

Diallo was already on his feet and crossed swiftly to Marguerite. He put his long black fingers beneath Marguerite's chin and slowly began to lift. "Take a deep breath."

She tried. She shook her head.

He kept lifting until she was standing upright once more, but her chest ached and she wanted to fall on her face and sob, something she never did. She just didn't understand the cause of so much terrible grief.

May I speak with you like this, telepathically? he sent.

She nodded.

I sense two elements that have converged, my dear. Be patient and listen. You are sad for those who have been enslaved and you are sad for yourself. Your life has been as unbearable as what these Seers are about to endure, and I don't just refer to your time of incarceration in the Convent.

She sent, *How do you know so much about me?*

His smile was soft. *Your arrival in the colony has been foreseen for decades—just a hint here and there so I investigated. I know what your life was, Marguerite. I spoke with your parents about thirty years ago. They told me of their religious beliefs and of their method of discipline. You are feeling all that evil right now, that sense of being powerless as a child coupled with knowing what it was to be trapped in the Convent. All this forges the basis for your current suffering.*

She had never told anyone about that, except Thorne. To have it acknowledged as evil changed something in her, and part of her lungs began to work again. She'd needed to hear that what had been done to her was pure evil.

Pure evil, he sent, as though understanding her exactly.

"And what Greaves intends to do," she said aloud, "is also pure evil."

"Yes."

She felt weak and sick but Thorne was there, his arms around her, the nubby feel of his loose-knit cotton sweater soothing against her bare arms. She leaned against him, her new fortress against all this evil. And on some deep level she understood something about their fated relationship.

She twisted to look up at him. He stroked her cheek with the backs of his fingers. She was as much his fortress as he was hers. She knew it in the depth of her being. They had been this to each other from the first.

She turned back to face Diallo but kept her back pinned to Thorne's chest.

"I hate that as Seers we have no rights. We never did."

Endelle took to her feet since everyone else was standing. She directed her attention to Leto. "What I'd like to know is, why are there five palaces? Do I take it that there is a purpose for them beyond just glorified prison camps?"

Leto had remained beside the couch, but with his arm slung over Grace's shoulder. She seemed to be holding him up. He said, "The structure was designed by the horticultural artist, the one known as Tazianne. And it is Greaves's belief, though untested, that the five palaces could operate as one in order to achieve pure vision."

"Tazianne. Why do I know that name?" Endelle asked.

Thorne said, "She's the one who created the live magnolia centerpiece in Medichi's villa, the one that always brings bees into his house. And Kerrick told me that Tazianne helped Alison communicate telepathically with baby Helena before she was born so that she wouldn't mount her wings during delivery."

Marguerite glanced back at him. This was one thing she knew to be true of Thorne—he knew the details of his warrior's lives, just as he knew the details of hers. She loved him for that.

Only what was she supposed to do with all of this new horrible information? What were any of them supposed to do?

She looked at Endelle. "So basically, if we lose the war against Greaves, all the Seers on two worlds end up in his Seer palaces."

Endelle snorted and flipped one of the shells of her halter. "Oh, I'm sure he'll only take the most powerful of the Seers. The rest he'll probably use as blood slaves to sustain and increase the death vampire portion of his army."

"Do you have to be sarcastic?" Thorne asked.

"Did you have to turn deserter, you bastard? I should have you arrested right now for this fucking stunt you pulled!"

Thorne felt the vibrations flow through him, but with his arms around Marguerite he couldn't quite recognize what they were or what they meant—until he realized he was nearly hyperventilating with rage. He was ready to speak, ready to say things he'd wanted to say for two centuries, but the woman in his arms suddenly spun around and put her hands on his face.

"Hey," she cried. "You're not helping here. We have a lot of other fish to fry."

He might have been okay, he might even have calmed down, but Endelle added, "Oh, so now you have your woman fighting your battles for you?"

That did it. Even Marguerite had the good sense to throw up her arms and step away from him.

Thorne whirled in Endelle's direction. "Just shut the fuck up, Endelle. For once, just shut the fuck up." He shouldn't have said it but he was pissed. The truth was he couldn't take it anymore, not any of it.

She stared at him for a long, hard moment, then said, "Fine. If that's what you want, I won't say another word." She waved a hand to encompass Leto, Grace, and Diallo. "Use all your brilliance and sort this out. When you've figured out how to win a war against two million trained warriors, let me fucking know." She lifted her arm and vanished.

Oh, shit. He was digging a goddamn hole. He wondered exactly how deep this was going to get before he was finished and whether or not Endelle would ever forgive him.

But that was trouble for another time. Besides, he wasn't sure he cared. Something had happened to him in the last few weeks, something that may have started over a year ago during Alison's rite of ascension, a wearing-down of his patience that couldn't be brought back. What he was feeling was not simple. It felt old, really old, centuries old, something that was birthed the first time he'd learned of Darian Greaves.

Thorne thanked Diallo for his time, for returning from a critical council meeting to be here with Endelle.

The man's eyes glimmered with understanding and just a little humor. He was a leader who understood the pitfalls of human nature. "I felt her power, but it seems more warrior-like than administrative."

"I think you just defined the problem exactly. She would have made a fearsome warrior, but on Second Earth she's the only ascender to match Greaves skill-for-skill so she's been held to this role for millennia."

Diallo nodded. "Well, I liked the sounds of the seashells when she moved."

Thorne chuckled. "Yeah. She's a piece of work."

"You love her."

"I do." He glanced at Marguerite, but was surprised to find that her features were soft, almost compassionate as she watched him. He had thought maybe she would be jealous, but she seemed to understand the exact nature of what he did feel for Endelle. He turned back to Diallo. "Endelle is . . . my family."

"I understand," Diallo said. "What do you wish for me to do?"

Thorne clapped the man's shoulder, a trick given the

disparity in height, but he often did the same with Medichi and the brother was six-seven. "To be patient. This is a moment of turmoil, but it will end and very soon no doubt. How can I reach you? Because I'm certain we'll need to coordinate strategies, especially if Stannett puts designs on your Seers here or in the other hidden colonies." He wondered again exactly how many colonies there were, how many Seers were living in exile.

Diallo smiled. "Let's keep it simple. I have an iPhone."

"I have a Droid."

"Interdimensional?" Diallo's brows rose.

"Of course."

Diallo nodded. Thorne laughed. He exchanged numbers with the man then said, "Let me know when your council decides to be completely open with Endelle. However, given Greaves's ambitions and how far along his plans are, the sooner the better."

"Understood." Diallo lifted his arm and was gone.

Thorne turned in the direction of Leto, who wasn't looking so good. Grace guided him in the direction of the couch. Leto didn't so much as sit down as fall into it. He reclined his head on the tall back and closed his eyes.

Shit, Thorne had no idea what to do for him, how to resolve a withdrawal from dying blood that seemed to be ending his life at light speed. Grace's blood had given him strength, but not for very long.

Well, one problem at a time.

He had a scorpion queen to deal with.

When Marguerite stacked the still-full mugs on one of the trays, then headed toward the kitchen, he followed her.

He knew what he had to do next but he wasn't sure what to do with Marguerite.

As she set the tray on the counter, his phone vibrated. He drew it from his pants pocket and read the text.

"What's going on now?" she asked.

He met her gaze. She lifted a brow and glanced at his phone. "Alison has invited us to Medichi's villa. She's putting a dinner together at five for all the warriors and their *breh*. She wants us both to come."

"Is that what you want to do?"

"Yeah. Will you come with me?"

She was quiet for a moment, then nodded. "I think I have to. Everything seems to be changing so fast.

"It is."

He glanced once more in the direction of the living room. "I need to let everyone know about Leto and about Greaves's army." He compressed his lips for a moment. "But what I have to do right now . . ." He couldn't even speak the words.

She took a step closer to him. "You have to go see Endelle."

"Yep."

"Uh, just so ya know, I have to be there."

He wanted to protest but she put two fingers on his lips. "My gut is screaming at me on this one, Thorne. I have to be there, but I'll keep my distance and I won't say a word. I promise."

At that, he smiled. "You? Not say a word?"

Her smile was crooked. "Well, I'll try to hold my tongue."

If it had been any other moment, he would have teased her about that, but yeah, right now he had to finish this thing with Endelle. He'd put it off long enough.

He focused on the link with Endelle deep within his mind. He'd cast an internal shield all around it to prevent a dialogue from the time he'd gone AWOL and dropped down to Mortal Earth. He very carefully began removing the shield, in part because he hadn't constructed one before and in part because he was afraid he'd hear nothing but Endelle's resonant shouting in his head and he'd drop to the floor crippled with pain.

But as the last of the shield slipped away, he opened the link. *Can we talk?* he sent.

There was a long, long pause. Finally, *Come to the palace. Now.*

Thorne knew Endelle could have brought them both

through security but because the silence told him she'd ended the discussion, he concentrated on his warrior phone sitting on his nightstand in Sedona. He folded it into his hand and called Carla.

"Central. How may I help?"

"I need a lift, for two, to the palace. She's expecting us." Well, she was expecting him.

"You got it . . . and . . . welcome home, boss."

"Thanks, Carla."

He thumbed the phone and sent it back to Sedona. He kept his arm around Marguerite and held on. Shit, he was nervous. There was so much that needed to be said and yet he hadn't really thought through any of it—why he was so fucking mad and, more to the point, what he needed from Endelle.

The vibration began.

What is left when the smoke clears?
Truth.
Awful, horrible, painful truth.

Collected Proverbs, Beatrice of Fourth

CHAPTER 16

James of Sixth Earth worked to hold his present form. It had been Luchianne's idea for him to interject himself into Second Society by taking on the persona of a short, gray-haired librarian with light blue eyes. But this shape required effort, since he was in many ways the opposite of this man, the one Alison had once said reminded her of an English country gentleman.

But that was because of the sweaters he wore, and maybe the bow ties.

Luchianne had thought that Alison would need a mild presence in order to accept his help and instruction. Perhaps she'd been right. He'd appeared to Fiona as well, when she'd been near death during the darkest part of a blood slave's death-and-resurrection process. He had been feeding pigeons when he spoke to her. He'd done some good. Now she was alive and living with Jean-Pierre as his *breh.* Yes, he'd done some good.

But as he waited for the exact moment to return to Second Earth, on strict instructions from Luchianne herself, he almost trembled at what was coming. This particular encounter between Endelle and her second-in-command had shaken even the High Seers of Sixth Earth.

If this ended badly, all could be lost.

So he had a job to do, and as he felt Thorne and Marguerite begin their folding process, he thought the thought and passed through the ether mist of four dimensions until he reached Second. He dropped down lightly to a space five feet behind Endelle.

"Hello, Endelle. Mind your temper."

Endelle turned around. "Shorty, what the fuck are you doing here?"

"Came to observe."

"I have a bone to pick with you, asshole. What the fuck is Greaves doing with a goddamn army of two million and how the fuck could you have let Leto build it?"

"Yes, it's a bit of a pickle."

She snorted. "A pickle? What the hell does that mean and just so ya know, I'm holding you, along with your fucking Sixth Earth friendship circle, accountable for having set Leto up like this. He's almost dead, you know. Being your spy, and having to take dying blood for a century, has just about killed him. I hope you're satisfied."

"We had to have the information Leto provided, all of it, in order to plot our course. Luchianne has a plan, but it's going to take some serious finessing. She said to tell you that Braulio would come by later for a little chat. Maybe he'll have an answer for you." He breathed heavily through his nose, then muttered, "Well, he'll have something for you anyway, if not an answer."

She was about to grab him by his skinny arms, shake him hard, and demand he tell her what the fuck was going on, but another voice, full of rocks, invaded the space. "Endelle?" She whirled back around and there stood Thorne with Marguerite, his arm around the other shorty in the room.

She stepped back until she stood beside James. "Thorne, I don't think you've met our oh-so-useless Sixth Ascender

Guardian. James of Sixth Earth, Gatekeeper of Third, may I present Warrior Thorne and Seer Marguerite."

"How do you do?" James offered.

She watched Thorne and Marguerite exchange a glance, brows raised, and why wouldn't they be? She hadn't known James was coming, either.

She turned back to him. "Why don't you tell us all just why you're here right now?"

"Just to monitor and report."

She glanced at Thorne then back to Shorty. "Wait a minute. Are you here to watch me take my second-in-command apart, because that's what I'm about to do unless of course you'd like to get involved."

"As you know, we have strict rules about interference."

"Well, how very *Star Trek* of you."

But James only smiled. He addressed the newcomers. "If you can, please continue as though I'm not here."

At that, Endelle met Thorne's gaze dead-on. "Yes, Warrior Thorne, why don't we continue as though James, and even your woman here, don't exist."

"Fine. Why don't we start, Endelle, with what you'd like to say to me."

She put her hands out in front of her, claw-like but facing each other, and as the energy began to spark, she shouted, "How could you have left me alone like this! How? What fucking possessed you to just take off, without a word to me, without thinking of me as a partner in all this shit?" She lifted her arm and as she waved, a red firework left her palm, aimed straight for Marguerite.

Thorne was quick, though. He stepped in front and took the sparks in the chest. He winced and she knew she'd hurt him, which meant he knew exactly just how badly she would have burned Marguerite.

His gaze became dark and hooded as he marched toward her. "Throw another one. Go ahead. Get everything off your chest."

She couldn't help herself. She launched repeated fireworks at him, one after the other, but he met each one with hand-blasts of his own, shunting them aside until the vast rotunda in which she stood, facing off her second-in-command, was full of smoke and lightning and showers of red, green, and blue sparks.

James had moved to stand beside Marguerite and set up some kind of shield to protect her.

But Endelle was just warming up. "And how dare you block our mind-link, the one we've had in place for centuries. Goddamn you, Thorne, treating me like I was worth a narrow stream of snail piss. Goddamn you."

The fireworks just kept getting bigger and bigger until even she felt the burn on her arms and shoulders as the sparks came down.

"I'm done, Endelle. I will no longer serve you in this capacity. No more, so I want you to break the fucking mind-link. I will not serve you as I have for the past two thousand years, not when Leto shows up and tells us that Greaves has built an army of two million warriors. How the hell are we supposed to battle that and win? How?"

She hated him now. Hated him for not understanding or valuing all that she had done. She'd never pretended to be a brilliant administrator, but who else could have stepped up and done her job? She said as much then added, "So suck it up, Thorne. I'm not letting you go. I'm not letting you walk away from your responsibilities."

She kept the blasts streaming and the fireworks bursting against his own hand-blasts.

"I'm not walking away, Endelle. I just refuse to serve you one more day like this. Not one more day, so break the fucking mind-link. Break it."

"No," she shouted, using resonance.

She watched him flinch, but he barely moved an inch from his present battling posture. He looked different, too, stronger somehow. He was definitely determined, but she was too angry to see straight.

She thought the thought and her wings flew from their wing-locks, but he must have anticipated this move because there his were, larger than before and lighter, more iridescent than she remembered.

Change had come to Thorne, which meant an increase in power. Maybe that's what his rebellion was all about.

She still didn't care what had brought all this on. He'd asked for it and she was dishing it up.

She began to fly in a circle and he matched her. The palace rotundas were enormous. Twenty death vampires could fly through and not touch one another.

"Break the link," he shouted, also using resonance.

It felt good to be in the air, to be flying, to be doing something other than reading emails and watching her world succumb to all of Greaves's machinations. How could Thorne possibly know what Leto's calm announcement about the size of Greaves's army had done to her? Or that he'd built palace prisons to reach pure fucking vision? How could he possibly know what it felt like to see that no matter what she had done, how little she had slept, how long she had served, how much of her life she had sacrificed, it would all, in the end, mean so little? Or that Greaves had ended up in a superior position, one that would allow him to win the war, and that the one she had come to rely on in everything had somehow decided that she was the real enemy in this whole equation?

So why the hell had she done any of it? Why had she given up her life?

She gathered all that rage, all that intense frustration, and did two things at once: She sent him a blast that would knock him hard into the marble and maybe ruin his wings and at the exact same moment she broke the mind-link.

There, she screamed telepathically, *satisfied?*

But as she watched Thorne fall, completely unconscious, through the smoke and sparks, she wanted to reach out to him, to break his fall. She couldn't. Something inside her had broken apart completely. She couldn't even move.

She popped her wings into parachute-mount and just hung high in the air near the rounded part of the ceiling where the smoke was thickest. She had to work to see anything below her.

At the last moment, it was Marguerite who folded beneath Thorne and sent her own hand-blast to stop his fall. He now hung suspended in midair.

Oh, God, Thorne. Thorne!

Endelle was sickened by what she had done, but still she just stayed there, rocking slightly, back and forth.

As Marguerite diminished her hand-blasts in stages, Thorne's body descended slowly until he lay inert on top of her, his wings spread wide in the full-mount position. Marguerite's feet stuck out at an odd angle beneath him. She coughed because of the smoke.

Endelle dropped swiftly to the marble floor and approached the pair. She wanted to know only one thing, so she focused on Thorne's bare chest: Was the bastard still alive or had she killed the most honorable vampire she'd known in her entire nine thousand years of ascended life.

His rib cage rose and fell.

Okay, so he was alive.

Fine.

Fucking fine.

She closed her eyes and folded to her meditation space.

She sat down on her chaise-longue and folded off her seashells and mini skirt.

She folded on her soft purple linen gown.

She was in her holy of holies and maybe she would just stay here until the earth blew apart into hundreds of trillions of tiny particles.

Sounded like a good plan.

Marguerite was stuck beneath 260 pounds of muscled vampire warrior and a pair of wings that were both making it hard to breathe and tickling her nose at the same time. For all their strength, wings were also fragile and when broken required a lot of energy to heal.

She'd only been stupid once while mounting her wings. She'd been drunk, of course, at college, or rather at one of the bars near the college, and had released her wings in too small a space.

Because she'd been standing on the bar, and her wings were huge, she'd broken them both at the apex, shattering a few bottles in the process because of her subsequent screaming. The university healers had worked on her for *hours*.

As she struggled to draw a deep breath under Thorne's weight, she hoped like hell he hadn't broken anything.

Through the feathers, a foot appeared; not hers, not Thorne's. Had to belong to James.

"Need some help?" he asked. His voice had a warm soothing quality, but even he coughed because of the smoke.

"No, no," she said. "We're fine. If he stays unconscious for about six months he might lose enough of his muscle mass for me to move." She turned her head and coughed.

James laughed, but suddenly Thorne's weight was just not there. Marguerite slid out from under the levitating body, then James lowered him back to the marble floor. "His wings are magnificent. Did I detect a flame pattern like yours while he was flying?"

Marguerite stood next to the short man, waving her hand back and forth against the thick cloud in the air. She really liked James's non-warrior, non-Supreme-High-Administrator height. "With all the smoke, fireworks, and sparks showering down like a monsoon storm, I didn't exactly notice the pattern of his wings." She turned to the side and coughed her lungs out. Her eyes stung from the smoke as well.

"I suppose not."

She glanced at James. "So is he okay?"

He nodded. "He's fine."

When she started coughing again, James waved an arm and *poof*, all the smoke was gone.

"Nice trick."

"Thank you." But his gaze was on Thorne.

"Why isn't he burned?" she asked. "There was enough energy in this room to set the whole northern Arizona forest on fire."

"I'm really not sure except that I believe he has emerging powers. If you'll remember, Endelle didn't get burned, either."

"She just knocked him unconscious during that last round?"

"Yep."

She turned a little in his direction. "So you're from Sixth. What's it like up there?"

Somehow she wasn't surprised when a look of long-suffering overcame his face. "It can be wonderful, just like here, but I have a very demanding boss."

"Then you and Thorne have the same problem."

"Sort of. I report to Luchianne."

Her mouth dropped open. "You report to the first vampire ever? The one who had first flight, who opened the gateway to Second Earth, who sported a pair of fangs before she could possibly have known what they were for?"

He nodded. "Those are the facts of the case."

"Sweet Lord in heaven."

She felt the strangest urge to touch him, to see if he was real. Instead, movement caught her eye. Thorne was coming around. If he moved too much, though, he'd do some damage.

She walked between the apex of his wings very carefully, knelt while avoiding any of the feathers, and bent over him. She put her hands on his face and sent, *Stay still. You're fine. You're at the palace with James and me.* She looked over her shoulder, but the Sixth ascender was gone. *Well, you're with me. Endelle folded somewhere. Try not to move. You're lying on top of your wings.*

His eyes opened and he looked up at her. "Hey."

"Hey, yourself."

"She got me pretty good."

"Yep. Anything broken?"

"Just my head. Maybe my heart a little. Holy shit, did I actually take her on? I'm lucky I wasn't blown into a thousand pieces."

"James said he thinks you have emerging powers."

"I have a fucking emerging headache. But . . ." He paused, then said, "She broke the mind-link."

She leaned down to kiss him, first his forehead, then his nose, then his lips.

He groaned but while she plucked at his lips, he sent, *You'd better stop that. I'm starting to move . . . in other places.*

She laughed. "Okay, fine. I'm going to fold away right now, just a few feet, okay?"

"Sure. Why?"

"If I back up, I might step on your wings."

"Oh. Yeah. Please don't do that."

She thought the thought and materialized ten feet from his left wing. The feathers were splayed out in a perfect span, so she looked down at it. She squinted. Maybe she saw a flame pattern. Maybe. So what kind of emerging powers could Thorne have that would put them both in even greater danger?

The next moment Thorne simply levitated from the floor, still stretched out on his back, and some of the tension left his face. It couldn't have felt good to be pressing against the wings, either.

While just lying in midair, he began moving the wings very slowly, wafting like he was doing the backstroke. He stared up into the vast dome of the rotunda and kept moving, easing first this way then that, apparently trying everything out. The beauty of his wings seemed odd against his nubby green sweater, blue jeans, and a brown pair of leather loafers, but the whole thing really worked for her. Even on his back, midair, in casual clothes and full-mount, he was one gorgeous vampire.

His small warrior phone appeared in his hand. "Hey, Carla. Thorne here. I'm at the palace and I need Horace. Can you get him here? A couple of my wings near the wing-locks have small fractures." He listened and nodded. "Apologize for me. I know he needs his rest." He then smiled. "Right back atcha. And thanks."

He drew in a deep breath and lifted up to a standing position, which of course put his wings on full display. Marguerite moved behind him and tried to see the flame pattern. Maybe it was the light, but she just wasn't seeing it.

"Enjoying the view?"

"Always," she said, moving to face him. "James said you had a flame pattern but I'm not seeing it. But man, your wings are beautiful. The apex has to rise five feet above your head. Wow."

She saw that he was sweating and his mouth was tight. "You okay?"

He gritted his teeth. "I'm fine but it just occurred to me that I would have fallen hard during that last round. I really should be worse off than I am."

"I kinda broke your fall."

At that, his eyes widened. "How?"

"I got underneath you and sent a hand-blast, not too strong, of course, but just enough to keep you from crashing. You landed on me."

"I landed on you." He laughed. "Did I hurt you? I mean, I can see that I didn't."

"No, but all that muscle weighs *a lot*." She moved in close and kissed him. "I mean *a lot*, but I liked it. Other than not being able to breathe much, I was just fine." She kissed him until his tongue was in her mouth, he had his hands on her waist, and he was dragging her toward him.

However, a warning vibration from behind her followed. Thorne spun her to his side, holding her close, and brought his sword into his right hand. His knees bent. He was red-faced and grimacing, but holding his posture as Horace materialized.

Marguerite felt his whole body relax, and the sword disappeared. She recognized Horace from the Superstition Seer's Fortress when Thorne and Jean-Pierre had busted her out of that shithole. They'd found Seers in every cell, badly abused, many of them pregnant. Horace had come to work his healing magic. Now he was here to help Thorne.

He bowed, an unfamiliar form of address, but Thorne had once told her it was an older ritual and he hadn't quite been able to break Horace of the habit.

Horace greeted her in a way that was very warm, something that surprised her, although she could see the respect he had for Thorne. That respect bordered on awe as Horace spoke to him and asked his questions about which parts of the mesh-like supporting filaments were causing him pain.

She was once more struck with her warrior. She stepped away from him and looked him up and down. He was gorgeous, muscled, powerful, and those wings. Magical.

Her gaze, however, landed on his pecs. Her mouth watered.

I'm smelling rose.

I'm admiring the view.

He smiled and slowly made a fist, then lifted his forearm and brought his bicep into one huge lump of man-meat. She felt her fangs emerge and—since Horace was completely screened by the wings—she flashed them at Thorne.

His eyes rolled in his head. The resulting wall of cherry tobacco that slammed into her put her flat on her ass. She laughed. The level of sexual cravings between them was ridiculous.

She shouldn't have, but since she was on the floor, she spread her legs about a foot and a half apart.

More cherry tobacco, but he looked away, staring up at the ceiling and taking deep breaths.

"Does this hurt?" Horace called out. "You've grown very tense."

"No, I'm fine. Really." He still didn't look at her.

Marguerite laughed but she rose to her feet and wandered outside to the balcony. If they didn't stop, pretty soon they'd be embarrassing Horace, healing or no healing.

Thorne could only look at her as she left the rotunda. He was grateful she'd left the room. He needed to settle down as Horace completed his work and he was at last able to retract his wings.

He worked his back muscles until they were completely thinned out and there was no pain whatsoever. He clapped Horace on the shoulder. "Hey, my man, thanks for getting out of bed for this."

Horace looked around, his gaze drifting up to the now

blackened ceiling. "May I ask what happened here? How many death vampires attacked?"

Thorne shook his head. "No death vampires. Endelle and I had a small disagreement on certain issues. I trust this will go no farther?"

He met Horace's gaze, and the man actually grinned. "I always wondered when the day would arrive that the last straw finally landed on your back. I used to make weekly wagers, but that ended in about AD 109. You have tremendous patience, Warrior Thorne."

"I don't know about that," he said. "The truth is, I've always understood her and I've respected her."

"As do I. Only Endelle could have kept Greaves at bay this long."

Thorne frowned. "We're in trouble, Horace. Greaves has an army two million strong."

"Oh, no."

"Exactly."

"And do you know this to be true for certain?"

"I had it from Leto this morning. And he would know because he built the army."

Once more Horace's gaze took in the ceiling. "Well, that wasn't just the last straw, that was the last bale." He met Thorne's eyes again. "What do I need to do?"

"A final battle is coming, the battle that could change the future of two worlds. And we're not prepared. Do what you can to recruit healers and train them fast."

"I will do that," he said. "And as always, I will keep everything we've just talked about, everything I've seen here completely confidential." He bowed then he was gone.

Thorne turned in the direction of the west-facing terrace. Marguerite leaned against the parapet. She held her face to the sun like she was drinking it in. Morning in late March was idyllic, with temps in the high seventies. As he drew up behind her, pressing himself against her and folding his arms around her, a breeze carried all the sharp desert scents up to the palace.

"This is heaven," she said. "I never saw enough of the sun this last century. I think I could stand here for hours."

"You'd be blistered."

"I'd heal."

"Thanks for breaking my fall."

"Hey, I told you. I have your back . . . literally, I guess." She laughed.

Marguerite seemed to enjoy laughing at her jokes, and he loved that about her. He'd never seen much of this side of her in the Convent. How could he have? They'd always rushed through their lovemaking for fear Grace would return, or one of the regulators, or God forbid Sister Quena.

He squeezed her and kissed her neck. "I want you to come home with me, to my house in Sedona. I have a big bathtub, room enough for two."

She moaned softly, and her rose-woman scent flooded the air.

I want to suck your wing-locks, he added for good measure.

She shuddered and groaned. *How about you suck mine then I'll suck yours.*

His turn to shudder. "Okay, we'd better go now."

"Can you fold us? I know the security here is tight."

"I think so. If not, I'll give Carla a shout." He squeezed her arms. "Ready?"

"Absolutely."

He thought the thought and there was no answering restraint, but rather a free glide so that the next moment he was standing with her in the foyer of his home in Sedona Two. He held her like that for a long moment, her back to his front, and let her just look.

"The arrangement is similar to Diallo's home." She pulled away from him. "You're on a promontory that has a two-hundred-seventy-degree view." She let her gaze rest on it for a moment then asked, "Which way to your bedroom?"

"The left wing."

She moved off to the left toward the room he used

primarily as his library, stepping up three steps, then across a hall to another bank of windows. He followed her, wanting her to explore his home. Maybe if she liked it well enough, she'd stay and she'd choose him over her freedom, over her deep fear of connecting with others.

She drew close to the windows and looked out. "This is the Mogollon Rim, isn't it?"

Again, he moved in behind her. The view had never been more beautiful because she was here to see it with him, the blue sky overhead and the tree-studded red cliffs opposite. Hawks soared above what was the gorge carved out by Oak Creek who knew how many millennia before his time.

"I think I could look at this view forever," she said.

How he wished that were true. His heavy sigh forced her to turn in his arms, look up at him, and stroke his cheek with her hand. "No sighing right now, Thorne. Please? Just be with me today, as though there is no other day, just you and me and the promise of a big bathtub."

"I can do that." But looking into her beautiful brown eyes, he suddenly felt so lost, so desperate that he kissed her hard.

She pulled back but still had her hands clasped at his nape. "So where's your bedroom?"

He jerked his head to the doorway and long hall on the left. "Over here."

She glanced in that direction and said, "Another flight of stairs?"

"I built this house on the hillside, so yeah, lots of stairs."

She glanced at the stairs then to her right in the direction of the foyer. "I'll bet this house looks beautiful from the front."

"The elevation is very pretty."

"Do all you warriors have big homes like this?"

He smiled. "Pretty much. We have to. We're big men."

Her hand found his groin and rubbed the length of him, all the way up. "I am so not going to state the obvious. How about you just show me your bedroom."

* * *

Marguerite didn't want to be feeling all that she was feeling: her absolute delight that she'd saved him the pain of damaged wings, her pleasure in his house and in his company, her wish that she could stay in this beautiful place for the rest of her life, as in forever.

But as he took her hand and drew her into the wood-paneled hallway, as she once more had an expansive view of the gorge and the rim and of the magnificent red monoliths everywhere, she slowed to again savor the view. This was one of those homes where every room had an astonishing vista.

She gave his hand a squeeze.

Maybe the design therefore was a perfect reflection of Thorne: The view from any perspective had always been amazing. Certainly on a physical level, the man didn't have a bad angle, and over the decades she had most definitely seen him from every angle possible.

Now a bath with him, another first of many over the past two days. Sweet Christ had they been together for only two days? It seemed like weeks had passed. Months, maybe.

As she climbed the steps behind him, as he squeezed her hand, she felt like she was being drawn into another world. She had an uneasy sensation and asked, "Thorne, have you brought other women here before?"

He looked back at her as he climbed yet another short flight of polished wood stairs. "No, of course not. You know the year I built this house. During that whole time, just how often did I fail to get to the Convent?"

"A handful of mornings, I guess."

"Exactly. So please tell me you know that I was faithful to you."

Her heart seized, one giant fist inside her chest strangling.

She stopped dead on the middle step so that now he really towered above her.

When she didn't budge, he turned to face her fully, releasing her hand. "What gives?"

"This feels like too much."

"Would it have helped if I'd brought other women here?"

Her fingers shaped into cat's claws so fast that even Thorne glanced at them and smiled.

"That's not the point and you know it." She lifted her hands to face him, still curled and ready for a fight. "This is the *breh-hedden*, nothing more."

He stepped down one step, but he was still like a giant against her five feet five inches. It then occurred to her in the most unholy way that these stairs had real potential.

"I thought we were fighting and now all I can smell in this confined space is a heavy wave of rose. Not that I'm complaining."

She was eye level with his stomach. She put her hand on his green sweater and looked up at him. "Get rid of this."

His eyes flared.

Sweater gone.

She drifted her fingers over his abs, and he tightened his stomach for her. She hooked her finger in the top of his jeans. Maybe there were many things about this situation that distressed her, that made her want to run screaming into the hills, but this wasn't one of them, the banquet that was Thorne.

His hand found her nape, one of his favorite places—and she knew why. He liked to exert control, or at least the appearance of it. And it turned her on as well. She rose to the next step, which put her exactly at pec level, one of her favorite places. He pushed on her nape, forcing her toward him.

She loved playing with him, playing with his body, touching him, sucking on him. His breath rose high in his chest, and that sweet cherry tobacco scent now clouded her senses and forced her mouth open to take in his nipple.

She descended on him like she hadn't eaten in weeks, sucking hard and biting, using her fingers to push all the muscle into a bunch so she could take as much of him in her mouth as she could gather.

"Oh, God," he groaned. "Jesus, what you do to me."

She took a turn on his other pec and by the time she was done, she was satisfied at how red the skin was, at the various bite marks she'd left, and how stiff and puckered his nipples were. She looked up at him. His hazel eyes were dark and seemed to flash in the dim hallway.

He stroked the back of her neck in quick rubs, up and down. She didn't dare touch him low right now, or he'd come. *You work me up.*

She smiled. *You need to settle down, Thorne. We're just getting started and I want you to last for me.*

He narrowed his eyes. *I'll fucking last for you.*

Oh, looked like she'd touched a sore spot, so she slid her hand low after all and stroked the length of his erection through his jeans, up and up, dipping her fingertips just below the crown before sliding off.

He arched forward and hissed.

She laughed. "I want my bath, Thorne. You said you'd suck me. You going to keep that promise or are you all talk?"

But he leaned down a little more, twisted sideways, and kissed her hard on the lips.

The thing was, she'd always loved his mouth. This time she put her hand on his nape and did some stroking of her own as he thrust his tongue against hers.

He sent, *Sex with you has been one of the finest experiences of my life.* He drew back and held her gaze.

She got that wiggly feeling again, the sense that she needed to run, that Thorne was asking things of her she couldn't give. At the same time, her eyes burned. *Sex with you kept me sane.*

He nodded. He closed his eyes for a moment, then in the distance she heard water running. No, not running, *gushing.*

"What the hell is that?"

"I don't like to wait long for the bathing pool to fill. I had it done special."

He turned and headed back up the stairs. He still wore his jeans, but his bare back had a gorgeous flare, angling to a narrow waist. She shivered watching him move up the stairs.

She followed, hopeless to do anything else.

The sound came from an arched doorway beyond the

bedroom. In the meantime, as he crossed to the bathroom, her gaze fell on the room and she drew in a deep breath. The entire wall behind the very large warrior-sized bed was made of slabs of rough gray stone. The bed had four massive posters of a dark rich-looking wood, maybe mahogany, and all she could think was that she'd like some rope looped around every post and around every one of Thorne's limbs. She'd like to tie him to the bed and keep him there to devour for a very long time.

Her tongue made an appearance.

"You have something else in mind?" he asked.

She shifted her gaze to the bathroom doorway, and her eyes almost popped from head. Thorne had lost his jeans and now stood completely naked, profile view, supporting a very firm cock in his hand. He thumbed the tip and smiled.

Marguerite began to tremble. Really tremble, and her body was on fire. What this man could do to her. She began to wonder how she could ever think of taking her pleasure anywhere but here.

She blurred the distance to him and before he could move, she slid between him and the doorjamb and dropped to her knees to take that beautiful head in her mouth and suck. It was a lot of head to enjoy. She pulled back and just let his cock float over her lips, her cheeks, her chin.

She looked up at him and saw pain in his eyes.

"What?" she asked, using her hand to support and steady him. She licked the tip.

He shook his head. "You please me so much, like you were made for me somehow. You couldn't have done anything else in this moment that I would have enjoyed more than to have seen you appreciate *all* of me."

She rose up. She could feel his distress. It matched her own. She leaned into him, pressing his cock straight up against his abdomen. "Back atcha, Thorne. But I'm scared."

He nodded. "I may have made a break with Endelle today, but you need to know that my job just got a helluva lot harder, not easier, and I don't know what's going to happen."

"You carry the load."

He nodded. "It's on me. It's been on me since I can remember."

He ran his hands down her wing-locks, which brought shivers streaking everywhere. "You're very wet," he said softly, his fingers playing with the moist apertures. "How about I give you that much-promised bath and we forget about all this shit for a while."

"Sounds like a plan." And right now she'd do just about anything to take that haunted look from his eyes. But she did know one thing that would help. She thought the thought and got rid of her clothes.

Water.
Take me to your bathing pool.
Keep me there until I am made anew.

—*Collected Poems*, Beatrice of Fourth

CHAPTER 17

Thorne growled at the sight of Marguerite all nice and naked, then did one of his favorite things: He slid his arm low behind her knees and picked her up to carry her. He took her to the side of the bath, which was really just one big-ass bathing pool. But hell, he was a big man and sometimes, after he'd been to the Convent, he'd just float and stare up at the lightening sky.

She looked first down then up. "If it was nighttime, we'd see the stars."

"I've never done that."

"Not once?"

"I'm always out battling at night, and this pool is only about sixty years old."

She looked down again. "Mind my head, but I'd love it if you just dropped me in there."

"You would, huh?" The pool had a shallow end and a nice platform for doing things he'd only imagined until now. But this part was five feet deep and eight feet across.

"Yeah, I would."

"Hold your arms next to your sides then. I don't want you breaking a wrist."

"Got it."

He tossed her in the air, watched her smile, then laughed as she crashed through the surface. A lot of that water cascaded over the sides, but like hell he cared. This was a day he never thought to have: *his woman* in his bathing pool.

She came up sputtering. He sat on the edge, swung his legs over, and dropped in. Because the water was deep enough, he let his knees go and went under. It was heaven. He came up and she was already on him, her arms around his neck, her small tongue in his mouth, her legs scissored around his stiffening cock.

Maybe it was the recent exchange about how this really couldn't work for either of them, but when he kissed her this time, his chest hurt, like maybe this would be the last time he would ever be with her. How strange to think that for a sudden strong moment, he wished her back at that hellhole of a Convent, safe inside her cell so that he could just keep visiting her in the morning. Now her safety was on his mind all the time, especially given her emerging obsidian flame power. But more than that, he feared she would just take off again.

He cupped her face in his hand and stared into her eyes. He wanted to memorize them, the different shades of brown that created the glitter he so often saw.

She caught his hand and pressed it against her cheek. "What is it, Thorne? Why are you looking at me like that?"

He shook his head and smiled. "Whatever else this might be, between us, Marguerite, I love you. I have from that first day. I want you to know that."

"I love you, too. You know, that right? I mean—" She looked down at his chest as though unable to meet his gaze. "—I mean as much as I'm able. I've never really known love, real love."

"And yet somehow you've overcome that."

"What do you mean?"

He thumbed her cheek. She had a beautiful complexion and full high cheekbones. "Because I know you. I know who you are. Grace told me you got her through a bunch of rough patches, helped her to make up her mind about things. And how about all those lashes you took for the other devotiates? And don't you think for a minute that I don't know how difficult it was for you to connect with Brynna as the only means of achieving pure vision. I know what you gave up. You gave up your freedom because you love my sister. I see that, sweetheart, and if that isn't love, then what the fuck is?"

"Thorne, how could I have done anything else?"

"You've just made my point. This is who you are. And now I made you a promise, and I'm going to keep it." He turned her around so that her back faced him. He shoved her gently in the direction of the shallow end until he could drop to his knees with his shoulders just above water level. While she was still standing, he settled his hands on her hips, his thumbs rubbing her ass. In that position, his lips came to the middle of her back. He slid his tongue in a line across one of her wing-locks and began to suck.

Her body arched immediately and she gasped. He reached low to slide a hand between her legs, pushing them apart. He turned slightly to get a good angle and slid two fingers up into her. She groaned heavily.

He worked her slowly, and the air filled with her rose scent. He licked the aperture and tasted the sweet liquid that released from the lock. Tasting her, no matter what part of her body, was like drinking in the essence of who she was, her wild spirit and her generous, sacrificial heart. He moved his fingers faster, wanting her to come, wanting to bring her over and over, to spend this time, this afternoon coaxing her body to a dozen orgasms, as many she could take.

Marguerite was moved. She didn't want to be, but she was. Thorne loved her and he valued her, things she wasn't even sure she felt about herself. There she'd admitted it, the deepest truths of her life and of herself. And how the hell could she ever be worthy of a man like Thorne? Dammit.

And here he was sucking on one of her wing-locks and oh, God, she could hardly keep standing. His fingers always seemed to find the spot in her body that couldn't get enough. Of course even his fingers were big and kept her satisfied.

The thought that he could put something even bigger inside her caused her to jerk forward. She would have fallen, but he caught her about the waist, held her steady, then searched around until he had a handful of her breast.

She could hardly breathe, just small gasps. She bent forward and put a hand on the side of the pool. Oh, Lord he was so going to bring her.

Prepare for a strike, he sent.

Oh, God, oh, God, oh, God. He was going to put a potion in her. *Do it.*

He struck. Because the wing-locks were sensitive, she once again jerked forward, but he held her steady and she felt the potion release from his fang near the aperture. The whole time his finger kept pumping, faster now. Pleasure began to seep over the wing-lock and into the surrounding tissue, the most pleasurable fire. Between his mouth, the rhythmic fondling of her breast, and his fingers pumping into her, she couldn't hold back. The orgasm caught her hard. She cried out, her body rolling and writhing, one hand gripping the edge of the pool, the other clinging to his forearm.

She panted and he released her wing-lock, kissing up her back. His fingers still worked her deep inside, but slowly now, in and out. She breathed hard.

He reached her neck and bit. *More?* he sent.

He knew her body so well. "Yes." Her voice sounded like she'd been swallowing grit.

He pumped again as the potion began to spread to the adjoining wing-locks. He reached down low with his mouth and sucked each aperture in turn.

She gave a strangled cry as the next orgasm descended on her, tugging low over and over, pleasure streaking over her and up. She leaned down and bit his forearm. Hard.

Thorne laughed and once more kissed and licked his way up her spine. He removed his fingers but didn't get very far as he caressed her ass.

He leaned over and kissed her neck. "Would you be open to something new?"

She flipped in his arms so fast, the water sloshed up the sides of the pool, sending a new wave onto the bathroom floor.

Her eyes were wide as she said, "I thought we'd done about everything there was to do."

He smiled. "Well, I've been thinking. You know that new power of yours?"

She frowned. "Obsidian flame? What the hell are you going to do with that? You want me to look into the future at our sex life?"

He smiled. Oh, his smile was so gorgeous, big even teeth. He met her gaze. "Obsidian flame is a place in your mind, a very deep place down a long dark channel. Sound familiar?"

"Yeah? You popped my obsiddy cherry. So . . . you're thinking . . ."

He shrugged. "I'd like to explore . . . some possibilities."

"You mean, you think if you did that again, it might not hurt? You think it might feel good?"

"Yeah." His deep gravelly voice got even deeper.

Her body started to tremble. As he pushed against her mind, she let her shields fall, which meant he fell inside and did a kind of lumbering roll as he righted himself. "Do I take that as a yes?"

"Hell, yeah, but I can't imagine what's going to happen. And by the way, it really hurt last time."

"I know and I didn't like that you were getting hurt, but I liked being in there. A lot." He rose up out of the water. "What do you think?"

She slid her arms around his waist and held on to him. He was very firm. In fact he was goddamn hard. She pressed up against him and wiggled so that his eyes did a roll and he sucked in air like he was breathing through a straw. "So what position do you want to do this in."

"Again, so my kind of woman." He began backing her up in the direction of the platform. "I want you up here, prone."

She looked behind her, and when he lifted her by her waist, she knew where she was headed. By the time her ass felt the platform, he'd folded a nice thick terry onto the hard stone just for her.

"You are so thoughtful."

"There's another one next to you in case you get cold. I'm still in all this warm water up to my thighs but"—he looked down her body at her bare mons—"you might get chilled because I'll be leaving most of you uncovered."

She smiled as she spread her legs wide for him and drew her knees up. "What do you intend to do?" she asked, as if she didn't know.

She watched a tremor pass through him. His mouth fell open. She dragged the extra towel, rolled it up, and shoved it under her head. She wanted to watch this, one big warrior planting his hands on either side of her hips and dipping his face right where she wanted it.

Do you like that I'm bare? she sent as his tongue made one long swipe.

God yes. At least right now, I do. I loved your thick hair as well. Aw, hell, Marguerite, I'm just so into your body. Addicted.

She knew exactly what he meant. His thick tongue began lapping at her, and everything low began trembling all over again.

Thorne?

Yeah, sweetheart. He groaned. *You taste of rose and woman blended and I'm hard as rock because of it. But, yeah, what do you want? More of this?* He flicked his tongue over her in quick little pats so that her back arched and he had to hold her pelvis down to keep her on the platform. His warm laughter rippled through the damp air.

Oh, God, she could so get used to this, being with him all the time. She felt him inside her mind as well, a strong presence. Her heart started to hurt all over again.

You said you wanted something.

She looked back down at his head bobbing between her

legs. *Actually, I was wondering, before you plunge into my obsiddy power, whether you needed some, you know, sustenance. Sustenance very low this time.*

He stopped lapping and groaned so deeply, pushing away from the stone, that she knew the thought of what she was offering had nearly brought him.

When he finally met her gaze, his eyes were at half-mast and his lips were parted as he worked to drag air in.

"Take me low," she said and she stretched her right leg out, pushing her knees even farther apart, and ran a hand slowly down along the side of her thigh.

He caught her fingers and kissed her hand but immediately settled his face into her groin and nuzzled her. Then he began to lick, long hard swipes to coax the vein to rise.

Her body began to tense because that kind of activity, so close to her clit, told her exactly what was coming. Thorne was no novice, either, and in preparation for what he knew this would do to her, he slid his fingers inside. *You're so wet.*

Of course I am. Oh, God, Thorne. I'm ready. Just do it.

He took his free arm and pressed across her lower abdomen in order to keep her anchored. Thank God he was strong, because as soon as he started taking her blood, she wouldn't be able to control her body's reactions.

One last lick, then he struck.

She didn't care how he did it, but she loved when he penetrated her: tongue, fingers, cock, fangs. Her body did exactly what she knew it would do, a full-body roll lifting her off the platform, but he was strong, and his left arm kept her pinned in place so that his fangs wouldn't tear her apart.

He drank hard and fast and she could hear his breathing take on a desperate quality, forcing his chest up and down in almost heaving gasps as he dragged air through his nose.

She was so close, but he suddenly rose up, his mouth covered in her blood.

She would have complained at the abrupt cessation, but she glanced low. His cock was a missile. She scooted her hips closer toward him, until she was almost falling off the side of the pool, but he stood breathing hard, his hands in fists.

His eyes were closed and he almost looked like he was in pain.

"Thorne?"

He held up one hand to still her. *Hold on,* he sent.

But for just a moment, as he stood there, that silvery white light poured over him until he was bathed in light, transfigured, a god once more.

Thorne didn't quite understand what the hell was happening to him. Shit, Marguerite's blood was suddenly a fire in his stomach, in his chest, in his veins, now flowing through his heart and setting his soul on fire, more than ever before.

He felt stronger, more fit for the world, ready to take on what was about to descend on Second Earth. Sweet Jesus, this was one helluva drug.

He was hard as flint and ready to come, but he didn't want to, not yet, not like this, not separated from her. And he wanted to delve into her obsidian flame power. He could feel the source waiting for him since he was within her mind, like a radiating heat not far away.

He opened his eyes and looked at her.

"Thorne, your eyes."

"What?" They felt warm, almost hot.

"They're almost glowing."

He nodded and moved toward her, toward all the swollen parts of her, opened wide and waiting. He wasn't exactly present. His need spoke for him, to be inside her as her blood was inside him, making him burn, making him hard.

He put one hand over her bare mons, savoring the feel of her. He took his cock in his hand and guided himself to her opening, holding himself in place. He began to push, his hips jerking forward.

"Sorry," he murmured.

"No, it felt good. Oh, God, Thorne."

He looked at her now and she dragged the towel from beneath her head so that she could lie flat. Her head rolled from side to side. "I love you inside me," she said, her voice breathy.

"I love being here so much."

She was so wet, so ready for him that three long pushes and he was buried deep. She accommodated him all the way to the end. She wrapped her legs around his waist as he moved over her, covering her because he was just that much bigger than her. He leaned down and arched to kiss the side of her head, her temple, her forehead.

She stretched and he found her lips, kissing her deep for a moment. It was the one thing they couldn't do because of the difference in their heights: really kiss face-to-face while doing this. But like hell he was complaining when she was everything he could have ever wanted in a partner.

He rolled his hips and drove into her, quickening his pace a little, groaning as she grew so tight, so close, so ready to come.

I want to dive now, he sent.

Oh, God, do it, Thorne.

If I hurt you, I'll back out, I promise.

I know you will, but I just have this feeling . . .

I know. Me, too.

He stretched out, settling his forearms next to her shoulders. In this position, his chest touched hers. She tilted her head, and her mouth found his neck. The groan that left him ricocheted around the rough dark stone walls. "Take my blood, Marguerite. Yes, do it."

He positioned himself as well as he could. She slid her arm around his neck to anchor him. She struck and the sensation caused his cock to jerk inside her. He tensed, holding back. Dammit, he almost came. He breathed light shallow breaths as she began to draw on his blood.

Whatever he was going to do, he had to do it quick.

He closed his eyes. *You ready?*

Yes.

Within her mind, he moved swiftly to her obsidian flame channel. He dove within and he heard her groans and it was all good.

Thorne. Oh, God, Thorne.

I know. I'm feeling it, too. Sweet Jesus all that sensation is going straight to my groin. He pumped faster. The tunnel was dark and long. Pleasure flowed all around him, teasing his mind, sending streaks of pleasure down through his torso and into his lower abdomen in pulsing streaks that built the deeper he dove.

He saw the pinprick of light that zoomed toward him opening suddenly and then he was inside her power, inside obsidian flame. All that pleasurable sensation intensified and the pulses quickened.

He could tell her orgasm was close.

Her screams were the first signal. The second was the bright flash of light. The third was the sudden energy that propelled him back up through her mind as at the same time he began to ejaculate. He pulsed and pumped and came, the orgasm taking him on a long, long ride all the way back up through her dark tunnel, now made light and brilliant.

He had never felt such intense pleasure, such a complete orgasm, still pulsing within him. She writhed beneath him. *Thorne, I'm still coming.*

Yes. He couldn't say more than that. He was still flying. His body stilled for a moment, but he threw his head back as another orgasm caught him and he came a second time, apparently to Marguerite's pleasure because she was screaming again, and arching her hips into him as hard as he was thrusting against her.

When he finally burst from her obsidian flame power it was like being propelled into outer space. He floated as the last of the second orgasm eased out of him, small twinges, sharp and perfect.

He was breathing hard as his body settled down on hers. *I'm going to withdraw from your mind.*

Huh? Oh. Sure. Okay.

She was breathing hard as well.

He withdrew, but it felt strange and rubbery until a final little *pop* separated his mind from hers.

She chuckled against him. "That was weird. Wonderful but weird."

"Yeah." He could speak. Sort of. "Wow."

"I know. My mind is full of beautiful rainbow-colored sparkles, like a shower of fireworks. I think I'm high."

"I know I am." He drew out of her so he could pull back and look into her eyes. "That was beautiful. What was it like for you?"

She shook her head. "I'm befuddled."

He smiled and leaned close to her, propping himself up over her with one arm. "Befuddled?"

"Bemused, confused, idiotic. My mind is like a slug right now, but it feels so good."

He kissed her, a soft pressure on her lips, then drew back.

"When you left the center of my power—"

"You mean when your orgasm propelled me out—"

"Is that what happened?"

"That's what it seemed like inside your mind."

"When you *flew* through that channel, oh . . . my . . . God. It was like a lightning strike of pleasure that kept coming and coming. I don't why I'm still alive. And you know what else?"

"What?"

"We are so doing that again. A lot."

He chuckled and kissed her. He spent the next several minutes just kissing her, thumbing her cheek, feeling her tongue on his lips, kissing her some more. He looked into her eyes and wondered how he could have ever thought of not having a life with her. He wondered if he should complete the *breh-hedden* with her—as in, maybe there was such a thing as destiny, maybe they even had a shared job to do, something together. Who else could have made love to her like this, traveling within her mind and entering her obsiddy power, as she called it.

It struck him as not insignificant that she matched him in power.

"What are you thinking about so hard?"

"You. Me. This thing between us. I'm trying to understand what it is. All this . . . power, especially my ability to handle all that you can give me."

She nodded. "Do you think it's more than the *breh-hedden*? More than that weird myth?"

"No. I think it *is* the myth." He held his hands out to her. She took them, and he drew her back into the tub to rinse off.

Marguerite splashed in the water, then floated. He pushed on her shoulder, hip, or ankle and spun in her circles, moving away from her as necessary. She giggled and released very deep sighs. She looked happy.

The bathroom had a grotto-like appearance, with all the dark, rough gray stone and deeply inset ceiling lights.

"Do you know what I'd like?" she asked.

"No. What?"

"A nap. Maybe all afternoon until Alison's dinner."

Some great happiness within Thorne's chest pushed at two thousand years of defensive bulwarks. An ease began to flow through him and he could breathe, really breathe. He helped her step out of the pool, followed after her, then folded a huge fluffy bath sheet into his hands to wrap her up.

She stood with her eyelids hanging low, but she was smiling. Her short blond hair was pushed straight back, which made her brown eyes appear huge in her face.

He dried off as well, then he led her to the bed, folding the covers back with his mind.

She looked around. "I need something to wear."

"Why?"

Her gaze snapped to his face, then she laughed. "A hundred years of Convent training. Well, fuck that." She dropped the towel and dove into bed, which gave him a fine view of her ass. He followed her.

Funny how she opened her arms and grabbed him, latching onto his neck with her mouth and sucking over his vein hard. At the same time, she pushed him onto his back, which was very easy for her to do since he sensed the direction of her thoughts and had no will to resist her.

Within a minute, he slid into all her beautiful rose wetness as she moaned and once more took his blood down her throat. He held on to her waist as he pumped into her, keeping her seated and enjoying the ride all over again.

Because he had come so recently, and all the nerve endings of his cock were still beautifully enflamed, this orgasm was almost more exquisite than the last two, which seemed impossible.

He held her for a long, long time afterward, keeping himself inside her and savoring that in such a position she simply fell asleep in his arms, satisfied and content.

He could stay this way forever, his woman in his arms, his maleness keeping his essence inside her, the soft mounds of her breasts warm against his chest.

He fell asleep and dreamed.

He led an army of thousands. No . . . millions.

Militia Warriors and a group he didn't recognize but he thought, Underground.

He flew at the head of this army that covered the skies for miles and miles both in depth and breadth.

He flew holding his sword aloft and in front, away from the vast sweep of his enormous silver wings. But the wings had flames now, dark iridescent gray against the silver.

He woke up with a start. He was now on his side, spooning Marguerite. He glanced at the clock on the dresser opposite. He'd been asleep for several hours; it was just after four.

He tried to recall the dream in its particulars, but he could only capture the images in brief flashes. All that he could really remember was the size of the army—vast—and the feeling that it was one of several armies all in flight, all at the same time, some under a dark night sky, others in full daylight.

The end of everything.

Or the beginning of peace and the eradication of all death vampires from two dimensions.

Purpose began to flow through his veins, a very deep abiding purpose, something large that filled his chest with fire and made the muscles of his limbs tense and release, tense and release.

Marguerite awoke with a start and pushed away from him, sliding from bed and staring at him. "What's happening to you? I suddenly felt like I was being burned."

He didn't know. The sensation was acute, however, and

full of heat. He slid to the side of the bed but remained seated, his feet flat on the cool stone floor. He put his head in his hands and took deep breaths. He felt sick to his stomach, and a pain began to build within his head.

Marguerite drew close and put a hand on his shoulder. "Thorne, what's wrong. Look at me. Talk to me."

He met her gaze through a veil of pain. "I don't know."

She put her hand on his forehead, then said, "Oh, God, I'm having a vision."

Marguerite felt the vision press in on her, but then stop and remain outside of what she now knew was her obsidian flame power. She called her power forth, as though wrapping it around her shoulders.

She saw the ribbon and knew that it belonged to Thorne, an elegant silver and gray, but iridescent. It rose to a vast height, something that generally the ribbons never did. She intuited that Thorne was in the process of change, big change, enormous change. She wondered suddenly if he was destined to ascend to Third Earth. He had been on Second Earth a long time, and he was very powerful. It was possible, but for the moment she set that aside.

Without hesitating, she dove inside the ribbon to see what the future streams were shouting about.

The vision came in slow steady images, of Thorne leading a huge army, in the sky, in the lead, his sword outstretched.

The vision shifted and there was Greaves's army led by a man she didn't know, who had waves of red hair flowing behind him. His eyes were a light blue, and power radiated from him in dark waves. She felt the weight of his darkness like a suffocating blanket in the future streams.

The image shifted back to Thorne and this time she saw the gray flame markings on his wings, and his wings had become enormous. They even billowed with what looked like silver flames from the tips.

Then she understood.

Obsidian flame.

By the time she pulled out of the vision, Thorne had dropped to the floor and was rolling in pain.

Thorne.

Oh, God. My head. There's so much pain.

Thorne, can you hear me?

Yes.

Thorne, I have to break through to your obsidian flame power.

What . . . the fuck?

You're obsidian flame, not the triad but some other kind. I need to pierce you and to release your power or you'll die.

A long pause, then, *Do . . . it.*

She pushed against his mind but couldn't get in. She shouted telepathically, *Release your shields.*

The shields began to lower and as soon as they did she felt what he was feeling. She recoiled. He was in so much pain.

She pushed on, however, forging her way through and searching for the source, the center of his mind. She found a pulsing ball of light.

Instinctively she knew what had to be done.

She summoned her obsiddy power, opening her mind and letting it release then sharpen, forging a kind of vast blade. *Now,* she cried.

She let the sword-shaped power release, straight at the enormous round structure. Her power split the membrane, which created a peeling-back effect so that light and power and heat released in a sudden broad stream up and up.

The nature of it catapulted her out of his mind so that she ended up being thrown back on the bed.

She felt disoriented but what went through her mind was: *How can he survive this?*

She sat up and saw the back of his head, because he was now sitting on the floor. She scooted off the bed and dropped down beside him. His eyes were wide as he stared at the wall opposite. He didn't seem to be aware of his surroundings.

She pushed at his shoulder. "Thorne, can you hear me?"

For a good long moment, all she could think was that she needed to get Horace here as quickly as possible.

Thorne's skin felt cool to the touch.

Way too cool.

She rose up, shaking. He wasn't present in his body. He had somehow left his body, which could only mean that if he didn't return pronto, he would die. She could feel it, sense it.

She had to get help.

Thorne kept his warrior phone on his nightstand. She looked around and there it was. She folded it into her hand and thumbed, as she'd seen him thumb.

"Central, how can I help?"

"Is this Jeannie?"

"Jeannie works the night shift, this is Carla. And you are—?"

"Marguerite. Thorne's in trouble. I broke open his obsiddy power but he's in some kind of death-like trance. I need Horace, maybe Alison. Endelle, shit, I don't know."

"I'm getting a fix on you now. Stay on the com. I'm calling all three entities. Thorne's house is a protected dwelling. I don't see any death vampire activity. Were you attacked?"

"No. It's his emerging power."

"Stay on the line."

A blankness began, a quiet that scorched every nerve in her body. She still sat beside him so she rubbed his arm, his shoulder, his chest, but he was getting colder by the second. "No, no, no," she whispered. "Stay with me."

"Marguerite," Carla said. "You have incoming. Horace and Alison. Behind you. Turn around please."

She whipped around and they both arrived at the same time. Alison's blond hair was in complete disarray and Horace's eyes were puffy from sleep.

Neither said anything, they just moved past her close to Thorne. Only as she stood there with the phone still pinned to her ear did she realize she and Thorne were both naked. As if she cared. Thorne sure as hell wouldn't.

But maybe the others would.

Carla came back on the line again. "Endelle's coming in three, two, one."

She shimmered to life right next to Marguerite wearing a very simple long purple gown.

Endelle looked her up and down and lifted her brows. "What happened. You fuck him to death, or what?" But for all that sarcasm, her eyes looked tight.

Marguerite wasn't certain whether she should reveal the truth about Thorne's new power to all three ascenders or not, but she finally just said it straight out. "Obsidian flame."

Endelle frowned, but she kept her gaze on Thorne. "You killed him with your obsidian flame power? I don't understand."

"No. Thorne has his own version of obsidian flame power."

"That's . . . not . . . possible. Wait a minute. When he and I were having our little tiff, and he was flying around, his wings had flames, very faint but they were silvery gray."

"There, you see?"

"Fine. All right, Alison, what have we got here? Horace, I need a report."

Alison leaned back. She wore jeans and an enormous T-shirt, probably one of Kerrick's. She shook her head. "He's not here."

"What the fuck do you mean?"

"He's not in this body."

Horace turned around. "His body is barely alive. It's as though his spirit departed. Can you tell us what happened?" His gaze flicked over Marguerite's body and his cheeks colored up.

She rolled her eyes and folded her leathers on. He released a deep breath. She explained, "Well, we weren't having sex, if that's what you're thinking. We'd done that earlier, of course, then we both fell asleep. The next thing I knew, my skin felt like I'd been torched and I jumped out of bed. Thorne was beginning this whole weird thing. He moved to sit at the edge of the bed and his head started to hurt really bad.

"I received a future stream warning that something big was going down, and this is what was going down. He was coming into his obsidian flame power, which neither of us knew about, and I had to do that thing that he'd already done to me and that Endelle had done to Fiona. I had to break open his power, it's part of the process. Maybe . . . maybe I punched too hard."

"Ya think?" Endelle sniped.

But Marguerite wasn't offended. She would own up to the truth, even if it meant she'd killed her boyfriend, but she hadn't. "No, Endelle, I knew what I was doing. And I would do it again. If you want, you can do a mind-dive and see the whole thing for yourself."

The Supreme High Administrator of Second Earth sighed heavily. "No, you have the smell of truth about you. Alison, you're up. What do we do? How do we get him back?"

Alison met Endelle's gaze. "He has to want to come back."

"What?" Marguerite all but shouted. "Are you saying right in this moment he doesn't *want* to come back? Oh, no, this is so not happening."

"You go, girl," Endelle murmured.

Alison sat back on her heels. She met Marguerite's gaze. "Yeah, that's what I'm saying. He doesn't want to come back."

Marguerite moved to stand in front of Thorne. He was dead. Sitting there, her vampire boyfriend was dead. And Alison was suggesting that it was because he didn't want to come back.

She knelt between his legs and put her hands on his shoulders. "Thorne, don't even think about staying wherever the hell it is you are! I need you here. We all need you." The sense that he wasn't present flat-out scared her, and she knew she had to do more than just beg.

She turned to Alison. "You'd better get out of the way."

Alison fell backward as though she had a premonition what Marguerite meant to do. This was going to hurt. She drew her right arm back and at the same time dove within his absent mind. She found the seat of his obsiddy power. It was still streaming, but in a thin stream, as though it had traveled a really long distance away from this body. In a coordinated move, she struck him hard on the face and shot her obsiddy power straight into the core of his bright shining ball of light.

"Get back here!"

Then she hit him again.

From Song of the Gods
Life is such a sweet agony,
How do the mortals bear it.
In the moment of perfect comprehension,
Death arrives to wash it all away.

—*Collected Poems*, Beatrice of Fourth

CHAPTER 18

Thorne floated. He was a long distance away, a galaxy away from his body, from Second Earth, from the woman he loved.

When Marguerite had ruptured the membrane surrounding his newly discovered obsidian flame power, his mind had gotten caught in a stream of energy so intense that he'd been catapulted a billion miles away. Or at least that's how he felt.

He floated, he felt one with the universe, he knew everything there was to know, the Creator was with him.

A man appeared beside him, a short man with gray hair and gentle blue eyes. Oh, James. He'd met James earlier.

The man swept an arm wide. "It's beautiful out here, isn't it? I confess I don't come here often enough. But then Upper Dimension work is rather time consuming, humanity being what it is, ascended or otherwise."

Thorne turned to look at him. He had an ethereal form, ghost-like. Out of curiosity, Thorne lifted his own arm; he, too, was opaque and unreal. He looked back at the stranger. "You're James, aren't you?"

He nodded and smiled. He was short, maybe five-eight. Endelle called him "Shorty." Thorne released a deep sigh, which was not quite a sigh because he had no lungs, but for the first time in twenty centuries he felt at peace. "I could stay here forever."

"One day, you just might, but you need to return to your body, the sooner the better."

"I don't want to go back."

"Of course not, but Second Earth needs you. The opening of your obsidian flame power has changed everything. In the coming months, your role in this world, and in the war, will alter significantly. You'll be able to do things you couldn't do before. And in the same way you've led the Warriors of the Blood, you'll become the anchor to obsidian flame. Once Grace joins with Fiona and Marguerite, once they experience the full expression of their triad of power, you will understand what it is to be their anchor, to bind them and to direct them. But even above all this, Marguerite needs you."

At almost the same moment that James spoke her name, a sharp stab of pain traveled through his entire not-exactly-corporeal being. "What the fuck?" Thorne winced.

"What's wrong?" James asked, but he was grinning.

"You know exactly what it is."

He laughed, although it was more like a ringing sound as though someone had struck a bell. "Marguerite has a lot of spirit. And power."

"And punch." His wildcat was after him. He could feel it. Suddenly her words reached him: *Get your ass back here, now.* His corporeal head started to hurt all over again. What the hell was she doing to him? *I didn't come this far to have you take off on some mystical adventure. Get back here.*

He looked at James. "Did you get all that?"

"The question is, did you?"

He smiled. "How much time have I got?"

"About fifteen seconds."

"You gonna help out with the war?"

"This is as much as I can do. Sorry."

There was a story in this vampire, but Thorne didn't have time to dissect it. "Later."

James nodded.

Thorne sighed, closed his ghost-like eyes, and began to stream back from whence the fuck he'd come.

When he reentered his body, pain shot through him because of Marguerite's thrust into his obsidian power and because the side of his face hurt like a bitch. Oh, so that's what she'd been doing to get his attention.

He opened his eyes, the ones with corneas, retinas, and lenses, which now rattled in his head. He saw her arm drawn back and her palm wide open; it was beet red from slapping him. "Hello, sweetheart."

She dropped her arm. "Oh, thank God, you're back."

He opened his arms and she fell into them.

Endelle understood something significant in this moment as Thorne held Marguerite close: Marguerite was the right woman for him. How many other ascenders could have brought him back from the dead like that? The woman had guts and strength, and by God she'd need both to live as his *breh*.

She had a sudden sense of the future, that these two would be up against the gates of hell in the coming hours.

She sent a silent message to Horace, telling him it was okay to take off. Horace offered her a slight bow, lifted his arm, and vanished.

Alison, a little red-cheeked, probably because Thorne didn't have a stitch of clothes on, turned away from the couple to face Endelle. "I'm going to leave, if that's okay with you." Her eyes had a drawn, pinched look.

Endelle rolled her eyes even though she knew what the problem was. Thorne was completely naked and once Kerrick saw the memories, something Alison would never be able to keep from him because of the bonding nature of the *breh-hedden*, Alison would have the devil to pay even though none of this had been her fault. Bonded warriors were notoriously protective of their women, and jealous as hell. Kerrick would not like on any level that Alison had seen Thorne in his full glory.

She knew Alison had been at the villa getting ready for

the coming-home dinner for Thorne. Big-fucking-deal. "I know you have things to do."

Alison frowned. "You can still come, you know."

"Don't think so." Jesus, her throat felt tight.

Alison nodded, lifted her arm, and was gone.

Marguerite drew back slightly and looked up at Thorne "What happened? I could feel that you weren't coming back. But why?"

At that, Thorne grew very still and stared at her. "You're right, I wouldn't have, if you hadn't been there. I got lost in the beauty and peacefulness of it. But you brought me back and that's what matters. I'm here. I'm not going anywhere. I'm here now." He drew her close once more and Marguerite burrowed her head beneath his chin.

Thorne met Endelle's gaze.

It was clear she wasn't needed here.

She nodded once, lifted her hand, and folded back to her palace to the west-facing parapet. The sun was heading for the horizon at this hour. The shadows had lengthened, a beautiful time of day.

Alison had asked her to come to the villa for Thorne's dinner, but she'd refused. She wasn't ready to speak to Thorne yet. She was still much too angry and there was a new pit in her stomach that she kept falling into, a real Thorne-shaped hole in her body that kept her as furious as she was sad.

She had never felt so alone in her struggles, so goddamn fucking bereft.

She could feel the scowl on her face as she released a sigh.

She felt the air next to her move and caught the shimmer from the corner of her eye, a large wavering of light and air that turned into a sizable vampire. But she was so not in the mood for Braulio's flirtations. Not today.

"Fuck off, Sixth ascender. Crawl back into your hole."

"Now, is that anyway to greet your lover."

She turned toward him and gave him a hard stare. "*Former* lover."

"Doesn't have to be."

"Bullshit. You're on an automatic timer that lasts, by my calculations, about three minutes, and that just ain't long enough."

"You never complained about our quickies."

She rolled her eyes and moved back into the rotunda. "What do you want, Braulio? Did you come to bust my chops about Thorne?"

He moved in close and took her arm. She wanted to shake him off, but the man was wearing that really nice cologne of his. Made her think of Obsession. He leaned in and whispered next to her ear. "I'm glad you got rid of him. That mind-link was a real *Thorne* in my ass."

Endelle snorted. "Oh, you are so funny."

He whispered in her ear, *"Every time he telepathed you, I wanted to kill him."* He'd used resonance, which made her tremble, and his breath sent shivers down her neck and sides.

But she still wasn't game. "Well, too fucking bad."

He moved behind her and pushed her hair away. She tried to move away from him but didn't get very far since he gripped both her arms and held her tight. He had the audacity to kiss her neck. She wanted to punch his lights out, but decided to just dematerialize instead, leaving him in the rotunda.

She folded to her meditation room, set up a trace-block, then set the walls aglow by mentally lighting all the candles at the same time. They now shone in a circle around the room, broken up by long lengths of burgundy velvet panels.

She turned to flop down on her chaise-longue, but there he was, stretched out as pretty as you please and not wearing a damn thing.

She was about to protest when it occurred to her: Other than seeing Thorne naked a few minutes ago, she hadn't really laid eyes on a warrior of Braulio's caliber in a *really* long time. Well, she had seen Marcus a few months ago, but he wasn't lying on his back, on full display.

She liked it.

Braulio had strong cheekbones, even stronger and more pronounced than Medichi's, and Medichi's were phenomenal.

Braulio's nose was somewhat narrow and sharp but perfect for his dark blue eyes and square jaw. He'd been birthed in one of the Germanic tribes eons ago and had ascended when he was just twenty, one of the most powerful ascenders of his day and for millennia afterward. Long before Thorne had arrived, Braulio had served as a leader of the Warriors of the Blood.

He had dark brown hair, which had changed over the millennia. She'd remembered a time when he'd been a streaky blond. But time changed a lot of things.

Her lips parted and as her gaze moved from all that dark beauty and settled on his pecs and on the light dusting of dark hair between, he shifted to slide one arm above his head. The move flexed so many different parts of his body that she actually stumbled on her stilettos.

He leaned up on an elbow. "Easy there."

"You . . . you should leave now." She hated how vulnerable she felt.

"Why? I've still got a couple of minutes left on the clock."

He began sliding off the lounge, and flexing his powerful thighs, which led her gaze straight to his cock. It was in that beautiful half-erect phase and still hung down but showed off every serious dimension.

The warrior was hung.

Her abs tensed and a long, rolling slide of sensation worked her so hard and fast that her breath caught and dammit, she almost came.

But she still wasn't in the mood to be humored by a man who was supposed to be fucking dead. She backed away from him and lifted her arm, ready to fold out of there, but he was on her again, from behind and holding her fast. Though she tried, she couldn't fold.

What the hell?

The next second her heels were gone, then the rest of her clothes. The Sixth ascender had power and lots of it—more than she did.

"What the fuck do you think you're doing?"

"Something I must do, Endelle, and you're going to hate me for it."

In the next instant, he slammed her down onto the chaise, facedown, and all the candles blew out so that the space was in complete darkness.

She heard him breathing, deep chuff-like sounds, strange sounds, animal-like sounds. He pushed against her mind.

But like hell she was going to let him take her.

Hell, no.

She erected her shields, holding them tight, but it was as though she'd constructed them of water and suddenly he was just in her mind, damn Sixth ascender.

Then her mind went loose and all she felt was pleasure, and she knew he was seducing her, stroking her mind. He'd put her in thrall and it felt so good, like she didn't have goddamn care in the world. Her body felt removed from her and yes, she knew he was doing something to her, but what did it matter? What did anything matter?

She lost herself in the mental thrall and in the way her body was experiencing sexual pleasure, even though he hadn't penetrated her. She could feel his rigid cock, how big it was, as he slid up and down her ass-crack, and it felt so good. She tried to shift her hips up so that he could find what was right now so wet and swollen for him, she ached up to her navel. But he had her pinned in a strange way, and she really couldn't move.

He felt bigger somehow, and his skin felt strange. However, given the mental distance, she just couldn't quite figure out what was going on.

His voice floated through her loose mind. *I'm sorry. But one day, you'll understand.*

Then she felt him bite the back of her neck hard, really hard. At first it felt so good then it started to hurt.

She whimpered because of the pain of it, despite the thrall. His breathing became ragged and rough and his teeth, bigger and sharper than usual, pierced her spine deep, penetrating the tissue, working between the vertebrae.

Fire began to flow up and down her spine, and it hurt.

Flames leaped through her, driving down to her tailbone then into her adjoining pelvis and leg bones. Up through her neck and into her skull, wrapping around her brain with fire, looping back to drive through the rest of her bones, her arms, wrists, hands, shoulders, and through her ribs until the deepest part of her, the marrow of her bones, was burning.

He had killed her—that was what she thought as the fire tore through her and completely engulfed her.

He had incinerated her to the core.

His voice floated through her mind. *You are more than vampire now, and you are mine. Mine.*

Then everything turned black.

Braulio looked down at the glowing body. He knew what this felt like, the burning agony, the fiery pain. Of all the assignments he'd undertaken, on behalf of the Council of Sixth Earth, this was the one he despised the most, that he'd taken the famous She'when'endel'livelle and done this to her without her permission, the woman destined to save two worlds from a monster, if only he could keep her alive.

He knew she'd reached the lowest point in her life. He could feel her despair as though it rolled in heavy waves off her unconscious body. He wanted to ease her, to comfort her, but her greater trials were in front of her, and yes, he had to somehow keep her alive, keep Greaves from destroying her before her own new powers emerged so that she could battle all the monsters to come.

He knelt beside the chaise-longue and took her limp hand. Bending her elbow carefully, he leaned in to kiss each of her fingers. "I'm so sorry, my faithful one. I'm so sorry. You are beloved in the Upper Dimensions, honored, and revered. They sing songs about you, about your service and suffering. Stay the course, my beloved, and you will win this war, but you must stay the course. Forgive me for this. Forgive me. Oh, God, how much I love you. How much I've always loved you. Be strong and be brave."

He felt the pull of Sixth Earth, but he resisted. The Council could go fuck themselves. He needed a minute. He closed his eyes and held the back of her hand to his cheek. He breathed and begged her forgiveness.

His cock was rigid and weeping. It had been all he could do to keep from piercing her, but he would not rape her, even though his body called to hers like ocean to earth. When he got back to Sixth, he'd give himself some relief, but it wouldn't be the same. To mark her neck as he had, but not come inside her, had been an agony beyond belief.

Sixth Earth pulled on him again, but he couldn't bring himself to move, to leave Endelle, to leave her without an understanding of what had transpired, to leave her all but blind for the coming weeks and months.

What he had done to her would change her.

Forever.

When Sixth Earth called a third time, it was with a resonant telepathic chime that about killed him. He released Endelle's hand and in the swooshing sensation of netherspace, he glided home.

Owen Stannett drifted a hand over the wave on the side of his head. His fingers trembled, but he couldn't exactly help that.

He stood in the center of Greaves's peach orchard on Second Earth, a high-security location, very private, with terra-cotta pavers and stone benches.

Casimir also stood near one of the benches, arms crossed over his chest as though he was embracing himself. No surprise there. That he faced outward, however, as though scrutinizing rows and rows of peach trees wasn't like him. He stood very still, almost statue-like, also not like him. Apparently, Stannett wasn't the only one rattled by the failure the night before at the Creator's Convent in Prescott Two.

Greaves was on his phone to Moscow Two. His extensive spectacle team, coordinated by a group of Beijing specialists, was working night and day to bring together every aspect of the forthcoming military review spectacle. There seemed to be some problem with the white tigers. One of them had gotten loose and killed several of his ALA Militia Warriors and even one death vampire. Two other death vampires had been severely wounded in the encounter. The greater misfortune, however, seemed to be that one of the tigers had died.

Greaves's face was red as he spoke into the phone. "You will secure a second tiger. *I am most displeased.*" He maintained his usual demeanor but there was resonance to his words that brought a knife-like sensation straight to the center of Stannett's brain.

Nausea afflicted him. He turned to the nearest stone seat, sat down, and put his head between his knees.

Greaves's ability to hurt with resonance was unlike any other ascender he'd ever known.

Stannett was sweating now, but it wasn't from the pain, which had already begun to ease. Nor was it from the necessity of offering a report to the Commander about their failure to off Leto and Thorne's sister.

No, what really troubled him had his heart pounding in deep terrible thrums.

Greaves ended his call. Stannett looked up at him, but the Commander shifted his gaze out into the peach orchard. All the rage dissipated, to be replaced by a haunted look in his very round brown eyes. "My mother loved peaches," he said, barely a whisper.

Ah, yes, Greaves's mother, the famous Beatrice of Fourth, Eternal Therapist of the Highest Order, memoirist, poetess, collector of proverbs. There were rumors that her relations with a death vampire had resulted in Darian Greaves, which of course would explain so much of the Commander's drive, his sociopath tendencies, and his power levels.

Greaves turned toward him, glanced at Casimir, then back to Stannett. "I do not know which of you is surprising me more in this moment. You, Owen, look so cast down as to appear utterly demoralized." He shifted toward Casimir but added just a hint of resonance to his words. *"And as for you, Caz, good God, what on earth has happened that not only did you send Julianna back to me, but your recent adventure in Prescott Two failed completely?"*

Stannett did his best to ignore the pain from that level of resonance, but he couldn't help but rock back and forth a little.

There would have been a time when Greaves fixing his attention on Casimir first would have brought Stannett a profound sense of relief. Now it just didn't seem to matter. None of it mattered anymore.

He saw no way out for himself—or Second Earth for that matter. Some higher roll of the dice had occurred, and he didn't think the play could be withdrawn.

Stannett watched Casimir shift to stare at Greaves for a long moment, his dark eyes almost glassy. Then he drew in a shuddering breath and his shoulders relaxed. He pursed his lips and he, too, sat down on the stone bench nearest him.

Casimir planted his hands on either sides of his legs on the smooth rounded edge of the seat. He leaned forward, which caused his mass of long hair to sway in front of him. That dark hair was his finest feature, but Stannett didn't envy him so much curl. His own waves were perfect for styling. Stannett couldn't imagine how much crème rinse the man had to use to keep his hair in order.

"So you want a report," Casimir stated. He didn't smile. That was also unusual for the Fourth ascender. The man always had a smile, or a sneer, or a lascivious glance, to throw around.

"At your *convenience*," Greaves said, using more resonance.

Oh, God, the pain. Stannett swallowed hard and took deep breaths. Stannett had a lot of power, but whenever he was around Greaves and was on the receiving end of the master's display, he was astonished all over again. He glanced at Casimir. Even the Fourth ascender had paled.

Casimir, however, lifted his chin. "I can't account for what the fuck happened. I created shifting mist—"

"And I was most impressed."

Casimir inclined his head at this significant compliment.

He continued, "But somehow the warriors arrived, as well as the obsidian flame Seer, Marguerite. There should not have been a way for them either to realize the mist was there or to pierce it. So no, I have no accounting for the failure of my plan."

"And I lent you a Third ascended death vampire, one of a rare group I have in my arsenal, and he did not report back to me."

"He's dead," Casimir said.

"How is that possible?"

Casimir shrugged. "He battled Thorne."

Thorne.

Stannett shuddered inwardly. Something was going on, something big, he could sense it.

At that, Greaves turned once more to face the peach orchard.

Stannett glanced out at the rows and rows of trees. The orchard was laid out in a vast circle above the Commander's Estrella Mountain military compound. Greaves had won several prestigious horticultural awards for his use of graded microclimates to sustain a single body of plants in twelve evolving stages of development. As a result, Greaves had ripe peaches every day of the year.

It was because of the orchard that Endelle called him "the little peach."

Greaves turned back to Stannett, holding his hands behind his back. "I was given to understand that this plan could not fail, that you would be in the future streams blocking prophetic information to the Seer Marguerite. I can only presume from what Casimir has told me that somehow she found her way into this stream, saw the future in every sharp detail, then relayed the rest to Warrior Thorne. Would that not be your take on it as well?"

Casimir, too, shifted to look at him. Stannett remained silent, clasping his hands together as he leaned forward on his knees.

So here it was, the moment he'd been dreading; he must now reveal this terrible truth. Nausea overtook him again.

Sweat poured. He tried to soothe himself by touching the wave on the side of his head, but now his whole hand shook.

"Good God, man," Greaves cried. "I won't kill you for telling me what happened."

He shook his head and looked up at Greaves. He was always surprised by those wide, brown, innocent-looking eyes. "I don't fear you, in this moment, Commander. I fear *her*, the one who achieved pure vision."

Greaves appeared to jerk and took a step backward. "No," he said very quietly. He shook his head. "That's not possible. You must be mistaken. Not pure vision."

Casimir was on his feet now and approached Stannett. Two pairs of deadly eyes stared down at him. "You're saying that the reason the warriors got into the Convent was because the Seer Marguerite achieved pure vision? You're lying. That's just not possible. No Seer that I know of, even on Fourth, can achieve pure vision."

"While I labored in the future streams, just as we planned, muddying the waters of the vision, I felt *her*. I was blocking the future, that peculiar ability that I possess, so that the efforts to slay Leto could not be seen, but I began to feel a disruption. The harder I worked to counter it, the less effective I became. I had no power to withstand what occurred. The only thing I can tell you is that she didn't do this alone."

"What do you mean?" Greaves asked. "Did you sense the presence of an Upper ascender in this fiasco?"

"No. An average vampire, a Seer. I saw the color of her ribbon and I pursued her future, but that, too, was clouded as though the combining of their forces created exponential power."

Greaves drew a deep breath but seemed to hold it. After a long moment, he released a hissing stream of air. "So let me understand what you are saying. Marguerite combined her power with another Seer and not only achieved pure vision, but also blocked your power in the future streams?"

Stannett nodded. His head fell but at least with the telling, some of his trembling had subsided. Thank God for that.

Greaves moved to stand directly in front of him. "I can

see your despair. Indeed, I can taste it like a sharp metallic bite on my tongue."

"Why wouldn't I despair?" he asked, looking up at Greaves.

"Because I have the potential to counter this ability."

At that, something inside Stannett grew very still. He searched Greaves's eyes. He wanted to understand exactly what the Commander was saying. Nothing with Darian Greaves was simple, nothing to be taken at surface value.

Greaves continued. "You have great power, Owen. I have felt it from you for decades now, ever since COPASS gave you the right to prevent Endelle from entering the Superstition Fortress. But we have a job to do, together, one that you must do for me, one that only you can do. And when this is accomplished, you will have your heart's desire." He paused, and it was this break in the flow of his speech that disturbed Stannett the most. Greaves continued, "In fact, I have a post in mind for you, one that I believe you are extremely well suited to fill."

"But not with autonomy."

Greaves shook his head. "No, my friend, not entirely. Those days are gone, I'm afraid. They ended last night and I know you understand because you do despair. But I would allow you autonomy within the various facilities."

Stannett nodded. A little flame of hope began to burn within his mind. "Autonomy *in the facilities*."

"Yes." Greaves then set out to explain the creation of five major Seer palaces as well as his plan to bind the Seers together in order to achieve pure vision.

Stannett sat up straighter. *Seers bound together.* He liked the sound of it, the *feel* of it in his mind. He was a Seer of power and he could intuit that Greaves's plan would work, perhaps in the same way that Marguerite, through joining with the other Seer, had achieved pure vision.

He also thought that he could continue his genetic experiment.

Greaves moved very close and settled his hand on Stannett's shoulder. "You would certainly be *free* to continue your scientific experiments. And of course, as you already know, I always reward my servants. Amply."

Yes, Stannett did know since a good deal of his personal wealth had come as Greaves had built up his fortune over the past century. "What would you have me do now, master?"

Greaves smiled, which gave those round eyes an even more youthful appearance. He removed his hand and took a slight step backward, turning in order to include Casimir in the discussion. "I think we need to shift our focus and put a rather large piece of bait into my now empty tiger's cage. But in order to do that, the focus must be on the bait and not on our super-powerful Seer. Otherwise I'm convinced that she will know what the future holds."

"And to what bait do you refer?" Stannett asked.

"To Thorne's sister, of course."

The mention of Grace, however, caused Casimir to emit a gasp, which turned into a ragged series of coughs.

Casimir had started feeling much better about the entire interview. He had not communicated with Stannett about the failed attack at the Convent because it hadn't occurred to him that the failure had been a result of emerging Seer power. He had assumed that Warrior Thorne and his band of merry vampires had somehow discovered a clever way to breach a kind of mist that was supposedly impregnable.

But now it all made sense: the timing of the warriors' arrival, that they knew where to battle the death vampires who should have overwhelmed Leto within the first fifteen seconds of the operation, even that Marguerite had found her way into the Convent at exactly the same time.

However, he couldn't quite bring himself to give a rat's ass about anything right now, except a certain scent that had bored a hole into his brain and kept his cock in an uproar. He hadn't been able to face the men for a long time because his erection was throbbing. He had a perpetual hard-on. Even the memory of Grace's meadow-wildflower scent was for him a triple dose of Viagra.

From the time that Marguerite had slammed that stool

down on his head, then folded Grace out of the Convent, Casimir's thoughts had been all about how to bring Grace under his control.

She was his. She belonged to no one else, despite some significant evidence that Leto was under the same weighty need and drive. Which begged the question: How the hell had the *breh-hedden* split off and decided that Grace was to have two *brehs*? That she felt an attraction to him was very clear. But she also had need of Leto.

The next question, however, was much more difficult to answer. What the hell was he supposed to do with this whole ridiculous situation? On a very deep level, he'd hoped that Grace would somehow end up dead; then he wouldn't be faced with his need for her. That she had lived changed everything for him. With each minute that passed, his need to possess her grew stronger.

Worse, when Greaves discovered that she was obsidian flame, the third leg of the triad, he would stop at nothing to destroy her.

And that, he simply could not have.

Grace at all costs must live and he must complete the *breh-hedden* with her before Leto did, because she must come entirely under his control. Nothing else mattered.

Greaves addressed Stannett. "I want you to dip into the future streams right now and see if you can find Grace in the immediate future, within the next few hours."

"As wish you, master."

Stannett closed his eyes. Seers often did so.

Stannett's eyes rolled back and forth beneath his eyelids. He was breathing hard, maybe even pushing into the future streams. He looked to be in pain.

Finally, his eyes popped open, and he stared at Greaves.

Casimir felt uneasy.

Stannett rose to his feet. He seemed calmer now, perhaps even hopeful. "I saw the devotiate, Grace, walking alone in the villa garden, in one of the garden rooms, the one with all the white blossoms. She was weeping."

"Which day and at what hour?" Greaves asked.

"Tomorrow morning, at the villa, before dawn. And at that hour, this one arrives." He jerked his thumb in Casimir's direction.

Caz recoiled. He even took a step backward. He didn't want Greaves to guess at what this was all about. He worked at calming his heart.

"And what does Casimir do?" Greaves asked.

"He holds her in his arms and comforts her. Then together they vanish."

Greaves turned to Casimir and smiled. "You must be very good at what you do, since apparently in this vision you have the capacity to slip through Endelle's mist, which still covers the villa. I am most impressed. It would also seem that our path is clear. You must abduct Thorne's sister."

"Yes." The fewer words he spoke, the better.

"When you have her, you will fold her to me."

Casimir turned toward Greaves. "I have a request, one that I insist must be fulfilled if you wish me to do as you've said."

Greaves grew very still, but he said, "Go on."

"I want the woman. I want her to live with me in Paris."

"Indeed?"

"Yes. I've developed a *need* for her."

Greaves remained still.

Casimir waited as the Commander searched his eyes. His shields were powerful enough to keep Greaves out, so he had that going in his favor.

Finally, Greaves smiled. "I suppose in your perverted world, taking a devotiate would be the ultimate adventure. Well, I see no harm in the plan. You have my . . . blessing."

Casimir didn't smile as he responded, "Thank you. I will do as you have said."

Greaves turned toward Stannett. "Please return to Mexico City. I would ask only that you work in the future streams to conceal Casimir's movements. That way, if the enemy should decide to look into our activities, at least we'll have this layer of concealment. Even if Marguerite is able to achieve pure vision, let's make her work for it." He glanced from one to the other. "You may both leave now."

Casimir didn't need a second invitation. He lifted his arm and vanished.

CHAPTER 19

At five o'clock, Thorne held Marguerite close as he folded them both to Medichi's villa on the east side of the White Tank Mountains. As he touched down in the large central foyer and he gave Marguerite a one-armed hug, he wanted to feel at ease, but he couldn't. So much had changed for him, as well as for the woman beside him, that coming back to Second Earth wasn't going to be easy. Nor was it a plus that this was essentially a social evening with the warriors and with those women bonded to Kerrick, Marcus, Jean-Pierre, and Medichi. Marguerite was all but gritting her teeth.

She wasn't happy about being here, but her situation was profoundly more complex than his. For one thing, she'd gotten into it with Medichi's woman a few weeks ago. They'd almost come to blows and would have if Endelle hadn't intervened, pulled a brief stasis stunt, and caught Parisa up beneath her arm. Parisa loved Medichi with a *breh*-based passion now and Marguerite's flirtation with Antony had not been well received. Understatement.

For another thing, socializing gave Marguerite the scratch. He was hoping Alison would show up sooner rather than later to maybe take charge of Marguerite since he had business to take care of with his men in the next hour or so, like essentially how to disrupt a military review spectacle.

He stood near the large central table, the one with the seven-foot-tall floral arrangement and the living magnolia flowers. The estate had a formal garden, a large pool, a guest house, an olive grove and press, as well as a vineyard and winery.

Medichi had bucks. He owned several massive public gardens that apparently brought in sufficient revenue to support several estates this size.

Thorne glanced down at Marguerite. He took her hand and asked, "You ready to do this?"

"Sure. Why not?"

"Thorne, you're here."

Alison's voice brought him turning around to face the north wing, which housed a number of communal rooms including the kitchen. She held a tray in her hands that supported several reddish drinks in martini glasses. Cosmos. Inside, he started to relax. Alison would have done this, would have made sure that Marguerite had her favorite drink at hand.

Maybe everything would be okay.

She set the tray down on the central foyer table and took his free hand. "I am so glad you're back." In a lower voice, she added, "You gave us a scare."

"I know. Sorry about that. But I'm here now."

"Yes, you are."

She took a glass from the tray and handed it to Marguerite. "I've heard you prefer these. I hope I made them right."

"Thank you." She took a sip but wrinkled her nose.

"I knew it," Alison cried. "I got the recipe wrong."

"Actually, that's not it." She put her hand to her stomach. "I just haven't been myself lately."

Alison nodded. "Well, that happens when you go through hell."

Thorne watched Marguerite grin. Alison took the drink back but continued, "So how are you? From everything Thorne has told me, you're squat in the middle of it right now."

He felt Marguerite's hand tense within his.

Marguerite didn't say anything for a long moment, just seemed to search Alison's eyes. She finally released a sigh. "I don't know. I don't know what to say. I'm just really confused about everything that's going on. You've heard about the hidden colony, right?"

"Shocked. We're just shocked. Three thousand years. Inconceivable. I think it's knocked Endelle a little out of stride as well."

Thorne saw movement in the room opposite and Kerrick appeared, supporting baby Helena over his left shoulder and carrying a diaper bag in his free hand. The baby wore a halter in case she mounted her wings.

"Thorne, you made it."

"Hell, yeah."

Alison turned and took the baby from Kerrick. Thorne eyed the brother for a long moment then thought, *What the hell.* He moved into him and the men embraced. Dammit, it had only been a few weeks, but it felt like centuries. But then the brothers had been battling together for a long time. Being apart, even for short stretches, well, it just felt weird.

Thorne released him and once more turned to Marguerite. "I don't know that you ever met Marguerite."

"Don't think I have. Nice to meet you. Heard you were in that shithole of a Convent in Prescott Two."

Marguerite laughed. "I like you, Kerrick. And shithole is exactly right. If that building wasn't made of stone, I'd say burn it to the ground."

Kerrick smiled. "I never could understand the mind of the religious zealot." He glanced at Thorne. "Even Grace. I mean I always knew that she had a more pronounced spiritual side than most." He frowned suddenly. "I heard Leto will be here tonight as well."

Thorne nodded. "In a bit. He's in rough shape. Hasn't taken . . . dying blood in a while. I wanted a chance to talk to everyone first. Grace is with him."

Kerrick's voice dropped. "Alison said it's the *brehhedden.*"

"It is." He shook his head. "Jesus. Leto."

The room got quiet.

Marguerite said, "Grace will adjust. I mean, the *breh-hedden*'s pleasant enough if you like a jackhammer to the center of your brain."

Both men busted up. "Exactly," Kerrick said.

Even Alison's head wagged back and forth. "It is pretty bad," she looked up at Kerrick, "at least in the beginning. But it's amazing, too." He slid his arm around her back and hugged her. He even leaned down and kissed her full on the lips. Helena had her head on Alison's shoulder.

The moment was so tender, so full of what the future could be between himself and Marguerite, that Thorne's muscles twitched. When Kerrick drew upright once more, Thorne really needed to move things in a different direction because dammit his chest hurt. "So, is everyone here?"

"Yep. I think Luken and Zach are in the pool room. Zach and Santiago are still feuding, but I guess you know about that. I tried to talk sense to them but it's just not my thing. Everyone else is in the living room." He jerked his head in the opposite direction.

"Okay, what the hell is this feud about that it wasn't resolved in about fifteen minutes over a couple a beers?"

Kerrick's smile was lopsided. "Well, if you must know, it's about you."

Oh, great.

Kerrick's smile broadened. "But I'll let them tell you all about it when they're in the same room and you can, I don't know, slam their heads together a couple of times. I know I wanted to." He grimaced. "But thanks for putting Luken in charge. I tried to fill your shoes for a couple of weeks and about lost my mind. I don't have that skill set or even a tenth of your patience. Luken has done a helluva lot better since he took over yesterday."

Marguerite watched Alison with her baby. Alison swayed from side to side. There was something mesmerizing about her, something she couldn't quite pinpoint, except that there seemed to be an almost visible connection between her and Kerrick.

Alison was at least six feet, very blond. She wore a black headband that held her long hair away from her face and down her back. She had on a sleek black strapless dress. Kerrick's hand naturally went to her back and shoulder, touching her often, very tender.

The baby, a little over three months, wore a halter. Thorne said this was typical since she often spontaneously mounted her wings, which were supposed to be a very pale blue, iridescent, almost fairy-like. According to the doctors, and oral tradition, her wings would likely change shape and the iridescence would disappear with age. Because Helena was an anomaly, Marguerite had a secret hope that she'd mount her wings tonight. Apparently, what you saw was the intricate mesh superstructure with just a thin layer of fine downy feathers. She thought it sounded beautiful.

The baby had soft skin with touchable rolls, and Alison's fingers ran in a soothing line up and down the middle of the baby's back. Maybe it kept her calm so she didn't mount her wings.

But Helena wiggled a lot and kept turning her head, almost craning her neck in Marguerite's direction. She hoped liked hell Alison wasn't one of those mothers who foisted their infants onto other women with the words like, *You'll love holding her.*

Like hell she would.

Marguerite was not especially fond of children. And babies gave her the willies. Without thinking she stepped closer to Thorne, and his arm found her shoulders. He and Kerrick were talking about the hidden colony's inadequate Militia Warrior setup.

Alison moved quite suddenly, crossing between the men, which caused a kind of social sucking movement that brought the warriors standing right next to each other. They kept talking as though nothing had happened.

Unfortunately, Alison turned in such a way that now Marguerite was eyeball-to-eyeball with the baby. Great.

"I'm sorry," Alison said. "I can see that babies aren't your thing, but she's been craning to get a look at you. Is that all right? I can take her into another room if you like."

Marguerite met Alison's concerned gaze. Well, put like that, how could she do anything but say, "Of course it's all right. But, yeah, I'm not exactly baby-friendly."

"I think you have to be around them, at least that's my theory. Before my sister had her baby I wasn't exactly enthusiastic. I mean I always wanted children of my own, but I so get not giving a rat's . . . I mean, not caring much about others." She lowered her voice. "We're trying to watch the language. It's a challenge."

She glanced at Kerrick then back.

No shit—she was bonded to a warrior. They talked like she talked, all salt with a little pepper thrown in.

Marguerite was surprised at how Helena stared at her. "Does she always do this?"

"No. That's what's so strange about it. She seems taken with you. Maybe it's your short hair, which I love by the way. I've been thinking about lopping mine off but apparently my warrior won't have it."

"I didn't exactly give Thorne a choice but he seems okay with it."

Helena strained in Marguerite's direction and reached out with her hand toward her. Alison got a funny look on her face. Her brow grew pinched. Her voice dropped to a whisper. "She's going to mount. I can always feel it. Her whole body gets tense—and look at her back muscles."

Even the men stopped talking. Marguerite moved so that she could see the baby's back. Yep, the muscles had thickened and the small apertures were weeping.

The baby gave a squeal and suddenly the miniature wings were just there.

Marguerite gasped. *Iridescent* was right. "They're so beautiful. And the feathers." She resisted the urge to touch them. Feathers were very sensitive to touch, and she didn't want to hurt her.

"Damn," Thorne said. "I don't think I'll ever get used to seeing that."

Kerrick beamed. "That's my daughter."

Helena kicked her legs and flapped her small wings. She used her voice a few times. After a couple of minutes she settled down and once more flopped against her mother's shoulder.

"It wears her out," Alison said. "Ah, she's getting ready to retract."

The baby's back relaxed and a moment later the wings thinned to fine points and flew back through the apertures. Another moment and the back thinned out.

Marguerite was fascinated all over again by life and by ascension and by the miracle of wings and flight. But the baby still eyeballed her then suddenly reached for her, extending both arms.

Marguerite took a step away.

Alison said, "I'll take her in the other room. Fiona's been begging for an armful."

"No. Wait." Marguerite may not have had much affinity with kids, but if for whatever reason Helena wanted a cuddle, she could give her that much. She could damn well make an effort, even if it killed her.

She slipped her hands under the baby's arms and hauled Helena against her left shoulder. The baby settled in as though she'd been waiting for this shoulder forever.

Alison moved to stand in front of the two of them. "Well, isn't that something. Wow."

"What?"

"I don't know. She just doesn't do this. Ever."

Fiona's voice came from behind her. "Marguerite, you're here. I'm so glad." She moved to Marguerite's right side and leaned in to kiss her cheek. Of all the women, Marguerite knew Fiona the best. They'd shared a couple of telepathic adventures together when she'd been in the Convent and later the Seers fortress. "Love your hair. I'm so jealous. I'll bet it's a cinch to maintain."

"It is."

She rounded Marguerite to stand beside Alison, but she scowled. "Well, how do you like that? How many times have I taken Helena in my arms and all she does is wiggle to get away from me . . . unless she's asleep, of course." She met Marguerite's gaze. "Again . . . jealous."

"You can take her now."

"I wouldn't dare. She's actually quiet and yet she's still awake. What are you, the baby whisperer?"

Marguerite felt a sudden need to sway from side to side, some sort of primal instinct. She felt Thorne's gaze on her and she shifted to look at him. Kerrick was looking at her as well, and grinning. These men were devilishly handsome. Kerrick had gorgeous green eyes but what the hell was that smile about?

Then she glanced at Thorne and understood. Thorne had that look, like he suddenly wanted her full of his child, her belly swollen with the results of what he'd put in her. Very caveman.

But she cocked a brow and sent, *Not in a thousand years, so wipe that look off your face. Got it?*

Thorne shrugged and released a sigh. *Fine.* He then directed Kerrick to lead the way to the living room. "I want to talk to Jean-Pierre then Santiago before I hunt down Zach."

Movement from the kitchen and a familiar voice made her cringe. Helena shifted her head and punched her fist in the direction of Marguerite's chin. Yeah, she was afraid Parisa was going to do that as well. She'd certainly tried the last time they were together.

But as Parisa moved to stand on Alison's left, the woman was more restrained than ready to do battle. "Hello, Marguerite," she said.

The last time the women had met, Marguerite's overture toward her warrior had sent Parisa into cavewoman mode. She'd actually launched at Marguerite; only Endelle's intervention had stopped a real catfight. She suspected that someone like Parisa, a librarian by trade and sedate by nature, would now be embarrassed by her actions. Maybe.

Parisa glanced from Marguerite to the baby then back. "I was prepared to dislike you," she whispered. "But since Helena thinks you're okay, I guess we're good."

Marguerite met Parisa's gaze and because of the baby, she spoke in a low voice. "I'm sorry for what happened. I didn't understand, not on any level. I was intent on one thing, and I caused you a heap of distress. For that, I apologize. This *thing*—" She paused and shook her head; maybe she even rolled her eyes. "Anyway, this thing is a nightmare."

Parisa glanced at her and a smile eased over her lips. "Thank you for that. I appreciate it and I apologize as well." Yep, color now touched her cheeks. "I've never acted like that before, so I guess it's a kind of warning. Even when you're bonded, the nightmare doesn't exactly end."

"Not much of an endorsement."

But the women laughed.

Helena sighed, like maybe she understood Marguerite's dilemma, which was absurd. The truth was, she kind of liked the weight of the baby on her shoulder.

Okay, so she and Thorne really needed to look into getting some condoms. She also thought she might liven things up and said, "So what's everyone here using to keep from getting knocked up?"

Thorne heard the laughter from the foyer and some of the tension he felt slid away. Marguerite was one prickly cactus, and he knew she wasn't comfortable. But for him, this was coming home, his family, and he needed to do what he could to get everything headed down the right path.

Medichi had hugged him. Marcus sat on the couch with Havily snuggled against his side. He held her fingers to his lips and kissed them. Santiago stood facing the backyard by the bank of windows along the west wall. The sun had already set behind the White Tanks but the sky was a lavender and rich orange color. Thorne made his way across the room, moving to stand next to him.

The Latin brother had his arms crossed over his chest. He'd barely acknowledged Thorne.

"Welcome home, *jefe*." Santiago generally had a light, teasing air about him, so these stiff words alerted Thorne all by themselves.

A lawn stretched at an upward slope toward the tops of the mountains. But the skyline was now a dark gray. A couple of deer fed at the perimeter. The usual.

"What gives, Santiago?"

"What the fuck do you care?"

And there it was. He was about to address the heart of the matter, when Zach's voice shot across the room "Are you going to fucking bust his chops, you asshole?"

Thorne turned. Zach had a fair complexion, but right now it was ruddy.

"He had to leave. Everybody else gets that but you. He didn't have a choice. His woman was in danger. He had to go after her."

Beyond Luken and Zach, the ladies flowed into the room, every expression somber.

Thorne felt his responsibility acutely. He'd caused this. He'd caused best friends to be at each other's throats. It was just one more cause-and-effect of his desertion.

"The trouble is," Thorne said, meeting Zach's gaze squarely, "Santiago has every right to be pissed. All of you do, because I did have a choice. Yes, I experienced a tremendous drive to follow Marguerite because she is my *breh*, but that's not the only reason why I left Second Earth."

Every eye was fixed on him, every expression dark; some worried, some hostile. Santiago moved up next to him, but his glare was accusing, a demand that Thorne man up and explain himself.

But how could he offer a reasonable defense? His thoughts hadn't exactly run deep on the subject. Just strong and unrelenting.

He crossed slowly in front of Santiago and sat in one of the many large antique chairs that flanked the room. Others sat as well. Fiona dropped down next to Jean-Pierre on the same couch as Havily and Marcus. Medichi sat down in a chair, held one arm out to Parisa, and she settled down on his lap like she'd always been there. Kerrick, Alison, and Marguerite remained standing.

Marguerite swayed from side to side, with the baby nestled on her shoulder. Her brow was furrowed as she watched him.

Luken looked a little grim as he leaned against the doorjamb.

Zach, however, didn't move as he stared down at Thorne. "What the fuck are you saying?"

"That Endelle or any of you has the right to try my ass in a COPASS court for desertion." He took a deep breath. "I left because I was sick of the war, or at least the direction the war was heading." There, he'd said it out loud.

A low rumbling flowed from couch to chair to doorjamb and ended up settling on Santiago. A stream of Spanish flowed from his mouth, words and meanings that he punctuated with a repeated toss of his arms.

Thorne leaned back in the chair and turned to watch him in these theatrics.

The man had style, even when he was enraged, a kind of loose Hispanic rhythm and movement that made the women swoon. His thick wavy black hair was combed straight back and caught tight in the *cadroen,* emphasizing all that dark masculine beauty. His brown eyes flashed. "And you, the leader of us all, to have betrayed us. We look to you for everything, *jefe,* for character, for purpose, for sacrifice, for what is noble and good in our ranks."

Thorne shifted once more and met Marguerite's gaze. She still looked serious, her brow furrowed. She rubbed Helena's back in a slow rhythm up and down the baby's spine. He was struck again how short she was compared with everyone else present.

But not in spirit, he thought. The woman had presence, something she probably didn't even know she had. She filled the space around her with her energy, her essential goodness.

He thought about what he'd said to her when he'd returned to his body earlier.

As he turned to Santiago, looking up at him, at the self-righteous fury on his face, he now asked the question he'd been asking himself: "Why are you here, my brother? That is the only real question you must ask and answer. You must be your own guide and model for what you value—because what if I die? What if this had been my death as opposed to my departure? What then? What would you have done differently?"

Suddenly Santiago's sword was in his hand, the ruby in the crossguard winking as he swiped the sword twice through the air. He swished it finally in a long strike in front of Thorne so that the point touched the carpet at his feet. "My fealty is with the Warriors of the Blood. I would never leave them or desert them."

Thorne nodded and a smile eased over his lips. "Well said, except for one thing: Man will always let you down. Even you might have to make decisions that will seem wrong to you."

Zacharius came forward to stand beside Santiago. He put his hand on Santiago's wrist. "This is what I've been trying to say to you. We are none of us perfect, and when one falters, the rest of us rise up and do what we must. You can't be so pigheaded about this. You've only served for a few hundred years. Thorne has served for two thousand years and look what Marcus went through." Marcus had left the brotherhood for two centuries because his sister had been killed by death vampires and he'd blamed Kerrick for the death. The war had taken its toll—and how was that a surprise? Marcus had fought death vampires as a Warrior of the Blood for four thousand years.

Alison spoke up. "Thorne, I think after battling for two millennia, you're allowed a few weeks off."

For some reason, the room seemed to settle down at her words. Even Santiago didn't look quite so mulish. But then this was Alison's primary gift, her empathy and her ability to give ease just by her presence.

Marcus's voice filled the space, which caused Zach and

Santiago to turn in the direction of the couch. "Zach's right. None of us is perfect, and each has a breaking point when things must change, or the future feels intolerable.

"But I do know this. I wasn't idle while I was away. I built an empire, and that has helped me to change Endelle's administration's profile to all of Second Earth." Marcus's efforts had slowly gained the confidence of the High Administrators still aligned with Endelle. For the past fifteen years, High Administrators had been leaving her alliance at an alarming rate thanks to Greaves's advanced PR methods. He was a genius at propaganda and as the owner of most of the mineral wealth of Second Earth, he had a monstrous fortune to throw at the heads of those wavering in their loyalty to Endelle.

Marcus had slowed the process of defection to barely a trickle.

Marcus met Thorne's gaze and asked, "What did you gain by being away?"

But it was Marguerite who spoke. "Thorne has emerging powers. We both do." All eyes shifted in her direction.

"What powers?" Kerrick asked, leaning to look around his wife so that he could see Marguerite.

Marguerite shifted. Baby Helena's hand now hung beside Marguerite's arm. She was fast asleep. Despite the subject at hand, a tremor went through Thorne, a quickening that stunned him, not of his groin, but of his heart. He felt a profound need to get children by Marguerite, as though this was part of his destiny.

He'd felt the same way earlier, when baby Helena had all but crawled into her arms, demanding her presence and attention. Sweet Jesus, what the fuck did this mean?

Marguerite said, "Obsidian flame. We are both obsidian flame, but Thorne's power is different. Mine is meant to combine with Fiona's—and there's something more. Grace is the blue variety of obsidian flame."

Alison whispered, "Oh, my God."

Santiago asked, "Is all of this true?" He turned to Thorne.

"Since you were gone, you have now become obsidian flame? What the fuck does it mean? And Grace, too, that gentle soul?"

Thorne rose to his feet and glanced at Santiago's identified sword. "How about you put your weapon away."

Santiago nodded. The sword vanished.

Thorne explained what had happened. Certainly not all of it, or that the breaking of the membrane had occurred when he and Marguerite were naked in his bedroom. "The truth is, I don't know the meaning yet. I don't know what value it will be to the war effort. It's all too new for that."

He met Marguerite's gaze. She nodded in agreement, but she looked so serious.

"Right now," he said, "we're taking this whole thing one horrible minute at a time."

A general rumble of understanding went through the couples who had already been through the enormous changes that came with the *breh-hedden*.

When the children are well-tended,
A society thrives.

—*Collected Proverbs,* Beatrice of Fourth

CHAPTER 20

Marguerite swayed and rubbed without thinking. The sleeping baby was a solid weight against her now. Still, she moved in a gentle comforting rhythm that must have been as old as time. It gave her as much solace and ease as no doubt it did the baby.

She glanced around the power-laden group, the warriors first, imprinting face to name and back again. She had never been in a room with so many muscle-packed men before.

But it struck her suddenly that she didn't feel like she would have just a few days ago, on the hunt and so hungry for masculine attention she could have killed for it.

Being with Thorne had changed that somehow. Perhaps being inside his mind, perhaps fighting with him, maybe even essentially bringing him back from the dead when she busted his power open.

She had the weirdest sensation that she belonged here, among these people—something she had never felt in her entire life. Pieces of her past began clicking into place, even the way her father's brutal concept of religion had forced her from that community forever. Even the way Grace's friendship and her nonjudgmental nature had made her feel comfortable in the woman's presence despite the fact that they were at opposite ends of the spiritual spectrum.

She felt the power around her as a living, breathing entity, as something that was unified while at the same time belonging to each individual separately. And she was part of that.

Thorne was part of that.

"Maybe you should tell everyone about Leto now," she suggested.

He nodded then proceeded to relate everything, beginning with Grace having pulled Leto out of Moscow Two at the exact moment that Greaves had planned his demise. He spoke for a long time, about the hidden colony, about Diallo, even a little about his fight with Endelle. That part of his story brought a heavy silence to the room.

He pressed on. He expanded on Marguerite's ability to reach pure vision with the help of the Seer Brynna, a vision that had led to yet another rescue not just of Leto but of Grace as well, since apparently Greaves had wanted her dead for interfering in his plans. Then he spoke of Grace as the blue variety of obsidian flame. Essentially the triad's members were now accounted for, he added, though no one really had any idea what their joined power could mean for the war.

He only slowed down when he got to Leto's revelations about the size of Greaves's army. Marguerite almost blurted it out but thought better of it.

It was Luken who finally prompted him. "So, what exactly did Leto do on behalf of the fucking little peach?"

"He built his army. Two million strong."

Marguerite glanced around the group. She heard faint hisses, a number of curses, then just a fearsome silence. The air in the room seemed to vibrate. When she glanced back at Thorne, she saw that it was coming from him.

What's going on? she sent.

I'm angry.

Well, you're almost glowing. You might want to calm down.

He laughed, but he put his forehead in his hand and rubbed the temples. He squeezed his eyes shut. Marguerite watched his shoulders rise in a deep breath until he let his hand fall away, opened his eyes, and said. "Leto had to do this in order to keep up the illusion. I don't fault him. How can I? He believed he was acting in the interests of all Second Earth. If any of us had been approached by a Sixth ascender, would we have refused? No, of course not.

"At the same time, I want him to come back to us, but he's not well. There's a good chance he won't survive his withdrawal from dying blood. He won't take it again and for some reason he's become very weak, almost at the point of death.

"Only Grace's sustenance has kept him alive over the past twenty-four hours, but just barely."

Santiago, still standing near Thorne, said, "But I thought it was impossible to die from a lack of dying blood, at least so soon. I thought you could starve to death, but that such a death would take months."

"Not in Leto's case, but we're not sure why—unless . . ." Marguerite once more watched him take a deep breath. "Unless it's because he's caught in the *breh-hedden*."

No one asked the who of it. News traveled fast among the warriors. Nor did anyone ask why it might be affecting Leto that way. The *breh-hedden* was no picnic.

The deep sigh she took lifted her shoulders and the baby with it. Helena shifted and sighed as well, but she remained in the heavy weight of sleep. Marguerite kept a slow gentle rub up and down her back like she'd seen Alison do.

"You okay with that, boss?" Luken asked. From the corner of her eye, she watched him push away from the doorjamb. He was big, this warrior, more muscled than any of the other men. "I mean, Grace is about the gentlest soul I've ever known. I never thought she'd hook up with a warrior."

Thorne's smile was crooked. "Well, she kind of put me in my place about it. She may be gentle and kind but she doesn't lack spirit. Make no mistake about that. As for if I'm okay with it, no, of course not, because it's one helluva rough ride and I wouldn't wish that on anyone I loved." But as his gaze made its way around the room, it landed on Marguerite.

"The truth is, I'm beginning to think there is infinite wisdom in the *breh-hedden*. I don't know of anyone who would have been strong enough to bring my obsidian power online, except for this woman." He didn't elaborate on how it all happened or that she'd all but brought him back from the dead.

Marguerite released another heavy sigh. She'd come a long way since she'd dropped down to Mortal Earth. Now here she was, looking at Thorne and wondering. It looked like Thorne was a little farther down the road than she was, though.

Her arm had begun to ache holding the baby in one position for so long. She crossed in front of Alison and Kerrick, then sat down in one of the large chairs and adjusted the baby. When Alison slipped a pillow under her elbow, she breathed a sigh of relief. In this position, she could hold Helena forever.

The baby once more sighed. Marguerite heard faint humorous grumblings from both Fiona and Parisa as they each stared at the sleeping baby.

Thorne continued, "What I need to know right now is where all of you stand on his activities as a spy for our Sixth ascender." Zacharius dropped to sit on the floor in front of the couch, within touching distance of both Havily and Fiona. Marguerite watched as both women reached toward Zach's hair then pulled away, each turning to meet the scowling gazes of her respective mate.

Marguerite thought the whole thing fascinating, but mostly she could understand why the women had reached for his hair. Zach's unusual curly black hair fanned out from his *cadroen* in an enormous mass. He was prettier than most of the men, his large cornflower-blue eyes and heavily fringed lashes giving him an outrageous appearance. He also had faint freckles and pale skin.

Okay, you've looked at him long enough.

She shot her gaze to Thorne. He lifted a brow at her.

Sorry. Guess I was staring. He really could be a model.

Yeah, so stop looking.

Jealous?

Hell, yeah, especially in this room.

Thorne looked away. Generally, it wasn't polite to hold telepathic conversations while in company. "Shall I give Leto and Grace a shout and bring them here? All in favor, say aye." It was unanimous.

Thorne drew his phone from the pocket of his slacks. Not jeans this time, but tailored dark gray slacks and Italian loafers. His shirt was made of fine cotton in a blue-green that enhanced those particular shades of his hazel eyes. Damn, he was handsome. Helena made a kind of cooing noise in her sleep and Marguerite murmured, "Exactly. But you just wait. Your day will come and then you'll understand."

The baby huffed a short dreamy sigh.

Thorne frowned as he said, "He's worse?" Pause. "Shit. But he still wants to come?"

Marguerite was just far enough away that she couldn't quite hear Grace on the other end. She had strong, vampire hearing, but it wasn't that strong.

Thorne hung up. "Grace wants everyone to know that Leto's in bad shape, and the fold will make it worse, so be prepared." He glanced at the couch. "He'll need to lie down."

Everyone rose as if on cue, even Zach who practically launched off the floor.

Parisa spoke to Antony. The next moment a blanket appeared on the couch, a very soft beige fleece, as well as a couple of pillows.

Thorne called out to Luken, "Carla's sending them into the foyer. He might need assistance."

"Got it, boss." Luken was right there so he immediately moved into the adjoining room.

A moment later Luken cried out a resounding, "Fuck, is he even still alive?"

Marguerite stayed put because of the baby, but otherwise there was a mad rush to the doorway, which meant that it was one major traffic jam. Everyone had to retrace their steps and resettle in different parts of the living room once more.

Luken had Leto's arm around his neck, his other around his waist, as he all but carried him to the couch. The vampire was pale and hollow-eyed. Grace followed behind, her expression calm, even dignified. Her lips, however, were pressed tightly together. She still wore the Convent gown, maybe thinking she would return after all this got settled.

Thorne joined her by the couch. "How's he doin'?"

"Not well. He was barely holding his own before the fold. He's going downhill fast, even though I've fed him twice." She shook her head and her voice trembled. "Once we arrived . . . he collapsed."

Thorne put his arm around Grace, and she turned into him until he held her tight in both arms. He turned slightly and met Marguerite's gaze over his sister's head.

Marguerite felt for all of them. Maybe she wasn't the most sympathetic person in the world, but she loved Grace and she loved Thorne and from everything she'd heard, Leto didn't deserve his present suffering despite his service to Greaves.

When brother and sister drew apart, Grace wiped her face with her hands then sank down on her knees next to Leto. His eyes were closed, his breathing shallow.

But an argument broke out near the doorway.

"No the fuck way," Marcus shouted. "Not for a thousand deserving men, Havily. No. That's final."

Marguerite had no idea what was going on. She glanced at Thorne but he had a stunned expression on his face and began making his way to Marguerite's side. For some reason, he sank down beside her, next to the chair, and took her hand.

"What is it?"

"Oh, man this is bad, but it might be good. But dammit, this is really bad. Shit. I don't think I could do it."

Havily's voice lifted to the tall villa ceilings. "Screw that, Marcus, this isn't your goddamn choice."

Marguerite lifted her brows and held Helena a little more

firmly. That was Havily? She hadn't thought the lovely woman, with the immaculate makeup and perfectly coiffed red hair, would ever utter such words. She began to like her a little more.

"You are so wrong about that, Hav. Warriors don't fucking share. You know that."

"We need to make an exception in this case."

"I don't think I could do it," Thorne murmured once more. He squeezed her fingers harder until she told him to let up, that he was hurting her. "Sorry."

"What's the argument about? What is it he won't let her share?"

Thorne met her gaze, but boy did his eyes look dark, almost hostile. "Her blood."

Marguerite recoiled. Even she got it. Even she understood the horrible nature of the idea. "She can't . . . do that."

He nodded in brisk pops of his head. "You understand, then."

"Sure. Of course. I'd kill a woman for taking yours."

But much to Marguerite's surprise Fiona moved to stand beside Havily. "You have to let her try, Marcus, you know you do."

"Okay, now I really don't get this," Marguerite whispered. But Thorne was rubbing her fingers and kissing them as though trying to soothe himself.

Alison moved closer to Fiona and put in her two cents' worth. "If you stand next to Havily and hold her, would that make it easier? He could take her blood at the wrist."

Marguerite was dumbfounded. Why Havily's blood? The warriors had begun forming a tight knot near the entrance to what looked like the library. Tension in the room seemed to be mounting.

Sweet Christ, what the hell was going on?

But when Parisa, who really didn't like to share, joined the group of women, Marguerite's mouth fell open.

"Marcus, we can all stand with her, surround her. Will that help?"

Marcus pushed his way through this feminine onslaught

until he stood before Thorne. "I can't do this. You have to order Havily not to do it."

Marguerite watched Thorne, wondering what he was going to do. He stared up at Marcus for a good long moment. His breathing was strange, really rough, like he was just barely holding himself together. He let go of Marguerite's hand and squared his shoulders. He rose to his feet and leveled his hard stare on Marcus, that commanding stare that Marguerite knew so well. Oh, shit. Thorne was going to allow it. What the hell?

Thorne put a heavy hand on Marcus's shoulder. "How about you and I and the boys go out on the front patio and have a smoke. Medichi has some great cigars and I've missed a lot of stuff over the past couple of weeks. Jeannie's kept me informed, but I'd like to hear what you've got going on."

"Shit," Marcus muttered. He put a hand to his face and shaded his eyes.

Thorne stepped in close and put his arm around Marcus's shoulders. He got the man moving in the direction of the foyer and kept him moving.

The women quickly flowed in to fill up the space behind, almost like a barricade to the couch where Leto breathed in small puffs of air.

Thorne signaled for the rest of the men to back him up and together, as one giant mountain of testosterone, they ushered Marcus outside.

Alison cried out, "Havily, make it quick."

Marguerite's mouth grew dry from having it so wide open as she watched female peer pressure orchestrate a move against one of the bonded warriors. It was no small thing that the rest of the warriors supported Thorne despite the fact that he'd been AWOL.

The next thing she knew, Havily dropped to the carpet next to Grace and offered her wrist to Leto. He moved his head around and wouldn't take it.

Grace got in close as well and began to kiss him and play with lips. She rubbed her face against Havily's arm several times, scenting it up. She then loomed over him, held his face in her hands, and looked into his eyes.

"Take it, Leto. Do it for me."

Marguerite couldn't see the strike from where she sat, but she watched Havily's back arch then settle down. Her shoulder began to bob.

After a few seconds had passed, Alison, who now stood behind the couch with Parisa, murmured, "Look how fast his color is coming back."

Parisa touched her arm and drew her away, whispering to her.

Alison drew back and met Parisa's gaze. "Oh, God, you're probably right. Oh, shit." This, from Alison. "Well, so much for dinner and welcoming either Thorne or Leto back."

Parisa leaned over the back of the couch and said to Grace, "You'll have the house to yourself for an hour or so. Do whatever you need to do. Everyone's taking off as soon as Havily's done. Uh . . . except that Antony and I will be in his suite of rooms, but I'll keep him there." Her cheeks had turned a dark pink.

Marguerite was so confused. She was trying to piece everything together and failing. Why was everyone leaving?

Alison approached her. "Will you continue to hold Helena for a couple more minutes while I settle things with the men?"

"Only if you tell me what the hell . . . I mean, what's going on?"

"Oh, that's right. You probably wouldn't know. Havily's blood has unique properties: It mimics dying blood. That's why there was such a dustup about this. Leto will probably emerge much stronger and, um, well, he'll have certain needs."

"Oh, my God."

"You got that right. So this"—she extended a hand toward the couch—"is going to get very interesting in about three minutes, maybe less. And our warriors just aren't going to handle this at all."

"I'll watch the baby."

Alison left the room, her heels clicking on the hardwood floor. Marguerite felt a rush of cool air from the front door opening and closing.

Parisa approached her, looking worried. "The men will have to head to the Borderlands soon, but once this is finished"—she jerked her head in the direction of the couch—"at the very least Marcus will need to assert himself with Havily, if you know what I mean."

"But she's just trying to help, maybe even save his life."

Parisa shrugged. "They're bonded. This is a big no-no, especially Havily's blood."

"I get that, but . . ."

Parisa was chewing on her lower lip, and her complexion was flushed. She kept glancing in the direction of the front door.

Finally, Marguerite understood. Parisa's complexion hadn't pinked up because she was embarrassed.

Alison came back in and called Fiona over. "We're going to have to break this up. Kerrick practically attacked me. Antony's shaking. Marcus is sitting in a chair with his arms tight around his chest and rocking like he's going crazy. Fiona, I'd suggest you go out to Jean-Pierre and take him home . . . now. He's pacing like a madman. It's as though whatever Marcus is feeling the rest of them are as well, even the ones that aren't bonded. Thorne sent Zach, Luken, and Santiago off to the Blood and Bite for some R and R."

Fiona didn't hesitate. "Got it." She lifted her arm and folded.

Parisa was next. A couple of seconds later she and Medichi materialized outside their bedroom door, way down the hall, at least thirty yards away. He was kissing her hard as he pushed open the door to what Marguerite supposed was his suite of rooms. He all but dragged her inside then shut the door so hard the walls shook.

Alison moved to the front of the chair. "I'll take Helena now. Sorry about this. I suppose it's not exactly a rousing endorsement for the *breh-hedden*. We'll catch up later, okay?"

"Sure." The blond beauty leaned down and lifted her baby oh-so-carefully, cradling her in her arms. "Thank you for holding her. It meant a lot." Then she was just gone.

Thorne reappeared by her chair so suddenly that she jerked away from him. If she'd been standing, his cherry tobacco scent would have knocked her flat. Sweet Christ the man was shaking.

She rose and slid her arm around his waist.

God, I need you, he sent.

"Do you want to leave?" she asked. "Maybe we should leave." His obvious need of her, and all that specific male scent meant just for her, was doing a serious number on her body.

"Roses," he murmured.

He looked down at her. She saw the raw need in his eyes, and his powerful tobacco scent powered over her. His eyes wered ilated.

Still, he shook his head. "Not yet. I have to see for myself how Leto's doing. Then we can go."

Havily backed up, holding her wrist. Marguerite caught a glimpse and realized Leto had all but savaged her. But as she turned to Thorne, she was smiling and her eyes were wet. "You'll see in a minute." She then drew a deep breath and lowered her chin like she knew she was in for it. "Now, for Marcus."

She lifted her arm and vanished.

Grace stood up. As she moved out of the way, so that Marguerite had a full view of Leto, she gasped. Even Thorne muttered, "Holy shit."

Leto sat up. His eyes were closed as he leaned against the back of the couch and touched his stomach. "Free," he whispered. "I'm free."

"You're out of pain?"

He looked up and met Grace's gaze, her exquisite green-gold eyes and pale lashes. "Yes. For the first time in weeks." He felt alive, really alive.

Healthy.

Strong.

Ready.

The scent of the earth rolled toward him in beautiful sweet waves. He was fully erect and what he needed was in front of him, the angel who had given her blood twice to save his life, the woman meant for him, his *breh,* and he would have her.

He looked past her and saw Thorne staring down at Marguerite, his body arched over hers, his hand at her nape. He leaned to her ear and said something. Then they vanished.

A shiver chased down his neck and spine.

Sex was in the air, in the room.

He took Grace's hand and pulled her toward him, between his legs. She shook her head.

"Yes," he responded.

Grace stood over Leto, willing.

Yet not willing.

Oh-so-ready.

Yet frightened.

All that she desired was in front of her. She was damp between her legs, and little shivers chased up and down her inner thighs until she was trembling.

Her lips were parted.

She couldn't breathe.

Her efforts at poetry had been one thing, but this banquet before her, this decadent feast, was quite another. He was a rich roast beef, smothered in wine sauce, when all she'd eaten for a century was sticks of celery and chunks of hard cheese.

"You're afraid of me."

"I'm afraid of this path."

"Do you want to go back to the Convent?"

She realized she hadn't thought of the Convent once since leaving with him, since her obsidian flame power had emerged in the form of the earth, rising up through her body, and guiding her to Moscow Two so that she could save him.

No, the Convent had not been in her thoughts. Yet the

reason for going there in the first place was. In her most essential being, Grace was old and very spiritual. Not religious, but she held spirituality as one of the highest forms of human existence, touching the heavens, the purest form of thought, the potential of the vampire nature.

The Convent had meant decades of serious study, of all the religions of Mortal Earth, and most certainly the unifying doctrines of the Creator's Church of Second Earth.

But the study of how man, whether ascended or not, always turned a form of spiritual enlightenment into the timber and plaster framework of communal worship was still not what drew her to service and devotion. What drew her was a love of the divine.

And yet . . .

And yet, the whole time she had been locked away, studying, seeking her own enlightenment through prayer on her knees for hours at a time, she had written her erotic verses. The dichotomy she understood very well: She was human, she was vampire, and she could not escape the call of passion and of joining, flesh-to-flesh. Even seeing baby Helena asleep on Marguerite's shoulder had brought an entirely new stream of sensations flowing through her body.

Now here was Leto, shedding his fragrant forest scent all over again, the one that had engulfed her in the infirmary at the Mortal Earth colony.

"You brought me," she whispered. "When you took my blood."

"You brought me as well," he said, nodding. "And you've saved me twice."

"Did Havily's blood heal you permanently? Are you well now? Can you move forward in your life and survive?"

"I don't know."

"Do you want to live?"

His gaze drifted away from her, his expression as stricken as if she had put a cup over his flame.

When he met her gaze again, he said, "I don't know, Grace. I know that I want you as I haven't wanted a woman before. I know this is the *breh-hedden*. I ache for you. I crave to take possession of you and I would take you now, if you would allow it. As for living, I'm not sure a future is what I deserve."

She turned away from him and the chasing shivers suddenly left her body. Her life had never been simple, and now this wasn't going to be simple, either.

She wanted to give herself to him. Part of her wanted to open her arms and take him to her breast, hold him fast, keep him forever. She had always admired the Warriors of the Blood because she shared with them the quality of commitment. Whatever their manly parts, their size and strength, their ability to wield a sword and slay the enemy, to battle and to kill, they were above all devoted and loyal.

Which led her back to Leto's traitorous activities of the past centuries. She felt the depth of his guilt and how his guilt now undermined his will to live. She felt it in each breath he took.

As for herself, the sudden presence of Leto in her life still only addressed one half of it.

The other half belonged to her most essential self, that part of her that was devoted not just to the Creator, or to service, but to true spirituality and growth.

She couldn't deny that this was who she was in her deepest self. And though she had certainly enjoyed sexual pleasure while lying in his arms at the Mortal Earth infirmary, while clothed and with a sheet between them, a surrender at this point would have significantly more meaning. To give herself to Leto now was a commitment.

She understood the *breh-hedden* perhaps better than he did because Thorne had given many reports of it, how it had afflicted Kerrick and Alison, and the other warriors and their women. She saw how it affected him now. It always brought change and—perhaps more important—a complete shifting of purpose and drive.

She had her purpose and she couldn't imagine that changing. Still, she smelled Leto and his primal scent worked in her body, reminding her of every poetic couplet she'd created over the past hundred years.

"I am unworthy of you," he said.

She turned back to him, horrified. "Is that what you think I'm pondering right now?"

"It would be natural." He held his palms out and stared at them. "I have so much innocent blood on my hands and even more in the future."

She moved to him so fast it was a blur of speed. And since she dropped to her knees, he jerked backward, stunned.

But she took his hands and held them tight. She stared into his clear blue eyes. "You are worthy, Leto, a thousand times over, a thousand times more than you believe."

His breath was ragged. "Do you know what you smell like to me? The most fragrant earth, clean and pure with just the faintest hint of sweet wildflowers." His hand found the back of her neck. She liked it there, almost possessive, very intimate.

"You're the forest to me, Leto, heavy and wild, dark, foreboding, exciting."

He groaned softly. "Let me kiss you."

She felt the pressure on her nape and she allowed him to pull her toward him until his lips found hers. A tingling traveled over her lips, so enticing. Her lips parted and his tongue dipped just a little, rimming her mouth, gliding over the edge of her teeth.

She had forgotten, truly, she had forgotten how wonderful it was to have the physical connection, the touch. She had loved kissing her husband and it had been a very long time.

He moaned softly as he pushed his tongue deep into her mouth. The little shivers returned to skate up and down the insides of her thighs, little guiding lights aimed at the well of life, the place where such swelling took place, such rising of pleasure to the point of ecstasy.

He dragged her up until she lay against the breadth of his warrior chest. This was the moment that brought home to her all the physical truths of what giving him up would mean. He kissed her hard now, his tongue working her mouth the way his cock would work the deep, dark part of her body. He held her in his powerful heavy arms so that she was pressed against his muscled chest and through the thin layer of his shirt and her gown, she could feel the dips and swell of him.

Her mind began to grow very lax, very loose, as though the scent that now engulfed her was like the heavy blanket of dry summer forest air. She couldn't quite think.

But as he kissed her, another image intruded, of a handsome face, dark eyes, and long curly hair.

Casimir.

A trembling began at the soles of her feet, pulling at her. She couldn't help that she drew slowly away from Leto until she stood upright and flat-footed on the woven antique carpet of Warrior Medichi's living room.

She closed her eyes and held her arms wide, her palms flat and facing upward toward the ceiling. The strange energy began to ripple up her legs, through her hips, and up through her torso.

Then Leto's hands were suddenly on her face.

She opened her eyes and for a moment, the energy diminished. But she shook her head. "Something is wrong, Leto. I can't explain it."

A strange collection of words suddenly flowed through her head, accompanied by an almost singing quality, almost like music: *To not love them both, is to lose them both.*

"I can't do this with you, not yet. I want to, but . . ."

"It's Casimir, isn't it?"

She nodded. "He's my *breh* in the same way you are."

Leto sank back down on the couch. He looked as though she'd kicked him.

To not love them both, is to lose them both.

"Leto, you must listen to me. Our fates are intertwined with Casimir's. I can't explain it but you must accept that. At all costs, he must live. And now, I have no explanation except that it's a message that has come through my obsidian flame power. Tell you understand."

Leto closed his eyes and leaned back against the sofa. "I have understood nothing for a hundred years. I've lived a life I've deplored, one that went against every belief, every tenet of my soul. Now the *breh-hedden* comes when I'm ready to pass from ascension, brings you to me, but I'm not allowed to possess you. So no, I don't understand."

Grace waited. The one thing she had learned in the Convent was the power of waiting, of patience. How her sister would have laughed at the irony that Grace had to go into a convent to learn to be her sister's namesake.

She waited now. She settled her spirit down, that part of her that wanted to crawl into Leto's arms, to touch him low, to give to him every erotic experience she had imagined through the decades. She drew a single deep breath and willed him, if not to understand, then to accept.

Finally, he opened his left arm. His smile might have been crooked and his clear blue eyes may have still been full of sadness, but she saw his acceptance.

She slid next to him and put her head on his shoulder as he surrounded her with his arm. How safe she felt like this, with his powerful muscles holding her close to his heart.

But she could feel the truth: that hell was about to break wide open, if not tonight, then in the early hours of the morning.

But she knew what to do.

She would rise early.

And she would pray.

"Do you know what I've loved?" Thorne asked. He lay flat on his back, in his Sedona bed, and Marguerite rode him, one of his favorite positions because he could see her. All of her.

"What have you loved?" she asked, tilting her pelvis just a little.

He groaned. It was getting difficult to hold back. When he'd been outside with Marcus and the rest of the brothers, he'd gotten so worked up. It was different now, because of the *breh-hedden*. A kind of communal response had resulted so that Marcus's suffering had become his, and shit how he'd needed this with Marguerite.

She dipped forward and kissed him. The forward movement of her body stroked him so hard that he could have come just like that, but he wanted the moment to last.

"What do you love?" she asked again, keeping her rhythm strong.

"This. Getting to make love to you anytime I want to. Sometimes when I had to wait until dawn I thought I'd crawl right out of my skin."

"I know exactly what you mean." Her back arched slightly, and the strength of her internal muscles tugged so that he hissed. Her deep rose scent flowed over him in a sudden heavy wave that plowed into his sinuses and brought his own back arching.

Marguerite eased back, slowing down. He took deep breaths. *Good,* he sent. He had his eyes closed. *I want this to last.*

Me, too. You're so beautiful, Thorne. Have I told you that? Have I told you how much I love just looking at you?

He opened his eyes. Her lips were dark, swollen, and parted. He wanted to rim her with his tongue but he feared moving. He was on the knife-edge of orgasm and it felt fantastic.

Marguerite smiled suddenly.

"What?"

"I just realized that if all your warrior gatherings end that way, you know, with all you men worked up, I'm in."

He laughed and his body bounced, but it eased him back just a little, which was good. "I want something from you?"

Her body shivered as she rose up and down on his column. *Anything,* she sent. She leaned closer and moved faster. "I think I know what you want. There's this ball of light—"

He closed his eyes and hissed. "Yes." He barely pinched the words out of his throat.

She started moving faster, and he put his hands on her hips. "You know the moment I touch your obsiddy power, you'll come."

He nodded. "Just come with me."

"That's what I've got in mind."

He'd been her lover a long time. He knew her body and she sure as hell knew what she was doing.

As she increased her speed and as he used his arms to help her pump, faster and faster, as she closed her eyes and began to moan, he lowered his mental shields so she could slip inside. He didn't have to wait long.

Suddenly she was just there. She focused on what even he could admit was so absurdly male, that big round ball deep in the center of his mind, he felt her power moving through him, flowing toward it. She was almost there.

The last time she'd pierced him, breaking open his power, it had hurt like hell, but he knew it would different from now on.

She reached the side of the ball.

Oh, God.

His neck arched and his back tightened in anticipation. Holy shit, this was going to be a ride.

Ready? she sent.

Are you?

A squeak of a moan left her throat. Now she was panting. *Oh, God, do it, Marguerite.*

When she slipped inside his obsidian flame power, it sent fire through his entire body, from his mind, down and down, over his torso, his hips, his legs, then rushed back up through his balls and cock.

By this time, she was tight around him, riding him fast and screaming her orgasm.

Pleasure began like a gripping flame that burned in the best way possible, at the base of his cock. As though time slowed, the pleasure expanded and intensified when he began to ejaculate. He had never felt so engaged with his entire body, as though ecstasy rode the veins of his legs, arms, and neck, as though he could feel the pleasure of his cock all the way down to his toes.

He heard a loud grunting, almost thrashing sound as he released deep into Marguerite. He recognized his voice and felt his throat open wide as he shouted, the pleasure streaking through his cock, again and again.

He opened his eyes. Marguerite was writhing on top of him. *Look at me.*

She popped her eyes wide then her back arched again and he could feel her pulsing against his cock once more.

He was breathing hard, but the thing was, he was still hard and he knew what he wanted to do. He pushed against her mind and she gave a loud cry and lowered her shields.

He dove straight into her obsidian flame channel, and when he reached the center he hit her hard. She cried out, her brows rising, her mouth wide. *Shit, I see stars,* she sent. *Oh, Thorne.*

Because she came again, she thrust him out, and that was the ride that brought him again. He shouted once more, pleasure streaking and straining and rocking him hard into her body, over and over, until at last he could feel her ease down and at last his own orgasm subsided.

She was panting and he dragged air hard as though he'd just run a marathon.

"Oh, my God," he whispered, sliding his arms around her and drawing her close.

"Ditto."

With his arms still around her, she slid to his side, her legs on his thigh. He smiled at how wet it was. He loved it.

He loved this woman and he wanted her with him, now and forever. That much he knew.

He thought back on the entire meeting. For whatever reason, Marguerite seemed to blend right in, even going so far as to hold a baby who generally didn't settle down with anyone except her parents.

His woman, without meaning to, had fit in.

Everything seemed to be adding up to one thing. The truth was, he had truly begun to wonder if maybe this was the right path for him after all, taking Marguerite as his *breh.*

Of course, other things were on his mind as well, like Grace and Leto, the war, always the war.

But as he stared through the wide bank of windows opposite his bed, at the monolith edge of the Mogollon Rim, black now against a dark night sky full of stars, his mind skipped around uneasily. All this emerging power, and he had no idea what it was for, especially his own obsidian flame power. Besides an incredible orgasm, what purpose did it serve and what exactly did this power encompass for him? He sort of got it where Fiona and Marguerite were concerned, since Fiona's ability to channel was enhanced exponentially, and Marguerite now had the power, with support from other Seers, to achieve pure vision.

But why the hell did he have this power? What ability of his would be enhanced, if enhancement was even the purpose in his case?

All in all, something didn't feel right to him, but when did it ever? The warriors would be out fighting now and he should join them, but he couldn't seem to leave this bed. He felt stopped dead, halted, immobile.

Marguerite plucked at the hair between his pecs. He had bite marks again, which he savored, something she'd done to him when they'd first returned from the villa. He loved the feel of her bare mons against his thigh. Her wax really worked for him.

First thing tomorrow morning, Greaves's massive military review would take place, morning in Phoenix but thirteen hours later in Moscow. He had meant to talk strategy earlier with his men, about concocting some means of disrupting the review.

Marguerite sat up and looked at him. "You're very tense."

He met her gaze. In the dark, her brown eyes were just a glitter. He could enhance his vision and bring her into perfect focus as though a light shone on her face, but right now he liked the shadows over her face and the glitter of her eyes.

He sighed. "Just thinking about the war."

She plopped down again and his arm once more held her tight. "Oh, that's all," she said, then she laughed.

"Yeah, that's all."

Though it was still fairly early in the evening, events of the night before, as well as the demands of the *breh-hedden*, tripped up his mind. Before he knew it he'd fallen asleep just like that, worrying about the war, with Marguerite in his arms.

When he woke up it was just before dawn, and the bed next to him was empty.

Connection is everything.

—*Collected Proverbs,* Beatrice of Fourth

CHAPTER 21

Marguerite stood by the window. As far as she could tell, there were no houses anywhere near Thorne's, so that her nakedness wouldn't be seen except by a couple of hawks circling over the gorge above Oak Creek.

Dawn broke on that side of the house, above the Rim, a beautiful clear pink that faded way too fast to the rising gray-blue of the day.

In a few minutes, yet thirteen hours away in terms of geography, the Moscow military spectacle review would begin.

As she looked out at the lightening sky, she thought it would be a wonderful thing to be on the wing right now, to be flying as the hawks were, catching air currents in the dawn, dressed in a warm flight suit of course, but flying free, without a care in the world, just letting the wind guide the journey and nothing more.

Her thoughts turned to her Convent days and how, on rare occasions, Thorne would unburden himself about the hideous depths of Greaves's overall plan for world-domination-via-death-vampire. What he couldn't have known was that afterward, when he dematerialized to return to this house for the day, she would be left in a state of despair and a longing to be free. She hated seeing her man so distraught, shoving his hand through his long hair as though he would tear out every last strand if it would just end the war.

But her short burst of freedom hadn't lasted very long and had basically ended the moment that second vision had crashed down on her at the Holiday Inn.

Now she was here, shacked up with Thorne, in his bedroom, in Sedona Two.

Although, to be fair, she wasn't exactly discontent.

She folded her arms across her chest. So what the hell was she?

Okay, maybe she was discontent. Maybe she still longed for her freedom and maybe, just maybe if she thought outside the box, she could still be a powerful Seer on Second Earth, still enjoy Thorne's oh-so-hot body, but chart her own course, go her own way. Hell, if she started practicing making her own mossy mist, maybe she could live by herself somewhere, a Seer hermit of sorts, on a beach in St. Croix Two maybe.

Thorne could come visit her and they could shake up the whole island with their obsiddy-based lovemaking.

"What time is it?" Thorne asked.

She didn't turn back to look at him. She didn't want to. She was frustrated and uneasy. She wanted an island paradise beneath a dome of mossy mist.

Yep, she wanted her freedom.

"It's time to get up," she said at last. "The little peach will be starting his puppets down the tree-lined avenue any minute now."

"You have a beautiful ass."

At that, she smiled, but she still didn't turn around.

"What are you thinking about so hard?"

"Nothing much," she responded. "How to craft my life, what I want to do next, where I want to live."

The silence that returned to her was so powerful that she finally turned around to look at him.

He was leaning up in bed, the covers hanging low on his hips, his massive chest on display, his long hair draped over his shoulders. He was an edible portrait, except for the hard stare in his eyes and the expanding and retracting of his nostrils.

"You're serious," he said at last.

"Yes. I'm serious. This life here is for shit. You know that."

"We're at war. The war is heating up."

"It's been heating up for decades."

"The review—"

"So what? A review today, maybe an air show tomorrow with ten gazillion death vamps flying in formation. I figure I could live somewhere else, like I've been doing. We communicate long-distance as it is, we could probably even do it through dimensions if we gave it a shot. We're both powerful enough."

"What about today? What are your plans today?" The man sounded bitter.

"I'm with you today, until this mess with Grace and Leto gets sorted out. Of course." When he didn't say anything, she added. "Thorne, please try to understand."

"What you're saying is that you're taking off as soon as Greaves lets the world know that he's ready and willing to subjugate everyone on Second Earth?"

"No. I'm saying we have options."

"Like hell we do."

"Hey, I didn't make this war. I've been locked up, remember? And I thought you wanted me to be happy."

He did want her to be happy but why should he be the only one with a responsibility here?

He hadn't awakened thinking about what he wanted. He woke up thinking about the military review and wondering what he could do to disrupt it.

Thorne leaned back and clasped his hands behind his head. He stared up at the black slate ceiling and the deep inset lights. He released a heavy sigh.

So his woman was still intent on taking off.

Great. Fucking great.

The trouble was, he understood her reasoning. He got it. The need to escape, to get away; hell, she'd been a prisoner for ten long decades. She should have her freedom. She should have what she needed. He wanted that for her.

But what about him? What about what he needed? When the fuck would he get a turn? "I want you with me, beside me, in my house. Why can't that be what you want as well?"

"Thorne."

"What?" He sat up. He recognized that tone of voice. "Another vision?"

She nodded. She moved back to the bed and sat on the edge. She put her fingers to her temples. That was new.

He scooted up behind her. "Are you in pain?"

She shook her head. "No. The vision is just a little unclear. Kind of fuzzy. I'm trying to focus better."

"Maybe I should look?"

"Yes."

He pushed inside her mind and there it was, but the image was wavy, almost blurry. Was this a result of her new decision to take off again? Did her emotions and her intentions distort her visions?

But after a moment, Grace came into view. She sat in some sort of cage, like a circus cage. She glanced around as though confused. She still wore her long Convent gown, so this had to be in the near future.

Then the vision sort of faded away.

"That's it? My sister in a cage?"

Marguerite turned to look at him over her shoulder. "I know. But I'm not myself right now. I'll try again."

Thorne got a really bad feeling. "We need to get to the villa."

He slid from bed and in a quick wave of his hand folded on jeans, loafers, and a long-sleeved T-shirt.

Marguerite followed suit and within another two seconds, she was dressed in her jeans, a red sweatshirt, and a pair of black flats. She ran her fingers through her hair a couple of times then nodded. "Let's go."

He folded her back to the villa, to the foyer.

"Leto," he called out toward the south rooms, his voice booming the length of the hall.

Leto moved in from another hallway that led to a couple of guest suites. He was showered, shaved, glowing with health, blue eyes crisp, his long black hair secured in the *cadroen*. He also wore jeans and a blue plaid short-sleeved shirt. "What's the hell's going on?"

"Marguerite had a vision of Grace in a cage. Where's my sister?"

But Leto paled and began walking toward them. "What kind of cage? You mean like a circus animal cage?"

"Yes," Marguerite said. "Black wrought iron. There was straw on the floor."

"Oh, shit. Greaves has a pair of white tigers in cages for the review. Can't be a coincidence."

Thorne felt himself weave on his feet. Oh, God. "Okay, but where is she? I take it she's not in the house?"

He waved a hand in the direction of the front door. "She went to the formal garden to meditate, I think. Is there something wrong with that? I thought with Endelle's mist, we were safe here."

Thorne shook his head. "I don't know." He didn't wait to discuss the matter further; he just wanted to make sure Grace was okay. He folded to the garden entrance near the pool. He felt Leto on his heels, Marguerite as well.

But trouble had already arrived.

The Fourth ascender had made his way through the mist. He had Grace in his arms and she was nestled into his shoulder. Had he put her in thrall?

"She has chosen to come with me," Casimir called out.

"Grace?" Thorne started to run. Leto blurred past him but by the time he got to her position, she was gone.

Leto tried several times to follow the trace, but was bumped back repeatedly.

Thorne whipped his phone from his pant pocket and called Endelle. If the Fourth ascender was involved, he needed her level of power to help get Grace back.

The phone rang and rang.

* * *

Endelle heard her phone ringing as if from a great distance. She pushed up with both hands then fell right back down on her *chaise-longue*.

At least she knew where the fuck she was. In her meditation room. But why was she here? Shit, she just couldn't remember.

Her bones were on fire and she had one motherfucker of a headache.

The room was dark. Why was it dark? Why was she here? What time was it? Where the hell was her phone?

She reached for it through nether-space, seeking it out, hearing the annoying ring, though faint, until she located it in her bathroom a couple of rooms away.

With a thought, she brought it to her hand. Alison had reset it to an old-fashioned phone sound. It about burst her head wide open when it rang next to her.

She touched the screen. "Yeah." Her voice sounded thick, like she hadn't used it in forever.

"Endelle?"

Thorne. Fuck. She cleared her throat, or tried to. "Well, if it isn't Your Majesty."

"What's wrong? Are you drunk?"

"Maybe." Had she been drinking? Her mind was fuzzy, like she'd had few shots of some really bad tequila. She rolled onto her back and became aware that she was stark naked. She rubbed a hand down her stomach and felt between her legs. Some moisture, but nothing more, nothing a male would leave in her or even on her. The back of her neck was killing her. She leaned up on her elbows.

Holy hell, why couldn't she remember what happened?

"We have a sitch, Endelle. You need to get over to Medichi's villa. Grace is gone."

"Where'd she go?"

A long pause. "Would I be calling you if I knew?"

That kind of made sense but she really didn't like his fucking tone. On the other hand, she just wasn't thinking clearly enough to tell him to go fuck himself. "No, I guess you wouldn't have called if you knew where she went." Her mind blanked out.

"Endelle?"

Why did Thorne's voice sound like it was at the end of a long tunnel? And why was she so tired?

"Okay. Give me five. I'll get my shit together and meet you over there."

What was that thumping noise? Oh, her phone just hit the floor. Whatever.

She struggled to her feet and with a wave of her arm folded to her bedroom. She touched down in front of her full-length wardrobe mirrors, but she had no knees to speak of and sort of crumpled until she was lying in front of the mirror staring at herself.

She lifted up on an elbow, a very wobbly elbow.

She had crusted blood in dried rivulets down both sides of her neck, and her hair looked like she'd walked through a wind tunnel.

She touched the back of her neck and winced. She'd been mangled back there. The skin was swollen and when she turned her head left or right, everything hurt.

Who had done this to her?

Part of the memory came back. Braulio.

Braulio.

That goddamn motherfucker, getting his kicks at her expense.

But what exactly did he do?

She couldn't remember much of anything except his weight on her, a lot of pleasure, then pain, so much pain all throughout her body. Maybe it was some kind of Sixth Earth coupling, which still didn't make sense.

She lifted her left hand and stared at it. Had he kissed her fingers?

Well, wasn't this one of the finest days of her life. Thorne took her apart this morning and the same day her former lover, Braulio, rapes her, or whatever the hell it was he did to her, and leaves her with a love-bite the size of the Sonoran Desert on the back of her neck.

And maybe he kissed her fingers. How fucking precious.

But she knew him and rape didn't quite fit. He was one randy sonofabitch and powerful as hell. If he'd wanted her, he'd have taken her. And he hadn't. She'd felt his cock rubbing up and down her ass, but nothing more. No, this had been about breaking skin and marking.

Marking.

He'd marked her, but what the hell for?

And she was so tired. She lowered back down to the floor so that her head rested on the cool marble. Yeah, the marble felt cool. Her eyes were so heavy and now she was dizzy.

She made a strong effort to reach for her phone and after a couple of tries brought it into her hand. Another round of serious effort had Thorne barking into her ear. "Where the fuck are you?"

"Sorry, asshole," she said. "This time you get to clean up the mess. You're on your own." She had meant to explain about Braulio and her neck and that something was wrong with her, but she forgot.

She lay there, trying to get her head clear. She had to. She had a sudden deep instinct that she would be needed.

She forced herself to sit up. One by one, she began clearing the cobwebs from her mind.

Thorne stared at his phone and frowned. Great. He was on his own. Well, didn't this feel familiar?

"What happened?" Marguerite asked.

He stared at his woman who wasn't really his woman and his irritation mounted. "Endelle's not coming and don't ask me why because I don't know. Guess she's still mad at me."

"And I guess you're still mad at me."

"Guess I am."

"So what are you going to do?"

"What I've always done. I'm going to take care of business."

Suddenly Thorne felt Grace close by. He turned in a circle.

"What is it?" Marguerite asked. "Shit, you're glowing again."

"It's Grace. I can feel her." He opened his obsidian flame power and let it flow. As the power released, Grace appeared in front of him. He could see her in an ethereal form. "Where are you?"

"Greaves has me in a cage, but it's a trap. Don't follow after me. Do you understand? I'll survive this." Her eyes closed. "I can feel Greaves. He's blocking my power." She vanished.

Thorne felt her trace and it was free of the block, but like hell was he not going after her. He had to. She was his sister and if he could get her back now, he could keep her from Casimir as well. Greaves wasn't her only enemy in this fucked-up situation.

He turned to Marguerite. "I have to go to her."

"I'll go with. Grace and I are sisters in obsidian flame. We'll have power together."

Thorne hesitated. As he stared into her eyes, he had a sudden sense of foreboding. "Maybe you should try reaching pure vision. We could call for Brynna."

But Marguerite shook her head. "I don't think it's necessary. We've already seen proof of the vision. We know where Grace is and we can get to her."

"Thorne."

He jerked his head in Leto's direction. "What?"

"I'm coming. Two swords would be better, much better."

Thorne shook his head. "I can't allow it. What if you have a relapse?" It was that simple.

Leto nodded. His shoulders slumped. "Tell me what I can do."

"Contact Marcus. Fill him in. See if he can get to Endelle. We're going to need her. That much I do know. She's in her rooms at the palace, but she didn't sound right just now."

"Got it."

He focused on the trace, but he hesitated a second time. That deep intuitive sense once more reached through his mind, touching him, warning him. He should wait, maybe contact Luken, get backup

He almost reached for his phone, but suddenly Grace

appeared once more in her ethereal form. As she did, she started to scream.

That ended all discussion.

He didn't have fucking time and besides, this was on him, like everything else was. "The hell with it," he said aloud. He turned to Marguerite. "I need you to stay put. This doesn't feel right."

She opened her mouth to speak, then closed it. She nodded.

But at the last moment, as he began to fold she touched his shoulder.

The ride through nether-space, even with Marguerite attached to him, was swift.

The moment he touched down on the straw of the cage, he didn't have time to yell at his woman. He took in several details at once: the cage was moving, fireworks boomed on both sides, geese and swans flew overhead, he could hear boots marching like thunder down the avenue, and Greaves held a very limp Grace against his chest.

In the next split second Greaves flung an insanely powerful hand-blast at him. He was shoved hard against the side rails of the cage.

Greaves vanished. In his place an enormous white tiger appeared.

What happened next was a blur of tiger fur, Marguerite's screams, his sword too long to be of any use, and his dagger struggling to find a vulnerable mortal spot in the tiger's torso.

He was able to get the tiger away from her, but how do you wrestle with all that muscle? At least he was vampire-strong, but in this Greaves-controlled space, he had no power to finish the beast off with a hand-blast. All he could do, as the claws shredded his arms and legs, was jab the dagger in repeatedly searching for the heart.

Greaves held Grace in his arms. He hovered outside the cage and watched the show. He had cloaked himself and the entire battle in mist.

He felt dizzy with pleasure on so many levels. It was

hard to pinpoint which felt the best: that he was watching the formidable Thorne being overcome at last by a creature he couldn't subdue—or maybe it was the sight of Marguerite lying facedown in the straw, bleeding out.

"And there goes obsidian flame," he said quietly, smiling.

He heard Thorne's grunts. He vowed he would savor the sound as long as he lived.

He wanted to wait for the exact moment of death, but he needed to be back on the platform since the cameras were still rolling.

He folded with Thorne's sister, however, into the bunker below the stage where Casimir waited. His servant deserved his reward.

"I didn't think you would return her to me."

"I wasn't going to, but she's no threat now. Marguerite is dying. Thorne will not survive this attack, either. You may take your prize back to Paris."

He held Grace out to him.

Casimir took her. Before Greaves had even blinked, the pair vanished.

But a chill went through Greaves, a prescience that all was not well, and suddenly he wanted his act of generosity undone.

Well, too late for that. He shook off the uneasy sensation, dismissed his concerns, and returned in a swift glide through nether-space to his preeminent throne-like seat on the platform.

As he stared down the long avenue, as his well-trained troops marched in rigid formation, as the handlers drove their squadrons of DNA-altered swans and geese along the route, and as the fireworks boomed, oh, yes, life could be magnificent.

Even as he watched, however, he used his voyeur window to keep tabs on what was going on in the cage. He kept his power-block intact. The tiger was dead now, not unexpected since Thorne had brought his daggers and sword into the cage, but he was near death, as was Marguerite.

Quite perfect and yes, magnificent.

* * *

Marguerite heard a strange cacophony of sound; the faint flapping of wings, the roaring of a crowd, and in the distance the boom of thunder.

Oh. The military review spectacle.

She had one thought: Why wasn't she dead? She hurt in so many places, all at once, that she couldn't focus on anything. And she was so weak.

She opened one eye and saw a beautiful bank of black-striped white fur.

Oh, God, the tiger, but she couldn't move. Neither could the tiger, apparently.

Where was Thorne?

Thorne? she sent.

No response.

Another roar of the crowd and shouts in what must have been Russian.

She pushed up on her elbows and shifted her head the opposite direction. She gasped. *No.*

Thorne leaned up against the side of the cage, shoulders slumped, head rolled forward, barely breathing, unconscious. Blood seeped from deep wounds down his chest, his arms, his legs. His usually golden skin was very pale. Too pale.

She *felt* that he was near death, almost gone.

Again?

Thorne.

Warrior.

Invincible.

She was close enough to reach out with her hand and touch his ankle. A tremor seemed to pass through his body, up his leg, abdomen, torso, which forced a deeper breath, a slight movement of the head, then nothing.

"You can't die," she whispered. "You can't die. Not now. Not like this."

In the distance, another round of thumping hit the air. Fireworks. Of course.

She was cold. She had on a sweatshirt, but the air was frigid; nighttime in Russia in March.

Thorne needed to get warm.

She tried folding the comforter from Thorne's bedroom, but she couldn't—as though she was blocked somehow. Of course she was blocked. Greaves would have had enough power to do that. She'd tried a hand-blast on the tiger and had failed.

Greaves seemed to have blocked most of their powers.

Awareness dawned. She would die here in minutes, from the cold and from the loss of blood. They would both die.

She laid her head down and stared at the bottom of Thorne's bare foot, smeared with blood. She closed her eyes.

How had it all come down to this, lying in a filthy cage, blood leaking out of her from a dozen wounds, and the man she loved dying? How had this become her life? Why was this her life?

Her mind flashed back and back, to her father's barn, the place where the animals shifted around uneasily while he laid the strap over her bare back and made her bleed.

She was still covered with wounds and bleeding.

Why?

Through her years at the Convent, sister-bitch had done the same thing.

So why was she still here—only this time she was about to die?

Why?

She opened her eyes again and watched Thorne's chest rise and fall in soft, almost panting breaths. She didn't want him to die. Of all the things that could happen in this situation, she didn't want him to die. He didn't deserve death, this beautiful warrior who had fought so hard, for so long. He didn't deserve to die.

Second Earth needed him. Deep into her bones, this is what she *felt*, what she *knew*.

Hell, she needed him. She caressed his ankle. "Don't die, Thorne. Not like this. Not ever. Stay with me. Please."

Her eyes burned but like hell she was going to cry. Fuck that.

Creator help me.

Odd to be praying, but shit, if she didn't get some kind of guidance or wisdom or strength or help, her man would die and Second Earth would fall to that monster.

She closed her eyes again. With her hand still resting on Thorne's ankle, she reviewed the past several bizarre, incredible days. She had started out on a man-hunt, looking for sex and enjoying her freedom; then the visions had started, all that emerging power that she hadn't asked for.

The need to whine about it rose up within her but she suppressed it quickly. She was pretty sure that her whining about how powerful she was had gotten her into this mess.

She had some chops, some serious chops, so why had she failed in this situation? After all, she'd gotten Grace out of the Convent without getting either killed or abducted by that freak, Casimir.

But why had that worked?

She thought back to how she'd gotten there in the first place and a very simple truth settled into her brain: pure vision.

She winced. Oh, God, she'd been arrogant, seeing only that she'd helped rescue Grace when in fact what had made the situation doable at all was that Brynna had connected with her and made the impossible, possible.

But when Thorne had asked just minutes ago whether she thought she should repeat the process, she'd insisted it wasn't necessary. The truth was, she hadn't wanted to connect with Brynna again, or any other Seer for that matter. She had come to view these kinds of connections, or any kind, as a stumbling block to her freedom.

She rubbed Thorne's foot. His skin was in that halfway place between cold and warm, not quite gone. Almost.

Okay, so a tear leaked from her eye, maybe two.

She drew in a deep breath.

She'd really fucked up. She'd been so stubborn and willful, so intent on living how she pleased, on pursuing her freedom, that now she had no freedom at all. Just death. And Thorne's death as well.

She opened her eyes and looked up at him.

She loved Thorne. She really loved him. She'd said those words before, but she'd qualified them saying that she loved him *as much as she was able*.

But now she understood something about herself: She was capable of love and worthy of love. That part of her that had been broken began knitting together, as though two parts of her soul reached across the chasm of all her past pain and began forging something strong and powerful. Her chest swelled as healing came to her and a couple more tears leaked out of her.

So what was she going to do now to get herself and Thorne out of this completely impossible situation? Was there anything she could do?

The thought ripped through her so fast, that her whole body jerked: *Obsidian flame.*

Hope flared.

She reached deep into her mind and released her power. It flowed through her in a heavy rush, then evaporated as though in this cage it had no power.

She heard laughter within her mind then Greaves's voice. *Did you think I would permit you to release your power? How absurd.*

Marguerite slammed her shields in place and felt the bastard leave her mind.

She was really sick of all these assholes having control, but dammit, what was she supposed to do now?

Thorne floated among the galaxies, so at peace, just like before yet not quite. He didn't seem to be as aware as he had been earlier in this state after Marguerite had split open his obsiddy power, which had in turn launched him into a true out-of-body experience.

James had been with him then.

Now he was just alone, as though he was neither here in this space, nor there, in his body.

But he was at peace.

Oh, yes, that much he could feel.

He waited for Marguerite, his wildcat, to start punching

at him, send lightning bolts into his obsidian flame power, forcing him to rejoin his body.

But nothing came, as though she were dead as well.

Yet he knew she wasn't.

Just him, in this floating place of peace.

No more responsibility.

No more war.

No more making love.

He would miss that.

Something moved inside his spirit at thoughts of Marguerite, of making love to her, of loving her. She had been his light, his sanity, his beacon. She didn't deserve to die in that cage, bleeding to death because Greaves was a monster.

He didn't deserve to die, either, yet how peaceful it was just floating among the stars.

His spirit moved once more: *Marguerite.*

He didn't want to leave her.

A wrestling began, a struggling between two worlds deep in his soul: a longing to remain, a need to go back and to finish what he had started.

But this sense of peace was not a new sensation. He had felt this recently while lying in bed with his arms around Marguerite, feeling her hair tickle his chin, putting his hand between her breasts to feel her heart beating, or yes, taking her, then taking her blood. In all those moments, he had felt peace, a mountain of it, he just hadn't seen it before.

She'd given him peace for a century but he'd dismissed the sensation as negligible. Yet here he was hanging between life and death, and understanding that there was nothing small about what she'd brought to his life.

She'd brought the tremendous force of all that she was, nothing held back. She'd kept him sane. Why had he believed that was nothing? Why had he always thought of her as just his Convent lay? In a century of sharing her bed, even for half an hour at the most each time, what was there she didn't know about him? Sure, they'd done their gymnastics and it had been great, but when all that was pared down, when he would finish inside her then look into her eyes, how many times had he thought: *I trust this woman.*

She had his back.

She'd proven herself over and over.

She'd doubted her ability to love but anyone willing to lay down her life knew a helluva lot about love.

She had laid her life down over and over.

She'd done it for him. And for Grace. And for a dozen Convent devotiates.

As he contemplated her, something else arose: that the love he felt for her had nothing to do with the *breh-hedden.*

He loved her.

Now she was dying and she needed him.

But how was he supposed to get back where he needed to be, as in back in his goddamn body, when he was all but dead?

He began to claw his way back, but it was like pushing against clouds. There was no resistance, no way to gain traction, not even a direction to find.

There was only one avenue that held the smallest bit of hope. He reached deep into his mind and flew toward the speck of light he'd come to know as his obsidian flame power. But even that source of light was dull. When he reached it, however, he dove within and felt a faint pulsing sensation. Maybe it was all he needed.

But what the hell was he supposed to do now?

Another question surfaced. Why had he failed in this situation?

For such a long time, he'd believed the war was on his shoulders, his alone. But in the past year what had happened? Alison had become Endelle's executive assistant and had calmed the scorpion queen down a lot. Havily's darkening ability had given Endelle more sleep, which in turn had eased Thorne because Her Supremeness was quiet in his head for a few hours every night. Marcus had taken over administrative duties and kept dozens of High Administrators from defecting. Medichi and Parisa together had an amazing power to

end a battle with the use of *royle* wings. Even Jean-Pierre
was increasing the powers of the Militia Warriors through
his own emerging ability.

No, he wasn't alone in this responsibility.

Then there was the untapped obsidian flame triad power.
Who the hell knew what gift the three women together would
bring to the table.

On some cosmic level, therefore, he finally saw that he
wasn't alone in this. He was surrounded by gifted ascenders,
each with a job to do. And he wasn't alone.

He wasn't alone.

And this wasn't just on him.

So what was on him, especially here, in this cage with his
breh dying?

Simple. He needed to make sure that she lived.

After that, whatever role he would need to play in the
future, he would embrace fully, but not as one who acted
alone and bore the sufferings of the world on his shoulders
alone.

Which meant . . .

He sent a very soft mental call to Marguerite: *Get Fiona.*

From deep with her mind, Marguerite heard the words, *Get
Fiona,* but she couldn't make sense of them. Had she fallen
asleep? Something smelled so funny, like blood and animal.
She opened her eyes. Oh, yeah, dead tiger.

Get Fiona, came once more, stronger this time and . . . it
sounded like Thorne.

Thorne was dying. Maybe dead already. She was close.
She was so damn cold.

Fiona. The gold variety of obsidian flame. Fiona, who
could channel things.

She'd made a connection with Fiona a few weeks ago and
in her way she'd helped Fiona and Endelle rescue twenty
thousand people from Dark Spectacle.

The connection was special.

She dove once more within her obsidian flame power and

this time sent a message to Fiona. As before the power seemed to dwindle to a weak stream. She couldn't do this alone. Greaves had blocked their power.

Thorne, she sent.

She waited.

After a moment, very faint, *I'm here, sweetheart.*

The sound of his gravelly voice, deep within her mind, strengthened her. *We have to combine power to reach Fiona. I'm coming to you, okay?*

Another long pause. Too long.

Yes.

Despite how weak he sounded, she pushed into his mind and at first was startled at how cold and empty it was. But she could feel some warmth and headed in the direction of what she knew to be his obsiddy power.

She arrived, shocked at how faint the light was, when before he'd been a ball of fire. Regardless, she pushed through the membrane.

The moment she did, it was as though she'd lit a match.

Thorne groaned. *Oh, God, you feel so damn good.*

So there's a little life left in you after all. But she sent him her love and she heard him draw in a strong breath and let it out.

You love me?

I do, more than I've understood, fool that I am. And that was the truth. Hard-core obsidian truth.

He sent, *So what have you got in mind, here?*

We'll do this together. My instincts tell me it will make a difference.

Do it, Marguerite, and no matter what happens, know that I'll love you forever.

She moved her power straight into his. She felt a deep kind of rumbling within herself, within her mind. She had felt this before, with Fiona.

And this was the truth about obsidian power: that it was all about connection, about joining forces, and about trust.

Call her now, Thorne sent.

She shot the message in a powerful thrust, wanting to make the most of it. Greaves seemed to have control of what happened inside the cage; she had no idea if they'd get more than one chance at making contact.

To be chosen, no matter how great or small the task,
Is to curry the favor of the gods.

—*Collected Proverbs*, Beatrice of Fourth

CHAPTER 22

Fiona dropped to her knees on one of the zebra rugs in Endelle's office and covered her ears.

"*Chérie*, what is it?" Jean-Pierre sank beside her and tried to pull her hands away from her ears, but she wouldn't let him.

And now her ears were bleeding.

"Hold on," she said to Jean-Pierre. "It's Thorne and Marguerite, I think."

She heard murmurs and gasps flow through the office. All the warriors and their women had gathered to find out what happened when Thorne, with Marguerite on his coat-tails, folded to what Leto had said was one of the white tiger cages in Greaves's spectacle parade.

Endelle, sitting at her desk but in a strangely weakened state, murmured, "Thank the Creator."

Fiona had heard Thorne's voice in her head, yet not his voice. More like Marguerite's, yet not hers, either . . . more like *theirs*.

She closed her eyes and focused on her obsidian flame power. When she dipped deep within her mind, following the dark channel that led to her power, she saw that the center of it was pulsing with light and heat. Whatever was going on, this was new.

She approached carefully and sent, *Marguerite and Thorne, if that's you, please not so loud. My eardrums burst again.* Jean-Pierre was now wiping at her face and neck with a damp cloth.

You're there, Marguerite cried.

She winced and she knew tears had popped form her eyes. *Gently. Quietly. Please.*

Sorry. This from Thorne.

You're both alive. Thank God. Where are you? What can I do? Leto let everyone know you were trying to rescue Grace. We're so worried.

We're in bad shape, Marguerite sent. *Thorne fought a tiger bare-handed and we're cut up. Greaves made it impossible to use most of our powers. Thorne is near death. I'm not far behind.*

We need Endelle, Fiona said. *Hold on. We're going to do what we did at Dark Spectacle and Greaves can just eat shit on this one.*

Jean-Pierre helped Fiona rise to her feet. She approached Endelle's desk and relayed the situation, then added, "Shall we go get them?"

Endelle nodded, but she remained seated. For this, Fiona's body would do the heavy lifting, but inside, it would be all Endelle.

Let's do this thing, Endelle sent. *Ramp up my power, Fiona, then I'll take possession.*

Fiona nodded.

The power flowed.

Endelle stared at Fiona. Her power began to merge with Fiona's incredible obsidian power. Her mind worked at lightning speed.

Now all she needed to do was possess the woman, and they'd get through anything together.

Hang tough, she said to Fiona.

She felt the woman step aside mentally. *I'm all yours, Endelle. Let's bring them home.*

Endelle leaned back in her chair and relaxed. She mentally took possession of Fiona and felt her powers expand exponentially.

She now looked through Fiona's eyes. She glanced around her office. All the warriors and their women were present. They all waited for her orders.

To Marcus, she said, "Get Horace here." He nodded.

She turned to Luken. "You're coming with. I want you to carry Thorne out."

He dipped his chin. "Let's go."

Endelle focused now on Fiona's connection with Marguerite. She could feel the woman's power fading, but she got a fix on her location. She moved to Luken and touched his shoulder. She thought the fucking brilliant thought.

Within the space of two heartbeats she touched down right next to the maw of a very dead, torn-up tiger. Luken turned, saw Thorne, then crossed in two long strides and picked him up in his arms.

Endelle did the same with Marguerite.

At the same time, she felt Greaves coming, a tornado of rage. She could feel the power-block he'd put over the cage. No wonder her second-in-command had all but lost this battle.

However, she slid next to Luken, touched his arm, and once more thought the thought. She traveled back through nether-space and with Marguerite in her arms, she touched down to face the same arc of warriors and their *brehs*.

She glanced at Thorne in Luken's arms. His complexion was now perfectly white.

She could feel that he was gone.

She separated from Fiona's body and returned to hers. It felt weird to be back. She opened her eyes and felt stronger for the recent connection to Fiona. She rose from her chair and moved with lightning speed back to Thorne.

Horace already had his hands over Thorne's body and

two other healers were working on the various deep cuts, but nothing was happening.

Endelle looked down at Thorne.

He couldn't be dead. He just couldn't.

Two more healers worked on Marguerite. She was unconscious but breathing.

"How we doin'?" she asked Horace.

"He's lost so much blood. There . . . just isn't anything left. He has no heartbeat."

Endelle shook her head, back and forth, over and over.

This could not be happening.

This was Thorne, her second-in-command, the one she had come to rely on in all things, the one who had helped her to not feel so alone for, oh, about twenty centuries. And he was dead.

Her throat ached.

This couldn't be happening, couldn't be real. She needed to do something, but what? She didn't exactly have the power to bring vampires back to life.

But this was Thorne.

Thorne.

Her closest friend. Her best friend. A man she loved with all her heart. Her family.

Oh . . . God.

She had to do something.

She glanced at Marguerite, then at Havily. If there had been any life left in Thorne, Havily could have brought him the rest of the way back. But a dead man couldn't drink, couldn't swallow.

"Feed Marguerite, or she'll die."

Havily raced in Marguerite's direction and before a handful of seconds passed, Marguerite nursed on her wrist drawing all that extraordinary power down her throat.

Endelle turned once more to stare down at a dead man.

Everything she despised about the war began to flow through her veins. Her mouth turned down, dragged down by all the hatred she felt, for all the ways this war had been a hopeless, useless endeavor for centuries, the never-ending creation of death vampires by the enemy, the incessant battling at night and wearing out of her warriors, the constant political manipulations by Greaves.

To end here, in this room, with Thorne dead, filled her with a fury the likes of which she had never known. She could feel the vibration of her rage. Her black hair swirled around her. A wind that only her ire could create moved in great swells and slammed into the warriors and their *brehs*.

She couldn't let this be the end.

She would not let this be the end.

She glanced at Fiona, then Jean-Pierre. "Get your woman out of here or her eardrums will bust open even wider than before."

Jean-Pierre didn't wait. He put his arms around Fiona. They vanished.

She turned to face the rest: Kerrick and Alison, Marcus, Medichi and Parisa, Luken, Santiago, Zacharius. "I want you to get everyone out of this building, then you must leave."

Marcus called out, "I'll take care of the building. Just hold on." He closed his eyes and a split second later, an alarm sounded. From her office she could feel the massive and abrupt folding of thousands of employees.

She glanced at Marguerite, who now stared at her wide-eyed, still sucking at Havily's wrist. She popped off with a sudden smack and pushed Havily's arm away. "I'm staying."

Endelle nodded. "Yes."

As Havily rose to her feet, Endelle gave her a shove. "Go with Marcus." Her voice trembled. Her arms shook.

No one challenged her. They just left one after the other, stricken, ill, frightened. She sent Horace and his healers away as well.

When the last of them left and when she checked the building and found that the high-rise was also empty of people, she waved a hand. The alarms grew silent.

Marguerite leaned over Thorne and kissed him on the lips.

Maybe that was the last straw in this horrible farce called

ascension. She wasn't sure, but she lifted her arms to the ceiling and she screamed long and hard then she called for James over and over.

The windows rattled, the walls vibrated. Her hair whipped around now, a pure reflection of her rage and of her determination.

When James didn't appear, she let her power flow from her in pulsing waves. The windows went first, blowing out into the desert.

"You will come to me," she shouted, splitting her resonance a dozen times. *"You will come to me now and you will give me back what was taken from me today or by God I will not hold back and my soul and my body be damned for what I am about to do, so help me God. Do you hear me, Luchianne? The vows I took, the laws I promised to obey, mean nothing to me if this man remains in this lifeless state.*

"I have served and I have been ignored and I will be ignored no longer.

"If you do not send your Sixth healers to me right now, then I will begin Armageddon myself. I will use every power at my command, including obsidian flame, and I will take this dimension down to ashes."

James appeared ten feet away, holding himself steady as the wind of her rage struck him first on one side then the other. "We all die," he said.

"Fuck that," she cried, splitting her resonance three times. *"Bring the healers now. Or I will destroy this planet, one rock, one drop of water, one ascender at a time if I have to."*

James winced then nodded.

Three women appeared, hooded in a way that led Endelle to believe they were being kept from seeing her.

He will need blood, one of the healers sent.

Endelle didn't give it a second thought. She dropped to her knees and offered her wrist. The healer closest to her moved to the top of Thorne's head and gestured with a draped arm for her to take up the position on Thorne's left.

She leaned down and put her hand on his face. "Come back to me, my friend, my companion. Please. I can't go forward without you. Second Earth needs you. We've always needed you. Forgive me for being the scorpion queen. Just please come back."

When the healing began, she closed her eyes and let the healers work. One of them took her arm. After half a minute when Thorne latched onto her arm, trashed her skin, then began to suck, she began to weep.

Marguerite knelt between two of the healers, reaching forward to touch the tips of Thorne's ice-cold fingers. With her free hand she kept wiping at her face. Havily's blood had restored her thoroughly. She felt more alive than she had in a long time, drugged almost.

And thank God for that, because having seen Thorne in this state, as in deceased, kept sharp claws tearing on the insides of her chest.

Worse. She kept looking at Endelle, whose face was a stream of tears over reddened cheeks. Her black hair hung in a heavy grieving mass down her back, quiet now as opposed to writhing with fury as it had been earlier.

She was an incredible ascender, so powerful and so passionate. Endelle loved Thorne, that much was clear to Marguerite, and the taste of that love felt passionate yet not romantic, which made no sense and yet every sense. They had never been lovers. Thorne had once said that it just would have been too weird even though at various times he said he'd been tempted. Endelle as well.

And why wouldn't either of them? They were both magnificent.

But Endelle loved him with a passion that transcended romance and sex. She would die for him.

Marguerite shifted her gaze back to Thorne. His fingers were warmer now. She gave thanks. The man she loved was being restored and returned to her. She felt humbled and changed.

Everything felt different to her now, but maybe that always happened when death was met head-on and somehow vanquished.

She leaned forward and slid her fingers farther down his palm. Did his hand twitch?

The stream of power emanating from the healers tingled the hairs on her arm. She looked down the length of his legs. His kilt was hanging partially off him, sliced through. His weapons harness was gone. The shallowest cuts were gone and the deepest ones were simply closing up. His skin wasn't nearly so pale. Some of the golden color had returned.

Endelle leaned back and drew her bleeding, torn up arm to her chest. Her eyes were bloodshot.

"Endelle, did you do this for me?" The gravelly voice hit the air, striking Marguerite's heart like a deftly swung mallet.

Thorne.

Marguerite drew in a long deep breath. He was alive. Sobs jerked her chest several times, but she kept them quiet. She just had a feeling.

"You're back," Endelle said, wiping at her face.

"Thank you." He turned to look at her.

Marguerite could hardly keep from pushing the healer next to her aside so that she could throw herself on Thorne, but she couldn't move, not with Endelle's face so contorted in grief and pain. The Amazon seemed hardly able to breathe.

Her lips however, did move, as though she was trying to say something, but couldn't.

She turned and met Marguerite's gaze. So much pain in those ancient, lined eyes. Her mouth moved once more, but nothing came from between her lips. Finally, she sent, *I give him to you, Marguerite. Take good care of him. He was the sun to my earth. I just didn't know it.*

Marguerite nodded.

Endelle turned back to Thorne, her mouth moving again so strangely, her still-bleeding wrist held against her chest. Finally, she just vanished.

Marguerite heard Thorne groan as though he was in pain. She knew he couldn't see her because of the robed figures but she could sense that he needed a minute.

This time, his stomach jerked uncontrollably.

She couldn't imagine what he was experiencing, but that it had to do with Endelle restrained her.

Thorne stared straight up into the ceiling of Endelle's office. He felt as though his heart had been ripped out of his chest; he just didn't exactly understand why. But when he'd re-awakened to life, he'd turned to look into Endelle's eyes and it was as though he could see straight into her soul, into every thought she'd ever had, into the absolute depths of her suffering.

Jesus. He hadn't known, he hadn't understood what her life had been like all these millennia. She was old, so old, and now, because he'd forced her to sever the mind-link, she was truly alone.

That was what he had seen, the painful breadth of her loneliness, that she'd been battling to keep Second and Mortal Earth safe for thousands of years, long before his arrival two thousand years ago, and that his willingness to serve as her second-in-command for centuries had made him her rock, the anchor that had kept her sane.

And now, he'd done the unthinkable to her: He'd abandoned her.

And yet he'd had to. In order to move forward in his life, perhaps even to save Second Earth, there was nothing he could do but break with her. Marguerite's presence in his life alone would have demanded it, but even if his *breh* hadn't shown up as she had, he'd have broken with her. New powers had emerged, and with those powers a new, larger purpose that moved him out of his role as her main support.

Yeah, he had a new role, and as he awoke to a new life, he saw it as clearly as if a vision had taken hold of his mind: He had to build an army and he had to build it fast. In addition, he could feel that his obsidian flame power was meant to serve as a sort of new anchor, but not for one woman this time. Instead, he would support three, and somewhere in all that support he might just be able to defeat Greaves.

He saw and understood all of this as the three hooded

figures continued to work on his wounds, to heal him, to restore his life completely.

What a complete miracle life was, this arrival in a body, replete with every emotion and sensation imaginable. To grow from infancy to maturity and to set a path, to walk that path, to stumble and fall on that path, to get distracted from that path, to face death on that path . . . yes, this was life.

And he'd been given a second chance.

He had a world to love and, God help him, a new world to build if . . . oh, God, if Endelle, the Warriors of the Blood, the Militia Warriors, and unknown allies could somehow bind together to forge an impenetrable wall against Greaves. But, oh, God, that goal seemed impossible.

But then it was impossible that he lay here, that three healers, not of this dimension, had just brought him back from the dead.

He couldn't exactly remember what had happened. He felt that there was a lapse in time, a few minutes maybe, for which he simply couldn't account.

For one thing, he didn't know how he'd gotten here. For another, Endelle had been weeping, the woman who never wept, like Marguerite.

Dammit, his stomach jerked again. So much pain moved through him that had nothing to do with a tiger ripping him to shreds. No, this was all about Endelle.

In a moment of clarity, he realized he was saying goodbye to her, to the strange shared intimacy that the mind-link had created.

Everything was changing.

He would no longer be the leader of the Warriors of the Blood. He would be something more. Much more.

He glanced at the healers, their faces completely cloaked. As one, they drew their hands back, bowed their heads, and disappeared.

Which left him with . . . Marguerite.

Her face was a mess as she wiped her eyes. Her white-blond hair was matted with blood and bits of straw. But her body was whole.

He'd died and come back to life. But unlike the other two times, he had no recollection of floating in space and experiencing the beauty of the galaxy. There was just a complete blankness.

"How did I get here?" he asked her.

She scooted closer and took his hand in both of hers. Despite the fact that her nose was swollen and her eyes red, she looked so beautiful to him.

"You don't remember?"

He looked back at the ceiling. "I remember the cage and the tiger. I remember telling you to get Fiona."

She filled in the blanks, ending with, "You were dead, Thorne." More tears tracked her cheeks. "But Endelle freaked, I mean she really freaked out." She told him the rest, leading up to this moment as she knelt beside him.

Only then did he realize he was feeling a whole lot of fresh air flowing through the room. He sat up and glanced around. All the windows had been blown out. "That glass was bulletproof. So Endelle did that."

"Yep. And she was exactly the woman you told me she was in that moment. She looked like a Greek goddess out for vengeance. I'm pretty sure if James hadn't shown up, she would have destroyed this dimension."

So Endelle had made sure he lived, despite the fact that he'd broken with her.

He squeezed Marguerite's hand. "There's so much I didn't understand until now."

She nodded. "I feel the same way."

He squeezed her hand. "I love you."

She nodded. He watched her swallow hard. "I love you, too, Thorne. I didn't understand just how much until we were trapped with that beast. I . . . I'm so sorry."

"For what?"

"For making your life a misery for the past few weeks."

He lifted her hand to his lips and kissed her fingers. He kept his eyes closed and pressed their joined hands to his chest. When he opened his eyes he wiped her cheeks, one after the other, and said, "I want to complete the *breh-hedden* with you. I want that more than anything else in the world but I would never force you. Never."

She put her hand on his cheek. "I know you wouldn't. That's something I finally figured out. I have freedom with you, Thorne. I have freedom with Endelle. She tried to tell me that the night you and Jean-Pierre busted me out of the Superstition Seers Fortress. She said she'd give me autonomy. I'd just never had that before and I honestly didn't believe her, but I know I was wrong. Endelle would have kept her word. And you? In all this time, you've never tried to corral me. Not once."

He leaned into her and kissed her very wet lips. "I love you so much. When we were in that cage together, it finally dawned on me just how much I love you—I mean really love you and need you—and how much wonderful peace you've always brought to my life. I was so weighed down with a sense of responsibility about everything that I didn't see all that I'd been given or how well I'm supported. You've been a huge support in my life. I see that now."

"Ditto," she murmured.

He kissed her again.

She took a deep breath. "I want to go all the way with you as well, no matter what the *breh-hedden* means. Even if it means we're joined at the hip." She lifted up and moved into him, sliding onto his lap until he held her in his arms and she was kissing him. "Even if it meant I had to wear a stupid ankle guard, Thorne, I'd do it for you and you know why? Because I trust you. With all my heart, I trust you."

He kissed her again but when she pulled back he said, "What is it? You've tensed up. A vision?"

She shook her head. "I guess I'm just a little worried about what the *breh-hedden* will mean, what it will be like."

"I know. I don't think either of us enjoys the unknown all that much."

Marcus appeared in the doorway. "Hey." He stared hard at Thorne, that slash of brows over light brown eyes. "Well, damn my ass, she brought you back."

Thorne twisted to look at him. Marguerite slid off his lap

and he stood up next to her. "Not sure exactly how it happened, but yeah, she did."

Marguerite said, "Healers from Sixth came and brought Thorne back. Once he was safe, Endelle dematerialized. She was pretty upset."

"Okay. Okay." He nodded several times, but he swallowed hard. "Shit, boss . . . we thought . . . damn . . ."

He crossed to Marcus and put his hand on the brother's shoulder.

Marcus released a rush of air then suddenly Thorne was just being hugged hard. "We thought it was over, all of it. You were so *gone*."

"I know. I know. But I'm here and Marcus, things are going to change. Let everyone know. Okay? Yeah, we've got a shitload of work to do, but things are going to change."

Marcus pulled back and jerked his head up and down a few times. He sniffed and flared his nostrils. He looked anywhere but at Thorne.

Thorne laughed. Marcus knew how to front. They all did.

"So what time is it? I mean how long was I gone? How long did this whole thing take?"

Marcus glanced at his Rolex. He shook his head. "Maybe forty-five minutes."

"So Greaves's little party is still under way."

"Oh, yes, it is. Coverage on every channel, on every continent. It helps to own most of the mineral rights of Second Earth."

"Is COPASS still holding to their position that they have his permits under review?"

Marcus lifted a brow. "Precious, isn't it?"

Thorne nodded. "Tell you what. Why don't you get the warriors back here. I think we have a fucking spectacle to disrupt."

Marcus's eyes lit up. "Hell, yeah, we do." He flipped his warrior phone from his pants pocket, thumbed it, and shot it to his ear. "Carla? Get all the WhatBees to Endelle's office pronto." He smiled suddenly. "Yeah, it's Gideon's fault. We've kind of taken to the nickname."

A few seconds later the men started folding in.

But it was Havily who, after arriving within seconds as well, made the most interesting suggestion. "Why don't we film this?" She met her *breh*'s gaze. "YouTube? Or at least the underground."

"That's a fantastic idea. Why don't we put Gideon and some of the Militia Warriors on that detail? That way, if Greaves wants to rumble, we'll have more men in the field."

And so it was decided.

Half an hour later Thorne flew at the head of the Warriors of the Blood, in a strict V pattern. Kerrick, Luken, Jean-Pierre, and Santiago were off his left flank; Leto, Marcus, Medichi, and Zacharius off his right.

He hadn't at first realized that the light illuminating the space as they flew emanated from his silvery white wings, but so it did. Raw obsidian flame power, unheard of on Second Earth, connected to his woman, and to Grace, and Fiona, strengthening all of his powers, including flight, which meant he'd had to slow it down a little to keep the squadron in tight formation.

He guided the flight pattern just below the swans and geese, which had the dramatic effect of frightening the birds and sending them soaring off into the dark, cloudy night, their handlers after them.

Thorne smiled as he pressed on, covering the first mile of still-marching warriors, furious all over again at the sound of the masses of hard boots on asphalt. Heavy orchestral music thundered through loudspeakers positioned at fifty-yard intervals. Cameras were set up everywhere.

The most bizarre features was that there were no crowds, just an occasional stretch of grandstands that housed a screaming mass, waving flags with Greaves's black, gold, and maroon insignia. At least six cameras surrounded each set of grandstands, filming the performers endlessly. Thorne didn't know how they kept it up.

Of course, as the Warriors of the Blood flew past, the audience, in stages, recognized them and all the ecstatic cheering turned to silence.

Good.

But they hadn't flown another hundred yards when all that shouting and cheering started up again.

When they neared the viewing platform, another set of grandstands was close by, this time containing dignitaries and notables, not the least of which was Daniel Harding, the head of COPASS.

Not unexpected.

As the geese and swans flew away, and as Thorne angled within thirty yards of the viewing platform, he focused on the loudspeaker system, summoned his obsiddy power, and sent a short circuit through the works. The occasional flash and pop traveled through the speakers until the loud orchestral music died.

He faced his palms toward the ground and sent a warning hand-blast among Greaves's marching soldiers, now stopped in their tracks and staring up at him and his men.

The moment the blast released, the army scattered.

That much energy would have hurt.

In the empty space that ensued, the Warriors of the Blood, except Thorne, dropped down to form a circle beneath Thorne, swords drawn, each man in his fighting crouch.

Thorne flapped his wings slowly and sustained his position in the air. He flew forward then called out in a voice that bore three split-resonances: "I hereby declare this spectacle illegal. You will disband at once or suffer the consequences." Because he'd split his resonance, dozens of screams followed. There were few ascenders powerful enough to withstand the combination of regular speech and split-resonance. If he'd added telepathy, he could have shattered some of the minds present.

He stared at Greaves and for one of the few times he'd known the bastard, Greaves appeared confused. But he rose from his chair very slowly then levitated.

He floated some ten yards in Thorne's direction.

Thorne knew in that moment that even if Greaves came at him with every power he had, Thorne would take him on. He didn't care in this moment if he died. He'd simply had enough of the direction the war had taken and he was taking his first stand.

If it was his last, so be it. He knew that his example would be honored and followed by a hundred good men, a thousand, a million.

Greaves waved his arm in an arc and the booming of the fireworks suddenly ceased. He called out, also splitting-resonance, "And I say that you are disturbing the peace, Warrior Thorne. This was a spectacle event, that is all."

"Bullshit. Send your army home, or by God we'll start sending them away for you." Fiona was on standby. If he needed to, he'd let her channel him, and start shipping the soldiers away by the tens of thousands, to all sorts of hostile environments.

Greaves knew that Endelle's faction had that power, since it had only been a few weeks ago that Endelle, inhabiting Fiona's body, had accomplished exactly the same thing.

Greaves started to float backward. He lifted his right arm. Thorne almost relaxed, assuming he meant to dematerialize.

Instead, three death vampires, all wearing Third Earth braids, began to fly in his direction, one from the east, one from the south, and one from the north.

He folded his sword into his hand and let his obsidian flame power flow through his body.

He felt the quickening of strength and speed, the one he had known when Fiona assisted him. But this time that quickening came from deep within himself.

He could also feel the warriors below him begin to spread out in an ever-greater circle, giving him space.

He could feel them all, his warrior brothers, on guard below him, protecting him. If he needed help, they were right there for him.

Luken entered his mind: *We're good here, boss. Take these three blue pricks down. We've got your back.*

And there it was, the truth more important than all the

other truths. He was supported, backed up, and not alone in this fight. His men would die with him if they needed to.

On the Third bastards came, each the size of Luken, but physically stronger and faster.

Thorne flapped his wings, twisted slightly, and began a slow spin, keeping each of them in sight. He saw the strategy. They would launch at him at once.

He sent a message to Fiona: *Strengthen my vision.* He felt her next to him, shoulder-to-shoulder, hip-to-hip, and it was as though he could see every infinitesimal shift of eyebrow, wing, shoulder, and hand of all three at once.

He knew he was glowing. He could see himself reflected in their eyes.

And so he spun.

The attack came, three blurring at him like lighting, swords whirling. But his enhanced vision saw each move as if in slow motion.

He sliced once to the south, once to the east, once to the north.

Down three Third Earth death vampires fell, one of them screeching loudly.

He stopped the spin and drew close to Greaves. He split his resonance again. "You will disband at once."

Greaves started to lift his arm and with the intuitive sense that came from his obsidian flame power, Thorne knew his foe intended to launch an even larger force against him.

But Thorne focused on Greaves's face and found the vibration that allowed his body to memorize the features, the size and shape of the head, the entire build—and suddenly *he was Greaves.*

The Commander's eyes opened wide. Even his lips parted.

Finally, the bastard was impressed.

He lowered his arm.

A rolling cry of astonishment spread through the spectators in the grandstands. Thorne wasn't surprised when people began vanishing. In ones and twos first, then in whole groups until at last, only Greaves, his generals, and his army remained.

Harding had been one of the first to leave.

"Well? What will it be, Commander?" Thorne smiled. His face felt different, his teeth, the shape of his cheeks, the arch of his brows.

Greaves returned to sit on his throne-like seat. This time he lifted his opposite arm and what do you know, his army began vanishing until at last even the generals were gone.

The floodlights faded as well so that in the end it was only Thorne and his silvery white wings that lit the space between them.

Greaves smiled. "It would seem you've changed."

"I have."

Greaves nodded. "I have only one thing to say. Take care not to mistake this night's work for a serious victory."

Then he was just gone, no lifted arm, nothing.

Gone.

The military spectacle review was over.

Thorne drew his wings into parachute-mount and lowered to the ground. But when his warriors caught sight of him, still holding Greaves's form, he had eight swords pointed at his chest and back.

He smiled as he morphed back, though he stumbled once. Morphing was no easy task.

"Shit," Luken cried out. "That was one fucked-up Halloween mask you had on."

As he drew in his wings, Thorne glanced from familiar face to familiar face. Affection swelled. This was his family and always would be.

The warriors drew in their wings as well.

Jean-Pierre suddenly called out, "Incoming." Thorne whirled in the direction of his sight line, had his sword at the ready, but it was only a frightened goose.

Strangely, the goose landed on Jean-Pierre's outstretched crooked arm and immediately settled down though breathing hard.

The men busted up.

Jean-Pierre stroked his breast feathers. "What can I say, *mes amis.* I have a gift."

Despite all the anecdotes surrounding the breh-hedden, *I'm convinced, having experienced it once myself, that it is love, soaring as if on wings, that forms the true mystery of vampire mate-bonding.*

—*Memoirs*, Beatrice of Fourth

CHAPTER 23

An hour later the warriors and their *brehs* milled around Medichi's villa foyer, sitting room, and dining room. Parisa had called in a couple of favors and an Italian feast had arrived. By noon everyone was well fed, and the warriors who had been battling all night found their beds calling to them.

Thorne spoke to each one, a hand on the shoulder, followed by a quick warrior hug. One by one they folded away with their women, as was the case.

After thanking Parisa and Antony for the food and the use of their home, he folded with Marguerite back to his Sedona home, back to the foyer.

And as his feet touched down, he had one singular thought: *There is no place like home.*

Finally, after three long torturous weeks, he truly felt as though he'd come home.

With his arm around Marguerite, he looked down at her and said, "I'm so glad you're with me."

Her eyes were shining as she met his gaze. "Me, too."

He smiled and stroked her cheek. "Will you be my *breh*? Will you take this enormous risk and complete the *breh-hedden* with me?"

She nodded and smiled. "I haven't changed my answer since you came back from the dead."

He chuckled. But she stood on tiptoes and kissed him on the lips, her hand on his shoulder. "Thorne, I don't have any doubts. Just some nerves about what's ahead for us. But this is my path."

He drew back and slid his hand behind her nape. He squeezed then leaned down to return the kiss. Jesus H. Christ, his chest felt full of fire, a kind of wonderful agony he had never known before.

This woman was *his* woman, now and forever.

They were completing the *breh-hedden*, something he hadn't believed they'd ever do. She had wanted her freedom and he hadn't wanted one more responsibility.

Now his view of life had changed.

"You look so serious," she said.

"I feel serious." He searched her eyes, the clear brown glimmer. "I love you, Marguerite. With all my heart. I need you to hear that, to feel it, to believe it."

"I do, Thorne," she said, twisting her neck to move against the palm of his hand.

He kissed her again. He wanted this so much, more than he'd wanted anything in his entire life.

He wanted to be joined to her, to feel her, to feel all her external sensations as she would feel his. The bonded men talked about it a lot. Jean-Pierre said he and Fiona had worked out a way to block it; otherwise they'd go crazy with worry. He didn't know quite what that meant, either the worry or the sensations, but he wanted it all with Marguerite.

"Where do you want to do this?" she asked.

He didn't hesitate. "In my bed, that place I've lived for so long, *alone.* I've loved having you there and I want you there now. I want this solemn deed done where we'll live together. But are you sure you want this?"

"I've already told you what I want. Twice."

"Marguerite, I want your happiness more than anything else in the world. I know what escaping to Mortal Earth meant to you."

She slid her arms around him and pressed her head against his chest. "Those days are gone."

"But you want them back."

Her head shifted rhythmically against his pecs. "No. I thought I would, but I don't. I mean, maybe there will always be part of me, that wild part, that wants to roam free. Maybe. I'm really not even sure about that anymore.

"But what I do know is that I belong here, on Second Earth, with you, with Madame Endelle, with Fiona, with all the Warriors of the Blood. This is home for me now. I feel it to my toes.

"When we were stuck in that cage, I realized that if I'd wanted to, I could have gotten rid of you a long time ago. I could have easily escaped to other parts of the world and you never could have found me. I could have gone to Hong Kong or even New York, anywhere with a big population, and you would have had the devil of a time finding me. Because of your sense of responsibility toward Second Earth, you would have given up the search.

"Don't you see? I wanted to be found.

"Beyond that, well, I kept thinking about what it had been like to connect with Fiona and with Brynna, even with you, whether it was my Seer power or my obsiddy power." She looked up at him. "I loved it. I mean, I was uncomfortable at first, but each time it happened, I started feeling more and more as though I'd come home after a really long journey. Do you know what I mean?"

He dipped down and kissed her again. "Yeah, I do."

"This is where I want to be, here, in your arms, in your house, in your bed."

"So we're doing this."

She tilted her head. "I wish I could have been there for you, Thorne."

"You were."

"No, I mean the last two thousand years. Now that I've really been inside your mind, despite all the women you've shagged, I've seen your loneliness. I wish I could have eased you in that way."

"You're here now," he said, setting her back on her feet. "That's all that matters. But I wish I could have stepped inside that barn and beat the shit out of your father."

She pulled away from him. "I don't know. I want to say this and I'm hoping you'll understand, but when I think back on everything that happened to me, because it led me here, into your arms, into your bed, I wouldn't change a thing. Not a damn thing."

"Do you know what I thought when you pulled that wretched gown aside and showed me your breast?"

She shook her head.

He chuckled. "I actually thought, *Here's the woman for me.*"

"You did not."

"The hell I didn't. Yeah, I was gone on you as well, but I was too lost in the war to know it. But I remember what I felt. Every night while battling, I couldn't wait to get to you. And yes, it was great sex and I mean *great sex*." She shivered because he'd added resonance and he knew she loved it. "But it was so much more. I was at peace when I was with you, and you always made me laugh."

She leaned against him again and once more he surrounded her with his arms. "I love you so much."

"I love you, too." He took a deep breath and let it out slowly.

He looked at the bed and tried to imagine completing the *breh-hedden* with her here, but he had a sudden prescience that this room was not going to be big enough. He recalled having made love with her in Diallo's garden. They'd both mounted their wings.

He rubbed her shoulders gently. He needed something more right now.

Yeah, he needed more room, lots of room.

Marguerite listened to Thorne's heart. She sighed. Could anything be more beautiful than this moment, being held by the man she loved and knowing that he loved her as well?

She was overcome. Her heart seemed to expand in her

chest. She was so warm, deep into her bones, into the marrow, into the blood.

She had never expected to feel this way, so content and fulfilled.

The *breh-hedden* had done this for her, brought this to her when she wasn't looking, even when she'd adamantly refused the gift.

A vision arrived, listing just off shore, waiting for her permission to enter. She opened her obsidian flame power. She was about to alert Thorne when she had a moment of prescience that told her this was for her.

She directed her obsiddy power to open the vision. It unfolded swiftly. She absorbed it and as she watched, as she saw her body entwined with Thorne's, she smiled. If there was a separate power that directed the visions, she sent a prayer of thanksgiving heavenward.

"Thorne, do you have a partially completed cabin or smallish home somewhere?"

He drew back and met her gaze. "Did you just have a vision?"

She nodded.

"Why are you crying? Did you see something bad?"

She shook her head. "No. Something beautiful, very beautiful." She stroked his cheek. "I think we're supposed to complete the *breh-hedden* there, in that place. It looked very open to the sky. I didn't really see a forest but it wasn't exactly complete."

"But was there a bed?"

She glanced at his bed. "Yes. This one. What do you make of that?"

He laughed. "Okay. I get it. Good." He was smiling.

He had such a beautiful smile. She leaned up on tiptoes and kissed him. "Take me there."

He glanced behind him, out the windows.

"Why do you hesitate?"

"It's at the Superstitions and there are no walls. Not much privacy."

"We could make mossy mist."

"We could. So you want to show me the vision?"

"Sure. Just dip inside."

He pushed within her mind. *That's it,* he sent. *My unfinished project. Shall I fold us there?*

Do it.

The vibration began.

It was exactly as she'd seen in the vision, but she hadn't understood the location until now. She stepped off the cement slab and walked over to what was the rim of the Superstition Mountain's leading monolith.

"You never told me you'd started a home up here?"

He joined her and put his arms around her. A cool breeze blew from the land below. The March temp was like heaven in the desert.

She felt him sigh. "We battle down there every fucking night. I don't know why I started building at a location where we battle."

Marguerite stared at the plain below. From here she could see Militia Warrior HQ in the distance, just a smudge on the horizon. The sun was overhead; it would be a long time before the night's battling began.

Even with all that, she felt the rightness of this place, as though destiny flowed over her in waves. She glanced up at Thorne, all six-five of him, all muscled warrior that she'd grown to love.

He seemed transformed to her, almost god-like, glowing with silvery light as he stared far out into the desert below. His hair flowed away from his face in long streams of gold.

Thorne, Warrior of the Blood, defender of the weak, anchor to obsidian flame, her *breh* through eternity, her lover, her man. After her raucous bid for freedom, after her stubbornness, after all her running, how could it be that she would receive this great and formidable blessing?

For now, however, they had a certain myth to bring into existence, so she tilted her head, looked him up and down, and said, "All right, Warrior. How about you show me what you've got."

He smiled then grinned. "You are so my kind of woman."

"And you're my kind of man but don't think for a minute that just because we're gonna bond and you're a Warrior of the Blood, I intend to lick your battle sandals. Don't even think it. And you do your own laundry."

But he brought her up against him hard. "You're gonna talk about laundry right now?"

"Just wanted to get a few things straight."

He pressed his arousal flush up against her. "This straight enough?"

Her chest warmed up. "How about you bring the bed over."

He smiled. "Done."

She turned and saw that he sure as hell had.

She pulled out of his arms and turned toward the half-built, weathered edifice. There was no roof, just three walls, framing a large room that might have been intended as the living room.

But his bed sat there. She looked up and up, into the blue sky. She'd had a preview in her vision so now she was achy everywhere.

As he had done so many times before, he leaned down, slid an arm behind her knees, and lifted her up. She slung her arms around his neck and kissed him hard. She wanted him to feel how into this she was, that she held nothing back.

He kissed her in return and thrust his tongue into her mouth. She moaned and leaned her head against his shoulder. So for the longest time, he stood there, holding her and kissing her.

But when he put her on her feet, she planted her hands on his chest. "Thorne, there's something I need to say to you before we go any farther?"

"What?"

"Well, I'm so very sorry about José."

He put his fingers on her lips. She was sure he meant to be gracious, but she really needed him to understand. She started to protest, but he said, "I morphed."

She blinked. "What?"

He shrugged. "Remember earlier at Medichi's when the

warriors talked about how I morphed into Greaves at the very end?" He let the words hang.

"Yeah, I thought it was amazing. But . . ." She broke off. She blinked. She put the pieces of the puzzle together.

"*You* were José, that big beefy Mexican?"

"Yep."

"What the hell?" She shook him off and planted her hands on her hips. She scowled. "What do you mean, you were José?"

He shrugged. "It's a newly emerged power. Uh, it emerged, I think, because otherwise I would have killed that bastard."

She screwed up her face. "You were José . . . ?"

"I was."

"Now you're freaking me out. But when . . . oh, yeah. You had him in the bed of his truck, didn't you? That's why you jumped down from there, but it was *you.*"

He nodded.

"Shiiiiit." She drawled the word. She was so conflicted on so many levels. Here it was how many days later and he hadn't confessed this really important truth to her, that he'd deceived her and let her wallow in all her terrible guilt feelings because she'd thought she'd cheated on him.

But another thought soared to the front of her mind, a really wicked one. "So you can morph. Huh. So, when I was with José, I was really with you?"

"Yep. Aren't you mad? I thought you'd be clawing my face off about now."

She could hardly confess the direction of her thoughts and she could feel her cheeks warm up. She couldn't exactly look Thorne in the eye.

"Wait a minute," he said. "What are you thinking?"

She finally looked up at him, drawing her lips in. She just stared at him, willing him to figure it out.

His hazel eyes widened. "Oh, my God. You're liking the idea."

She put her fingers on his arm, playing with his muscles. "I . . . I think it has possibilities."

"I'm smelling roses. You're outrageous, you know. God, I love you."

She thought there was only one way out of this, so she folded off her clothes. He laughed.

He carried her to the side of the bed and mentally pulled the comforter back then laid her on her back.

"Take your clothes off," she said, stretching an arm above her head, letting it rest on the pillows. "Let me look at you."

He got that look on his face, that *Thorne* look that was just a little bit arrogant because the man had confidence. He knew he was built, stem-to-stern, and he also knew just how much his body pleased her.

As he folded off his clothes, she leaned up on her elbows. His long warrior hair flowed over his muscled shoulders and arms. Some of the strands hung over his thick pecs.

She shifted position and knee-walked to the edge of the bed. His gaze slid over her breasts and straight down to her bare mons. His jaw trembled as he sucked in a long stream of air. She pushed his hair back and put her hands on his chest. The man was stacked. As she ran her hands down his arms, she leaned forward, took his nipple in her mouth, and suckled.

He pushed his chest toward her and moaned.

Her hands ran to his fingers and she held on as she suckled. His body rolled beneath her mouth.

Thorne, I love tasting you . . . everywhere.

You do me in. One touch, one lick, one good suck, and I'm ready for you.

As she continued to suckle, she released his hand and slid her palm over his hip, his thigh, back up in an arc over his lower abdomen, then down until she felt the hard base of his cock and the curls that framed him. He was right. He was ready for her.

She drew her hand up his thick stalk and caressed the tip with her thumb.

Roses, he murmured.

His scent, so very male and infused with just a hint of that sweet cherry tobacco bouquet, had the same usual effect. She wept for him.

His hand found her chin and he lifted her up so that she popped off his nipple. When she met his gaze, he said, "I need you sucking something else."

She shuddered, a sensation that tightened her internal muscles. *Oh, yeah,* she sent. She never needed much encouragement.

He pushed her head down in the right direction, but she had a different idea and dematerialized behind him. She gave him a good hard shove so that he lost his balance.

But being a quick vampire, he flipped onto his back at the last moment, falling down on the bed and laughing with a chuckle. She caught his hands and pulled him to a sitting position.

She folded the comforter beneath her knees and spread his legs so that all that size and beauty was displayed just the way she liked it. She ran her hands up the insides of his thighs.

Play with my mouth while I do this, she sent.

He groaned and, using one finger, he rimmed her lips. She didn't know the why of it, but it made her tingle just about everywhere. He must have liked it as well, because a roll of cherry tobacco almost pushed her backward.

She suckled his finger as she kept moving forward, her hands massaging his thighs until she reached his sack. She moved higher, leaning forward, and as her tongue touched down on all that hardness, Thorne kept his finger-massaging her tongue and alternately rubbing himself.

She followed where he rubbed, nipping at him, licking, and sucking until his finger reached his tip. She got so hungry she took him inside, sucking him and savoring the wet sounds. All the while, his hand moved over her cheeks, her lips, and sometimes she brought his finger in her mouth while her tongue played over his cock.

His hips rocked into her and he moaned heavily. But after his breath caught on a solid hitch, he pushed her shoulders away from him and did some deep breathing.

"God, I don't want to come, not yet, but you feel like heaven to me."

She leaned back and withdrew her hands. He was so close.

"Thorne."

He opened his eyes, his lips parted, his chest still dragging in air. "Yeah." But he smiled.

"I love doing this with you. I love it so much. Damn, I was such a fool."

He leaned forward and caught her beneath her arms. He dragged her to recline on top of him. "Hold on. Let me get us more comfortable." In a quick motion he glided them both up the bed so that he could lie flat.

She straddled one of his thighs, careful not to touch him when he was so aroused. She put her hand on his face and kissed him. "I love you."

"I love you, too. God, I love you so much. I can't believe I was such an idiot not to have seen this sooner."

"I know." She kissed him again, then stayed connected with his lips until they were fully engaged, mouth-to-mouth, his tongue sweeping inside her mouth the way she loved.

I'm really hungry, he sent. *Downright starving.*

Then you should eat, she responded.

He left her mouth and moved with such speed that before she could blink, he had taken her very bare mons in his mouth and sucked, his hand pushing on her ass.

"You're gonna make me come like this." She was breathing hard.

Exactly what I want you to do. Your blood tastes better when you've come a few times.

She shivered at the thought of sharing blood. To complete the *breh-hedden,* they'd both be taking blood at the same time.

He opened his mouth wider and took as much of her in his mouth as he could. With him using alternating sucks and licks, along with the pressure of her ass, the orgasm was suddenly there, traveling like a streak of lightning along her clitoris, up into her well, catching her hard. She opened her mouth and groaned, as he worked the orgasm, sucking on her faster until her hips settled down.

Heaven, she sent.

He licked her lightly then shifted to raise up on his elbow so that he could look up at her. "I love how you taste," he said. "I always did but now there's this flavor of roses and it gets me every time."

She reached down and thumbed his lips, then dipped inside his mouth. He suckled.

You're frowning, he sent. *What's going on?*

*This is a virgin experience for us, isn't it? The first time we'll complete the*b reh-hedden.

Yes, he responded, but he kept tonguing her thumb.

Do you know what I'd like you to do?

At that, he released her thumb and looked at her, suddenly intense. "What?"

She smiled and leaned up as well. "Come up here."

He moved to stretch out beside her again, facing her and cupping the back of her neck. "What? I'll do anything. You know that."

"I do know that." She loved that about him. He was so present with her and so willing.

"I want you to go deep inside my obsiddy power again."

He closed his eyes and trembled, head-to-foot. When he opened his eyes, he smiled. "Is it possible we won't survive this experience?"

She leaned into him, sliding close and pressing as much of her up against him as she could. "That would be one helluva way to go. I say we give it a shot. You do my obsiddy power then I'll do yours."

Again, he trembled, his shoulders jerking.

She kissed him hard. *Fuck me, Thorne. Fuck me hard and fast like you'll never get another chance.*

And before she knew what he meant to do, he pushed inside her mind and was suddenly diving down the long tunnel of her obsidian flame power. Pleasure flowed so that she hardly noticed when he pushed her onto her back and pierced her low.

He was rocking into her when he reached the core of her power. Once there, he did something amazing as he flew all around the edges of it, grazing the sensitive sides until she was moaning against his mouth and then his wrist was just there so that she grabbed his arm and held him in position. She licked in quick swipes to draw the veins forward then struck.

His entire body jerked over her.

Oh, God, this feels so good.

She slowly twisted her head for him while keeping his wrist pressed to her mouth. She sucked greedily but was in agony as his tongue made long sweeps up her neck. He was grunting as he struck. Her body rolled as the burn of his fangs and ensuing suck pulled her internal muscles tight.

There was so much going on that she didn't feel as though she was inside her body. Pleasure built low, dragging down her clit, rippling up inside her, then returned with each thrust of his cock inside her. His scent flooded her mind. He was still teasing her obsiddy power and now he was sucking at her neck.

She groaned against his wrist as she pulled more of his blood into her mouth. She had fire in her body now, down her throat, between her legs, and in her chest.

Marguerite, I love you so much.

His words did her in, gripped her so that the orgasm began like a heavy streak of lightning pulling up and up, swelling into a heavy wave, then releasing in a swift flow up through her chest. She cried out but still kept her fangs buried in his wrist, her hips pumping as the orgasm spun and spun.

When she at last settled down, she realized that this orgasm hadn't pushed him out of her obsiddy power. She could feel him swirling around deep inside it, meaning there was more pleasure to come.

But how the hell was he lasting?

Thorne had never felt so alive. Marguerite's blood down his throat had flooded him with power, an increase in strength so that not only was he able to last through her orgasm and the tightening of her body around his cock, but he knew something huge was waiting to erupt from them both, and it wouldn't just be his ejaculation.

He kept his thrusts into her body steady and strong. Once more she writhed under him as she sucked on his wrist and took his blood. He could feel her strengthening as well.

I need to look at you while we complete this, he sent.

I don't want to let your wrist go.

I know. I feel the same way about your throat, but can you trust me enough in this? The blood part of the ritual is complete.

She didn't answer him, she just released his wrist. He let go of her throat and pulled back. He rocked his hips into her. She pushed back. She put her arms around his neck and he looked down at her, locking her gaze with his.

But the sensations were all so powerful that he couldn't speak, so he sent, *Can you reach my obsidian flame power with your mind? Can you be inside my power as I'm inside yours?*

I'll try.

Good. He drove into her, harder now. He knew they were close to the *breh-hedden.*

He felt her mind cross into his and it seemed like a small miracle that he was able to stay within her obsidian flame power, but he stayed there as she sought him.

He watched her eyes. She blinked and her eyes rolled. *The pleasure is almost too much.*

I know. Find me. Hurry. This is it.

Okay.

When she got close, he nodded. *Yes. Almost there.*

I can feel it, she sent in a rush. She smiled. *Oh, God, there you are.*

And then she was just inside his power.

The sensation of her being there rocked him.

He was thrusting hard now but her eyes were closed. *Look at me.*

She opened her eyes and that did it. He couldn't hold

back and the orgasm swelled not just from his balls but from his obsidian flame power. He held her gaze as he cried out.

Thorne, you're flying up my power again. So he was, or thrust out of it by her orgasm.

Only this time it was different because, dammit, he could feel her pleasure. He shouted at the sky as he ejaculated, as his obsidian flame power exploded, as hers exploded, and as all that pleasure gripped her lower body.

He couldn't believe the sensation she had as she gripped him.

When a second orgasm began to rise, he shouted once more and as had been happening to him lately with her, his balls reloaded and all that exquisite pleasure began to pump out of him.

"Thorne, I can feel you come. How the hell is that happening?" Then she was screaming, her body slamming against his. She kept crying out and when a third orgasm began to build, his body began to grow hot, hers as well.

This time he put his hands on either side of her face and pinned her. She gripped his forearms and held on tight.

Are you feeling this? he sent.

She nodded between his hands. He was breathing hard.

Let it go, he sent.

She did, and her orgasm barreled through her and through him and back and forth, but this time somehow the obsidian flame power flowed together in a single continuous stream. He reached down and kissed her hard as pleasure swirled, flowed, and erupted all at the same time.

He'd never ejaculated so much. She was a hard tug on him, in familiar pulses.

But as the physical pleasure eased, her body grew quiet, and his hips settled against hers, the stream of power that flowed through each mind brought a continued pleasure and intensity. She smiled and he smiled in return. He kissed her again. She kissed him back.

"My wings," she said.

He nodded. She slid her legs up high, up around his waist as she had done before, in Diallo's courtyard garden.

He lifted them both up to his knees. He levitated until he could put his feet on the cement. "Stay connected," he said.

She nodded. "I can feel it, too, what needs to be done here."

"Go ahead."

She held on to his shoulders, pushing back just a little. He clasped his hands low around her waist, well below her wing-locks, and bent his knees for support. She arched her neck and closed her eyes. Her body rolled sensually and he could feel her wings release, which made his cock twitch all over again. Damn, the release was exquisitely sexual, no question about that.

And her wings, black with red flames, were so incredibly beautiful and powerful in appearance, enormous. Each flap moved his body as well. If he wasn't as strong as he was, he would have been airborne, but he kept her anchored.

She relaxed, her wings still moving very slowly. "Your turn—and Thorne?"

"Yeah?"

"Did you feel my wings release?"

His voice deepened. "Oh . . . yeah."

"I can hardly wait to feel yours."

His back was a mess of weeping so it took but three deep breaths and his wings mounted. He groaned at so much pleasure. But the mount didn't feel anything like before, almost as though . . . his wings were bigger now.

Marguerite groaned as well then opened her eyes. "That was amazing." Her eyes widened as her gaze drifted from one wing to the next. "Oh, my God, Thorne. Can you see your wings?"

He flapped one forward then almost lost his balance. They were as large as Endelle's—a span of forty feet. And the gray flame pattern was even more pronounced against all the silvery white expanse.

"Take me into the air," she said, drawing closer so that she could wrap her arms around his neck. He smiled, drew his massive wings back, bent his knees, and with one strong downward sweep launched heavenward.

* * *

This was the vision, she thought, *the reason we needed to be here in the open air.*

Thorne flapped hard and she could feel with each powerful thrust of his wings and movement of his body how much he was taking pleasure in this flight, as though it were his first—and perhaps it was. This was their *breh-hedden* flight.

She held her wings in a close-mount position, which allowed her to keep her face against his muscular chest. Every sensation, as connected as they were, body-to-body, arms-to-arms, in flight, was a kind of ecstasy all in its own.

She held the sensation close and because she was still connected to his mind, she drew close to the round ball of his obsidian flame power and stroked.

He groaned softly. *I love you this close,* he sent.

She smiled against his warm body. She let him do the work as she kept her legs wrapped tightly around his ass, and because the air grew chill, she manipulated her wings to surround her. His body was on fire, a typical man.

She savored this flight and the depths of its meaning in her life, in their lives.

When they were far above the earth and the wind blew steadily, he popped his wings into parachute position, which rocked them back and forth.

I'm going to withdraw from you now, he sent.

Yes.

When he pulled his cock from her, she would have been sad but she knew what was coming.

He didn't.

What is that sound? he asked.

The future.

She began to flap her wings and took his hand as she moved away from him.

The wind began to blow from the west in a steady warm stream. She stretched her body out to mimic his.

The future arrived and suddenly she was gliding beside him in an ever-increasing flow, faster and faster, until soon they were crossing the Pacific Ocean. The journey moved north to the Japan Islands then China, swinging south to Indonesia and Australia then east once more to India and upward, crossing the Himalayas, Tibet, and into Russia, zig-zagging to cover the continents, on and on. As night fell, streams of light connected until they were circling the earth over and over, the light streams flowing and flowing until the earth was a ball of interconnected light.

She had a tremendous sense of purpose and she felt that Thorne was having a similar experience.

At last the journey began to slow until once more the earth appeared below, the vast expanse of the Sonoran Desert and the Metro Phoenix Two area, and the rim of the Superstition Monolith in front of the half-built dwelling.

Thorne touched down and her feet felt the earth once more. He held her in front of him as she retracted her wings, then drew her close once more.

But he didn't withdraw his wings. They were glowing, as was he.

Within his mind, she drifted away from the seat of his obsidian flame power and looked up at him. He nodded.

She explored his mind until she found what held him captive, what had set his body and wings aglow, his eyes on fire, that which had transfigured him.

He was now the man in charge . . . of everything.

His future was clear. He would soon become Supreme High Commander of the Allied Ascender Forces. More would follow—that was what she felt and knew.

I'm to build an army, he sent.

Yes.

There is more. But I don't want to think about it.

She nodded. *And I'm to work on behalf of Seers all over the world, working for their freedom.*

He hugged her. *That makes such beautiful, perfect sense.*

Isn't it strange? That my pursuit of freedom might be the vehicle to free so many others?

He held her close, his deep breaths moving her body in peaceful swells.

She had never been happier. Whatever the future brought, she would remember this moment as long as she lived.

Finally, she said, "How about you start filling that bathing pool of yours?"

"Let me get this straight. We both just experienced incredible, multi-orgasmic sex, we traveled the entire globe in some kind of blended vision and real life, and you're thinking about the bathing pool?"

"Hell, yes, Warrior. I want a warm bath, I want you to take me on that well-designed and super-convenient shelf next to the pool a couple of times, then I want to sleep all spooned up with you for the rest of the afternoon. As for the night, well, we'll just have to wait and see."

She felt his body relax and he hugged her hard. He retracted his wings and, without saying a word, he had her flying through nether-space.

To make peace with a dragon,
Persevere in the presence of the beast,
with respect and affection.

—*Collected Proverbs*, Beatrice of Fourth

CHAPTER 24

A week later, Thorne entered the Militia Warrior complex at the security landing platform. Jean-Pierre waited for him, smiling a very warm smile with a knowing look in his gray-green eyes—his ocean-eyes as Fiona called them.

Thorne thought he understood. It was the look of a brother who had been through the exact same thing, knowing by experience both the suffering before the *breh-hedden* and the glorious mysteries after.

Right now he felt the cool tile beneath Marguerite's feet and the warmth on her palm from the bottom of a ceramic mug. Now she was sitting down and probably staring out at the Mogollon Rim because she loved doing that. Brynna would join her soon and they would discuss the future of the Seers Fortresses of Second Earth.

If he pressed hard, he could enter her mind and see what she was seeing, but they were each learning to keep some boundaries. With so much intimacy now, some strong separation was necessary for them or one or the other would go mad.

So he set up a block and sighed.

But Jean-Pierre held his gaze, his crooked smile accompanied by a knowing nod.

Thorne nodded in response. Nothing needed to be said. No doubt there would be conversations in the future, about the *breh-hedden,* about handling the powerful women they'd been given to mate with, about ways to accommodate so much extraordinary intimacy without destroying it.

Hopefully, there would be centuries.

"Thorne." His French accent eased over the name.

"Jean-Pierre."

"So, what is this news you have for me?"

He glanced at the Militia Warriors who worked the landing platform. There seemed to be more than the usual contingent present. "Let's go to your office."

"Or yours. Seriffe cleared a space for you while they remodeled the north wing. Apparently you and Seriffe will both have offices when the work is finished. There is to be a large conference room and a new command center. Very impressive. Havily's architect helped with the design."

As they moved into the hallway that led in the direction of the offices and the HQ grid, Thorne said, "I noticed the extra security."

"What do you mean?"

He jerked his thumb behind them. "At the landing platform."

Jean-Pierre grinned, all those big teeth of his. "That was not additional security. Several of the men wanted to see the new Supreme High Commander of the Allied Ascender Forces."

Ah, yes, his new duties. Endelle had bestowed the title on him in an official ceremony. The problem was, they still weren't speaking. Endelle had become withdrawn from him, and he wasn't sure what to do about it.

"You are different now, Thorne. Everyone speaks of it. Your eyes are clear, of course. I take it you are no longer such intimate friends with Ketel One."

Thorne smiled. "No. Not so much."

He glanced down the length of the hall and saw that Seriffe stood outside his office, the largest one on the premises.
Eight Section Leaders of the Thunder God Warriors were
lined up next to him, a formal greeting. He knew the men, of
course, since they'd begun taking their squadrons to battle
at the Borderlands during what had become a major time of
transition for the Warriors of the Blood.

There was talk of merging the Section Leaders with the
Warriors of the Blood, for the purposes of planning and strategy. But it was Gideon and Duncan who fought the merge
the hardest. As close as they were to Warrior of the Blood
status, they showed one of the most dominant traits of the
elite warriors: territoriality, to the point of obsession.

It made Thorne smile, nothing more. That level of bull-
headedness only confirmed his belief that they were ready
for the grade bump.

Yes, everything was changing.

Seriffe welcomed him aboard and shook his hand.

He hadn't seen Seriffe since his own status had changed,
but the famous warrior, too, met him with a knowing look in
his eye, the look of a man who'd been in charge of thousands
of warriors for a very long time.

Seriffe gestured to the open doorway. "I want you to use
this space until your offices and the new executive command center are ready."

Thorne started to protest but instantly felt the restraining
voice in his head, the one that connected to obsidian flame
power, the one that gave him better insight, better understanding, and a longer vision of what the next few weeks,
days, and months would have to be.

Thorne was now the Supreme High Commander, the one
who would have the final say in everything that related to the
coming battle between Greaves's ALA and Endelle's AAF.

This room was only fitting, and it spoke volumes about
Seriffe's character that he stepped aside so easily and allowed another man to take what had been his seat of command for a very long time.

He glanced at Gideon and Duncan. His first order would

be to summon Militia Warrior Section Leaders from all over the world to begin the necessary army training.

But not today.

Thorne thanked Seriffe for the office. He invited him in, but Seriffe said he had a meeting scheduled with his men.

Thorne moved into the space. Jean-Pierre followed him in.

He inclined his head toward the door. "Close that, Jean-Pierre. I realize we have a lot discuss, but first I want to talk to you about the hidden colonies and another more personal matter."

He moved to the desk and noticed that it had been completely cleared out and made ready for him. There was even a fresh memo pad with a wing watermark, something Havily had created as one of her first steps in changing up the quality of Endelle's overall staff operation.

Jean-Pierre remained standing. He wore flight battle gear since for the remainder of the afternoon, yeah, he was training Militia Warriors.

Thorne decided to lay it out. "I met your great-grandson at the colony in Mortal Earth Washington—the Seattle Colony as it's known."

Jean-Pierre's brows rose. "You must mean Arthur."

"Yes."

"We were not certain where he was. He just seemed to have disappeared, although he let his father know that he was well and safe, but he was not coming home. I suppose this is good news."

"The thing is, Arthur is Warrior of the Blood caliber." He then described the battle and the level of Arthur's skills.

"Merde," Jean-Pierre murmured

Thorne couldn't help but smile. "He reminded me of you . . . a lot. So, I suspect it's a genetic thing. But he's really unhappy because of the death of his fiancée."

"He was too young to be thinking of such things. Only nineteen."

Thorne shrugged. "I wouldn't know what to say about that. He seemed to have loved her very much."

Jean-Pierre drew in a deep breath. "Is there something you wish me to do?"

"I'm not sure. He says that he has four other friends at his level of battling skills, but they all refuse to have anything to do with the war. Since he's your blood, I wanted you in on the decision making. This network of colonies will not remain secret much longer. We're respecting their choice to remain as they are and to not accept our protection or involvement, but I'd hate to think what would happen if Greaves decided to get involved on any level."

"Did you have a sense of what ought to be done? Given all the changes in the past few weeks, I believe I should take this dilemma to my family, especially to Arthur's father."

Thorne tapped deeply into that power that was fast becoming his greatest ally. He let the vibrations flow up through his body until he knew he was glowing.

He saw Jean-Pierre sit back in his chair, eyes wide.

"Better get used to it. Apparently it's my new fucking look. I'm hoping at some point that this damn thing will settle down." Jean-Pierre nodded, but he didn't exactly close his mouth.

Thorne turned inward and held his last memory of Arthur firmly within his mind. He closed his eyes and just let the young warrior's image rest, his strength and ability for one so young, that leanness of youth, the crooked smile.

Oddly, Leto came to mind. He knew enough, even after only a week, to follow his instincts.

Thorne met Jean-Pierre's gaze. "I heard that Leto has been having some issues." Thorne hadn't seen the brother in several days. He'd been staying at Medichi's villa, but apparently had taken a liking to Antony's limoncello. He was battling all night at the Borderlands, like the rest of the warriors, but apparently not sleeping well during the day.

Jean-Pierre shook his head. "He is not right. I cannot explain it and I think it is more than the *breh-hedden*, more than just losing Grace to Casimir. Luken has questioned whether he should be fighting at all." There was a long pause.

Thorne waited. A shiver went down his spine. Finally, he said, "Tell me."

"Last night, he was in Awatukee. When Jeannie could not reach him on his warrior phone, she sent Santiago to see if he was all right. Santiago found him tearing a death vampire to pieces with his hands. He was deep in the chest. He ripped out the heart . . . and other things. Santiago said he was crazed. Leto did not even notice he was there. And when he did seem to come back to himself, he shouted into the night sky for a long time."

Leto. His mentor for centuries.

"Maybe Leto should go to the Seattle Colony. The Militia Warriors need to be trained, and he could work with Arthur."

"I think it would be best if he did not battle death vampires just now. He needs time to heal and to adjust. In the meantime, I will speak with my grandson, Arthur's father, about the situation and see what he wishes to do." He leaned forward in his chair. "Now there is something I would like to know. When are you going to make peace with Endelle? None of us like this person she has become. She is changed and very unhappy."

"I know. I haven't known what to do."

"Just speak with her, Thorne. You knew her better than anyone else, but to my eye she is just very, very sad at losing such a good friend as you were to her all those centuries, *non*?"

He didn't need to tap into his obsiddy power to gain clarity on the subject. He already knew Jean-Pierre had it exactly right.

"I'll speak with her."

Jean-Pierre rose to his feet, that same crooked smile on his face. "Now, I think, would be an excellent time."

"Point taken."

Jean-Pierre left. Thorne made his way to the landing platform.

After some searching, he found Endelle at one of her

favorite gardens in the White Lake Resort Colony. But he didn't approach her right away because she seemed lost in thought behind a heavy dome of mist.

Endelle leaned on the wrought-iron railing overlooking the replica of the Mortal Earth Butchart Gardens. This was one of a hundred enormous gardens that flanked either side of White Lake. The man-made lake was fifteen miles long and stretched the entire length of the White Tank Mountains, at the foot of the western slopes.

On either side of the lake, famous hotels and public gardens made this location one of the most visited places on Second Earth. She only wished she'd had enough foresight to invest in the colony at its inception a few decades ago, but that's what happened to overworked Supreme High Administrators. They were just too busy keeping bad guys from taking over the world to see to their own futures.

Whatever.

She rubbed her neck and still felt nauseated. What the hell had Braulio done to her? She had scars at the upper end of her spine now. Horace had looked at them and believed them to be permanent. The depth of his concern had almost been her undoing. She could feel that Braulio had marked her in some way that was permanent, as in Upper Dimension permanent. She just didn't know why, or what it would mean for her.

What she did know was that at odd times her muscles and bones would ache, as if she had some kind of virus at work in her body, which was impossible given that she was an ascended vampire. Hello, no such thing as a virus for the near-immortal.

She clasped her hands together and shifted her feet. The iron was cool beneath her forearms. Butchart Gardens Two was one of her favorite places. She couldn't imagine how many tons of dirt had been removed to create the deep, sunken space. A lot.

She often came here to think. She'd pulled a nice cloak of mist around her to keep from being approached or recognized. Or even, she supposed, to avoid giving Greaves a chance to have a pair of his pretty-boys attempt to off her, especially now that he'd found some way to employ the Third Earth bastards. Right now, she just didn't want the grief.

She had a hole in her chest about three feet wide and twelve feet deep. She couldn't remember the last time she'd felt this way, maybe when Braulio had died, or not died, or what-the-fuck-ever had actually happened to him.

She sighed. She sure as hell wished she had someone to turn to in this situation, but who would understand what her life had been like, what it was like as the Supreme High Administrator of a world that had been at war for a couple of fucking millennia? Or even how important Thorne had been to her, that she had shared a mind-link with him, that she had always counted on him. The role he'd played in her life had been . . . crucial. She'd just never seen it before.

Now that he'd moved on because of his emerging powers, she should rejoice that he would be able to make a serious contribution to the war effort. Instead she felt completely lost, which made no sense but there it was.

The mind-link with him had kept her sane and strangely content, had helped her to feel not quite so alone in her struggles.

Now he was gone, he was a bonded warrior, and he had a new role to play.

Thorne had really dragged her over the coals then back again. She didn't quibble with his complaints; they were all true. She knew her limitations and she knew she should have been removed from this job eons ago.

But the problem was, who could have taken her place? Anyone of lesser power would have simply been eliminated by Greaves, and he'd have owned both Second and Mortal Earth a long time ago.

Of all the changes that had been rolling through her administration, the last she had expected was Thorne emerging as some kind of Olympian god.

Suddenly she realized she wasn't alone and hadn't been for a few minutes. Thorne. Shit, how had he arrived without her knowing. He'd even penetrated her mist, a turn of phrase that ordinarily would have pleased her bawdy soul, but not today.

"Thought we should talk," Thorne said, that deep gravelly voice digging more chunks out of the hole in her heart.

"What for? Seems like everything's settled." She didn't look at him. She couldn't. She didn't want him to know what she was feeling, and dammit, she was hurt, something she never allowed herself to be.

"Marguerite has been after my ass to come to you."

"I protected you both, you know. I knew about Marguerite from the beginning."

He remained silent but moved to mirror her position, settling his forearms on the wrought-iron railing a couple of feet away from her. "She thinks I'm being ungrateful and stubborn."

"Sounds like she knows you."

He didn't answer right away, but finally said, "Thought you needed some time, is all. Also, I didn't know what to say to you."

At that, she rose up, taking air into her lungs like she hadn't been breathing. "Why are you here? You said you'd be setting up shop at Militia Warrior Headquarters. Don't you have work to do?"

She towered over him in her stilettos. She'd worn them all these centuries, or some version of them, to give her an advantage over her warriors. Now it didn't seem to matter. Though Thorne was still six-five, he had changed. Something in his entire being now towered over her, and she could hardly bear it. She could hardly bear so many sudden changes: all this *breh-hedden* shit, the discovery of blood slaves, obsidian flame, and now an entire network of secret rogue colonies on Mortal Earth that protected Seers. It was all just too much.

"You can't stay mad at me forever."

"Can't I? Why the hell not?" She sounded like she was about five years old, and still she pressed on. "We're immortal, right? Unless a bomb takes us apart. And according to you we have a lot of bombs in our future. I don't see why I can't be pissed at you until at least then. Bound to be one of them with my name on it . . . or yours."

He narrowed his eyes. "What the fuck is wrong with you?"

"Nothing."

"You're acting like a goddamn woman."

"I am a woman."

He snorted.

Her anger ruffled over her shoulders. She jerked a few times as her temper rose. "I didn't want any of this. But I made do. I did my job as best I could. I thought . . . I thought you valued the mind-link we shared. I never thought you hated it, abhorred it . . . despised me."

"Take off your shoes."

"What? No."

"Take them off. There's something I need to say to you and I'll be damned if I'm going to say it with you towering over me and raging at me like a Greek fury. Take 'em off. Meet me, just this once, eye-to-eye."

Her throat ached. "Fine." What did she care?

She folded them off and dropped barefoot to the cool cement walk, but she felt like a warrior who'd just removed his suit of armor. So . . . shit.

He took a deep breath and leveled his gaze at her, straight-on because now they were exactly the same height. Even his eyes looked different, and not just because they were no longer red-rimmed. He looked . . . powerful in every respect.

"Do you know why I never complained, until yesterday?" he asked.

"Too chickenshit?"

He lifted his hands like he wanted to put them around her neck and squeeze hard. "God, give me patience with wild women. No, not because I was too chickenshit, as you damn well know. I never said anything because I knew you were doing what you knew how to do and I respected the hell out of you. Do you remember in, I don't know, I think it was sixteen or seventeen hundred? We'd just come back from getting our asses kicked by about twenty death vamps that Greaves had set up as an ambush. Santiago had been sliced through the stomach and he was dying, bleeding out because the cut had hit an artery. Remember that? Out at the Superstitions?"

She sought back through her memories and frowned. Nothing about that particular event struck her as exceptional. "Yeah, I think so. I held him on my lap, as I recall." It was a rare time when one of her warriors even got close to being on the sucky end of a mortal wound. She could count them on both hands. "What about it?"

He smiled. "You don't remember what you did. I want you to think back and tell me what you did."

She shook her head. "I remember sitting in the dirt out there and holding him. I put my hand over his stomach. Some of his right lung was exposed and bubbling. I remember that my healing gifts weren't strong enough to do much good but I did what I could until Horace got there."

Thorne shook his head. "You kept repeating that stupid Spanish phrase you'd had him teach you about the goat fucking the pig until midnight. You kept repeating it every time you felt his spirit fade, and I'd say that was a good hour. Every time you said it, something in Santiago's spirit lit up. You kept saying, 'Don't leave us, Warrior.' You kissed him on the side of his head several times."

"No I didn't."

"Yes, you did. You kissed him. You kept him going while Horace healed him. And the whole time, though he couldn't see you, tears streamed down your face. And the whole time, you kept sending to me, *I hate this fucking war.* But you never said it to him, just that stupid phrase in Spanish. He would have died without you there, keeping his spark alive until Horace could get the job done.

"Endelle, I have a thousand stories just like that one. The latest? When Fiona was doing her recitation in front of Rith's cage and you knelt beside her for two hours while she spoke the name of every blood slave who had died in Burma. You are *that* person. And I would die for *that* person."

"You would die for me?" Shit, her voice sounded small.

"Of course I would."

"Aw, holy hell."

She wasn't certain where the impulse came from, but she didn't care. She stepped into him and slung her arms around his neck. He was a big man and though she was tall, when his arms folded around her, it was like she almost disappeared.

She heard earthmoving equipment in her chest and felt big dump trucks backing up, with those stupid alarm-beeps sounding as they unloaded all that earth back into the pit of her heart.

I couldn't bear it, Thorne, if you hated me.

He rubbed her back. *I could never hate you. I've wanted to kill you on occasion, but I could never hate you. You shouldn't have been abandoned to fight this bloody war alone. I've never understood what the Upper Dimensions were thinking. This was never fair to you.*

She drew back and nodded. Like hell she was going to shed a tear, not in front of the Supreme High Commander of the Allied Ascender Fucking Forces. "All right, fine. So we're agreed, we don't hate each other. What now? How the hell is this supposed to work?"

"What exactly did you think was going to change?"

"Well, you're taking over, aren't you?"

His brows lifted. "No. I'm putting together an army, which we've needed for a goddamn long time, to face Greaves when the time comes."

"It sounded . . . no, it felt like more to me. A helluva lot more." She frowned and a light seemed to surround Thorne, the one she'd seen before. She *knew* this was much more than just the directive to create an army.

"Well," Thorne said, "maybe it is, but right now it doesn't matter, does it? We all know where this whole thing is headed and we have to prepare. Jean-Pierre's in deep with the Militia Warriors now. Shit, he's almost got both Gideon and Duncan up to Warrior of the Blood speed, plus half a dozen more."

"We have a long way to go."

"Yes, we do, but I'm hopeful, Endelle. I know what needs to be done and I'm going to do it."

She met his gaze and nodded.

So be it.

But there was one thing she wanted to say to him. "I like your woman, by the way. She has great spirit. I'm thinking of giving her the rank of Supreme High Seer of Second Earth. That she decided to take on COPASS tells me she has some balls."

He chuckled. "That she does."

"Much good it will do, I mean taking her complaints to COPASS."

Thorne sighed. "She understands the point of bringing the issues before the committee. She knows it's just the beginning of a very long road, since Seers have never had rights before."

"Is there any chance she, or the other Seers out of the Superstition Fortress, will be willing to offer their services to me?"

"She needs light hands, Endelle. They all do after what they've been through. But yeah, I think it's a real possibility, especially if you let Marguerite design a proper working model for the environment Seers really need in order to do what they do best."

She nodded. "Well, as Supreme High Seer I think she could write the handbook. It might be a good place to begin."

"Marguerite would eat that up."

"Well, good. We'll do that then."

She saw movement in the garden. Two kids, about ten, had stripped off their shirts and were mounting their wings. They'd just launched into some low-level flying, starting a chase, when a voice came over the loudspeaker, "No mounting of wings in the garden. Cease at once, or you'll be taken to the security office."

But the boys were apparently really game. They turned and headed in the direction of Endelle and Thorne.

"Let's get 'em," Endelle said.

Thorne laughed. And it was a good sound.

The boys were smiling, their eyes wild with excitement.

Just as they breached the first row of protective railings,

one of a series of three and just twenty feet away, Endelle dropped her mist.

By that time the boys were at full speed and rocketed right into them. Thorne caught his prey easily by the hand and, with a whirling motion to keep from damaging the wings, swung him in a circle going slower and slower until he could set the boy on his feet.

Endelle did the same.

"Warrior Thorne," the shorter of the two cried. He didn't seem in the least afraid but stared up at Thorne wide-eyed, mouth agape.

"Yep, that's me. What the hell were the two of you thinking?"

The other kid pushed away from Endelle but not to escape. He was clearly determined to join his buddy and engage in a some much-deserved hero-worship. Both boys looked at each other and with incredible speed retracted their wings.

"We want to be Warriors of the Blood," the taller boy all but shouted.

"Really?" Thorne shifted his gaze to Endelle and winked. "Well, then the first thing you'll need to learn is to be very respectful of authority."

They both almost fell over themselves apologizing to him. "I wasn't referring to myself," he said. He jerked his head in Endelle's direction. "I believe you owe an apology to the Supreme High Administrator, Madame Endelle."

Both boys turned, shock-eyed, and backed up against Thorne as if for protection. More apologies then silence as they stared at her. Thorne put a hand on each shoulder, and a strange look came over his face. Endelle understood. Shit, as soon as these men found the right woman suddenly they wanted kids.

Goddammit.

Oh,w hatever.

"So you boys want to be warriors?" she asked.

But they'd grown very silent and they were both eyeing the octopus tentacles that covered her boobs. "Can we touch those?"

She laughed.

Well, they had the brass of warriors.

She opened her mouth to say something unholy because she couldn't resist but Thorne called out sharply, "She'when'endel'livelle," clicks and everything. Thorne was the only ascender capable of pronouncing her birth name.

She shrugged and rolled her eyes. To the boys, she said, "The two of you had better get out of here before I call security, or better yet, your parents. Now git."

They took off running.

What is the measure of a man,
But to wield his sword with power,
Yet to hold his family,
Like the greatest treasure,
In the palm of his hand.

—*Collected Proverbs,* Beatrice of Fourth

CHAPTER 25

Grace lay in bed with Casimir. She had been his lover now for a little over a week. She touched his face, memorizing the line of his nose, the indentation above his lip, his chin.

Though his eyes were closed, he smiled. He whispered, "I can't believe I'm saying this, but you've made me happy, more than I had ever believed possible."

He was a difficult man, very difficult. He had a thousand techniques for shunting any serious subject aside. And he had little belief in himself. In his power, yes, but not in himself, not in what lay deep within his soul.

He satisfied her in bed. How could he not, when his mulled wine scent filled her with desire and when he treated her so gently. When he made love to her, it was as though he intended to find every means possible by which to bring her to a place of ecstasy.

But of all the paths she had ever walked, this one was the hardest. What she hadn't told anyone was that she had seen his death. It was that seeing that kept her touching his face, his lips, his nose, and reaching down even now to kiss him.

In a week, she had grown to love the man, because in one

swift brilliant moment well into the future, he would become all that the Creator had meant him to be, and for that reason she had given herself to him, body and soul.

But her heart was already breaking.

Two weeks after she had completed the *breh-hedden* with Thorne, and officially become the *breh* to the Supreme High Commander of the Allied Ascender Forces, Marguerite stood on a wooden platform in Prague, addressing COPASS.

She addressed each of her points: the need for better evaluation of all Seers Fortresses around the world, for Seers rights, and for a document to outline such rights. But what good was it doing?

The committee was very quiet, perhaps because Madame Endelle had introduced her by her new designation as Supreme High Seer of Second Earth.

So no matter how enthusiastic or strident she became, the committee members looked almost bored.

She had practiced her speech a hundred times and had asked Thorne to look it over and offer suggestions. She had taken his ideas and worked up several variations. Both Fiona and Havily had offered further concepts, which she had incorporated as well.

But as she stared out at the way the committee rustled papers, shifted in seats, and actually yawned, she realized she was talking to a group of men and women who already belonged to Greaves.

Besides that, she was sweating and really felt nauseated, like she would throw up any minute now.

When one of the committee members actually flopped backward because he'd fallen asleep, then awakened with a shout that he wanted his Scotch, she'd had enough.

Though she felt an impulse to flip them all off, she took a deep breath, thanked the committee for their time, and stepped down from the platform. She didn't look back. The fight wouldn't be won in a day and her stomach was doing some serious flips.

Once she was out of the stuffy building, she began swallowing hard and her cheeks had that telling cramping quality. Fiona had come along, so she was glad for the support, but she couldn't even open her mouth to thank her.

She lifted her arm and folded back to administrative HQ.

She barely made it to the bathroom before she threw up a very nice tuna salad.

Fiona, of course, had followed her. "Are you all right?"

Marguerite looked up at her and for one of the first times in her life, she started to cry. "No," she wailed.

Fiona's eyes went wide. "No? Oh . . . no. Really?"

"I'm not sure. I don't know. Probably. Oh, God. What am I supposed to do now?"

But Fiona didn't try to answer the question. Instead, she sat down on the floor next to her, put her arm around her shoulders, and held her.

It might have been because of obsidian flame that Fiona knew exactly what to do in this moment, but Marguerite suspected it was just because Fiona was a really wonderful person.

"Aw, shit," Marguerite said.

"Well, before you get all worked up, let's hit a drugstore just to be sure."

Greaves dreamed that he was wrapped up in something so angelically soft, his whole spirit gave a fine-grained shudder, he ad-to-toe.

A force moved around him, walking in slow steps, very measured, as though not wanting to wake him. He felt love, an overpowering wave of love, flow over him with each soft step. He breathed as he had never breathed in his life, as though his lungs were just learning to work and the air was fresh, and clean, and good.

What was the measure of a man?

What prompted each man down his chosen path?

What forces shaped that path and all subsequent choices?

How was a man responsible for those choices when they were predestined by the early years of love or the early years of torture?

In the end, how much of a choice did a man ever really have?

Greaves was not blind to his faults, the great chasms in his essential character, so great that each one had spawned his need for power, for control, for transforming the world into something safe and beautiful that he could command. He wanted to do for others what he'd been unable to do for himself when he was young. And so he was building a new world—two new worlds, and eventually six.

He was a visionary.

There would be lives lost but that was completely inconsequential to the end result, to the magnificence that would emerge, where all young children would be protected from evil.

The dream took a turn, as dreams do, and he rose from his swaddled, safe bed and was dressed in a long black linen gown, very soft, very expensive. In the distance, he saw a woman, very clearly, and he knew the woman. She was glowing with light and iridescence, supremely majestic.

He didn't want to move toward her because he hated her and blamed her. She had been the cause, the root of all the evil that had happened for years after she abandoned him.

But she held out her hand and she smiled.

Mother, he sent.

Come to me, my son. Let me love you again, as I did when you were very young.

He didn't want to move forward, but he felt compelled by a deep call in his soul, by what he remembered of her. His feet shuffled in her direction because he could not stop them.

When he drew near, he saw that tears ran down her cheeks and from her mind to his mind, he felt how deeply she begged for his forgiveness for giving him up to the fosterage system of Mortal Earth.

But as much as he wanted to forgive her, he realized forgiveness wasn't necessary. Only obliterating what had happened to him could change the course of the future now— and that was impossible, one of the few things in the ascended dimensions that truly could not be done.

Everyone had to live with their past.

How unfortunate.

You must cease this madness, Darian. Indeed, you must, or you will be lost forever.

Forever is a very long time, Mother.

I have a place you can come to. The Council of Fourth has given me permission to bring you here, if you will agree to come to me now.

You mean the place that Casimir calls the Lake of Fire? You wish to baptize all the evil out of your son?

I wish you to be healed and to become whole.

His being shook with sudden fury and he spoke aloud and with all the resonance he could summon, *"I am whole."*

The woman who was his mother, the poetess, the healer, the memoirist of Fourth Earth, fell to her knees, her hands to ears. He could see the blood flow, which meant this was not truly a dream.

Darian Greaves, Commander of the Ascenders Liberation Army, leader of death vampires, architect of a new world, lifted both his arms and drew into his body all the power he could summon. He let that power flow and aimed his hands at her, releasing a rumbling of hand-blast energy that echoed through the dream and shattered the illusion.

He stood in his Geneva penthouse, naked, pain slicing up both arms from the repercussion of having delivered so much directed power in one blast. His only surprise was that he had not taken out the entire side of the building.

But then again, his aim had been very specific. He had hit the mark. The stench of burned flesh now filled his bedroom.

He crossed to the window and mentally opened it. The air was cold and felt wonderful on his skin.

He had made his choice long ago.

How dare the woman invade his dreams and try to persuade him to be baptized. He'd rather become a death vampire a thousand times over than submit to her form of therapy.

He looked across the land and saw the future he was

building, the vision he held in his mind of some of the greatest architecture ever imagined in the course of humankind.

And he saw that it was good.

Beatrice lay trembling, a charred remnant of the woman she had been. Her stomach churned but she couldn't vomit because she was curled up, her flesh having been seared into that position.

"Madame Beatrice," her assistant cried. "Dear Creator. Dear Creator."

She wanted to tell the woman to please stop moving around her and to summon the healers, but her jaw was burned in place as well.

The pain was beyond bearing and yet her ascended mind was far too powerful to allow her to faint. Waves of agony flowed and blinded her. Or maybe her eyes had been destroyed in the atomic force that had come out of her son's hands and decimated her.

But her ears worked.

There was a consistent shrieking. In the distance she could hear running feet, faster and faster. Why was anyone running when they could just fold to her and begin to help her?

Not running feet, then.

The pounding of drums, the signal of danger, of something gone awry.

She could hear voices around her now and she caught phrases as the conversations looped in and out of her hearing.

". . . no attack, not on the property . . ."

". . . looks like hand-blast damage . . ."

". . . I saw no one folding in or out . . ."

". . . is this the work of the son, perchance . . ."

Yes, the work of the son, the least she deserved.

Oh, God, the pain, not of her flesh, but of her heart. She had held the babe who had been Darian Greaves in her arms. She had suckled him at her breast. She had read books to him, and played with him, and prayed that his biological father's death vampire nature would not have any place in his DNA.

As the healers placed their hands above her skin, and healing flowed, only then did her mind release, like the snap of a taut rubber band, and she flowed into the bliss of unconsciousness.

As she drifted away, she heard her second assistant say, "She failed and now we are lost. All six dimensions are lost."

"No, there is still hope, the one who is to transform."

Blackness engulfed her.

Marguerite sat on the cool tile floor in the powder room of Thorne's Sedona house, not far from the toilet. She'd known the truth for a while; she just hadn't been willing to accept it, or even to approach it, until she had tangible physical evidence.

Fiona had taken her to Walgreens Two and bought her three different tests.

Each one had been positive.

So there it was, staring back at her: *yes*.

The test actually used the word *yes*.

She so could not be pregnant. This could not be happening. She wasn't meant to be a mother. Given how she'd been raised, how was she supposed to raise a child of her own? And now she had a job to do, a big job. She was the Supreme High Seer of Second Earth.

Her stomach boiled all over again and once more her cheeks cramped up. Surely there couldn't be any tuna salad left after the episode at HQ?

Apparently, there was.

She twisted around to face the toilet and hurled so hard that she bounced forward and missed the toilet bowl completely. Oh, God.

She retched and retched and retched.

When she was done, she sank to the floor opposite the toilet then used her folding power to clean up. Thank God for Second Earth powers because she kept her eyes closed the whole time except for the occasional single eye squint to see what she'd missed.

She doubted she'd ever eat tuna again.

So the Supreme High Seer of Second Earth had been impregnated by the Supreme High Commander of the Allied Ascender Forces.

She banged her head against the bathroom wall a couple of times. A little harder and she would crack the tile. Oh, she really should have thought about birth control sooner.

Goddamn that Thorne.

Thorne sat on the edge of his leather couch, a towel around his hips and one draped over his head. He'd showered, but he hated blow-drying his long hair—hence the towel and pretty soon just the dry Sedona Two air. Right now he still dripped.

He had been blocking Marguerite's physical sensations so that he could concentrate on the task in front of him. As much as he'd come to cherish experiencing what she experienced, a break now and then wasn't a bad thing.

His knees were spread wide so he could make use of the laptop sitting on the coffee table. He was scrutinizing a number of geographic survey maps of Second Earth. He needed to understand some basic things about the planet: how many plains there were where massive armies could gather, the elevations of these areas, which hemisphere they were in—and therefore the corresponding seasonal weather—the wildlife. All the elements to consider in planning a war.

So it had come to this. He shook his head and the towel on his head swayed. All-out war would come soon, and it was his job to get the allied forces battle-ready.

He'd already sent out a summons to hundreds of Militia Warrior Section Leaders from all over the world. Seriffe would fold them directly to Endelle's palace, where they'd be secure. Tomorrow he would begin forming his command organization, all those departments that would establish lines of communication, provide weaponry and ordnance, place orders for uniforms, create medical units, and of course maintain a food supply.

Every army needed a well-stocked supply train. Always had. Always would.

He only realized, however, that Marguerite had been gone an unusually long time when he heard her footsteps down the hall, her bare feet padding along the hardwood floor. He reopened his connection to her and felt the cool of the wood beneath her feet and the damp of her hair against her face.

She seemed to be moving strangely slowly.

He pulled the damp towel off his head and dropped it to the floor beside his feet. He turned in her direction, focusing all of his attention on her. She'd just recently returned from Prague and a demoralizing response to her well-prepared speech before an indifferent committee, so he knew she was a little down.

But as soon as he saw her face, he realized something else was wrong. Her eyes even looked red-rimmed. Nor did she meet his gaze.

"You've been crying?"

Marguerite never cried.

She shifted her unfocused gaze toward him then stopped in her tracks. "I'm pregnant."

Thorne stared into beautiful brown eyes and his life seemed to just stop. His heart paused. His mind grew very, very still as though time had a new meaning all its own, something only he could see. A vision slid through his mind, of a boy and a girl, same age. Yes, twins. Both with brown hair like Marguerite's, but with his hazel eyes. They were young, maybe two, walking in a field, tugging on flowers. Both had wings. He'd filled his woman with twins, wing-bearing twins.

A third child flew past them, laughing. She had long black hair and bigger wings. She was a little older.

Helena.

He blinked and time resumed.

"So you're sure about this?"

She nodded, moving to stand next to him.

"Well, I'd say I'm sorry but I always wanted a family. Guess you're not getting away from me now."

At that she stilled and looked down at him. Her body relaxed as she frowned. "Is that what you think? That I still want to leave you, want to live my life of freedom, that I have regrets?"

It wasn't exactly what he meant but maybe it had been the right thing to say, to bring forward. "Do you have regrets?"

And suddenly he wished he hadn't asked because his heart started pounding. He wanted her to be happy more than anything else in the world. He'd always thought that she deserved a thousand years of unbridled lust-driven activity for the hundred years she'd been incarcerated in the Convent. But the thought of her doing that was about as pleasant to his soul as a slap on a sunburn. Yet what if she still needed to leave?

She rolled her eyes. "You are such an idiot to even ask me that. Haven't I said enough, done enough to prove that I want to be here? I haven't *resigned* myself to this life, Thorne, if that's what you think. I've *given* myself, one hundred percent."

At that he smiled, stretched out on the couch, and pulled her down on top of him. "Just checking. I want you to be happy."

"I can't believe I'm pregnant."

His body responded to that truth, a wonderful electric vibration that passed through every muscle and landed in his groin. He'd already been half firm with her body pressed against his, but now he toughened up, got really warrior-strong as he said, *"Yeah. You are."* His voice carried resonance, which brought a gasp from her throat.

"I love your voice, like a flow of water over coarse gravel. And the resonance. Do it again."

So here was one important truth about Marguerite: As a sexual being she matched him perfectly. She had from the first. He'd never really known a woman like her, so game, so ready, so earthy when it came to lovemaking. He thought it a great irony that her parents had tried to beat the sin out of her, which had instead given her a ripeness for life that made her just right for him.

He slid his arms around her and pulled her up higher on

his chest, dragging her body over his erection. So good. When her legs were tight around his cock, he pressed his mouth against her ear and with three resonances whispered, *"I'm going to fuck you again."*

Her whole body shivered and she so kindly rubbed her legs up and down his cock. She was too short for him to enter her in this position and still keep his mouth against her ear, but over the decades they'd made a lot of things work.

She lifted her left knee up and he smoothed his hand down the back of her thigh. He entered her with two fingers. She was so wet, always wet for him, and now she carried his babies inside her.

Life got no better than this.

Do it again, she sent.

He didn't exactly know the why of it, but his resonance always worked her up like nothing else, and it never seemed to hurt her.

So he said, *"I can feel the pleasure my fingers are giving you."* He moved them faster and her body started gyrating over his. She was panting into his shoulder, her ear pressed to his mouth.

He split his resonance a few more times and just groaned into her ear. She cried out but sent, *You can make me come faster than any man I've ever known.*

"Wrong words, Marguerite. Never talk about other men to me. Ever." He was pissed, but he felt her smile and then he understood. Dammit, she'd said that to him on purpose.

He withdrew his fingers and flipped her over in a smooth arc that brought her onto the couch beneath him but on her stomach, one of his favorite positions.

He lifted her up so that he was poised behind her hips. "You're being very bad and I'm going to have to punish you."

She turned and looked back at him. "What are you going to do to me?"

He let her feel the tip of his cock at her opening, then he spelled it out for her. When her legs started trembling, he shoved himself in deep.

She balanced her hands on the arm of the couch and spread her legs wide. He set up a rhythm; then he leaned down and she stretched out her neck for him, ready to take her punishment.

He bit her hard, which brought her internal muscles wrapping tight around him and spasming. She cried out over and over as the orgasm rocked her. He released chemicals at the same time that, because of his new ability to feel her, caused shivers to race up and down his spine the way they were racing up and down hers.

His orgasm followed as he pumped into her, a streak of profound pleasure because she climaxed again and he could feel at the same time what his hard cock was doing to her. The combined sensation was like fire. He released her neck and roared as the orgasm rolled and rolled, on and on, until he'd spilled himself inside her and at last her hips grew quiet.

He collapsed to his side, taking her with him, keeping himself connected. He was breathing hard, trying to figure out which sensations were his and which were hers. Her lungs gulped for air; his cock twitched. His legs were sweaty against the leather; so were hers. Her nose itched. The muscles of his shoulders flexed.

He held her close, loving this, loving sex with his woman, loving that she was game, that she was here, that she belonged to him, that love had found them both. He hugged her and she caught his arms and held them, pressing them against her chest. He felt her breasts flex from the inside and he smiled.

"I love you," he said.

"You work me up."

He laughed. "Ditto, sweetheart."

She sighed. "How the hell am I supposed to be a mother?"

"You'll be fine. The woman who brought me back from the dead, twice, will do just fine with anyone and anything. Two babies? Piece of cake."

He felt her stiffen. "What do you mean, *two* babies?"

Thorne could have kicked himself for not being more diplomatic. He'd have to work on that.

But after a few more seconds, he felt her relax and something more, a vibration that clicked with his own obsiddy power. He could feel her power moving within her body, deep within her mind. He could sense that she was having a vision.

She turned slowly in his arms so that she was now face to face with him and her eyes were lit up. "I saw them, both of them."

He nodded. "With baby Helena?"

Marguerite smiled. "They were walking hand in hand. You saw them, too?"

"Helena flew above them."

"Yes." She put her hand on his face, then kissed him. "More than anything that's happened in the past few weeks, that image gives me hope, Thorne. Real hope. Our kids had to be at least two, maybe three, don't you think? And they had wings."

"Yes. Wings."

"Do you think the war will be over by then?"

He drew in a deep breath. "I hope so, sweetheart, but if it isn't, we'll figure it out."

She dipped her chin and snuggled close so that her head was buried against his neck. *Together, we'll figure it out,* she sent.

"Yes, together."

Together. The sweetest word he'd heard in a long, long time.

ASCENSION
TERMINOLOGY

AAF pr. n. Allied Ascender Forces, Endelle's army.

ALA pr. n. Ascenders Liberation Army, the name Greaves assigned to his army.

answering the call to ascension n. The mortal human who experiences the hallmarks of the *call to ascension* will at some point feel compelled to answer, usually by demonstrating significant preternatural power.

ascender n. A mortal human of earth who has moved permanently to the second dimension.

ascendiate n. A mortal human who has answered the *call to ascension* and thereby commences his or her *rite of ascension*.

ascension n. The act of moving permanently from one dimension to a higher dimension.

ascension ceremony n. Upon the completion of the *rite of ascension*, the mortal undergoes a ceremony in which loyalty to the laws of Second Society is professed and the attributes of the *vampire* mantle along with immortality are bestowed.

the Borderlands pr. n. Those geographic areas that form dimensional borders at both ends of a dimensional pathway. The dimensional pathway is an access point through which travel can take place from one dimension to the next. See *Trough*.

***breh-hedden* n.** (Term from an ancient language.) A mate-bonding ritual that can only be experienced by the most powerful warriors and the most powerful preternaturally gifted women. Effects of the *breh-hedden* can include but are not limited to: specific scent experience, extreme physical/sexual attraction, loss of rational thought, primal sexual drives, inexplicable need to bond, powerful need to experience deep *mind-engagement,* etc.

***cadroen* n.** (Term from an ancient language.) The name for the hair clasp that holds back the ritual long hair of a *Warrior of the Blood*.

call to ascension n. A period of time, usually involving several weeks, in which the mortal human has experienced some or all of, but not limited to, the following: specific dreams about the next dimension, deep yearnings and longings of a soulful and inexplicable nature, visions of and possibly visits to any of the dimensional Borderlands, etc. See *Borderlands*.

Central pr.n. The office of the current administration that tracks movement of *death vampires* in both the second dimension and on *Mortal Earth* for the purpose of alerting the *Warriors of the Blood* and the *Militia Warriors* to illegal activities.

the darkening n. An area of *nether-space* that can be found during meditations and/or with strong preternatural darkening capabilities. Such abilities enable the *ascender* to move into nether-space and remain there or to use nether-space in order to be two places at once.

death vampire n. Any vampire, male or female, who partakes of *dying blood* automatically becomes a death vampire. Death vampires can have, but are not limited to, the following characteristics: remarkably increased physical strength, an increasingly porcelain complexion true of all ethnicities so that death vampires have a long-term reputation of looking very similar, a faint bluing of the porcelain complexion, increasing beauty of face, the ability to enthrall, the blackening of *wings* over a period of time. Though death vampires are not gender-specific, most are male. See *vampire*.

dimensional worlds n. Eleven thousand years ago the first *ascender*, Luchianne, made the difficult transition from *Mortal Earth* to what became known as Second Earth. In the early millennia four more dimensions were discovered, Luchianne always leading the way. Each dimension's ascenders exhibited expanding preternatural power before *ascension*. Upper dimensions are generally closed off to the dimension or dimensions below.

***duhuro* n.** (Term from an ancient language.) A word of respect that in the old language combines the spiritual offices of both servant and master. To call someone *duhuro* is to offer a profound compliment suggesting great worth.

dying blood n. Blood extracted from a mortal or an *ascender* at the point of death. This blood is highly addictive in nature. There is no known treatment for anyone who partakes of dying blood. The results of ingesting dying blood include, but are not limited to: increased physical, mental, or preternatural power, a sense of extreme euphoria, a deep sense of well-being, a sense of omnipotence and fearlessness, the taking in of the preternatural powers of the host body, etc. If dying blood is not taken on a regular basis, extreme abdominal cramps result without ceasing. Note: Currently there is an antidote not for the addiction to dying blood itself but to the various results of ingesting dying blood. This means that a *death vampire* who drinks dying blood then partakes of the antidote will not show the usual physical side effects of ingesting dying blood: no whitening or faint bluing of the skin, no beautifying of features, no blackening of the *wings*, etc.

effetne n. (Term from an ancient language.) An intense form of supplication to the gods; an abasement of self and of self-will.

folding v. Slang for dematerialization, since some believe that one does not actually dematerialize self or objects but rather one "folds space" to move self or objects from one place to another. There is much scientific debate on this subject since at present neither theory can be proved.

grid n. The technology used by Central that allows for the tracking of *death vampires* primarily at the *Borderlands* on both *Mortal Earth* and *Second Earth*. Death vampires by nature carry a strong, trackable signal, unlike normal *vampires*. See *Central*.

Guardian of Ascension pr. n. A prestigious title and rank at present given only to those *Warriors of the Blood* who also serve to guard powerful *ascendiates* during their *rite of ascension*. In millennia past Guardians of Ascension were also those powerful ascenders who offered themselves in unique and powerful service to Second Society.

High Administrator pr. n. The designation given to a leader of a Second Earth *Territory*.

identified sword n. A sword made by Second Earth metallurgy that has the preternatural capacity to become identified to a single *ascender*. The identification process involves holding the sword by the grip for several continuous seconds. The identification of a sword to a single ascender means that only that person can touch or hold the sword. If anyone else tries to take possession of it, that person will die.

Militia Warrior pr. n. One of hundreds of thousands of warriors who serve Second Earth society as a policing force for the usual civic crimes and as a battling force, in squads only, to fight against the continual depredations of *death vampires* on both *Mortal Earth* and Second Earth.

millennial adjustment n. The phenomenon of time taking on a more fluid aspect with the passing of centuries.

mind-engagement n. The ability to penetrate another mind and experience the thoughts and memories of the other person. The ability to receive another mind and allow that person to experience one's thoughts and memories. These abilities must be present in order to complete the *breh-hedden*.

mist n. A preternatural creation designed to confuse the mind and thereby hide things or people. Most mortals and *ascenders* are unable to see mist. The powerful ascender, however, is capable of seeing mist, which usually appears like an intricate mesh, or a cloud, or a web-like covering.

Mortal Earth pr. n The name for First Earth, or the current modern world known simply as earth.

nether-space n. The unknowable, unmappable regions of space. The space between dimensions is considered nether-space as well as the space found in *the darkening*.

preternatural voyeurism n. The ability to "open a window" with the power of the mind in order to see people and events happening elsewhere in real time. Two of the limits of preternatural voyeurism are: The voyeur must usually know the person or place, and if the voyeur is engaged in *darkening* work, it is very difficult to make use of preternatural voyeurism at the same time.

pretty-boy n. Slang for *death vampire,* since most death vampires are male.

rite of ascension n. A three-day period during which time an *ascendiate* contemplates *ascending* to the next highest dimension.

royle **n.** (Term from an ancient language.) The literal translation is: a benevolent wind. More loosely translated, *royle* refers to the specific quality of having the capacity to create a state of benevolence, of goodwill, within an entire people or culture. See *royle adj.*

royle **adj.** (Term from an ancient language.) This term is generally used to describe a specific coloration of *wings:* cream with three narrow bands at the outer tips of the wings when in full-span. The bands are always burnished gold, amethyst, and black. Because Luchianne, the first *ascender* and first *vampire,* had this coloration on her wings, anyone whose wings matched Luchianne's was said to have *royle* wings. Having *royle* wings was considered a tremendous gift, holding great promise for the world.

Seer pr. n. An *ascender* gifted with the preternatural ability to ride the future streams and report on future events.

Seers Fortress pr. n. *Seers* have traditionally been gathered into compounds designed to provide a highly peaceful environment, thereby enhancing the Seer's ability to ride the future streams. The information gathered at a Seers Fortress benefits the local *High Administrator.* Some believe that the term *fortress* emerged as a protest against the prison-like conditions the *Seers* often have to endure.

spectacle n. The name given to events of gigantic proportion that include but are not limited to: trained squadrons of DNA-altered geese, swans, and ducks, *ascenders* with the specialized and dangerous skills of flight performance, intricate and often massive light and fireworks displays, as well as various forms of music.

Supreme High Administrator pr. n. The ruler of Second Earth. See *High Administrator*.

Territory pr. n. For the purpose of governance, Second Earth is divided up into groups of countries called Territories. Because the total population of Second Earth is only 1 percent of that found on *Mortal Earth*, Territories were established as a simpler means of administering Second Society law. See *High Administrator*.

Trough pr. n. A slang term for a dimensional pathway. See *Borderlands*.

Twoling pr. n. Anyone born on Second Earth is a Twoling.

vampire n. The natural state of the *ascended* human. Every ascender is a vampire. The qualities of being a vampire include but are not limited to: immortality, the use of fangs to take blood, the use of fangs to release potent chemicals, increased physical power, increased preternatural ability, etc. Luchianne created the word *vampire* upon her *ascension* to Second Earth to identify in one word the totality of the changes she experienced upon that ascension. From the first, the taking of blood was viewed as an act of reverence and bonding, not as a means of death. The *Mortal Earth* myths surrounding the word *vampire* for the most part personify the Second Earth death vampire. See *death vampire*.

Warriors of the Blood pr. n. An elite fighting unit of usually seven powerful warriors, each with phenomenal preternatural ability and capable of battling several *death vampires* at any one time.

What-Bee pr. n. Slang for *Warrior of the Blood,* as in WOTB.

wings n. All *ascenders* eventually produce wings from wing-locks. *Wing-lock* is the term used to describe the apertures on the ascender's back from which the feathers and attending mesh-like superstructure emerge. Mounting wings involves a hormonal rush that some liken to sexual release. Flight is one of the finest experiences of ascended life. Wings can be held in a variety of positions, including but not limited to: full-mount, close-mount, aggressive-mount, etc. Wings emerge over a period of time from one year to several hundred years. Wings can, but do not always, begin small in one decade then grow larger in later decades.

Y pro nai-y-stae **n.** (Term from an ancient language.) The loose translation is, "You may stay for an eternity."